The Twistical Nature of Spoons

Also by Patti Grayson from Turnstone Press

Core Samples
Autumn, One Spring

The Twistical Nature of Spoons

Patti Grayson

TURNSTONE PRESS

The Twistical Nature of Spoons
copyright © Patti Grayson 2023
Turnstone Press
Artspace Building
206-100 Arthur Street
Winnipeg, MB
R3B 1H3 Canada
www.TurnstonePress.com

All rights reserved. No part of this book may be reproduced or transmitted in any form or by any means—graphic, electronic or mechanical—without the prior written permission of the publisher. Any request to photocopy any part of this book shall be directed in writing to Access Copyright, Toronto.

Turnstone Press gratefully acknowledges the assistance of the Canada Council for the Arts, the Manitoba Arts Council, the Government of Canada through the Canada Book Fund, and the Province of Manitoba through the Book Publishing Tax Credit and the Book Publisher Marketing Assistance Program.

This novel is a work of fiction. Names, characters, places and incidents are either the product of the author's imagination or are used fictitiously, and any resemblance to actual persons living or dead, events or locales, is entirely coincidental.

Printed and bound in Canada.

Library and Archives Canada Cataloguing in Publication

Title: The twistical nature of spoons / Patti Grayson.
Names: Grayson, Patti, 1957- author.
Identifiers: Canadiana (print) 20230447937 | Canadiana (ebook) 20230447996 |
    ISBN 9780888017710 (softcover) | ISBN 9780888017727 (EPUB) |
    ISBN 9780888017734 (PDF)
Classification: LCC PS8613.R39 T85 2023 | DDC C813/.6—dc23

for
David

Lying, the telling of beautiful untrue things,
is the proper aim of Art.

—Oscar Wilde, *Intentions*

Liar, liar, pants on fire …

—Unknown

The Twistical Nature of Spoons

1

Blisse

unknown prone

The hunt for loose change in the bottom of my backpack is not primarily driven by hunger, but by my craving for the sensation of hard metal pressed against my fingertips—metal that is not formed into a spoon. I will not touch the spoon. It is difficult to deny myself its comfort. It beckons. I resist. I have no intention of reaching into my parka pocket to be assuaged by its calming influence. I may never touch the spoon again. Perhaps, in the spring, I will donate my coat back to the secondhand store without first emptying it of any personal belongings. Who would suffer more from the loss of the cheap souvenir—Ina or me?

The quarters and dimes feel sweaty in my palm. I debate whether I should be wasting them, but then deposit their sum into the vending machine. At least there is the reward of the slide and clink, the accompanying *ka-thump* as the spiral coil releases my D4 choice into the lower trough. As I retrieve my purchase, I think, *This confection is real.* This candy bar is chocolate and nuts and caramel, not a concoction of subterfuge and fabrications. As

Patti Grayson

I settle into a vacant waiting-room chair, I delay unwrapping the treat. I rifle through my backpack again to locate a tube of cherry lip gloss and apply the dregs. Accosting me are stomach-churning wafts of disinfectant, the flickering of the muted television set, and the unsettling code announcements spewing from the intercom. I would prefer them all vanished. Nevertheless, I will sit and wait in their midst, even if it takes all night and necessitates skipping my Brit Lit lecture and French lab in the morning. And when my mother begins her story—*my* story—I will hear her out this time, listen to her full explanation. I can control my inner seething long enough to listen.

The problem is that now, not only do I expect Ina to address my bewilderment with respect to the fiasco she created with the spoons, she also must explain why she insisted on scrambling into the back of an ambulance with a complete stranger. Especially since the man appeared to be raising his voice at her in protest right before he collapsed. My mother keeps to herself at the best of times, so why would she feel responsible for a random individual who shows up at her gallery opening? Unless he is an art critic and she was trying to woo his favour. But if his judgements and responses are that intense and overblown, who would pay attention to him anyway? It is not as if Ina's work requires a shock-value disclaimer like some trauma-inducing performance-art installation. At worst, some of my mother's pieces might gently haunt you when you close your eyes at night. So what was his complaint?

Ina must have lied to the paramedics to be allowed to accompany the man. Some cock-and-bull story. But crazed invention is, after all, my mother's specialty. Which begs the question, why am I sitting in this hospital waiting room expecting her to provide me with a truthful explanation? Odds are Ina's story will be questionable at best. It would be better for me to try and answer my own questions.

I debate removing the wrapper from the chocolate bar,

The Twistical Nature of Spoons

anticipating that the sweetness might just sit in my stomach like a stone. As I dither, I do not notice the nurse approaching until she touches my shoulder.

"Excuse me, Blisse? Are you Blisse Trove?" she asks.

I blink and nod.

She looms over me in her pastel scrubs, a folded piece of paper in her hand, and continues, "You're the daughter of the woman who rode here in an ambulance? Ina?"

I nod again.

"Your mother asked me to give you this. Her companion might require emergency surgery. We're running tests. She said you should go home for the night. There's no telling the duration—"

"Her *companion*?" I shake my head. "My mother is not his …" I stop myself. Who knows what Ina has told the hospital and why? I would like to inform this messenger that, to my knowledge, Ina has not gone on a single date since my birth, and it is doubtful that, prior to this evening, she had ever laid eyes on the man who might require life-saving intervention. So *companion*? Highly unlikely.

With a vague gesture, the nurse coaxes me to take the paper. I do not.

Instead, I press for answers. "Where is my mother? Could you ask her to come speak to me herself?"

The woman squints at my bangs to avoid eye contact. "She went up to the cardiac unit. She basically begged me to persuade you to go home and get some sleep." She chances a pointed glance to assess my reaction. Her lips are configured into rehearsed sincerity as she continues, "She doesn't want you staying here alone. You have classes in the morning?"

I rub my knuckles across my eyebrows. I want to point out I would not be alone if Ina came out from wherever she was hiding in the bowels of this hospital. Does this note-bearer not find it odd that my mother is avoiding me? Or has Ina revealed that I have been unwilling to speak to her for weeks now—even eluding her

Christmas overtures—and is thus justified in her own behaviour? I would like to present my side of the story: the version in which Ina drags me into a corner of the gallery while ambulance attendants load a stranger onto a stretcher, at which point she prepares to abandon her exhibit on opening night, while insisting—her face full of anguish—that I hail a cab and follow her to the hospital so she can explain, as if I should just leave our own unresolved crisis simmering on the back burner.

Ina urging me out the fire exit was made even worse by Tweed Halverden scrambling toward me from across the gallery, in a state of uncharacteristic agitation. What Tweed was doing there, I cannot imagine, unless he was trying to impress a date: *Just on the down-low, I know the artist's daughter intimately, and let me tell you, she is a wacko!* And now that I am here at the hospital at my mother's bizarre request—my heart lamenting a missed encounter with Tweed—Ina simply instructs another stranger to tell me to go home and toddle off to university in the morning.

When I was a child, I sometimes resented Ina's preoccupied flurries of activity; in my early teens, it was her ever-hovering physical presence; but tonight's weird little disappearing act tops it all. Bile rises to the back of my throat. I desperately need to believe that the shame and humiliation I have been lugging around are all Ina's fault, but there is a nagging fear that should someone, anyone—perhaps even this coerced courier—be privy to both of our stories, I might not be perceived as totally gullible and innocent. My behaviour, especially my recent actions, might place me within blame's reach.

I lower my gaze to the folded paper. If Ina is choosing to be absent, the note will have to suffice. I reach for it. My mother's messenger hands it to me, then hesitates, her palm remaining upturned, the pose of a religious icon. For some unknown reason, I place the chocolate bar in her hand.

She looks down at it, tries to give it back.

The Twistical Nature of Spoons

I say, "Would you please take it to my mother? I doubt she ate much today."

"Sure," she agrees.

"Thank you," I say. "I am certain you have more important things to do than deliver candy. I appreciate it."

When she turns away, I consider sneaking along behind her. Instead, I yank my backpack out from under the chair, shove the note into my pocket, and slink out between the hissing automatic doors. "Go home and get some sleep," the nurse relayed. But perhaps Ina should have specified which home. The one I have lived in with her my whole life? Or my Mr. Fluxcer-acquired temporary lodgings?

And what of poor Mr. Fluxcer? What am I supposed to say to him? He was more insistent than Ina that I take the cab to the hospital. "Imperative" was the word he used, before wringing his hands and inexplicably mumbling, "I should have known the minute I laid eyes on him." Perhaps I can avoid Mr. Fluxcer. I dig my bus pass out of my backpack and head to the stop, hoping the wait will not be long. The midnight air is stunningly cold, and I cannot afford another taxi. Thankfully, the transit shelter is vacant, but even within its glass protection, my breath rises in puffs of icy fog.

I slip into the right-hand seat at the front of the bus. It is my preferred spot. I like that there is little to obstruct the seat's view at the same time as it provides the closest proximity to the assured *thwap* of the doors' rubber edges sealing closed behind the passengers. I am torn between sitting back and savouring my luck or reading the note. A dull lump turns over in my stomach despite having relinquished the candy bar. I dig the note from my pocket and unfold it.

Its surface is covered in a hurried scrawl:

Patti Grayson

Blisse,

I wanted to explain when you got here, but it has to wait. Don't return to the hospital for now. (Thank Knowlton for staying back at the gallery for me when you see him.) Not that I blame you, but hating me won't solve this.

Ina

It is a good thing the bus ride is short. I cannot wait to ball Ina's cryptic blather in my fist and toss it into a snowbank. And how dare she expect me to thank Mr. Fluxcer for doing her bidding? We both owe him inexpressible gratitude. She should be thanking her lucky stars for his help, not ordering me to deliver her platitudes.

I practically sprint the two blocks from the bus stop. By the time I reach the porch, my bare hands are so cold, I can hardly crank the key in the lock; still, as I push open the door, I have the urge to turn tail and run back out into the frigid January air. After weeks away, I had anticipated a feeling of familiarity to wash over me upon entering the foyer, but I neglected to brace myself for the brash reminder of my sudden departure. Although Ina appears to have made an effort to hang some lanterns for Chinese New Year, the foyer is still brimming with Christmas decorations. One entire section of the yuletide display lies in a jumbled mess. My heart pounds. In the midst of the disrupted corner, Santa's elf trio sit like injured accusers awaiting the return of the culprit to the crime scene. I half fear they might begin to tremble in my presence, but they remain inert. One no longer grips his toy hammer. The middle one, with his perfect, merry little elbows-out symmetry, is missing his elfin hat—severed raw porcelain marks his hairline in its stead. I assume the third has not sat upright since I bolted from the house. His arm lies detached; I can see into his hollow cavity. My tears well up as much for their wrecked state as for the violent streak I had not known I possessed. I mirror their blank stares as I

The Twistical Nature of Spoons

remove my boots and make my way to the kitchen. It is better not to look. I refuse to remember Ina toppled in their midst, calling after me, "Please, can I just have your forgiveness, Blisse?" Just? Why would she ask for the hardest thing to give?

I head straight to my bedroom and drop onto the narrow mattress, reaching my hand under the bed to feel the hard edge of the canteen. Ina must have picked it up and stowed it away again. There are traces of her jasmine perfume—her one personal splurge—on my pillow, as if she was lying in this same spot not long ago. I imagine her ransacking my room for clues to track down my whereabouts. Over the past weeks, while lying awake tossing and turning on Mr. Fluxcer's pay-by-the-month-hotel daybed, I have wondered how long it would be before she found me.

I breathe in and out slowly. The house creaks from the cold; the furnace blows a warm, albeit hollow, emptiness to compensate, its mechanical rumble oddly comforting. I cannot remember many occasions when it was just me and the furnace alone in the house. There was always someone renting the upstairs rooms, and Ina seldom left to go anywhere once I arrived home from school each day, unless I was in her company.

My ribcage contracts with a sudden thought. Perhaps Ina could not bear the solitude after she evicted Mr. Fluxcer from his rooms and I flew the coop. Despite her widowed declarations that she would never love another man, her isolation may have driven her to take a lover. Is my mother having a tryst with the man who collapsed at the gallery? Perhaps "companion" is an apt description. I cannot know what Ina has done in my absence. Maybe she was trying to end their relationship earlier this evening and he was reacting to that, not her work. He did seem to be spewing nonsense; she might have decided to be rid of him. Everyone, including me, had turned to stare when he shouted something that sounded like "sock and buskin!" Perhaps he had a stroke and his words were all garbled; but then again, I heard him clearly pronounce Ina's name seconds before he collapsed. So much chaos ensued—I swear a scarlet aura was pulsing around him before I realized the ambulance had arrived, its red lights flashing through the windows and splashing across the gallery walls.

I sit up to switch on my dresser lamp. It flickers like the bulb might be dying. Willing it to remain lit, I tap the shade, knowing that my actions are senseless, perhaps as futile as hoping that Ina's testament of undying devotion to my father's memory remains intact—that she has not fallen for another man—and that her past behaviours can be explained by her deep and lasting grief over my father's passing. This is the one consoling fundamental I have clung to for weeks now. But it is just as likely that the man from the gallery is actually her lover, and that she has already done something to deceive him—as she has me.

I jump off the bed and dash to the bathroom, desperate to not find an extra toothbrush in the glass by the sink. I feel like a crazed intruder rummaging through the medicine chest, but if there is evidence that a man occupies space in Ina's life, I need to know. It is not just that she is ultimately the reason Tweed thinks I am an out-of-my-mind freak—it is that for my entire life, she swore her everlasting love for my father. She swore she would go to her grave his widow and with her life fulfilled by their love. She told me that when she repeated the until-death-do-us-part vow, she meant until her own death, not just should death separate them. And I believed her. I took solace in the romance of it even when I felt disadvantaged by not having a father. And when I was finally deemed old enough to hear the tragic details of his demise, I believed that the strength of her love must have been the one thing that allowed her to carry on. Just as I believed in the origin of the spoons.

I sweep the contents of the under-sink cabinet onto the floor. There are feminine products, body lotions, and empty shaving-gel containers, all pink and pastel. Not a masculine product in sight. I shove the items back in helter-skelter and head to her room.

The Twistical Nature of Spoons

Putting my nose to her linens, I sniff around for a whiff of something that suggests Ina has invited a man into her bed. There is jasmine eau de toilette, but nothing more. A fringed shawl that she must have decided would not be part of her evening's outfit lies strewn across the bed, next to the ratty peach chenille housecoat she has worn ever since I can remember. Mornings were always Ina in that matted mess of a garment. There is no hint anywhere in the room of a man come to call.

I make a determined beeline for the basement stairs but sit down halfway to the bottom. Ever since Ina stopped using the kitchen table as her crafting space and moved her work down a floor, she became protective of what she christened her "cellar sanctuary." I sometimes whined about not being invited into her workshop, but it was not as if I wanted to watch her string glass beads or paint pet rocks; it was simply my exclusion that goaded me. That, and I missed hearing the little intermittent humming sounds my mother made when she was busy at her task. She never installed a lock on her workspace. "I don't need to bolt the place down, Missy Blissey. Because I trust you." If there was one singular, crystalline priority in my childhood, it was the code of trust. There was no option, Ina insisted. In that confidential hush that only applied when we spoke of my father, Ina declared that she and I shared a secret that could never be revealed. If I decided to trespass into Ina's workspace below, it came with the risk of diminishing my A-plus level of trustworthiness in her eyes. It had made good sense to avoid that breach.

But what has Ina been hiding down there? Earlier this evening, seeing her recent work all gathered into one gallery space for the first time—instead of in a craft-show booth or stacked up on our kitchen counters—it was evident that her work has been—as Ina might describe it—"kicked up a notch." And although there is no indication of a man's presence in the house, some transformation has taken place in her workshop. There are obvious hints of new inspiration in her most recent pieces. Perhaps I should not have kept my distance at first when I arrived at the opening and saw her standing with her unknown "companion"; I should have marched right up and made her introduce me to the disgruntled man the minute I spotted them together. Would they have cringed under my scrutiny?

Because one thing has become clear to me over the past weeks: trust has been abandoned like a glass slipper at the ball. Ina claims she wants to tell me the whole truthful story, but I am prepared for more subterfuge. What I must attempt is to piece my own memories together, comb through the pertinent spoon details, and try to make sense of all that I understood and came to believe. Perhaps something buried will come to light and help elucidate how I ended up here tonight, in my present state, on these cellar steps. If nothing else, I am certain my dredging will serve as a reminder for me to remain on guard. As should you. When Ina starts telling you her side of things, be aware that she is capable of elevating deception into an art form. Pay close attention. There is nothing up *my* sleeve, but as for Ina's? Do not say I did not warn you.

Ina

encounters

Nineteen years ago, a man walked into a bar. If you're waiting for the corny punchline, better brace yourself. This is more on the scale of a cosmic joke. Cue the drum sting anyway, *ba-dum tss!* Although it's almost two decades back, it's not as hard to remember what happened, as it is to remember why. Like, who was I back then? And why was I so stupid? You can't just sidle up to a library shelf and expect to find the answers to those kinds of questions. Blisse probably told you I'm going to spin a yarn—try to pull the wool over your eyes—but I've been laddering down on my mistakes, and I don't intend to repeat them. What I'm about to tell you is the honest-to-gawd's truth.

It was an unseasonably warm early spring evening in the late 1970s and a man walked into the Three Sheets Tavern where I worked. I glanced up when the glass chime tinkled at the door, but my eyes shifted back to the bar's front window, out to the lights of the Lakehead Harbour beyond. The port had started hopping again. First the icebreakers, then the freighters making their way in and out, headed through the Great Lakes and down the St. Lawrence.

The man who walked in regained my full attention when he stalled in the entrance—as if making up his mind about the place. He turned as if to leave. At that point, I pegged him for a crewman or a stevedore. Sculpted cheekbones, five o'clock shadow, dark hair that hung past his earlobes and fractured at his collar. Unkempt. But not cheap-campfire-wieners-on-a-stick unkempt. Think sizzling appetizers tossed haphazardly on a platter.

He glanced around both halves of the bar before dodging away from the midweek pool tournament on the one side, beelining for the table set closest to the back on the other, the one next to the men's room. None of our regulars sat there unless it was the last table in the place. You could smell the disinfectant pucks in the urinals from that table—a gross addition to the two-for-one combo of stale beer and cigarette smoke. Not that I smelled rosy myself after struggling to haul down the oversized playoffs banner for my boss Antony's defeated Maple Leafs on an unexpectedly balmy day. It was the time of year when warm temperatures trick you into believing you've seen the last snowfall, but the furnace won't knock it off because it can't believe its own thermostat. I would have appreciated the man-who-walked-into-a-bar taking a vacant stool up front, saving me the extra steps to serve him his poison. But I forced a smile as I approached the back table because Antony insisted that the Three Sheets creed was to try and show even the unruliest drunk some courtesy. "If a guy can leave with some dignity, he won't be cursing my place with the evil eye or nothing." Antony's superstitious nature could only be matched by my mother's, and since she had good reason for her beliefs—with my father's life ending under a construction ladder when I was still in diapers—I figured I shouldn't question Antony's precautionary wisdom either. So I concentrated on relaxing my scrunched-up nose as I crossed the bar, and beamed as if I hadn't a care in the world.

The Twistical Nature of Spoons

I placed a cardboard coaster down in front of the man, courtesy of Molson Export Ale. I liked working in an establishment that provided coasters. And these, with their nautical theme, made me feel as if I could smell a stiff ocean breeze filling canvas sails. Not only did they do a bang-up job protecting the tables against water rings, but they also showed off our cheap bar glasses to their best advantage.

"What can I getcha?" I asked the stranger tucked next to the men's room door.

Without looking up at the smile I was offering, he responded, "Vodka, neat, please." He then fiddled with the coaster until it was perfectly straight, square to the table's edge.

Right off the hop, I tried to guess why this guy wouldn't look me in the eye—painfully shy, culturally divergent, simply rude, or something to hide? Call me an idiot—because what did it matter?—but there was an urgent need for me to know. I didn't, for one second, consider what I would do with the information once I had it. Did I want to teach him some manners or offer comfort for whatever had driven him to a guarded life? A few minutes earlier, as I'd wrestled with the Leafs banner, I'd been focussed on the end of my shift and walking home to a nice bathtub soak with the stack of front-cover-removed crafting magazines I'd lucked into earlier that week in the back alley behind the drugstore. But that instantly changed. I felt an inexplicable need to grab the attention of the man-who-walked-into-a-bar. I forgot about my sore calf muscles and platform-heel-pinched toes and decided to make the most of the stranger's presence.

I straightened my back, lifted the damp curls off my neck and let them fall over my shoulders, before repeating his order to him, "Vodka, neat." And then added, "How refreshing. Lotsa loner guys come in and order something 'up' just to watch me shake their drinks."

This caused him to sigh and rub at one of his eyebrows with his middle finger, his index finger and thumb left hovering delicately over his forehead. His hands looked rough enough to have recently loaded ship cargo, but with that genteel hand positioning, there was only one conclusion. Artistic type. That explained it. And that practically sealed his fate for me too. Though I could totally relate to the aching desire to create, I'd sworn off fraternizing with artists. My past encounters with them and their ilk had more often than not left me to personally clear up their tabs at the end of the night amidst their grateful, shit-faced promises to paint me, sculpt me, take me on tour when they secured a record deal.

Without looking up, the stranger said, "If I wanted my vodka chilled, I'd merely place it here, over my heart." His left hand clutched his down-filled vest over his chest.

Wow. A statement like that was shouting one thing: poet. And poets were the worst kind of artist. Rarely flush. What poet gets a big book advance to squander? But even though his sappy line should have made me turn tail, there was something so raw and naked about his delivery that my breath caught like a hiccup. As I hesitated, it was as if his heart's chill seeped through his ribcage, skin, shirt, anorak, and down vest to make me shiver in my own perspiration. He was clearly cold from the inside out, unlike half of Thunder Bay's population, who had donned shorts to delight in the feel of wan late-April sunlight striking their gooseflesh, despite the snow piles still melting in parking lots. The illogical notion struck me that, even with all those layers of protection, his heart was suffering from frostbite. I felt compelled to upgrade his free peanuts to a warm bowl of roasted cashews, on the house. When I turned to do just that, he raised one finger to stall me.

Reaching into his jeans pocket, he placed a twenty on the table, staring at it intensely as if memorizing its serial numbers. "Make it a double, please?"

I'd heard that line a thousand times. The request for a double often expressed more than a drink order. There could be

The Twistical Nature of Spoons

accompanying desperation, loneliness, jealousy, joy. So much of the bar biz was fuelled by citizens celebrating or folks down on their luck. But right in the middle, there was a no-man's-land where a person just wanted a strong drink. My stranger's request seemed to originate there, but with an extra twist. It was a drink request with subtext: *if I order a double, will you leave me alone?*

I still hadn't moved, so he finally looked up at me, his regard so piercing that I glanced away. And then, who knows what possessed me? I said, "Before I can serve doubles, I need your name."

He sighed, more audibly.

Why was this guy getting to me? First he inspired kindness. Now he was provoking me to be a pain in the ass.

Fiddling with his coaster again, he mumbled, "Your northern liquor laws are peculiar." He turned it perpendicular to the table.

"It's not policy," I responded. "I just can't risk messing up the orders. You can see I'm run off my feet here tonight."

He glanced at the smattering of patrons, none of whom were beckoning me, and then proceeded to trace his finger around the edge of the coaster, like a runner on a baseball diamond. Around and around. Half a dozen home runs. At some point, he decided to play. "Taras," he said.

"Pardon me?"

"My name. Taras."

"Ter-race, like a garden?"

"You have the syllabic emphasis incorrect." He repeated, "Taras."

"Tear-ass?"

"You can rhyme it with 'harass,' if it makes it easier for you," he said, motioning with his hand as if bestowing permission.

My cheeks flamed. "Humph," I said, letting him know I thought his gesture patronizing.

"Though it would rhyme better with 'hair loss,'" he stated. "Ta-ross. My father named me for a famous poet from our homeland. Taras."

Nail on the head! Poet. Just as I suspected. I wanted to ask what homeland that was—Terre-Oz? He displayed no trace of a foreign accent, except maybe when he said his own name. Nothing un-Canadian about him, but obviously not a local. Instead, I relented. "A neat double vodka it is, Tear-oss."

"But wait," he insisted. "Where do I find reciprocity? You have not offered up your own name and I feel cheated."

"Cheated?" I snorted.

"An unpleasant sensation. One should experience it, but not repeatedly. I think the cause of ulcers and lunacy—"

He would have gone on, but I interrupted him. "Ina."

"Eye-nuh?" he repeated, trying my syllables on for size. "Diminutive of what?"

I stared at him.

"Is it short for Angelina? Katarina? Delphina? But then, I suppose you'd pronounce it, *Ee*-nuh, not *Eye*-nuh?"

"It's just plain old Ina," I repeated, not about to reveal that Ina was actually short for Regina—not pronounced like royalty, but rather like the Saskatchewan city where I suspected I'd been conceived, since my mother, without a shred of irony, had bragged about seeing the Mountie Musical Ride while on her honeymoon. Out loud, I said to the man-who-walked-into-a-bar, "Just say to yourself, 'Ina … rhymes with the private part.' Hard to forget that way."

He blinked several times, as if I'd managed to embarrass him, but then he tapped his temple and said, "I have committed it to memory, Ina-Rhymes-With. Never to be forgotten."

Unwilling to give him the last word, I said, "Well, with introductions out of the way, does Mister Genius still require a beverage? 'Cause if so … I-na gonna get your drink now, Tear-oss."

As I turned toward the bar, a reluctant sideways grin laced his face, compelling enough to make me wobble on my heels.

I'd barely set the glass down on his table when he reached for it

The Twistical Nature of Spoons

and shot it back like a drink of water. His bottom lip quivered for a split second, but otherwise there was no response to the bite of booze at all. I waited. This was the time when your hardcore drunk usually said, "Another, please."

"You spiked my drink."

"Huh?" I said. "No, I didn't."

"Oh, but you did, Eye-nuh. Perhaps only an eye-dropper's worth. But I can taste it." He nodded with appreciation.

"Taste what?" I demanded.

"It is either hapless compassion or … soulful yearning. Or both? They can taste similar mixed with vodka. Indistinguishable—like a melody one is hearing for the first time." He looked up and searched my face. "Ina, may I enquire? What is the secret of your uplifting concoction?" he asked.

"It's straight booze, like you ordered."

"Until *you* served it," he countered in a tone way too earnest for a pick-up line.

"Riiiiight," I said, shaking my head at him. I reached my right hand out to clear his glass, but he caught me gently by the wrist.

He said, "I'll keep the glass. I like to stare into them when they're empty." Then he turned my hand, palm-side up, and ran his own hand over mine to flatten my fingers, which I'd unconsciously balled into a fist. Before he released me, he peered at my palm; his head drooped, and he gently curled my fingers back into a fist and let go.

I swiped the twenty off the table. *Ass-crack weirdo*, I thought in an attempt to summon some defences. Even for a poet, he talked insanely. But his words had touched a nerve. And his touch had unnerved me. Go scrub my hand or never wash it again? Antony, although careful to be courteous about it, did not put up with the clutch-and-grab crowd in his establishment—he could turn politely menacing if push came to shove. The regulars knew this and kept their hands to themselves—one of the reasons I stayed on at Three Sheets. But Antony was kicking back with his buddies on the other side of the bar, cleaning up at the pool table, leaving me the run of the place with him only a shout away. I should have called him over right then and there.

When I returned with Taras's change, his empty glass had been refilled. The coaster was cockeyed beneath it. I squinted at him and then at the clear liquid contents. For some reason, I glanced over my shoulder as if some imaginary barmaid had come and refilled it for him. It couldn't have been Antony; the click of colliding billiard balls still sounded amidst jeers and cheering. Water from the bathroom tap? But I hadn't noticed Taras vacate his chair.

"What the hell?" I said, angry that I couldn't pose a more intelligent question.

"I beg your pardon, but I thought we had an agreement," Taras responded.

I squinted even harder at him.

He added, "When I made it a double and you decided to leave me alone back here."

"I didn't ... I wasn't ..." I sputtered. How could my fleeting thought have become a verbal contract? I took a step back from him.

He smirked into his glass before he downed the contents a second time, but any sign of glee was wiped away by a second wince. Not tap water, then, unless he had an aversion to chlorine. Continuing to clutch his change in my right hand, I stuck out my left and motioned for him to give up the glass.

He ignored my gesture, methodically reached into an inner pocket of his vest, and produced a small silver flask.

"Hey, you know you can't do that in here!" I hissed, checking over my shoulder a second time. "Antony is a good guy, but he doesn't put up with shenanigans."

"Go ahead, call your boss. By the time he ambles over, the evidence will have vanished." He unscrewed the cap, poured out a stiff four fingers, and took it in two gulps. He waved the glass at me in

The Twistical Nature of Spoons

a salute. "But at least you can feel saved then, yes? Perhaps you are secretly in love with the boss. Trust that he will leave his wife and children?"

There wasn't an ounce of truth in his taunt, but it irked me enough to ensure I wasn't going to call Antony over. "Give me the glass and head home, Tear-oss." Disappointment crept into my voice, though I couldn't say why. "Wherever that might be." I signalled again for him to hand it over.

At the sight of my outstretched hand, he jolted forward. He was staring at my left palm, eyes narrowed. I wondered if he'd emptied that flask and was about to pass out, but his focus remained fixed on my hand. I withdrew it as if it was in danger. That provoked him, and he sprang from his chair. I opened my mouth to call for Antony, but Taras shook his head vehemently, and pressed his hands together in a pleading gesture.

"Wait!" he insisted. He pointed a finger to hold me there. "Don't," he said, a cross between a plea and a warning. "How did you get that scar on your palm?"

I whipped my hand behind my back. "I accidentally broke a bottle."

Taras winced. "Working here at the bar? Or at some other pursuit?"

I shrugged. It was none of his business that a year earlier I'd been down at the harbour, as had been my habit at the time, launching an emptied lemon gin bottle with a message stuffed inside it. Glass bottles had become my obsession, and I'd been brainstorming ways to transform them into artsy objects. My creative ventures didn't include shatter-proofing. Having polished off the dregs of the gin that evening, I was slightly tipsy on the rocky shoreline.

"Freaky," I said, remembering, "because one minute, glass is so smooth and enchanting. The next, it's deadly. Know what I mean?"

His intent focus redirected to my face. "Unyielding, even though we see right through it."

"But we can also see our reflection in it," I said.

"At light's behest," he agreed.

"Yes, depending on the light."

"Exactly!" His tone turned intimate. "And the wound? What was to blame? Labour or love?"

I snorted, wondering how he sensed there was a story to coax out of me. But I still wasn't about to admit to the strangest of strangers that I'd been attempting to send a message with an elaborate pen-and-ink-sketched border to an as-yet-unmet future husband. It was bad enough cramming my vulnerability into a bottle for art's sake; I wasn't about to compound that by confessing to it. That week's criteria had been a man with respectable career ambitions; I chose a Buckingham Palace guard, hence the gin. Back then, my plan had been to save tips, travel the world, seek out artistic wonders, and cross paths with the finders of my messages. That particular blood-splattered note never did get launched.

Taras interrupted my thoughts. "Did you faint? Cry? Swear? Scream to the heavens?" he persisted.

I was back in the bar. Pool balls clicked. Glasses clinked. "I caught the bus to the hospital," I said. "I can tell you, Taras, the driver wasn't keen on letting me on with my hand wrapped in a blood-soaked sweater. Took five stitches."

He mumbled, "So this is her pronouncement."

I thought he was referring to me mangling his name. "Tell me again how you say it."

He ignored my request and gestured for me to display my palm.

I shook my head, offering him his change which I'd retained in my other hand. "You should leave," I repeated.

"I must see it," he said, and then muttered in a self-deprecating way, "I checked the wrong hand." When I refused to cooperate, he drawled, "Eye-nuh, free will is a philosopher's fabrication. You think you choose not to show me? There is no choice. There

The Twistical Nature of Spoons

cannot be. I did not choose to find you here tonight. Yet here we are. Inescapable fate, Ina."

He shrugged, with a hint of apology, a layer of acceptance, as if we'd both been victims of some scam for which there was no recourse. His lopsided grin flickered in and out of regret and mirth.

I glanced around the room to avoid the expression on his face. The patrons who had craned their necks when Taras had sprung from his chair had already lost interest, turning back to their drinks, their companions, the muted TV with its sports stats scrolling across the bottom of the screen. The room, although familiar, also seemed unrecognizable. Like the feeling you get when you return from a holiday, and there's your chair and knitted throw just where you left them, but it's as if they've been having a life of their own without you, changed in some subtle way, so they don't feel like yours at first glance. That's the shift I felt while Taras waited for me to show him my hand, as if maybe time had passed in the room, and I hadn't been there to experience it.

I thrust his money at him. "Take your change and hit the road," I insisted.

He awkwardly juggled his empty glass in an attempt to accept his bills and coins. A quarter fell between our hands. We watched it roll across the plank floor, neither of us moving to retrieve it.

"As you wish. But you can't alter the outcome any more than you can erase that scar—your extra lifeline."

I turned to see Taras's face, but he was already staggering toward the door, bellowing, "Amethyst. From the Greek *amethustos*—not intoxicated! Never give up your gem before the night is done." He laughed maniacally.

An extra lifeline? What was he talking about? But before I could check my scar, I realized that deposited in my right hand, in place of his change, was a small spoon. The kind you buy at a souvenir shop. Taras had somehow put it there, but I hadn't felt a thing. The silvery bowl was stamped *Thunder Bay*. There was a mangled twist in the handle and embedded at the end, an amethyst stone the colour of grape Lik-M-Aid. Teetering on my heels, I zigzagged between the tables in pursuit of him. I wanted to tell him to shove his poor excuse for a tip up his poetic derrière.

His stagger turned nimble as he approached the exit. He flung the door open. The temperature outside had dropped, and fog had rolled in from the harbour. The Three Sheets neon sign blinked a blue sheen, first illuminating Taras in the enveloping fog, and then casting him in eerie dimness. Blink. Blink. In one fluid motion, he toasted the air—"*Dai Bozhe!*"—and smashed the glass on the sidewalk. The door swung shut behind him. When I shoved it open again, the sidewalk was littered with glass shards, glittering under blue neon. Blink. Blink. Taras was nowhere to be seen.

2

Blisse

spoon croon

Although I have blips of early memory concerning the spoons, my first prolonged, vivid recollection is attached to a particular day. I am six years old. Ina is allowing me to ride my bicycle, independently, up and down a short section of our quiet back alley. My outings behind our house make me anxious. The rear edges of people's properties are often the most neglected, sprouting reminders of the world's fragility: tufts of weeds, the glitter of broken glass, amputated pieces of furniture. Our back lane, although not quite sinister, has a claustrophobic air to it.

It is a Saturday in April, my fingers chilly on the handlebars of my bike, leaf buds peeking out from the branches of the neighbourhood's trees, not quite ready to burst into the verdant hue that borders on neon. I ignore my back-lane misgivings when I spy the wooden box on a pile of discarded items, including a steam iron and some yellowed kitchen curtains, a few houses down. I brake well before the heap, knowing that although Ina shops regularly at the local thrift store, she would not approve of me picking up other people's castoffs. I recognize that the dark wooden chest is for holding silverware; I saw others like it at a store downtown when Ina took me to help browse for gift ideas in the off chance her recently engaged cousin Charlene got around to setting a wedding date. During that excursion, Ina informed me that a whole box of silverware is called a canteen. I thought a canteen was just the cubby in my school where the bigger kids bought chocolate milk and erasers.

As I sit on my bike in the alley, a lot of thoughts fill my head at once. Cousin Charlene lives in the city of Thunder Bay, and we shop at Hudson's Bay, but I have never seen an actual bay. Ina says maybe I will see Thunder Bay if we can ever afford to take a holiday. I know in my heart that would be special because I would see both a bay and the original spoon's city. In the meantime, there is a wooden box, just like the one at The Bay, right in our alley. My spotting it suggests a profound symmetry to me, like life is not just willy-nilly; that everything in the world happens for a reason, because that cast-off box would be perfect to house my spoons. The idea makes my heart thump as if I have just uncovered a treasure chest on a tropical island.

There are seven spoons now. I recently made them into a family, and I imagine them living in the wooden enclosure. Daddyspoon, Mommyspoon, Daughterspoon, Sonspoon, Babyspoon, Grannyspoon, and Petspoon: a family quite distinct from my own, which consists of Ina and me. Before I christened them, the spoons served other numerous purposes. I practised my first counting skills with them, ate my cereal with the one that has a U-bend in the handle—the one I call Daughterspoon. The spoons made great bubble scoops when Ina saw fit to add a drop of dish soap to my bathwater. They also served as excellent noisemakers, and I loved licking the bowl of the one with the simplest right-angle bend—Sonspoon—and sticking it to my nose—transforming myself into a Seuss-esque caricature.

The Twistical Nature of Spoons

The box beckons. I inch my bicycle closer and recognize the hurdles to acquiring it. First off, the thought of garbage picking makes me feel ashamed. Secondly, I know my plastic basket is not large enough for the box's heft, and my training wheels have only been off for a month. I do not trust my balance. If I simply grab the box and run home, it will mean abandoning my bicycle, and that borders on felonious. My bike was cheaply purchased at a police auction the previous spring, a day when I caught a rare glimpse of Ina flirting. The officer on the receiving end of her attention had kneeled down and reminded me to take care of my new purchase and lock it up if I left it unattended. When he stood again, Ina concurred, batting her eyelashes at him—an awkward and unsettling moment for me—but one which I intuitively understood: his ship-shape, conformist grooming and the factory-fresh, authoritative squeak of his leather gun holster demanded a response that was outside the norm. Much to my distress, Ina's submissive regard appeared to evaporate shortly afterward, as she never bothered to acquire the promised bicycle lock—mostly because she spent the next week transforming our porch into a monument of national pride for upcoming Canada Day, scooping up every free or ultra-cheap miniature maple-leaf-flag product available. My bike security was shuffled down the list of priorities. But on that evening after the auction, she did inform me it was time I stop referring to her as Mommy and call her Ina instead. I would be going to kindergarten, she reminded me, and that was an indication that I had earned the right to be a big girl and call her by her given name. When I protested that even older children called their mothers Mommy, she responded, "Yes, Blisse, but you're pretty darn special. I've told you that since you were born. And so, you don't always have to do what other kids do."

It is possible I may have created Spoonfamily to ensure there would still be a mommy in our home.

In the back lane, I check over my shoulder. A calico cat is

soundlessly slinking down the length of a fence. Birds chirp, oblivious. The tinkle of my mother's glass wind chimes can still be heard. I pedal hard to the pile, dismount, and snatch the box up. It weighs more than I imagined, and the wooden surface bears scratches that explain its discarded status. Sensing it is empty, I open it to glance inside. The royal-blue felt part of the lining is covered in lint, but the white satin is pure and intact and provides a formality to the interior. Upward mobility harkens—my spoon family can move out of their cereal box! Struggling to hold my bike upright, I prop the open chest over my basket and handlebars. I remount and attempt to shove off, but I wobble so severely that I have to abandon the pedals and roll myself forward, my sneakers slipping on the gravel, akin to a hapless thief who has neglected to fuel up the getaway car. I am certain someone is giving chase but dare not check behind. I am frightened I will topple and smash the box to smithereens. Somehow, I make it to our yard.

 Toting the chest, I muscle it through our back door and kitchen, then pass directly into the front foyer, which doubles as my play space. My bedroom, which was originally the walk-in pantry off the kitchen, is only large enough to house my bed and small dresser. And although the foyer is the main focal point for Ina's seasonal decorating—which means I am often crammed in and competing for space with the revolving bevy of reindeer and bunnies and ghouls—I love the tall mantel fixed over the fake fireplace, the two stained-glass panels that Ina made before I was born, which hang from thin chains in the narrow windows on either side of our front door, and the bookshelf in the corner that is not stacked with how-to craft magazines, but is all mine. Best of all, by planting myself here, I can see our lodger arrive at our front entrance or descend the staircase to leave. She cannot come or go from her own rooms without passing by me. Presently, I am enamoured with Miss Chen, a foreign student who Ina said chose to move out of her rowdy university residence to our quiet second

The Twistical Nature of Spoons

floor. I love the melodic intonation of her accent and believe if she already speaks two languages and has come to Canada to study, she must be the smartest person I will ever hope to meet. I want to enquire about the ceramic cat she has placed on the first landing to her suite. It has one paw raised, as if it is beckoning me to come and play. I wonder if Miss Chen ever imagines that the statue might come alive, but I do not dare ask in case she finds me silly.

I was less fond of Mrs. Gardinier, who had previously presided over the suite. She had a beak-like nose and always seemed to know the neighbourhood's business, unlike Ina, who remains aloof from other people living around us. I did, however, recognize the singular pipeline into adult matters Mrs. Gardinier provided, so whenever she came downstairs to lament her personal affairs or deliver some gossip to my mother, I tried to remain in close proximity. One day, she came down without invitation, nudged her way into our kitchen, and started speaking to Ina in a near whisper. From where I sat playing in the foyer, I could still catch large snippets.

She said, "Well, if she was my kid, I think it'd be high time to get her checked."

"For what?" Ina responded.

"Well, they know stuff nowadays. Doesn't seem normal, you know?"

"Normal?" Ina's voice was growing louder.

Mrs. Gardinier's volume increased too. "Talking to spoons like that? Making up voices for them. I heard her. More than once."

"She's playing. She's an imaginative child," Ina declared.

Mrs. Gardinier sniffed at my mother. "Well, there's another thing. She doesn't talk like a kid. Uses such big words. And why not play with dolls? Surely you can afford one for her. If not, put your name on the Christmas Cheer list. Why spoons? Cripes, what's next? Knives?"

I heard Ina's footsteps thudding toward the door. I tucked myself between the wall and the bookshelf and slid my little wooden chair in front of me in hopes that I would not be spotted. When my mother flung the kitchen door wide open, I suspected I was in trouble. Ina does not want me to draw attention to the spoons. I peeked through the chair spindles.

My mother's face was registering dread, but the words she directed at Mrs. Gardinier were fearless. "Don't ever talk about her or her spoons again."

Mrs. Gardinier exited our kitchen. "Suit yourself," she said and shrugged. "No skin off my nose."

Ina's voice lowered into a growl. "Right, it's not. Maybe your nose should stick to its own family's business. Find out why your own kids won't visit you."

Mrs. Gardinier practically screeched, "My kids are ungrateful."

Ina muttered, "Well then, why would I take your advice on how to raise mine?"

I wanted to chime in, "So there!" But I knew better than to draw attention to the fact I was crouched there listening to every word. Mrs. Gardinier huffed up the stairs to her rooms, and later that evening, gave Ina notice she was moving out. Ina did nothing to dissuade her. Instead, without any explanation, my mother told me to change back out of my pyjamas because we were going out for ice cream, despite it being my bedtime. I did not hesitate. The sound of the wind in the treetops and the rushing night traffic helped erase the earlier conflict. Ina held my hand all the way there and all the way back. She didn't let go even when we needed our other hands to hold our cones.

As I carry the chest into the foyer, I am relieved Mrs. Gardinier no longer lives in our house. No doubt she would accuse me of stealing it. I am concerned enough that Ina might make me return it to the back alley. I can hear my mother in the basement doing laundry, so I quickly use Scotch tape to dab the lint out of the box lining, collect the spoons from their cardboard container, and arrange them in the chest. The spoons look so replete nestled in

The Twistical Nature of Spoons

their new abode. At one end lies the oversized Daddy serving spoon with its handle bent in a complete circular loop starting right at the neck; and last in line, the souvenir spoon with its handle's single twist and little purple stone embedded on its tip. It is the smallest spoon, the one I named Petspoon and which Ina refers to as "The Original." The one she sometimes also calls "the proof—witnessed with my own eyes." It is the only spoon that technically belongs to her and not me, but it is never apart from my collection. She entrusts it to me, she says, because when I was teething, I rejected all the rubber rings and freezer-gel gizmos and only found relief if that spoon was in my mouth: "How you never choked, or swallowed that amethyst, Blisse, I will never know. Well, I do know, actually. Or at least, I believe I know."

I fail to hear Ina enter the foyer until she yelps, "For the love of Javex, where did that come from?"

I whirl around and jump aside, as if by not touching the canteen, I can avoid association with it. At the same time I want it to be in full view.

She looks puzzled and demands, "Did that old meddler leave that here?"

"Mrs. Gardinier? No. I found it in the alley. It was at the house with the shiny metal garbage cans, but it wasn't touching the garbage."

Ina runs her hand through her tangled curls and then, noticing she has a hair elastic wrapped around her wrist, sweeps the whole mess into a ponytail and secures it. She circles the chest. "You got that home by yourself? And you're sure it was thrown out, Blisse?"

I nod my head, my lips pursed so I do not break into a smile. Even at that age, I seem to understand that Ina cannot bear to see me unhappy, but I also sense she loves to be the one who cajoles happiness out of me.

"Well, that's impressive, Missy Blissey."

My grin cracks open.

"Makes the spoons look extra special, doesn't it?" she says, nodding with positive assessment.

"I can keep it?"

She shoots me a sideways glance. "Sure." She shrugs. "Why not? You'll have to vacuum the thing out, but it's a good find."

I throw myself at her and hug her legs. She picks me up and twirls me in a tight circle, my feet flying out toward the mantel and banister.

"While you've got the vacuum out, you can run it around the foyer for me," she says when she puts me back down then returns to the laundry.

It is vital I obey Ina's vacuuming request, but I also want to celebrate with my spoons. I place the canteen on my bookshelf in the foyer. *Really favourable digs,* Daddyspoon congratulates me with his polished tone. Sonspoon does a few backflips while Petspoon barks with pleasure, causing Grannyspoon's gale of laughter to surrender to a tarnished coughing fit. Mommyspoon bestows a silvery kiss atop Daughterspoon's head.

With being swept up in my afternoon chores, I only have time to wave to my metal family as Ina and I later head out the door for our once-a-week fast-food supper. I ignore the niggling at the back of my head that reminds me to put the case back in my room before departing. My happiness convinces me that my good fortune is untouchable, and so I do not even stop to shut the lid. I did not imagine we would return to the house, stuffed with fries and milkshakes, to discover one of the spoons missing.

Ina notices it as soon as we walk through the front door. She goes straight to the case. "Blisse, did you bring a spoon with you to McD's?" she asks.

I shake my head, uncomprehending.

"Where's the spoon?" she cries out, as if it has been thrown down a well and she can hear it in the distance, pleading for a rope.

I shut and reopen the lid. Check behind the canteen. Shuffle

The Twistical Nature of Spoons

some books out of the way. Mommyspoon is missing. It is the only one with a straight handle and a transformed bowl. The sides of it are bent upwards toward the middle, giving the spoon the appearance of having a mouth if you hold it sideways. It also resembles an oyster shell that could house a pearl within its folded edges. The ornate filigree on its handle and tip lends it a regal air—a spoon fit for a mermaid queen's table.

Ina unlocks our kitchen door and grabs her key ring for the upstairs suite. I scamper up behind her as she takes the stairs two at a time. After banging so hard on Miss Chen's door it bounces on its hinges, Ina unlocks it and flings the door open. The change in room pressure pastes the thin curtains against an open window. That sight further fuels Ina's fury; she always counsels our lodgers to close their windows when leaving the house. I watch as she scatters papers from Miss Chen's makeshift desk and whips the neatly made bed into a jumbled pile. Amidst the mounting chaos, I spot Mommyspoon sitting atop the battered dresser, alongside a pair of chopsticks in a bowl of instant noodles. Miss Chen has clearly borrowed it.

I tug at the edge of Ina's shirt and point. She stares at it for a moment, and instead of simply retrieving the spoon and exiting, Ina grabs hold of the top dresser drawer, pulls it completely out, and dumps the contents onto Miss Chen's floor. She springs to the open window, removes the screen, gathers the heap of socks and T-shirts from the floor, and flings them out, watching them parachute from the second storey down. For good measure, she dumps the contents of another drawer on the floor and then, as if she is drained of all energy, she lurches back toward the staircase and down the steps. At first, I remain frozen in place. I survey the room's damage before inching to the gaping window. I peek out to view Miss Chen's garments strewn across our lawn, one piece snagged on the overhang which protrudes from the front porch. Some vagrant socks have made it as far as the row of wooden tulips that Ina plants on our lawn to welcome spring. I turn from the window and pick up the spoon—a single remnant of sticky noodle is caught in the place where the pearl should be—and I wish I had paid attention to the niggle at the back of my head earlier and put the spoons back in my room where they belong. More than that, I wish I had left the wooden chest in the alley. If I had, I am sure none of this would have happened.

I long to run about our front yard, picking up our lodger's clothing, but I suspect Ina would not be pleased if I did. At least Miss Chen is all finished with her exams; I overheard her tell Ina they went well. It is Ina's behaviour that does not make sense. A few months prior, she went out of her way to lessen our student's possible homesickness by hanging lanterns in our foyer to celebrate Chinese New Year. I cannot reconcile Ina's punishment with the transgression, as I doubt Miss Chen had any intention of stealing the spoon, but merely wished to use it to eat. Her only misdemeanour was forgetting to return it. That, and leaving her window open.

As I wash the spoon in Miss Chen's bathroom sink and pat it dry on my T-shirt, a thought lodges in my head. The spoons that I receive on my birthday each year, fashioned for me by my father before his death, must be more special than Ina has ever admitted. Otherwise, why such a fierce reaction to one gone missing? Although Ina has assured me that every family has a secret that they never, ever reveal to anyone—it is the extra glue that binds a family—and that ours just happens to be the origin of the spoons, I can now see that our secret must be far more significant than even the most ultimate cross-my-heart pinky swear. Ina clearly feared that just by eating with one, Miss Chen might guess our spoons' secret. I tuck Mommyspoon into the crook of my neck, lean against its solid, cool touch, and close my eyes. An involuntary giggle wells up inside me from the intensity of my newfound knowledge. What I accepted as normal is not so. There is a blindingly wondrous enormity to being the daughter of a man who could bend spoons with the power of his mind.

Ina

tracks

As I stepped out to sweep up the remains of Taras's smashed bar glass from the sidewalk, his words swarmed in my head. Could the scar on my palm really be considered an extra lifeline? My brain started itching. Second lifeline? Just what had I been doing with my first? Where had my see-the-world plans flown off to?

When my cousin Charlene first urged me to move east from Winnipeg to live with her in Thunder Bay, her ultimate plan for us was to save some funds and do some global partying together. I was up for escape. I'd already axed the idea of college. When people, including my mother, wanted to ridicule studies they thought were a waste of time and money, they called it "majoring in basket weaving." But that was the exact thing I wanted to do—basket weaving or sponge painting or gluing layers of collage. Crafting stayed on as my pastime, but I stuck to serving jobs, and Char, to hairdressing. We socked away all our tips in preparation for sailing out of Lakehead Harbour, and I started to fantasize about visiting the Louvre or gazing up in the Sistine Chapel. That was when Char figured I might not be the ideal travel partner after all. Partying with students on the Left Bank? Yes. Watching them paint? No.

Not long after, Char found herself a caveman boyfriend, which at first made me more determined to leave on my own. But then, for a year or two, when Unibrow was sluggish to propose, I thought Charlene would give up on him, freeing us to go as planned. I doused my impatience, dabbling in macramé and découpage. I borrowed from my tip fund and signed up for stained-glass classes. But Charlene stuck it out with the mammoth hunter, and what happened to adventure-seeking Ina after that? I went on a blind date with gravity and turned into static Ina, that's what. Apart from the odd excursion down to Duluth for cross-border shopping, and a dutiful return to Winnipeg for Christmas every other year, I'd become as grounded as the Sleeping Giant—that slumber-posed peninsula that defined our harbour view. Somehow, three more years passed, and I seemed as likely to leave as the rock giant was to rise and yawn himself awake.

Standing outside the Three Sheets doorway, the chilly night air started to seep into my pores. I took a deep breath to counteract my shivering—an oily whiff of wharf tar mingled with a sprinkling of winter rot. In the distance, out on the harbour breakwall, the fog tried its best to blind the lighthouse beacon. I bent over the glass shards with a dustpan. The spoon Taras had placed in my hand earlier, which was stowed in my jeans pocket, dug into my hip. I dropped the dustpan and fished it out. Its twisted handle disturbed me. Grabbing both ends of the spoon, careful not to dislodge the mounted gemstone on its tip, I attempted to straighten it. Despite a fragile appearance, it was rigid. Didn't budge. It struck me how odd that someone had palmed me a bent spoon, but I sure wasn't about to get sentimental about it. I closed my eyes and pitched it as far as I could. There was a metallic ping as the spoon struck something, but I refused to even glance down the sidewalk in its

The Twistical Nature of Spoons

direction. With glass slivers gritty beneath my shoes, I finished sweeping up the shards. They glittered in the neon light, almost as if they were tittering about a joke I wasn't in on. As if they knew the alluring punchline to the man-who-walked-into-a-bar. I stomped back inside and dumped them in the trash, knowing I was probably tracking some glass dust underfoot. No kicking off my shoes at the end of my shift for cash-out. Antony, a look of concern pasted on his face, barrelled toward me, demanding to know what was going on.

After I told him about the guy who smashed the glass, Antony insisted he'd be sending me home in a cab that night. He knew I preferred the five-block walk home, even at 1:00 a.m., so after we closed up and cashed out, he followed me out the door, whistled for the taxi waiting outside the lounge down the street—our only neighbourhood competition—shoved some cash at the driver, and told him my address, adding, "Keep the change." I shot Antony a look of resignation. There was no point taking my frustrations out on him.

I slid into the backseat of the cab and something on the upholstery jabbed into my thigh. "What the ...?" I fished out the offending object, holding it up to the cab's overhead interior light. The mangled spoon glinted, and its tiny purple stone winked.

The driver, glancing in his rearview mirror, apologized. "Whoa, sorry 'bout that. That's from my last fare." He turned to take it from me.

"No!" I insisted. "No, this is my spoon. I chucked it down the street earlier. How did it get in here?" I imagined the fluke of it sailing through an open taxi window.

He shook his head. "Well, loco as it sounds, the guy asked if I wanted to see him bend that thing." He hesitated. "Though I swear it was straight then. Anyways, I says to him, 'Another time, man,' 'cause it's clear he's pretty loaded. And then I tell him they mine those amethysts not far from here, and he proceeds to tell me if you carry an amethyst, you stay sober when you're drinking. And

Patti Grayson

I says, 'I guess that stone's too small, man.' Maybe that's why he left it on the backseat." Pulling out from the curb, the driver chuckled with self-satisfaction. "The guy called me 'an amusing sire.' I been called worse."

"This is mine," I insisted. "Your last fare was my customer, and he gave me this spoon when he left the bar." Did Taras watch me pitch the spoon, or did he happen upon it later?

The driver shook his head in confusion. "Dark hair? Down vest? Drunk?"

I nodded.

"Same guy, then," he shrugged. "Well, keep it if you insist. It's too effin' weird for me to explain …" He chuckled. "Spoons, for cripes' sake. Still, can't top the guy last week with the boa constrictor. I kid you not, gets into my cab with a baby boa under his leather jacket! Pedal to the metal on that ride." He lifted his hands off the wheel in a gesture that indicated he alone was both doomed and entitled to drive the world's weirdness around.

"Where did you drop tonight's fare?"

"Say what?" He regained control of the steering wheel, keeping his eyes on the road.

"Where did you take Spoon-Man?" I repeated.

He concentrated, as if checking his blind spot demanded his full attention, before answering. "Can't say. Company policy and all that jazz."

"Okay, don't say. Just drive there."

"Hey, your boss-man said two-twenty Elgin and now we're less than a block away …"

At that moment, the static crackle of his dispatch radio broke through the air. "One-five-eight, can you head back to LU? Pickup at Centennial, main door."

The driver hesitated. His eyes shifted from his rearview mirror to his dash before lifting the radio mic. "Roger that," he muttered into it.

The Twistical Nature of Spoons

I pondered. LU. Lakehead Univeristy. "Campus?"

The driver said nothing, but his index finger tapped the steering wheel repeatedly.

I said, "You can drive back with no fare, or I stay in your cab and pay you on top of what Antony handed you."

He took a hard left. "Hey, doll. It's your life. But a drunk with a spoon fetish? Cripes," he said, shaking his head, sounding as if he'd prefer something cold-blooded and venomous in his cab over the likes of me.

Part of me agreed with what he was saying, but I was suddenly more troubled by what awaited me if I simply went home: darkened doors and windows, save for the porch's single bulb; Charlene either sound asleep or spending the night at the caveman's; the cramped front entrance with its scramble of shoes and boots to stumble over. Its stagnation filled me with dread. Plus, the longer I held on to the mutilated souvenir, the more jittery my pulse grew. I'd never sleep. It made no sense tracking Taras, but alternatives escaped me. And hey, look me in the eye and tell me you've never done something rash in your life.

Due to the additional layer of fog that had set in, or his preoccupied reluctance to have me in his cab, the driver overshot the entrance to the Centennial Building. As he U-turned in the middle of the street to head back to the parking lot, the cab slid sideways on the damp pavement. I groped for the door handle to maintain my balance. That's when I spotted the lone figure in the distance. For a moment, I'd doubted what I'd seen: a silhouette of a person, arms outstretched as if attempting to fly, hovering over the campus lake. I was certain it was Taras.

Before I could lose sight of the figure, I yelled at the driver to stop, tossed some bills into the front seat, and bounded out of the cab. I cursed my stupid platform shoes, charging ahead with minced steps, afraid I was about to go ass over teakettle on the damp grass as I approached the walkway. From my new vantage point, I realized the elevated figure was balancing on the handrail of a footbridge, but the fog made it feel as if I'd stumbled into a place where people could float if they knew how. As I got closer, the lights from the surrounding walkway lit him up like a circus tightrope walker. This was the point where a hush would fall over the crowd, and they'd hold their collective breath. Only thing was, his safety net was a concrete spillway. Lake Tamblyn had been man-made to moderate the river's spring flooding. I broke into a half run.

When I was close enough, I yelled his name across the expanse. Not my best idea. His arms windmilled and he teetered. I rushed forward. He managed to regain his balance, and then, lifting off the railing, he landed upright on the bridge as if his life had not been endangered seconds earlier. He waited there, hands in his vest pockets, as I panted my way toward him. The sound of rushing water underfoot made my pulse leap into my throat as I trekked onto the bridge.

For a moment, neither of us spoke.

He seemed quite sober when he drawled, "Eye-nuh. It is enough to contemplate how you found me, but the deeper mystery is why you wish me drowned?"

I thrust the spoon toward him, ignoring his taunt. "I needed to return this to you."

His mouth turned up with slight amusement. "Instincts like a homing pigeon. Lately, I've been wishing I could stop feeling compelled to bend them. I think they object. There is a resistance these days, as if they sense my coming and brace themselves." He took the spoon from my hand and made a fist around it, knuckles down. I observed his closed eyes, the slight backward tilt of his head. A crease appeared between his eyebrows. I was uncertain if he was in pain or just concentrating. As he opened his eyes again, he rotated his fist and splayed his fingers open. The spoon sat flat, restored.

My breath caught and then released in a puff of visible air. "How did you …? What in the name of …?"

The Twistical Nature of Spoons

I reached for the spoon in his open palm, but he closed his fist around it a second time. I glanced up, but he was staring past me. I checked over my shoulder.

His voice grew anxious. "Souvenir spoons are not meant to conjure drab memories … but rather evoke the thrill of exploring new milieus." Unfurling his fingers, he revealed the little spoon with a twist in its handle again, but at a slightly different angle, closer to the bowl.

I blinked hard, willing my eyes to see it whole and pristine. "Okay, this is too frickin' weird! How, Taras?"

He tapped his finger to the side of his forehead and shrugged.

"Yeah, right," I declared and guffawed, but then I took a good, hard look at his face. "Hey, you're not that guy who's on TV, are you?"

A smirk appeared on his face. "I have asked myself, why the bestowment if not to exploit this meagre entertainment?" His amusement disappeared. "I think there is another answer. Until I discover what it is, I choose a low profile."

"If you don't want to draw attention to yourself, why bother showing me at all?"

He tapped the spoon against his chin as if considering his next words carefully. "I had hoped, Ina, it might prompt you to continue to stare at me with your look of blissful wonder."

"Oh," was all I could manage to say.

"Unless it's a ruse," he said, as if talking to himself, "and you agree with my no-longer wife that my life's pursuits are foolish." He held up three fingers. "Her trident of insults includes: one, trifling; two, child's play; and three, waste of precious time." He made as if to leave the footbridge, then paused. "Do you concur, Ina? If so, why does your gaze illuminate and make me forget my own limitations?" He offered me the spoon again. "Take it. My damaged heart beseeches you."

I looked from him to the bent metal. "Your no-longer wife?" I repeated. Taras had just insinuated he bent a damn spoon with his mind, and that I was some kind of light source, but I was somehow more distracted by the word "wife."

The energy that had seeped out of Taras seemed to be retained in the spoon. It was as if it was challenging me to take it up. I plucked it from his hand and shoved it in my coat pocket, where I could feel its warmth lingering. My hand remained wrapped around it, and the fog and chill of the night shifted into something wondrous. As if just being alive in that single moment could be enough.

Once the spoon was in my pocket, Taras nodded at me. His voice remained flat. "It was the first time in three years that she didn't complain I had to tour. She wasn't without her reasons. I fell short. She is not to blame for finding me lacking. Yet I didn't suspect she'd slink behind my back with her doctoral thesis advisor and make a cuckold of me. He, an expert on the 'active voice,' of all things, and a walking billboard for machismo, as evidenced by his repulsively hairy hands."

In my inability to sift through my feelings at that moment, I blurted, "My cousin dates one of those. She wants his hairy hand in matrimony." I snorted. "His voice is not active. But gawd, my cousin says he's an expert at tongue action."

Taras cocked his head at me. I knew I was rambling—attempting to cover up my desperation to learn how recently Taras's wife had become a no-longer wife. Not only was he strange, but he was on the rebound. I took a step away.

He didn't seem to notice I had thoughts of fleeing. He leaned on the bridge railing and looked over the spillway. "Hairy Hands is ensconced in my marital bed as we speak. She took it when she moved in with him. Heightens the eroticism, no doubt," he stated, with strangled bitterness. He yanked his vest zipper up. "But I try not to begrudge her decision."

I realized I'd just minimized his marriage with my juvenile comparison. Under my breath, I chastised myself, "Take the front

The Twistical Nature of Spoons

seat in ass-class, Ina. It's all yours." That was my exit cue. "Ack, sorry," I said. "Your wife's betrayal is not in the same category as my roommate issues. Not the same at all." I turned my back to leave.

"Perhaps similar enough?" he called. His words stopped me. "Do you consider it rare or common to encounter hands that are hairy enough to warrant this much scrutinous observation and comment, Ina?"

"Well, I'm talking about hands that need daily shampooing. So yeah, rare!" After a moment, I added, "My cousin and I had travelling plans until Paws came along."

Taras reversed his position on the handrail. He leaned back against it before asking, "And where, Ina, would you have ventured?"

"Oh, maybe Italy ... France. I know it's a cliché, but I want to see the *Mona Lisa*. Not just to gawk at her ... They say her eyes follow you around the room, right? Well, I want to know how it feels when a masterpiece checks me out."

Taras quipped, "Platonically or otherwise?"

"No! Like, *observes* me. Trains her mysterious look on me."

"Ahhh!" he acknowledged, and then, as if inquiring on behalf of the entire universe, he gestured broadly. "And with said connection made and knowledge obtained, what then, Ina?"

What then? I tucked my chin into my coat collar, acutely self-conscious. "I don't know. And anyway ... my cousin chose *Fur*-ance instead. Faithful to the *fur*-de-lis."

Taras looked disappointed, but then brightened. "Exceptionally hairy hands posing impediments to others' happiness—perhaps that is uncommon enough to connect us? A link perhaps as significant as great-grandmother's hand pronouncement."

My thoughts clamoured for the puzzle-talk to stop. "Your great-grandmother, Taras? On top of hairy hands, your ancient granny connects us?"

Patti Grayson

He stepped closer and leaned toward me, taking on the posture of a confidant. I expected to catch a whiff of vodka aftermath and a body odour that matched his slightly unkempt appearance. Instead, I detected a trace of cedar soap and lavender fabric softener. I breathed him in as he began.

"When I was five, my parents and I emigrated from Ukraine. Before departing, we paid a final visit to my grandparents in their village. It is my most vivid childhood memory, more defined even than landing in our new country. My great-grandmother, who resided with my grandparents, was revered, but also feared in her village because of her psychic abilities. She read palms. The story goes that out of an obscuring mist, she appeared one morning in their village, unaccompanied—except for the devil riding on her shoulder, some villagers swore, half hidden in her long tresses—and that she bewitched my great-grandfather into taking her for his wife. He was betrothed to another but forsook her. If he hadn't been the community blacksmith and unschooled animal doctor, he likely would have been run out of the village for his immoral behaviour, but his services were depended upon, so the community tolerated the scandalous union.

"During our last visit, *Prababusya* took me aside and read my palm. I remember her sucking in her breath and exclaiming in her native tongue, 'Choose the wrong wife and a curse will come.' She pointed to her own palm, traced her gnarled finger across it, and whispered, 'Seek a hand with an extra lifeline. Not born that way. Seek her.' And then, wagging her finger and smiling wide enough to display several gaps of missing teeth, she emphasized, '*Prababusya* knows. Remember. Beware the curse.'" Taras paused.

I shoved my hands deeper into my coat pockets, closing my scarred fist, tightening my grip on the spoon. I was relieved Taras was at least coherent, despite the fantastical claims he was making.

"She spent much of the remainder of our visit cooing Ukrainian endearments to me and kissing my forehead," Taras continued.

The Twistical Nature of Spoons

"I would not have been described as an excitable child up to that point, but each time her dry old lips touched my forehead, I swear I felt an invigorating, amplified buzzing in my brain. On our final day there, I was staring at a teaspoon lying on the patterned oilcloth that protected the kitchen table. The spoon slid of its own accord across the oilcloth's design. Where it had been atop a rooster to start, it came to rest on a hen nesting on her eggs. I swear I heard the tabletop hen cluck in protest. When I asked the adults if they'd heard the chicken commotion, only *Prababusya* responded in the affirmative, her crooked shoulders shaking with mirth. Everyone else shushed me and told me to go check for eggs in the real henhouse outside." He paused. "If I hadn't believed she was the cause of the spoon phenomenon, I doubt I would've remembered her predictions or taken them to heart."

Without warning, Taras grabbed the bridge handrail and vaulted on top of it, hands outstretched, rising from a crouched position to stand fully erect. He began to inch his way across the rail.

"Come down from there!" I blurted.

"You cannot make me," he responded childishly.

"Fine then," I replied, deciding I'd had enough. I turned in the opposite direction and started walking off the bridge. "I should've stayed in that cab Antony insisted I take home."

From atop the rail, Taras called after me, "You're leaving with my spoon?"

"It's my spoon!" I declared.

"Unless I continue to wish you to have it, there's no telling what havoc it might wreak."

I withdrew it from my pocket and placed it on the final metre of the railing. As I broke contact with the spoon, I suddenly felt the damp night air sink all the way through me, down to my toes. "Fine. Come and get it. But while you're up there tempting fate, think about this: She'll feel guilty at first—your wife. Boohoo, poor beautiful Taras! How tragic. Her active-voice education will pay off when she repeats the story of how you splattered your amplified brains out on this spillway. But in the end, she'll have ol' Hairy Hands consoling her. And don't you think you're just playing right into his furry claws with your double vodkas and death wishes? I do. That's what I think."

Taras lithely ran the length of the thin rail, and as he leapt down onto the bridge, he scooped up the spoon, held it aloft, and blocked my way to the footpath. "Ina, how very unkind," he murmured, clutching his heart as he had done earlier that evening in Three Sheets. But he didn't look hurt. He looked transfixed.

My lips twitched. "But I made you come down. Easy-peasy," I asserted triumphantly before he took a step forward, slipped the spoon into my coat pocket, and stopped up my mouth with his own.

3

Blisse

resplendent tenants

I realize that something is afoot in the morning. Ina seldom shifts into high gear until later in the day, but she is tidying the kitchen at a frantic pace, wiping the counter behind the toaster and tea tins, emptying the overstacked dish rack. The kitchen is all a-clatter. As she clears her latest craft project off the table, she dictates a list of what I need to pack for school. Lately, she has been leaving that up to me, insisting that it is the end of my kindergarten year and I should be acting more like a big girl, making decisions for myself. She no longer dips down onto one knee to fuss if my sneakers are on the wrong feet. I assume it is because she worries she will not finish painting sunflowers onto the stacks of glass votive candle holders in time for the summer markets if she does not delegate some chores to me. This morning, her actions make me anxious, as I have no explanation for our routine's disruption, and I harbour the specific concern of her reverting back to verifying my backpack's contents for herself. Will she discover I have adopted a spoon-of-the-day inclusion? She has always expressly forbidden this. "Too many prying eyes. Too many questions." I had stashed Daddyspoon, with its roller-coaster handle, into an interior zippered pocket. It will be hard to miss the collection's biggest spoon bulging next to my lunch bag. And although I am now expected to remember my clean gym clothes, and to plastic-wrap my own sandwiches, Ina still enforces the rules.

   Recently, I have been very cautious, keeping my spoon family in their put-out-with-the-trash wooden chest, ensuring it is well hidden under my bed each day behind a pile of books. I reason that Ina finds this safekeeping measure justifiable, considering that the Mommyspoon fiasco caused Miss Chen to move out, despite Ina's apologies. Knowing it will take a suspicious and deliberate search on my mother's part to discover a spoon's absence, I have summoned the courage to disobey her. Smuggling a member of my silvery family to class gives me a sense of security. Even though I keep them stowed in my backpack throughout the day, their adjacent proximity boosts my learning. The spoons often seem to be involved when I acquire some new awareness—like the first time I printed my entire name, after seeing it on the stiff tag that accompanied Daughterspoon on my fifth birthday. *Blisse Sterling Trove.* It seemed important to learn the correct order of all the letters for myself because, that day, Ina told me that it was my father who had chosen my middle name before I was born—before he died—and that even if I had been born a boy, my middle name would still have been Sterling. I doubted Ina would have kept Blisse for a boy's first name. But what would she have chosen instead? Blister? I was never thrilled when Ina called me Missy Blissey, but Mister Blister would have been far worse. I turned the tag over and spelled out my entire name without once peeking, happy to be born me.

   When a spoon is nearby, I also find it easier to imagine our conversations. *Be nice to the other children, Blisse, even when they're being mean to you.* That is Grannyspoon's sage reminder. *Good work!* I savour Mommyspoon's praise. And Sonspoon never fails

The Twistical Nature of Spoons

to dish up distraction when the monotony of waiting in line and lying on blankets becomes tedious. *Knock, knock! Who's there? Canoe. Canoe who? Canoe help me with my schoolwork?* And that *clap, clap, clap* is the applause that Daddyspoon provides in my music and gym classes.

My evasive tactic—squirreling my backpack stash to the front door so Ina cannot discover Daddyspoon—is what allows me the opportune first glimpse of Mr. Knowlton Fluxcer's arrival. Through the hazy May drizzle, I see his ancient wood-panelled station wagon pull up on the wrong side of the street and park, nose backward, at the curb in front of our house. Secured on the roof rack with bungee cords are a soggy assortment of cardboard boxes. He switches on his flashers. Struggling out from behind the steering wheel, he holds a spread-open newspaper aloft in an attempt to keep his balding head dry. He momentarily abandons his makeshift protection to pat down his corduroy pants pockets; his keys are still in the ignition, however, and he leans back into the car, retrieves them, and grips them between his teeth as he restores his newsprint tent. He closes the car door with his foot. As if this was not enough of a struggle, I have the sense that parts of him are falling off, and he is forced to retrieve them to piece himself back together again. In reality, Mr. Fluxcer is intact and hearty enough, with no apparent physical limitations, so my Humpty Dumpty impression of him is hard to explain.

He looks up at our porch and spots me observing him through one of the windows adjacent to our front door. Taking a deep breath, he draws himself up to stand straighter. At that moment, I believe I witness him exhaling. I will eventually learn that others ascribe the term "aura" to what I am observing, but I have no words for it at the time. If it is indeed an aura, it is my first. A dozen years will pass before I see a second. Mr. Fluxcer's aura is the greenish-yellow colour of a fading bruise. Having seen it, I cannot unsee it, even though it rapidly evaporates.

"Ina!" I call to alert her that a stranger is making his way onto our porch.

She barges ahead of me to open the front door for him.

"Oh, come in, Knowlton. Wouldn't you know it would rain, of course?"

Mr. Fluxcer reaches into his jacket pocket and produces an envelope. He bobs his head as he speaks for emphasis, "The first and last month's rent. Plus damage deposit. An extra hundred dollars, correct?"

Ina summons some nonchalance as she receives the envelope, but I recognize an undercurrent of relief.

He continues, "I'm afraid, if I carry everything upstairs, I'll be late for class. Could I leave the boxes on the porch, out of the rain, until after four o'clock? I will need to take the doves upstairs, however."

"Best to tuck the boxes into the foyer here. I'd hate for someone to walk off with your stuff."

I take a step out from behind Ina. "Doves?" I ask. "You have birds in your car?"

Ina cuts in before he can answer, "Knowlton, this is Blisse, of course. Blisse, this is Mr. Fluxcer, who is taking the upper floors as of today."

Mr. Fluxcer pats at some wispy remnants of hair on the side of his head and says, "Very pleased. Happy to make your acquaintance, Blisse." Then he nods with barely contained enthusiasm. "Yes, I have three doves. They'll live on the third floor. Less disturbance. They like to coo. The sound is soothing to some. Not so, to others." He glances at Ina in alarm and then addresses me, "You're not afraid of birds, are you?"

I shake my head.

He breathes out with relief, and I brace for visible colour tinting the air around him, but there is nothing more than coffee breath mixed with wintergreen mint.

The Twistical Nature of Spoons

I ask, "What are their names? Did you catch them or buy them?"

But Ina shoos me off, saying Mr. Fluxcer will be late for work if we hold him up any longer. And then, with a bright enthusiasm which is clearly meant for his benefit, she adds, "And, Missy Blissey, time to be off to school yourself."

Mr. Fluxcer looks disappointed for both our sakes. He removes a pocket watch from his corduroy pants pocket, flips it open, grimaces, and resolutely heads out our front door. I jam on my rain boots and jacket, grab my backpack—thankful it has escaped inspection—and follow him as far as the sidewalk. From the back of the station wagon, he withdraws a large, covered cage.

I cannot see the doves, but Mr. Fluxcer, as he hurries past me, chants out, "Mortise and Tenon and Dovetail."

"Pardon me?" I call.

"Their names ... that's what I've named them."

I walk the two and a half blocks to my school that morning and mull over what kind of person names a dove Dovetail. It is like naming a dog Dogtail, a hamster Hamstertail. It would be comparable to calling a member of my spoon family Spoonhandle. Only when I give serious thought to Horsetail and Cattail do I cut Mr. Fluxcer some slack. Horsetail and cattail plants were pointed out to our class recently when we visited a marsh outside the city. I was more interested in the ducks and red-winged blackbirds, so they could have pointed out a dovetail plant when my attention was elsewhere. Or perhaps "dovetail" has another meaning altogether? Who is to say? Even with Daddyspoon in my bag, I do not have the courage to ask my teacher. Instead, I turn my attention to the details of my schoolwork, somehow understanding that pondering multiple meanings for words goes hand in hand with my favourite subject: practising letters. To me, that is why the same word refers to both the casting of charms and the correct arrangement of letters—"spelling" is magic. Concentrating on printing my rows of capital and lowercase Ys provides the necessary distraction for me to avoid obsessing about Mr. Knowlton Fluxcer, his visible breath, and his doves. I do take comfort in recognizing that at least doves can fly if Ina decides to dispense of our new lodger's personal belongings in the same manner as Miss Chen's, and then I force myself to focus on the calming sound of pencil lead scuffing across ruled white paper. I know that when the bell frees me to dash home, my first order of business is to ascertain why birds are now permitted to live on our third floor when Ina has a strict no-pet rule.

•—•—•

"They aren't pets," Ina declares to me as I step around the cardboard boxes, careful to hang my rain jacket overtop of my backpack until I can retrieve Daddyspoon and put it away.

She continues, "The birds are part of Mr. Fluxcer's job. Not his paying job. He teaches shop classes at Belroad Tech, where I went to high school. The birds relate to his self-employment. And we finally have a lodger who is well-enough employed to afford rent, plus extra for garage space. All this time, I've had to pay insurance for that ramshackle thing to store a rake, a shovel, and a pair of bicycles. Now I'm receiving rent for it. My life has become a whole lot simpler, birds or no birds."

I venture, "Is he self-employed at making peace, then?"

"What?" Ina says, peering through the front door window, expectantly waiting for Mr. Fluxcer's after-school return.

I say, "Doves are a symbol of peace. Our librarian told us that last fall when she hung origami doves everywhere to celebrate a new special day of the year. So does he go around with his doves making peace?"

Ina takes a long, hard pause. Then she drops down to my level and draws me in close as she swipes at the corner of her eye. I cannot

The Twistical Nature of Spoons

tell if this rush of Ina emotion is sadness that she missed a foyer-decorating opportunity, or happiness that her life has become simpler.

In a tone that sounds like a strangled laugh, she says, "Oh, Blisse! You truly are something else." When she lets me go, she flicks her finger under my chin, beams at me, and turns away to start dinner.

"But Ina, does he?" I say, trailing after her a few steps before remembering Daddyspoon in my backpack pocket. I do not hear her answer as I turn back to remove it while her attention is elsewhere.

When evening sets in, I fall into reciting *One fish, two fish, red fish, blue fish* to the rhythm of Mr. Fluxcer's footfalls on our staircase. I want to hang out in the foyer and be of some assistance, but Ina insists I take an early bath and play in my pantry bedroom. "You need to stay out of Mr. Fluxcer's hair," she insists. When I attempt to confirm if she recognizes he actually has very little hair, she is not amused. "Enough lip, Missy Blissey!" Realizing I have managed to erase the positive remnants of her earlier emotional display, I stay put and leave the bedroom door open a crack, so that it appears closed, but still allows for a degree of household noise to reach me.

At first, my recitation rhythm is lively, but before long, the pattern grows sluggish as Mr. Fluxcer's steps become laboured. I am forced to pause more and more often midphrase in anticipation of his next step: *red ... fish... blue ...* In the interval when he drives off to retrieve a second carful of belongings, I creep out, ensuring Ina is engrossed in her craft-sale-glass-votive painting, and sit on the bottom stair, listening for the cooing of doves. There are no sounds emanating from the upper floors. This evokes a keen disappointment in me. I reason, yawning, that they go to bed earlier than I do. The next thing I know, Mr. Fluxcer is standing over me, the front door ajar, as cool evening air raises gooseflesh on my pyjama-clad skin.

When he speaks, it is in a whisper, alarm evident in his tone, and I am sure that his hands adjust his lips to the correct angle on his face before he can manage to say, "Has my renting of these rooms left you with no bedroom? No bed to sleep in?"

I rub my eyes. If not Humpty Dumpty, then at the very least Mr. Potato Head. My disorientation dissipating, I shake my head. "I was listening for your doves. Are they asleep?"

He nods. Concern still registers in his expression, along with a dog-tired weariness.

Staring at his scalp, I confess, "Ina said I have to stay out of your hair, but I had no plans to ever be in it."

He reaches up and runs a hand over the wispy rim of hair, then chuckles. He scoops up a wooden crate that he must have placed inside the door when he first caught sight of me. I jump up to see what the crate might be storing, and when I realize it holds a jumble of hand tools, I sit back down on the floor. Mr. Fluxcer shoots me an inquisitive look as he starts up the staircase.

I say, "I thought you might have an extra dove you had not mentioned before."

He rests the crate on the step in front of him and straightens his back. "Go ask your mother. Ask her permission. I'll show you the doves if she says so," he states.

Ina, still seated at the kitchen table, has reached a robotic state from the repetitive brushstrokes required to mass-produce sunflower petals. She looks as alarmed as Mr. Fluxcer to see me standing next to her and swings around to check the clock on the stove. "What are you still doing up? It's after nine, Blisse! I thought you were in your room."

"I was asleep, but then I woke up." A perfect truth. I smile. "Mr. Fluxcer asked if you would allow me to meet Mortise, Tenon, and Dovetail? I promise to go right to bed after."

Ina squints at me, uncomprehending.

"The doves. I just want to see them. All day, I have been wondering how they look."

Ina starts to shake her head.

The Twistical Nature of Spoons

I blurt, "I am supposing they smell bad."

Ina is highly sensitive when it came to foul smells. I think she considers them a personal affront, as if they have been created for the sole purpose of offending her. Even before she agrees, I am proud of my strategy.

"Oh, all right. But you get one peek in and then you beat it to bed," she exclaims.

I nod happily and dash for the staircase. Ina follows, calling apologies up the steps to Mr. Fluxcer as I turn on the first landing and bound up the next short flight.

There are two rooms on the third floor. Mr. Fluxcer stands, blocking the doorway to the one in which the doves are dwelling. He says, "Doves are sensitive. When moved to a new environment, they need time to adjust. Limited commotion."

"Oh," I say and stare at the knees of his corduroy pants, which have been rubbed shiny from the day's physical endeavours.

Perhaps he notices my face fall, for he sighs heavily. "You seem trustworthy to me, Blisse. Do not run. Do not speak loudly. Avoid sticking fingers in the cage. Agreed?"

I nod like my neck is on a spring.

"Then you are welcome to look in."

The oversized birdcage sits in the middle of the room on our large, antique-looking table. Three doves perch inside. Two are pure white, and the other is grey with a narrow ring of greyish-black around most of its neck, as if it requested that some adornment be painted on. I take cautious steps forward and stare at them. They seem to stare back, their eyes shiny as polished gems.

"The one with the ring is Dovetail," Mr. Fluxcer announces, as if he is a tour guide in an exotic locale. "She's been rescued, I suppose. Her mate passed on. Her callous owner debated freeing her … releasing poor Dovetail to her own devices. She wouldn't have lasted a week. A hawk's or cat's lunch. I took a lesser risk introducing her into the cage. Luckily, Mortise and Tenon seem fine with her. They lived with other magician's doves before residing with me."

"They were magician's doves?" I exclaim.

"Now semi-retired," he says with emphasis. "We do the odd trick together. If you look closely, you will see that Tenon is a bit larger than Mortise. That's how you tell them apart."

"Is Tenon a boy, then?" I ask.

"Yes, he is. And Mortise and Dovetail are the girls. Two males would not be workable. I am relieved this trio seems content." His gaze drifts off, as if he is speaking to himself. "I have always preferred uneven numbers for some inexplicable reason." He admits this as if even numbers are a troubling issue for him.

I do not care that much about numbers, so I am not sure how to relate. I stick to bird questions. "Two boy doves would fight?" I ask.

"Likely. And the one without the mate might never stop singing," he adds.

This also seems to be an issue beyond my experience. I do not want to leave the doves, so I offer another observation instead. "Some boys in my class will not sing, ever, but they sure fight."

Mr. Fluxcer smiles down at me, and then turns to Ina, who has joined us in the room. "Precocious."

Ina shrugs as if she is puzzling over something. "She never talked much to the other adults who lived here."

Mr. Fluxcer is about to respond when one of the doves starts to croon. *Croo-CROOK-croo.* He nods then. "Ah! A good sign."

"Is a 'koshus' like a kilogram?" I ask Ina quietly.

"A what?" Ina says.

I turn to Mr. Fluxcer. You said 'per koshus.' Is that like per kilogram?

"Astute question," he chuckles.

Ina jumps in before he can answer me. "I live with a three-and-a-half-foot-tall professor!" She then shakes her head, but not in

The Twistical Nature of Spoons

a mean way, and addresses me. "No, 'koshus' is a code word for bedtime."

Despite not answering my question, Mr. Fluxcer seems quite tolerant of my asking it, so I dare one last request, attempting to maintain my voice at a near whisper. "When they have adjusted to living here, may I touch them, or do they bite?"

"You may," he answers. "Once they're settled. They were hand-trained at a young age, and I handle them often. They're quite gentle. Gentleness is in a dove's nature."

With that, Ina clasps me by the shoulders and steers me toward the staircase.

"Mr. Fluxcer, you are a lucky duck to have those birds! Thank you for showing me."

His hand shoots up to his mouth, muffling his words. "You are welcome. And welcome to come by again." He removes his hand. "Thank you for not startling the doves."

Once in my bedroom, I dig the canteen out from under my bed and feel a quandary sink in. Could Grannyspoon be converted to a Lodgerspoon? I never met my Granny, as she died and left us her house just before I was born. "Saved our asses," I once overheard Ina admit to Cousin Charlene on a long-distance telephone call. A traitorous feeling wells up in me to even consider replacing poor Grannyspoon. Besides, it is very delicate with its half twist—likely all it could sustain with its dainty, narrow, embossed handle. It does not match Mr. Fluxcer's actual lumbering presence. I am slightly crestfallen. My birthday is more than half a year away, and how can I be certain that my father has left me a more appropriate spoon? How much effort did it require to bend a spoon with his mind? Perhaps the rest are delicate like Grannyspoon and will not match the bulkier nature that a Lodgerspoon requires. I could try to ask Ina about my father's bequests, but she generally does not welcome too many questions if they pertain to our family secret. Sometimes she clams up, but instead of admitting she is reluctant to talk about it, she usually finds something amiss that must be straightened or fixed right that second. I wish she was as willing to answer my questions as Mr. Fluxcer.

Perhaps it falls to Sonspoon to give up his familial status. Sonspoon is the most average-sized teaspoon, and its tip reminds me of the ace of spades from a card deck. Its handle has a single right-angle bend that renders it rather useless, but I like that its bent part seems respectful, like a salute. I am fond of its willingness to be unassuming, and that it is never too busy to share a laugh.

A faint *croo-CROOK-croo* reaches me. A sound destined to pacify, a night lullaby, and just calming enough to wipe away my sense of betrayal in renaming a spoon. I reason that if my classmates get babies added to their families, then families are not necessarily meant to remain static. It falls to Sonspoon to give up his flatware familial claim. I pray that Lodgerspoon knows some good knock-knock jokes. As I make the renaming official with a silent proclamation and a small kiss on the tip of the handle, I have a jolt of realization that Lodgerspoon is connected to a real living person with whom I have made acquaintance. As real as Mommyspoon and Daughterspoon. After the wonder of that realization, it does not feel traitorous to imagine Petspoon giving up its bark and sprouting wings. As I drift off to sleep, I relish my own daring.

Ina

unmasks

Taras slipped us in a side door that was propped open with a thin strip of leather. "Come. I want you to bear witness."

"Witness to what?" The rush of warm interior air spelled relief. I slipped my feet out of my platform heels and wiggled my toes while muttering under my breath, "I feel like a criminal."

"Nothing criminal about a propped-open door. Anything that could be deemed criminal occurred before your arrival. You have no involvement, Ina the Innocent." He tried to usher me toward a corridor. "It can also be argued that picking a door lock is not criminal if there is no intent to commit a crime. I'm merely working late. University staff are never discouraged from working late."

"You picked the locks?" I declared in a hushed whisper, refusing to budge from the doorway. "If you work here, why don't you have a key?"

"I don't work here," he responded.

I closed my eyes and wished the doublespeak had not returned. My eyes flew open when I felt his face near mine.

He spoke softly into my ear, his breath warm on my cheek. "Ina, your concern is misdirected. It's our very own hearts we should fear. The darkness that abides in them despite our best intentions; the things we wish done and undone." Before I could contradict him—confess to having sensed a purity in his heart—he shrugged and stated, "And trust me, the sleep-deprived on-duty security guard will be more terrified than either of us should he find us here. Those paid to be brave have more to fear." He proceeded to pull out an ID tag on a lanyard from beneath his vest. "But fortunately, I have the necessary credentials to reassure him."

I squinted at the tag marked *Visitor* and shook my head, bewildered again. On the bridge, Taras had apologized for the kiss and begged me not to leave. He insisted he would not be taking another single liberty: "I kissed you to appease my great-grandmother; to assuage her spirit. But even she would not have me behave like a rogue to test her prediction." He'd placed his hand on his chest, as if swearing a solemn oath. I was about to tell him he was full of it when he murmured, "Oh, Ina, do you intend to banish the winter from my heart?" I'd turned my back to him, afraid he'd see my confusion; certain if I looked at him, my lips would take matters into their own hands out there on the footbridge. It was as if I was disoriented in a Taras-fog. And the only beacon in sight to steer me through was his intrigue. How could he be both the danger and the safe harbour?

I glanced down the corridor behind him before pointing to the tag. "Well, that's great, but I don't have one."

Removing the security pass, he draped it around my neck. "Now you do."

I opened my mouth to state the obvious.

He shushed me, then patted at his vest and intoned as if explaining to someone official, "I forgot mine at the hotel." Then he paused, reached forward to finger the tag around my neck, and explained in a tone that proved he was capable of *some* non-nonsensical

The Twistical Nature of Spoons

statements, "The very same hotel I can't afford on account of the pittance I am being paid to conduct this workshop. Dirk, an old friend who generously secured my plane ticket and a measly honorarium, offered to put me up, but his wife just gave birth to twins and can't forgive Dirk for this calamity. I begged off for their sakes." Then he added, "I am sleeping here with my masks."

"Your masks!" I guffawed. "And your lock picks! What is this workshop? Petty Theft 101? Oh, but I shouldn't forget your handy flask and your tiny spoons. Serious course materials."

"Eye-nuh, where do I find your sarcasm off switch?" With his question, he glanced down at my footwear, which still lay abandoned next to me. He bent down and shoved his hands into my platform heels. Positioning the pair side by side, and with his fingers sloped deep into the toes, he kicked his legs upward into a handstand. He took a few tentative upside-down steps before he began to topple forward. He leapt upright again, waving his arms in mock bewilderment. "However do you walk in these things?" he demanded, his face contorted with quizzical confusion.

Laughter bubbled up in me. It was nearly 3:00 a.m. I was punch-drunk, and I laughed until I shook, until tears welled up. I swiped at them. There was enough time between bursts of mirth to tell myself I was an idiot for not grabbing my shoes and running. For some reason, that made it all the more funny. While I laughed, Taras stood smirking, arms folded across his chest, my shoes tucked under his armpits. A snort erupted from him at one point as I doubled over with hilarity. When I eventually ceased, he placed my shoes in front of me, withdrew an actual handkerchief from his vest pocket, and dabbed at my tear-dampened cheeks. He gestured again toward the hallway. I swept up my shoes and trailed barefoot behind him, careful to avoid the damp marks his hiking boots were leaving on the floor.

He led me down several halls to an unlocked room and switched on a single row of overhead lights. My eyes darted to the shadowy corners, the nearest of which was crammed with a jumble of wooden easels; behind them were open shelves, mostly bare. In the opposite corner, a large industrial-looking workstation was surrounded by ducts and vents, and beyond that, an opening to what looked like a small storage alcove. Under the lit part of the room, there were two rows of chairs assembled to face a bank of sturdy tables. Whatever was on the tables was covered by draped black cloth.

Tara swept his arm out, indicating the expanse of the room. "Behold, Dirk's playground!"

I wanted to remain close to the door, where a quick exit was still possible, but the place had a magnetic draw. I was standing in an honest-to-gawd studio where people studied art. A definite cut above the back booths of restaurants where I'd sketched on paper placemats, and the artisan's unheated garage where I'd taken my stained-glass classes. I inched my way forward as Taras strode through the open space.

He went straight to the tables, reached beneath the black cloth without looking, and withdrew an object. Cradling the item in both hands, he stared at it for a moment, as if making a decision. With his back still to me, he said, "I make these. That's why I'm here. Leading a historical art workshop of sorts. Normally, I don't instruct on their construction. I perform in them. *Commedia dell'arte.*" He glanced over his shoulder at me.

I stopped midway across the room. "You're an actor, then?"

He kept his back to me, but continued, "I am reminded all too often that it's not a sensible career path—trying to make a living from improvising on stage with centuries-old stock characters. But who will keep the art form alive if there is no one to dedicate themselves? The world will be diminished if it spins on the axis of synthesizers and blue screens alone." Then, as if repenting for a sin, he admitted, "Lately, our troupe has taken more liberties with the tradition to bolster our relevance."

The Twistical Nature of Spoons

"Well, show me already," I demanded. "What's in your hands?"

As he detected my determined approach, he brightened. He turned fully toward me and held out the object. "This ... this is Arlecchino."

Taras was holding a leather mask. A half mask. Nose and forehead. The forehead had arched eyebrow ridges; above its bulbous nose, a small lump—a boil—bulged out. These sculpted features were defined and amplified by variations in its burnished colouring, from reddish brown to black. At first glance, I could only assume Taras had lifted the lid of the underworld to create the thing, but it was also all too human, with its air of puzzlement. Lifelike. I reached out a fingertip. The leather was surprisingly rigid. I drew back. "Arle-what?" I asked.

"Arlecchino." His mouth stretched into a broad, tight smile as he overemphasized the second-last syllable, "Ar-le-*keeee*-no." He added, "Lowly servant—he has come to be popularized by his descendent, Harlequin."

"Like the Harlequin romance novels?" I asked.

His expression clouded, and he moved to slip the mask back under the cloth.

I didn't want that. I tried to undo my dumb remark, but all that came out was more blather. "My cousin, the one attached to Hairy Hands, borrows Harlequins by the bagful from the library. I feel as if that little black-and-white clown figure on the cover is our third roommate. Sometimes I score her the discard books from the back lane behind our corner pharmacy, but the covers have been stripped off those. They're half as appealing without that little Harlequin, if you ask me, but she reads them anyway."

A half smile flicked across Taras's face. He offered, "Yes. That little Harlequin descended from Arlecchino. Italy, sixteenth century. Some associate him with the devil, but I avoid that particular slant. As a character, he is a tad hyperactive, not typically bright, often mistreated, with an artful persistence for food and sex and simple survival." Turning away, he donned the mask. As he twisted to face me again, his body transformed, as if his energy was pinging from his opened hips and pronounced rump to his yearning chest and back again. He sashayed away from the table, knees bent and bouncing; the heels of his boots barely making a sound when they touched down on the floor with each exaggerated step.

I'd watched *The Lone Ranger* and *Zorro*, trick-or-treated in October. But the man in the mask in front of me loomed from an unknown world, ridiculous and joyful. I wasn't simply seeing something unique; it was as if I'd been given new eyes to see it. I blinked hard. A shiver ran down my spine to my bare feet.

Taras's brooding eyes watched me from the depths of the mask. His mouth alternated between mirth and anguish. It was the same mouth that had kissed me, but it didn't seem to belong to the man-who-walked-into-a-bar any longer. From behind the mask's dark leather, Taras seemed to be seeking my approval as a performer from his audience; but I also had the strange sense that I was the one for which admission had been paid. That I was the one to be watched—to engage or disappoint—to be booed or applauded. And that Taras, peering out through Arlecchino's eye sockets, could really see me. Ina Trove. Unmasked.

He struck a pose, his rump protruding, and then he shifted the stance with the flat of his belly straining toward me. "Ah, *bella* Ina. Have you come to serve in Pantalone's household?"

"Panta-who?"

"Pant-a-loan-ay. The old miserly coot!"

I cocked my head at him.

He shrank back and then recovered, "*Ehemm*, I mean, my distinguished, wealthy master. The gentleman is demanding his evening's fortified drink. An early riser, he is to bed by sunset, so he requests you bring the spirits directly to his bedchamber." I opened my mouth to stop his play, but he cut me off. "Cast off concern. He will pay dearly for his attempt to lure you."

The Twistical Nature of Spoons

I shook my head at him. "Humph!"

The strangeness thickened as Taras began to circle me. "Fear not. I, Arlecchino, have a plan. Bring Pantalone his wine. Ply him with it." He shifted his weight from one foot to the other as if the floor were too hot. "Be coy. Pretend you welcome his lecherous intentions. Pour more wine and take note of the sack of gold he guards on his belt. *Ehemm*." He rubbed his hands down the front of his thighs as if to admonish himself and then continued, his finger pointed skyward. "Soon after Master imbibes, his ancient eyelids flutter. Lullaby him to dreamland." He held an upright pose before his final point. "When Pantalone starts to snore, snatch several gold coins for your trouble. Perhaps enough to spare Arlecchino a penny for his excellent plan?"

The leather mask beckoned me to step into its zany entertainment. Wondrous, disarming, grotesque. Perform or shrivel. Perform and die. All I had to do was allow myself to fall off the earth. Taras and resurrection beckoned.

I replied, with my most shaming tone, "You want me to steal an old man's money?"

Elation flashed across Taras's features, and then Arlecchino rubbed his belly. "Only as he starves us half to death!" He switched to hold the small of his back in a state of lamentation. "Beats us with sticks!" He recovered and posed again. "While his humble servants remain ever faithful."

"What if he wakes and beats me for stealing his gold?" I yelped, turning my back on him.

He leaped in front of me. "Ah! Arlecchino is no nincompoop! There is more to my cunning plan." He tapped the temple of his mask.

"Okay, what is it?"

"He will not catch you."

"That's your plan? That's not a plan!"

"He will not catch you because you are a wondrous beauty."

"What do my looks have to do with not getting caught?"

Confused, he two-stepped in a circle before declaring, "You can outrun him. He only shuffles in his decrepitude."

"What?"

"His aged sight is weak. He will not catch you because you can hide right in front of him," he beamed. He swiped his hands together, as if nothing could go wrong. "Shall we shake on this deal? Seal it with a kiss?" Lips puckered in anticipation, he leaned forward so far as to teeter in the air, windmilling his arms to remain upright.

"What? You said no more liberties," I exclaimed.

He leaned even farther forward and then somersaulted out of his awkward tilt. He jumped up and looked around with a frantic air. He stuck his tongue out past the bottom edge of the mask and stared cross-eyed at it. "Has someone been putting words in my mouth?" He mimed brushing his tongue with his hands. "Out! Out!"

Laughter burst from me.

He turned his back and removed the mask.

"Aw, why'd you do that?" I demanded, unable to hide my disappointment.

Taras stood with the mask dangling from one hand, his hair mussed, expression unreadable. He shrugged, "The *lazzo*. It's realized."

"I beg your pardon?"

"I made you laugh," he stated.

"So make me *lazzo* again."

"Ah! *Lazzo* is not the action of laughing, but the action that brings about the laughter. The comic business. The gag."

I sniffed.

He brightened. "Would you like to trick the old miser?"

I faked nonchalance and shrugged. "Pantalone?"

He raised an eyebrow at me and I nodded. He reached under

The Twistical Nature of Spoons

the black cloth again and located the next mask without looking. When he turned to me, mask affixed, I let out a squeak of unexpected delight. The elongated nose and obscenely long greying eyebrows that framed the half mask transformed Taras into an old man. Back hunched, he shrivelled in front of me.

I laughed and he wheezed in response. He headed straight for me, his feet shuffling in a great flurry, making little headway; his elbows tucked close to his body but his hands whirling as if they were paddling him forward through the air. I backed up to avoid those hands, but he continued his advance. I turned and took a few steps toward the door. This fuelled his determination, increased his shuffle speed. I squealed and skipped forward. His wheezing amplified. No matter which direction I darted, he adjusted his line of pursuit. When I decided to play it cool, he seized his opportunity and lunged, encircling me in his arms.

"Aaahhh-haaa!" he wheezed out in triumph.

As I tried to escape, he nuzzled my neck with the mask's pronounced nose and croaked, "So, *bella* Ina. You resist Pantalone, ay? I have chests of gold, no? A nice sack of coins in my pantaloons."

I threw my head back and laughed. "Just how many women have you seduced in that mask, Taras?"

He released me, turned, and removed Pantalone. "You would have been the first," he said with mock regret. He returned the mask to the table. "But that," he added, "is only because you didn't know in advance that it's not in the *commedia* cards for Pantalone to have success in seduction."

"He chases that hard but never gets the girl?"

"His efforts are fruitless."

"But you would've duped me? My ignorance makes me easy to trick?"

He tilted his head as if I'd hit a nerve. Then, with a dose of cruel mockery, he said, "You say that as if lying won't get someone what they want. Does your innocence run that deep, Eye-nuh?"

He stopped himself and asked again, his scorn replaced with awe, "Does it, Ina?"

I was taken aback by his initial cruelty. I wanted him to continue *seeing* me with his mask removed. "I prefer honesty," I replied, "but obviously have a hard time spotting it."

"Whew," he breathed out. "And there's not a single unscrupulous soul willing to take advantage of your naivety?"

I straightened my back. "Who said that?" I spat out.

He continued, but gently, "Eye-nuh, I don't need chickens on a tablecloth to tell me you currently have no man in your life."

I shrugged. "So? What of it?"

He nodded. "Your loneliness plays inside me like a cello."

My breath caught. I didn't want to admit how much his words were affecting me so I taunted back, "I'd rather be alone than with someone who thinks it's okay to use poor decrepit Pantalone to his advantage. You could have killed the old guy."

He stared at me. There was a long silence. I broke first and looked away. I had the urge to fling back the black cloths. Expose and jumble his beloved masks. Sweep them off the table with intent to maim.

When Taras finally spoke, it was as if he was explaining something to himself. "In the *commedia*, so much of the story is expressed through action and the energy of that action. But to feel the emotion under the mask is vital for honest work. Sometimes that doesn't happen; sometimes the audience is satisfied anyway." Then, as if an invisible mask dropped over his face, he added, "As in life, a person can play—say, the devoted spouse—through their actions: make meals, pay bills, have sex. But if it's not what they *feel* … then what?" He looked at me, but continued without waiting for my reply. "What then? When does the audience stop being satisfied?"

I didn't know the answer. Instead, I said, "She hurt you bad. Your wife."

The Twistical Nature of Spoons

The invisible mask slipped away. "Damaged the past, absconded with the future."

I searched for something consoling to say. "I'm sure everyone feels that way when they're betrayed." I realized my comment sounded flat; I didn't want to be talking about his wife.

A trance-like despair seemed to settle over him. "You said on the bridge that my wife would shed tears if I fell and dashed out my brains. Your prediction is highly unlikely. My once bewitching bride now wants me dead. Curses me to death in the most sinister and inventive ways."

I was glad I was still wearing my coat. I tugged it tighter around me. "Well, maybe she secretly resents you're not trying to win her back. Ever think about that?"

He flinched. "I suspect the source of her powerful malevolence originates elsewhere."

What could I say to that? At a loss, I retreated to my wisecracking corner. "Sure! You oughta know, Taras. I hope you're not letting your stock of talismans and antidotes run low. Buckle up. Always opt for the flight insurance."

He cleared his throat. The corners of his mouth twitched. I couldn't tell if my sarcasm had wounded him further or if he was actually amused. His next words did nothing to shed light. "Your concern for my well-being overwhelms me."

I offered a smile.

With his next breath, he uttered, "Show's over, Ina."

My voice quavered, "Yup, time to haul my ass out of here."

"Let me get you a cab home," he said.

I let out a long, slow breath. Our spell was broken, the mood drifting off as dejectedly as the smoke from fireworks. I clung to the remnants and confessed, "Well, even though your demon of a wife thinks it's a precious waste of time, you should know that what you've created here is … it's, um … extraordinary."

He didn't respond, but he paused halfway across the room.

I started to blather again. "I'm still in the habit of saving my tips in case I ever get to travel, but I'd empty my jar at the end of the week to buy a ticket to one of your shows."

Taras turned to me. "You are a born flatterer, Eye-nuh," he drawled.

I still wasn't sure if I was continuing to insult him or not. "Hey, some weeks that's pretty good money. Weekends can be profitable."

He moved back to the table and ran a hand over the black cloth that covered the masks. "Your compliment suffices. Ample payment," he said.

I sensed I should stop gushing, but the thought of the impending cab ride pushed me to keep talking. "So tell me, was it solely for the masks' sakes that you brought me here?"

He didn't answer at first. Then, as if he was reciting lines, he replied, "Art feels incomplete until it communicates. The masks live for an audience." A breath later, raw emotion ripped across his face. "We all need out from under our suffocating black shrouds."

Now I ask you, and forgive me for putting you on the spot, but would you call that a satisfying answer? I was hoping he might be a bit more obvious—maybe admit that I was at least registering on his attraction meter, since he'd been making my own needle jitter off the scale. But maybe he truly just needed an audience. Any audience. Especially since his wife's betrayal seemed to have him relying on his art more than was healthy. Ina and her scarred palm were handy and available. A barmaid who'd tracked him down for the sake of a spoon, sure to be impressed and applaud.

As if he was reading my thoughts, he shrugged, and his playful smirk resurfaced. "How pompous and absurd is that, Ina? In light of the fact that art has served two masters tonight, I beg the masks' pardon for my misuse of them, but more importantly, yours." When I didn't respond, his attempt at levity seemed too heavy for

The Twistical Nature of Spoons

him. He concluded, "I must trust that the masks at least forgive me, having earned your praise."

I glanced at the dark drapery on the table. The masks were starting to feel like my only real allies in the room. I stepped forward and lifted the edge of the cloth. Taras caught my hand, his eyes imploring. I couldn't pinpoint the source of his reluctance. Did he think the masks were vulnerable, lying lifeless on the table, or did he not want to risk my disenchantment? I removed his grip, determined. Reaching under the cloth, I grabbed the first mask my hand touched. I held Taras's gaze as I slipped it onto my face; a musky funk of leather and sweat filled my nostrils. I breathed deeply. The upturned nose that protruded below my eyes took the same breath.

A smile twitched at the edge of Taras's mouth. "Tartaglia," he said with a gentle nod. "His role is defined by his stutter." He added, "And limited eyesight. What exists in front of him is dim."

My tongue suddenly felt swollen and ineffective. For a long moment, I stared at Taras through the owlish rims of the mask's eye openings. He seemed to go in and out of focus. The tension I'd felt from that first moment I'd served Taras at Three Sheets wound even tighter. I could feel a red flush creep up the exposed skin of my neck below the mask; Tartaglia's leathery jowls could only obscure part of my yearning.

"You feel the character's nervousness," Taras confirmed. "Tartaglia stammers but can't give up on words. It's such a relief to finally get them out. Like a sneeze. Like an orgasm. So now, confess. What is it you beseech of me? That I go to hell? That I uncover the last of what it is you're masking?"

"I … I w-w-wa … my tongue stumbled around the words.

"Tell me," he encouraged. "Spit it out."

"I w-w-wa …" I stopped and took a deep breath. "I th-th-think I'm f-fal … Oh, blast! Y-y-you already kn-kn-know!"

A flicker of gratitude crossed Taras's face, like the first appreciative titter that escapes a reserved audience. He eyed my lips below the leather covering and said, "Is my resistance doomed, Ina? You are taking the words right out of my mouth."

There was the slightest hesitation before he slid Tartaglia up and away.

4

Blisse

wicked ticket

*I*n the week or two that follow Mr. Knowlton Fluxcer's arrival as our lodger, I have high hopes for a second visit with his winged companions. I cannot stop thinking about the doves, as I am beyond curious to know what magic tricks they have been taught. How does anyone learn magic, let alone a bird? Do magician's doves have to be magical themselves? When I met them the first time, they seemed of this earth, but perhaps it was too short a visit for me to detect otherwise. Racing home from school to ensure I arrive first, I hang out in the foyer or on the front porch. I pass the waiting time with my canteen. Sometimes I read to the spoons from picture books borrowed from the public library; sometimes we just rehearse their Spoonfamily lives. When Mr. Fluxcer arrives home, I quickly set everything aside and rush to greet him, and although he responds with a kind and civil greeting, I do not have the courage to ask to see his avian trio, and he does not offer.

One day, upon arriving home near the end of the school year,

I find a dove feather in the foyer, lying on the bottom step of the staircase that leads up to Mr. Fluxcer's suite. It is pure white and the same length as my hand. I bend down and blow lightly on it, and it stirs before settling again. When I pick it up, its delicateness is a marvel. I hold it above my head and let go, watching it flutter downward before I catch it again. I am thrilled. It seems crucial that I ask Mr. Fluxcer's permission to keep it since technically it belongs to him. There must be some way to demonstrate that I will treasure it always if he allows me to become its owner. I run to my room and grab my canteen. I arrange the spoons to the outside slots and place the feather in the centre. I am confident that when Mr. Fluxcer sees the special place the feather commands, he will appreciate my keen interest and invite me for a dove visit.

I sit and wait on the same step where I found the feather, the canteen closed and situated at my feet. I am relieved that Ina is cooking dinner and not paying attention to my stakeout. When Mr. Fluxcer comes in the front door, I can hardly contain myself. I tell him I have a surprise and I flip open the lid.

He takes one look and turns away, as if the sight has made him squeamish. He clasps his hands on his chest as if to keep them safe there, while his Adam's apple bobs up and down, then appears to wobble sideways like it has loosened in his throat.

Despite his reaction, I feel I must not waste the opportunity. I grab the feather and approach him, blurting, "I would like to keep this if you do not mind? And visit the dove that lost it."

Mr. Fluxcer does not look at the feather. He glances at the open canteen and away again. As if it pains him to say it, he answers, "I am afraid … I am very tired this evening, Blisse."

Crestfallen, I offer him the feather.

He looks contrite when he insists I keep it. I do not understand. He was very tired the night he moved in, but he showed me the doves. And if he is not angry I took the feather, then why is my simple wish being denied? What kind of unjust universe prevents

The Twistical Nature of Spoons

a girl from visiting with doves—especially magic-act doves—when they reside in her own house? As I watch Mr. Fluxcer climb the stairs to his suite, I fume that it is a cruelty to have introduced me to the doves and shared their birthrights, but then not allow me back into the croo-crook room.

I place the feather back into the chest and try to console myself with my good fortune in finding it. It will be in good company with my spoons. That is when it strikes me that perhaps Mr. Fluxcer has overheard my spoon conversations and—like our old lodger, Mrs. Gardinier—thinks I should be playing with dolls instead. The very thought that Mr. Fluxcer believes I am odd and should not have an audience with the doves prompts me to rush to my room, fling the chest onto my bed, gather the spoons, and toss them onto the floor. They clatter in protest. The feather looks abandoned. I cross my arms and stare at the jumbled heap of metal.

The urge to make amends quickly overtakes me. I cradle Babyspoon first. It is always the most helpless of the bunch with its diminutive size, in addition to the fact it was originally constructed with a loop in its handle for a baby's grasp before my father's powers bent the entire curved handle a second time. The handle now sits over the bowl like a lid, making it resemble a silver sphere as much as a spoon. I gently pat it, as if burping a baby, and then reach for the other spoons, one by one, tracing my fingers over their bends and twists, and place them back in the box until they are neatly arranged and I am calm again. None of our lodgers have seemed to appreciate the spoons' wonder the way I do. Perhaps that is what my father intended all along. He made them especially for me. Ina has insisted on the need for secrecy about their origins, but perhaps it is best not to share any part of them at all.

On the last day of school, I am exuberant after earning an attendance award for no absences all year. The principal's thick, slanted signature on my certificate emboldens me. Dashing into the kitchen when I arrive home, I wave the paper at Ina and interrupt the packaging of her sunflower-adorned votive holders. She pauses to beam at me with a hint of self-satisfaction, and I do not hesitate to try to bring her on board. "Do you think now that Mr. Fluxcer is on summer holidays he will show me the doves again?"

Setting the half-filled box aside, Ina indicates I should sit down at the table. "Good job on the award there, Missy Blissey."

I do not take her praise bait.

A tad miffed, she meets me head on. "You are not to bug Mr. Fluxcer, okay? We don't want him moving out, right? He teaches kids all day; I'm sure he wants a break from that at home."

"But he teaches big kids. Teenagers. It is different."

"Look, Blisse, he's going through some bad stuff."

"What bad stuff?"

"Bad grown-up stuff," Ina replies.

I wait.

She says, "You don't need to know about it because you're not a grown-up."

"You said I was grown up last year when it was time to call you Ina instead of Mommy."

She sighs in exasperation. Ina hates it when I use her own words to my advantage, but it sometimes makes her vacillate. I raise my eyebrows at her.

She frowns back. "Look, you shouldn't bug Mr. Fluxcer. That way, you can't accidentally say something that makes the bad stuff worse, right? Easy-peasy lemon squeezy. Nothing can go wrong."

I stop and ponder. "He is just like a stranger, then? And I should not talk to strangers because they might be bad people."

Ina shakes her head, growing more annoyed, and insists, "No, Blisse. I don't believe Knowlton is a bad man or I wouldn't have let the rooms to him." There is a pause as she seems to reconsider her approach. "Look … he had a wife … and she had a gambling problem."

"What does that mean?"

The Twistical Nature of Spoons

"It's when you buy way too many lotto tickets or go to grown-up places like horse racetracks or Las Vegas casinos and eventually lose all your money."

I feel panic rising in me. One time, Ina bought a lottery ticket and let me crack open the little cardboard tabs to try to win some money. I loved the *phhfflltt* sound of the detaching tabs. I loved the feeling beforehand—that if I wished hard enough, I could make the symbols match. When I watch the man who announces the lottery draws every week on TV, I feel that same notion of possibility, despite the fact Ina never buys a "Winsday" ticket. I have often thought she should because she worries about money and that seems like an exciting way to get some. We could be rich. Am I a gambler? I do not want to admit any of this to Ina, especially now that a gambler's husband has moved in upstairs.

I try to steer the conversation away from tickets. "But horses are nice, Ina," I gush. "Remember my pony ride at the Red River Exhibition? Oh, but you said The Ex was full of money swindlers too."

"Yes, Blisse, but that's not the same. We save up to go have some fun once a year at The Ex. Gamblers give their money to swindlers every day until they can't afford milk." She pauses to see if I comprehend. "We have milk money, right?"

I nod, but am not convinced. I do not actually know the answer, because I am uncertain how milk money varies from other kinds of money.

Ina must sense that my growing unease is an opportunity to drive her point home, because she stops reassuring me. "Knowlton sold their big belongings—boat, camper, workshop tools—to pay off her gambling debts. But gamblers believe their bad luck will change. And you know how I feel about that, right?"

"There is no bad luck, only bad decisions about good luck," I recite. "Is that really right? It is hard to understand," I insist, craving specifics.

She ignores my confusion. "Next, he was forced to sell their house. And then, his wife up and left him."

"Where did she go? He tried to help her!"

"Exactly, Blisse. Poor Mr. Fluxcer, right?"

"He is sad, then?"

"Yeah, and they're not married anymore. Divorced. To get back on his feet, he moved into our suite with his birds and his few measly belongings. It is awfully nice for us, but also pretty darn sad, Blisse."

"Is divorce as sad as death?"

"What?"

"Is he as sad about his wife and divorce as you are about my dad and his death?"

Ina's eyes bulge. Then she turns her attention to closing and reopening the box of candle holders. She looks inside and not at me. "I don't know for sure, Blisse." She takes a deep breath. "It's sad either way. You aren't with the person you love anymore." Then she brightens. "But maybe Mr. Fluxcer will find new love someday."

"So then maybe it is the same sad? Because maybe you will find new love someday too, Ina."

"Oh, doubters, Blisse," she exclaims. She turns from the box, sits down at the table with her hands clasped in her lap. "Your father … Petro," she pauses, as if just saying his name pains her. "He was my one true love, and I have extra sadness that you two never met. But your dad is always in your heart because you're part of him." Then she scrunches her eyes at me, as if my understanding is of utmost importance. "And I am fortunate because, through you and with you, I get to continue loving Petro forever and ever, even though he is not here."

I beam at her. Imagining my parents in love is one of my favourite things to do when I close my eyes at night. I like it when Ina reminds me about it.

She continues, "And you always have a symbol of his love in return."

The Twistical Nature of Spoons

I nod and recite, "Knowing I was going to be born, he was so excited that he bent twelve spoons for my birthdays, which was a lot of spoons."

Ina nods, "Exactly. Amazing Petey!"

I dig my knuckles into my eyebrows to keep from giggling. I find it ridiculous that Ina calls my father by a nickname. "Petey" sounds like a kid's name, and Ina never knew my father when they were kids. Whenever she says it, I think I hear birds chirping, like he is a Petey Bird. When I stop to surmise that I named Petspoon without even thinking that my father's name started with the same three letters, it gives me goosebumps.

I ask, "But why did he die?"

Ina sighs and looks worried. "I'll tell you when you're bigger," she says, then slips into our familiar adage. "But when he was alive, he knew how special you'd be, and he wanted you to know how much you were loved, so he bent those spoons, which we don't …"

"Tell anyone!" I confirm with a conviction that reaches right down to my toes.

Ina nods her head once, and then she reaches out and hugs me hard. I do not want her to let go, but even with her arms around me, the disloyal thought rises up in my brain that it would be nice to have an *alive* dad too. I speculate whether, despite his divorce, or maybe even because of it, Mr. Fluxcer might be interested in being a dad, even though he seems quite a bit older than most kids' dads at my school. I know I cannot say these words to Ina either, so I keep them to myself as well. She has told me I should be grateful because dads can also be deadbeats who sell drugs, rob banks, and even wallop their kids. At least I do not have a dad like that.

Ina breaks into my thoughts with an abrupt warning. "Anyway, I need you to not pester Mr. Fluxcer. It takes money to keep this roof over our heads. His rent payment helps with that."

I nod from my squished quarters against her chest, but instead of releasing me, Ina holds me tighter and confesses, "And I know

I'm the one who chased off the last lodgers. So Blisse, do as I say, not as I do."

I feel her shudder once before she releases me to straighten her shirt. My hair is mussed all about. I swipe at the strands obscuring my vision and understand it is best not to bother Mr. Fluxcer for now. My desire for a dove visit is officially rendered out of bounds.

July descends, muggy as a sweaty palm. In that first week of summer holidays, Mr. Fluxcer's appearances are infrequent. When he does leave his rooms, he returns with bags of clinking glass or sacks of fast food. I am certain Ina is not fond of the wafts of fryer grease that cling to the humid air. I start to worry that if parts of him should fall off, an ooze of milkshakes and macerated fries will follow. In order to obey Ina, I stop acknowledging him altogether. I stare away into middle space or focus on the paper flags Ina has tied to the porch railing and that remain there after Canada Day passes. With only peripheral vision, I cannot confirm if he glances in my direction or if he is relieved to ignore me in return.

One day, Ina takes me downtown and we return on the sweltering bus with a new fan for him, something Ina has never bothered to provide for past tenants. Because she does not want to disturb Mr. Fluxcer in his suite, she puts me in charge of notifying her when he descends on his own. I entrench myself in the foyer. At the first glimpse of him exiting from the upper levels, I jump forward and hail him. He looks so taken aback that I have misgivings he might disintegrate on the landing. As I rush past him to get Ina, I notice he has cut the legs off his worn corduroy pants to make shorts. The ragged strings on the unhemmed edges hang limp in the hot, close air, and I imagine them all aflutter from the new fan.

"What is it? What's wrong?" he insists.

The Twistical Nature of Spoons

When I retrieve Ina and she presents him with the fan, his relief is tangible. He clasps his hands together and peers out past the porch's overhang to the breezeless afternoon before accepting it.

"How thoughtful. And even though the doves ... they shouldn't be exposed to drafts, I will indulge myself. Thank you."

Ina immediately heads back to our kitchen, and once Mr. Fluxcer has returned to his rooms, I position myself at the bottom of the stairs. I cannot risk Ina hearing me, but I hope Mr. Fluxcer will. I cup my hands around my mouth. "I wonder why doves cannot be exposed to drafts? Do they not normally fly in the wind?" There is no reply, and although I play out on the porch that evening until mosquitoes serenade the dusk, Mr. Fluxcer does not reappear. I crawl onto my bed that night and lie atop the covers. If I lift my head and strain to listen, I can just perceive the whispered whirr of the upstairs fan. As I drift to sleep, my ears fill with the imagined rustle of wings flapping against air currents.

•—-—•

The next morning, when I pad out to the foyer, I hear the distant roll of thunder and the faint cooing of doves. I cannot hear the fan blowing, but there seems to be a draft of Mr. Fluxcer's sadness drifting down the staircase anyway. I head to the kitchen and Ina pours my cereal into a plastic bowl. Whether wafts of his sadness are burdening her as well is not obvious, but she allows me to take my breakfast out of doors with only the weakest of warnings that she can smell rain coming, and that I should get my butt inside if there is any sign of lightning. I sense the porch will be highly concentrated with sadness, so I grab Daughterspoon and head out the back door. The sun is obscured by low-hanging clouds, and the air is eerily calm. I wedge myself between the garage and our scraggly caragana bush for a sense of secure containment, hoping the overhead garage eaves will provide some protection against a downpour. The hedge's yellow blooms are all but spent, replaced by funny little pointy pods; the bees that still hover are like guests who have arrived too late for the lunch buffet. They zigzag over my sugary bowl, and then move off, their soft buzzing devoid of complaint.

I say to Daughterspoon, "Poor Mr. Fluxcer. I don't think that fan can blow all of his sadness away. He will continue making more."

What if he's too sad to take care of the doves? Daughterspoon demands in a voice that is often louder and bossier than my own.

I do not shush her, but respond quietly, "I would do it. And I would build them a big outdoor cage right between the house and garage where it is sheltered from drafts."

You're too small. And the rest of us are spoons. And anyway, Ina won't let you. She wants you to do everything and nothing at the same time.

Those words are risky. "Shh! Do not be mean. What if she hears you?" I admonish.

The caragana hedge rustles with the upstart of a breeze. Thunder rumbles its proximity. I plunge Daughterspoon into the dregs of my bowl's soggy remains. She comes up sputtering, and says, *If you want Mr. Fluxcer to stop being sad, buy him a Winsday ticket. When it wins, he can get his boat and camper back.*

I stop to consider her suggestion. "Good idea. Maybe he will be so happy that he will take Ina, me, and the doves camping in the woods."

Daughterspoon nods and dances around the edge of my cereal bowl.

"But wait a minute," I exclaim, and she halts her celebration. "That is crazy!"

Daughterspoon ignores my protest and replies, *Hop on your bike and go right now to the corner supermarket—*

The Twistical Nature of Spoons

"Gambling is the reason Mr. Fluxcer is sad in the first place," I interrupt her. "It is doomed to backfire."

That is because his wife lost.

"Well, it cannot be that easy to pick the winning numbers."

Daughterspoon's response is so intimate, I am uncertain if I speak it aloud. *Your Dad bent metal with his mind. You must have special powers too. So do it. Use your mind's powers to pick the winner.*

"But how will I pay for the ticket? I only have pennies in my piggy bank."

She replies in a silvery whisper, *Take money from Ina's craft-sale cash box. Her float has one-dollar bills.*

"Steal them?" I squeal. "What if Ina catches me? What if she takes you all away as punishment?"

Daughterspoon taps the side of the bowl as if her patience is running out.

I muster my courage. "Okay," I agree, "but when we win all the lottery money, you can never, ever tell the secret of how I did it!"

A rusty squeak startles me, causing me to drop my bowl and Daughterspoon. The garage's side door opens.

In the next heartbeat, Mr. Fluxcer is standing over me, his cheeks coloured by a ruddy blush and his forehead perspiring. "What were you saying just now?" he demands, but he keeps his voice low. It is clear he does not want anyone but me to hear him.

When I remain stock-still in my wedged quarters, he paces a few steps before turning back to me and speaking just above a whisper. "Did your mother tell you about …. What was she thinking?" He stops and shakes his head at me. "Blisse Trove, gambling is no joke! Children aren't allowed—"

I interrupt him, trying to match my voice level to his, "Please do not tell Ina!"

"How can I not?" he sputters. "Zounds! Keeping secrets? Plotting to steal money!" He lifts an arm to wipe his brow and the underarm of his shirt is wet with stress. "Making matters worse," he mutters to himself, his hand all atremble.

I hope his fingers will remain intact and not be shed onto the sunburnt grass with his eyebrows stuck to them. Collecting my bowl and Daughterspoon, I wiggle myself out from between the garage and caragana, just in case I have to dash inside and call 911.

"I will be in big trouble if you tell her, Mr. Fluxcer," I admit, throwing myself at his mercy. My brain jangles with the potential losses. What if, due to my stupid plan, Mr. Fluxcer chooses to move out? Then the true contest for saddest-of-them-all would take place between Ina, grieving for the rent money scattered on the wind, and me, bemoaning the promise of doves caught in an updraft of never-see-them-again. Daughterspoon pats at my leg in a weak attempt to offer reassurance, but it is obvious she knows that we are in scads of hot water.

Ina

waits

*A*fterwards, just before the sun came up, and while we still lay entangled in a heap of our discarded clothes, Taras reached for the Tartaglia mask. It had been abandoned on a low shelf next to us in the studio's cramped storage vestibule—an empty-eyed witness to our frantic pairing-off. Taras held the leather mask over his face momentarily, breathed deeply, and said, "Despite Tartaglia's impediments, he has managed to retain a hint of your enticing perfume." He then turned it, arm's-length above our heads. As the mask stared down at us, I flushed with a modesty I hadn't been feeling a moment earlier. I turned my head away from Taras's bare chest, anxious to put my clothes back on, but could still detect his ragged breathing.

His question stalled me. "Why, Ina?"

I slumped against him again to avoid looking in his eyes. "Why what?" I said, my lips brushing his skin.

"Why didn't you allow me to get you a cab?" He lowered the

mask again, just inches above his face, so that his own expression was screened.

"Why didn't you just get the cab anyway?" I countered. How was I supposed to explain what, prior to our coupling, he had seemed to already know? Or was he just messing with me again? I resorted to my cure for self-consciousness—straight-up smart-ass sarcasm. "You know, if I'd got in a cab, poor Tartaglia would have been left here alone, struck dumb from having to watch you masturbate. Stammer, shmammer. Forget him ever speaking again, period. Perhaps those past occurrences account for his limited eyesight."

Taras's chest vibrated with silent mirth. He cleared his throat. "I'm grateful your tongue was not that harsh during our love-making. But, sweet Eye-nuh, don't fret about the masks' innocence. It's their centuries-old birthright to be imbued with bawdy knowledge; it renders them incorruptible."

"Okay, then. How about this, Taras? I didn't leave because I had a burning desire to find out if you still spoke in your stagey, dramatic way right after sex." I reached for my undergarments and wrestled them back on.

Taras did not move. He spoke into the lowered mask, "I think what your tongue wants to say is that you believe I know you, Ina."

I gaped at him. "You don't say?"

He nodded and set Tartaglia aside. "Yes. What defines ultimate intimacy in our lives? Not sex—it's a close second. The real wallop of intimacy comes from being known and understood by another human being. Someone from whom hiding yourself is futile. You were convinced I knew you, Ina, before I even left the bar last night."

Our eyes met for a long moment. He seemed to be seeking the coordinates of my soul before he asked, "The thing I want to know is if you know me."

I swallowed. "I feel as if I've never *not* known you, Taras. Does that count?" He gave no reply, so I plunged in. "But you prefer being *unknowable*."

The Twistical Nature of Spoons

When his only response was a sharp exhalation, I grew impatient. My shirt half on and half off, I blurted, "Let's be honest here. You don't even *know* my last name."

He looked away, muttering a foreign lament—"*Bozhe, Bozhe.*"—and then said, "Nor you mine."

"Makes us even."

"I'd like to hope."

On the topic of his surname, he remained mute. Were normal introductions too commonplace for him? Blah, blah, syllables. Or had my comments—added to the raw edge of his orgasm—left him feeling overly exposed? I wasn't about to share first.

I said, "So do we know each other, or have I just become the butt of a one-night-stand joke?"

"The punchline eludes me, Ina," he countered.

"Really? That's your answer?"

He pushed himself up to a sitting position and reached for his shirt.

I shook my head. "Well, aren't *you* the master of sidestepping. You do with your words what your little Arlecchino freak does with his feet."

He winced. "Freak?"

I jeered, "I get the feeling, despite your proclamations, that close-second rebound sex is fine and dandy." I thrust my legs into my jeans and stood. "You can dial up that cab now, Tear-*ass.*"

He agreed, dressed, and strode out of the studio to place the call. As I gathered my shoes and coat, I noticed the dull whoosh of forced air pushing through the building's duct work, the breaths we'd exhaled in fits of pleasure so easily displaced. I closed my eyes to lock in the memory.

A moment later, Taras's voice startled me. "Do you work tonight?"

I didn't answer him.

"Ina, will you be there when I come to the Three Sheets Tavern tonight?"

I shrugged an affirmative.

"Good," he said. "Although I fear you've already been exposed to a lethal dose of my heart-ice, Eye-nuh."

I stared at him, but he fumbled with his belt and didn't meet my eyes.

He added, "Well, at any rate, you'd best be gone before campus wakes up."

"That's the first sensible thing you've said all night," I muttered, and then felt guilty as I looked out of the storage room toward the rows of chairs, the covered tables, and the hidden masks. "You haven't slept …"

It was his turn to shrug. "It's our final day. My workshop is their last assignment before exams. They won't notice my sleep deprivation due to their own." He stepped in front of me and rubbed the space between my brows with his thumb. "Don't fret, Ina. It makes your forehead frown." Then he reached for my scarred palm and brought it to his lips.

I tried to ignore the way his touch ignited my pulse, but I knew he wasn't fooled. I wondered why he wasn't gloating. If anything, he looked contrite as we made our way out of the building. Panic swelled inside me. I didn't want to leave the man-who-walked-into-a-bar. I'd never known such a wild desperation to take hold of me. It stemmed from not knowing if I could even risk having feelings for him, while those very same feelings were now indelible. There was a gaping space between what I felt and what I could bring myself to confess. I blurted, "Which version of me do you think you know? The me before or after you?"

"Eye-nuh …" he drawled, and I suspected he was about to bust out some philosophical nonsense to ease the blight of dread on my face.

"You've changed me, Taras. Do you understand?"

The Twistical Nature of Spoons

He swallowed. I watched his jaw muscles tense and relax before he reached for me. He held me tightly against him, kissing my eyelids, as the sun crept over the horizon.

"Nothing of your essence is changed, Ina. I know you crave the possibility of surpassing yourself, but … how to overcome fear and grasp the nettle?"

I tried to pull back far enough to see his face in the dawn light, but he did not ease his encircling hold until the taxi arrived.

When the driver pulled up, Taras released me, urging me into the cab, and shut the door. Immediately, he opened it again, and asked in an urgent tone, "Do you have the spoon?"

"Yes," I said, as I shifted sideways to remove it from my pocket. I clutched it, waiting for him to request its return.

Instead, he nodded and murmured, so that the cabbie could not overhear, "When I've bent a spoon, I often brace myself, because its twistical nature can be tortuous; but that one … that one, Ina, proves that life can take a glorious turn when you least expect it."

My cousin Charlene must have been sneaking into my room to raid my closet just before she set off for work that morning.

She shook me awake. "Ina, what the hell …?"

I squinted at her through the doping of half sleep. I'd been dreaming. *It was time for the spring smelt run. I stood just below the campus bridge, waiting in the dark, holding a tiny spotlight and a black cloth for a net. The waters suddenly seemed to boil with the school's arrival—hundreds of silvery flashes, fighting upstream. I dipped my cloth and realized I wasn't catching little fish; I was capturing spoons. Spoons swimming their way up from Lake Superior to spawn. I understood I didn't have a valid licence for silverware fishing, but I knew that poaching spoons was far more valuable than netting smelt. The threat of imprisonment loomed while I filled a bucket with their luminous, unfilletable bodies.*

Panic from the dream pressed on my chest. Charlene's yammering battered me. I covered my head with a pillow.

Char yanked it away. "Ina! Seriously, eh! Did you go on a bender after work?"

I wanted her to shut up so I could finish the dream. I placed my arm over my eyes to screen out the light.

She rattled on. "I come in here, you're wearing your clothes from last night, makeup a smeared disaster, and you're, like, passed out on the bed. I ask myself, 'Is she dead?' I spent the night at Denny's place, so I wasn't here when you got home. He just dropped me off."

Images jumbled in my head. Denny's hairy hands netting smelt collided with Taras flexing the fingers of Pantalone's lust. I shivered and then flushed.

"Are you, like, major hungover?" Charlene pulled my arm away from my face and surveyed me. "Damn, did you get laid?"

"Char!"

"No, what's the skinny? You look like you got laid."

"Don't you have to be at work?"

She grinned. "'Bout time."

"What, are you keeping a calendar?"

"Tippity-tapped Ina," she proclaimed as she swung her hips around in a circle.

"Char! Can you grow up?"

"Yeah, you're lucky I have to go to work right now. Catch you on the flip side. And later, details." She was out the door with one of my sweaters in her hand.

"Don't wait up," I called after her, not knowing if she heard.

The Twistical Nature of Spoons

Later, my night was defined by *waiting*. For much of my shift, when I wasn't pacing, I loitered by the Three Sheets front window. The dusk light faded. In the distance, the harbour lights blinked as if powered by my anticipation. The regular customers loved that I was distracted and overpouring. Every time the door swung open, I braced myself. I wanted to witness Taras's expression change from uncertainty to relief when he spotted me. It was the first time since I'd started working there that sailing out didn't cross my mind. All I wanted was for him to bustle in.

Part of my anticipation was not just from a desire to see him, but also because I wanted to become the fully knowable Ina Trove to him when he appeared. No more sarcastic concealer. I wanted to drop all disguise. A mask-maker would understand the depths of that commitment. Wouldn't he?

As I leaned over to unload a tray of draft glasses, I felt the familiar jab in my hip from the little twisted spoon in my jeans pocket. I didn't remove or shift it. I depended on its frequent prods to keep me in kilter. Each little stab was proof that the previous night had happened. How could I have survived the waiting without them?

At the end of my shift, after I'd stood outside Three Sheets and scanned the street in all directions, I steered myself back in and deliberately left the lock and deadbolt unlatched when I switched off the *Open* sign. Antony had started to cash out, and I offered to stay late and help. He said he thought I should "hit the road and hit the hay" because I'd seemed a little "off" that night. To delay a little longer, I skittered into the ladies' room. In the stall, I noticed that the spoon jabs had caused three tiny bruises to colour my upper thigh; coin-sized commemoratives to mark the occasion of Taras's no-show. I swallowed down my sobs. It was crucial my boss not hear me. I turned on the cold-water tap and let it run alongside my throbbing, silent spasms. There would be no bearing it if public shame was piled onto my private one-night-stand humiliation. Plus, what if Antony took it into his head to fire me? He hired a

Patti Grayson

cab to take me home the night before to ensure I avoided the dubious character that I'd chosen to follow instead. Ina the Idiot. And blubbering about it to boot! I splashed water on my face, dried it with a harsh paper towel. Antony was up front doing inventory for reorders, and I snuck by while his back was turned, shouting a quick "goodnight" from the door. He never saw the fresh tears welling up.

You might wonder if I'd realistically expected a different outcome. I have to admit, I did. It was like being blindfolded and spun around and still believing that you're going to stretch out your arm and pin that tail right on the donkey's ass.

And so I hoped and waited the next night, and the one after that. I tried to keep perspective. I wasn't waiting for a loved one away at war, for an organ donor, for word from relatives at an earthquake's epicentre. I was just waiting for some guy who'd come along and mesmerized me. I stopped waiting on the fourth day and stuffed the little spoon into the bottom of my purse. For several weeks, I didn't wait. The technicolour of my encounter with Taras started to fade. At moments, I questioned if he had really walked into the bar at all, but the empty ache in my chest confirmed it. How could Taras have walked off with parts of me that I hadn't even known about until I met him?

And then a new cycle of waiting began. It was midday on a Sunday. Charlene and I were still in our pyjamas, eating toast at the chrome kitchen table. A heavy spring downpour was beating against the window.

"Char," I said, the dry toast sticking in my throat. "Don't fly off the handle …"

My cousin looked at me and set her coffee mug down without it making a sound. She could become eerily quiet when someone else turned serious.

"I'm more than several weeks late," I breathed out.

Charlene placed her hands in her lap. "Are you sure?"

The Twistical Nature of Spoons

I raised an eyebrow at her.

"Oh, fudge, Ina," she yelped, her right hand jerking up to cover her mouth. Behind it, she muttered, "Oh, I told you to get on the pill."

"Not helpful, Char."

She grabbed her coffee mug with both hands as if to anchor herself. "So I take it he didn't use a rubber? Or did it … break?" she trailed off.

"Neither of us were planning to end up in bed."

"Oh, yeah," she said with a slight edge, "I forgot your intentions were totally innocent when you followed a good-looking hunk to return a cheap souvenir spoon he dropped." She shook her head. "Shiiit!" she added, stricken. I braced myself for her to launch into a health-risk lecture. Charlene was a big fan of the word "crabs."

Instead, she turned her concerns inward, muttering, "I am never forgetting to take every single pill every single cycle from now on."

I responded so quietly, with my chin nestled into my collarbone, that she had to lean in to hear me above the rain thrashing the windowpane. "You do that, Char."

"Sorry, Ina," she said, but then couldn't stop herself from shaking her head. "But geez, no rubber?"

There was no point in trying to explain it to Charlene. How could I tell my cousin, without sounding like an utter flake, that protection hadn't seemed like a concern when just being with Taras felt so otherworldly? When I was with him, I was immersed in a mystery that had no foothold in the real world of venereal afflictions or making a baby. Still, I clung to a slim hope. "Maybe it's just a fluke. I'm not totally regular every month."

"Ina, it's too late for praying," she blurted. She looked at my face and relented, "Well, it's possible … " But then it all seemed to become too much for her. "Ina, this is so, so not copacetic. You need to go to the doctor for a pregnancy test. God, Denny will not set foot in this place if there's a bawling baby here."

I couldn't blame Char for worrying about how my potential pregnancy was going to screw up her life too, but if push came to shove, she could toss me and my little embryo out the door and get on with her life. I stood up to refill my coffee. At first, I thought the sensation in my chest was from having carried overloaded trays of draft the previous night, but then it dawned on me that the new tenderness in my breasts had nothing to do with muscle strain. I snuck a hand along the front of my pyjamas and lightly pressed. I winced. I wasn't going to need a doctor's visit to confirm my pregnancy.

A week later, as I was washing some saltines down with weak tea, Charlene paused with her hand on the doorknob as she was heading out to work. She made a stab at trying to convince me to move back in with my mother in Winnipeg.

I sputtered, dry crumbs flying out of my mouth. "Char, do you not recall her parting words to me?" When I'd first moved to Thunder Bay, I'd repeated the statements to Charlene for her amusement: "Whatever you do, don't let your cousin give you one of those hideous perms that are all the rage. It'll wreck your naturally curly hair. And don't put me in an early grave by coming back home knocked up unless you're flashing a wedding ring." Charlene had shaken her head in disbelief. Neither of us knew how our mothers were sisters. Before Char's mother lost her brutal battle with cancer, she'd been sweeter than a Tootsie Pop. My mother, May, was the sibling blessed with the salt-in-the-wound demeanour.

Char knew my phone calls back home to my mother were infrequent. I didn't return every Christmas because May took all the holiday shifts offered to her, claiming, "Someone has to feed the travelling wayward souls and single fathers doing their best." As a child, I'd spent Christmas Day in the back booth of the Nobleman's Hotel dining room, eating on-the-house turkey dinner or curled up asleep, while my mother waited on customers and insisted on reading them their horoscopes from her pocket-sized zodiac

The Twistical Nature of Spoons

guide. "Forewarned, forearmed," was her favourite saying when she served up the predictions. She swore that bestowing her little holiday gift earned her bigger tips, never assuming that people might just be more generous at that time of year. It wasn't a tradition I needed to uphold into adulthood, and May never objected to the years I chose to be absent, likely because her biggest joy came from chance encounters with those who appeared or confessed to be unluckier than her.

In response to my spewed-out reminder, Charlene offered, "Well, okay, I get it. Aunt May won't be laying out a red carpet. But listen, I'm not telling anyone, least of all Denny, about this right now. So I can be discreet and ask around at the salon. Women know where to turn in these situations. I could get an address."

"I appreciate you keeping the lid on it. I don't want anyone knowing. Not Denny. Not Antony. Not anybody. But I don't think you should ask around. Whoever you talk to might think it's you who needs it. Not a good idea, for your sake."

I had to admire Charlene's restraint that day when she merely nodded her goodbye and headed off to work. I figured it wouldn't be long before she launched a blunter verbal attack and stated that if she wanted to be living with a baby, she'd have had one. Gratitude for the postponed ultimatum didn't prevent the swell of morning sickness. A moment later, I was sitting on the bathroom floor, clenching my molars against a wave of nausea. From my unique vantage point, staring at a spot behind the toilet tank, I noticed an accumulation of hair and that fine white dust that results from the unfurling of toilet paper rolls. I was surprised the grunge didn't increase my nausea. Instead, I found it oddly comforting. Something I could clean later, after I knew my saltines would stay down; an activity to undertake. I could remain one dust bunny ahead of a full-blown panic attack.

As I spit the last dribble of bile into the toilet bowl, the thought that the pregnancy might end on its own flitted in and out of my brain cells. What were my odds if I didn't take matters into my own hands? What were the chances of my pregnancy in the first place? Why was I knocked up after a single night with Taras when other women tried for years to have a baby? My mother's warning swirled in my head, but it was suddenly overtaken by Taras's great-grandmother's words, and I was struck by the feeling that she had preordained this pregnancy. What had she told Taras? Seek the hand with the extra lifeline. What if my extra lifeline didn't extend my own life—maybe it just meant a second life? What if this child—the one growing in my uterus and making me want to puke weak tea and crackers—was my fate? She spoke of a curse. Would a curse befall me if I didn't live out my destiny of giving birth to Taras's baby? I blamed flooding hormones for these cockamamie thoughts and squirmed at my superstitious ridiculousness. I'd vowed I wouldn't turn into my mother. I was about to *become* a mother! And that was the surprising relief: the only reprieve from the panic of the pregnancy came when I stopped long enough to imagine the tiny human being that was to be. I wondered if Taras, wherever he was, would feel the same.

5

Blisse

dove love

When Mr. Fluxcer notices me tapping nervously at my leg after I have climbed out from between the garage and caragana hedge, he clasps his own hands together to stop them from shaking. I am relieved. His firm clenching might prevent his fingers from falling off. There are, however, other potentially errant body parts, so I am grateful for the day's gluey humidity. It is much more likely Mr. Fluxcer will remain intact on a sticky summer day than during a spell of chapped-dry prairie winter.

My bigger problem still remains. If he marches in and tells Ina he overheard me talking about purchasing lotto tickets, I cannot imagine what will happen. She will believe I am undermining, not supporting, our lodger's recovery from sadness. I have to stop him, so I decide to come clean. "Please do not be angry. I wanted to visit your doves, and Ina said I had to leave you alone because of your troubles. She only told me so I would know not to bother you." I pause to take a breath, then add, "And I did not realize you were listening to me."

"Well, we both had a belief ... an expectation of privacy, then. And thank goodness I *did* overhear you!" He paces in a tight circle.

I attempt a diversion. "If I promise to leave you alone, will you please not tell? You can trust me, Mr. Fluxcer. I will tell you a secret in exchange, and then we will be even-steven. Come on," I urge, my words accelerating, "I will introduce you to my spoon family. It is a good year to meet them as there are seven. You like uneven numbers, right? If you wait, there will be an even number, and you might not like them so much."

Mr. Fluxcer recoils from my statements. The remaining tinge of colour drains from his face.

I realize I have made matters worse by bringing up my spoons again. Desperation takes hold. Perhaps he will be assuaged if I pretend to realign myself—create a division between me and my silver family. I thrust Daughterspoon forward like a stop sign. "It is all this spoon's fault. She is what my teacher calls a meddler. It is a bit like a tattler, but not quite. 'Meddlers always have to be in the mix of things where they have no business being,'" I quote. "I *do* promise to leave you alone, Mr. Fluxcer. I swear it," I say, using Daughterspoon to make an X across my entire chest and abdomen. "Hope to die!" I add for emphasis.

He squeezes his eyes shut and holds up his hands as if to defend himself. Turning away from me, he exhales. I half expect to see a belch of greenish-yellow breath exude, as I did on the first day he arrived, but the air around him remains visually normal. I feel encouraged even though his face has flared from wan to beet red.

A gust of wind rustles the caragana bush and thunder rumbles again. Mr. Fluxcer raises his hand, flattened palm up. The first oversized raindrops land. Several hit my head, and as I look up to Mr. Fluxcer, one catches my eyelid and soaks my cheek. At this, he collects himself and motions toward the garage door. We flee inside as the skies open in earnest. With the rain battering the garage roof, we stand in the cramped space in front of his station

The Twistical Nature of Spoons

wagon. Ina occasionally talks about the garage collapsing someday, and I wonder if the storm might cause such an outcome. She could not be mad at me if I am buried under the rubble of beams and shingles. I clutch Daughterspoon tighter to my chest.

Mr. Fluxcer shakes his head. "Your mother asked me to transport her crafts to the rec centre in my car," he says, as if he owes himself an explanation for eavesdropping on me. "I was tidying it. To be ready for tomorrow."

"I did not know you were in here," I repeat to assure him I had not meant to cause him upset.

He glances over. We stare at each other for a moment before he reaches for the doorknob, as if he has made the decision to head back to the house.

"Please, Mr. Fluxcer, do not tell Ina!" I plead.

He mutters to himself. Only the odd word reaches me, something about "what's best."

I feel tears welling up. Desperate to stall him, I shout, "Two wrongs do not make a right!" My shouting causes a commotion. There is a flutter and a rattle of metal, and my first thought is that Mr. Fluxcer is finally flying apart for real. Then I realize he is rushing to the back of his station wagon, and there on the roof of the car is a small birdcage with Dovetail in it.

"Hush. Hush. All's well," he coos to her.

When I realize that, aside from the trouble I am already in, I have also now startled his gentle bird, my forlorn heart constricts. Tears flood over my already damp cheeks; my chest heaves with sobs. At that moment, the garage side door flies open. Ina rushes in, her shirt and jeans splattered with huge wet streaks.

She takes one look at my tears and demands, "What's going on in here?" There is a bright intensity in her eyes when she shoots Mr. Fluxcer a look of distrust.

If it is possible to cry harder, I do.

Mr. Fluxcer abandons Dovetail and comes forward. His eyes

dart from Ina to me and back again before he commences. "It's all my fault. Completely my fault. Without thinking, I asked Blisse if she might be interested in becoming a magician's assistant. My helper. Pending your approval, Ina, of course. I have a few shows booked. City libraries. Day camps. Children involved in magic inspire other children. And I foolishly … I unwisely said that one day I would like to learn to saw an assistant in half."

Mr. Fluxcer has levelled his gaze at me and raises one eyebrow. It amazes me how firmly affixed to his forehead it appears. For the first time, I feel assured that no part of him will go catapulting off. This reassurance, combined with the intrigue of his on-the-spot lie, reduces my tears.

He continues, "I believe she wanted to be my assistant. Until she realized she might be cut in two. I scared … frightened the daylights out of her. I apologize, Ina." He turns to me, but his glance is skyward. "I swear I will not saw you in half, Blisse."

Ina turns to me, laughter bubbling in her voice. "That's just a magic trick, Blisse. No one gets sawn in half for real," she adds with bravado.

Dovetail sings out from her cage, *croo-CROOK-croo,* as if she is adding to the merriment.

I want to rush back and see the ring-necked bird, but there is something about Ina's tone that worries me. Her words lack honest conviction. Although she is obviously relieved to hear Mr. Fluxcer's explanation for my tears, she is still on edge. She glances from Daughterspoon, clutched in my hand, to my eyes, and I dare not look away in case she is about to provide a clue. She knows as well as I do that there are unexplainable things in the world. Does she secretly believe an assistant's head and torso could be separated from their hips and legs if the magic fails?

Ina finally says, "So what's your answer?"

I stand with my mouth agape. Those words are not what I am expecting.

The Twistical Nature of Spoons

"Do you want to be a magician's assistant?"

It is too enormous a question. "I do not know. I think I do," I answer so quietly that I am sure the drumming rain on the roof drowns me out.

Ina frowns. "Well, do you understand your responsibilities? And did you talk about pay?"

Mr. Fluxcer asserts, "Ten dollars per show. That includes prep time. Mortise and Tenon need to be acquainted and comfortable with you. The order of the tricks must be memorized. Also, you must swear an oath to never reveal how a trick is done. So if you can't keep a secret …" His voice conveys the direst warning.

"Oh, I can do that," I say, bobbing my head. I hold my breath, hoping that Ina will confirm my ability, but she neither substantiates nor refutes my claim, and I know how close I came to breaking my secret-keeping promise to her just moments earlier. The relief that I did not share our spoon secret with Mr. Fluxcer makes me suddenly giddy.

Outside the garage, the rain's barrage continues. In a matter of minutes, the threat of Mr. Fluxcer moving out of our house due to my reckless behaviour has transformed into a job offer that includes earnings and a chance to be with the doves! The one time Cousin Charlene visited us from Thunder Bay, I overheard her say that when her boyfriend, Denny, opened the box to her engagement ring and offered it to her, she was so shocked, she did not know whether to "shit or go blind." At the time, I covered my ears against the vulgarity, but here, standing in the garage, I experience a sudden appreciation for what Cousin Charlene meant. My future holds a most desirable thing, but it also feels more frightening than ever before. Aside from the threat of sharp saws sectioning me off, how can I ever stand up in front of people and help a magician?

Ina cuts through my growing queasiness, her voice overly bright. "I always said you were special, Blisse. Here's more proof. How many six-year-olds get an offer like this?"

Mr. Fluxcer proffers an out. "You don't have to, Blisse. Perhaps you'd rather be riding your bike. Playing with friends."

I want to assure him that is not the case. I have no real friends on our block, and my friends at school, Lisa and Matthew, seem more intent on competing for my friendship and making me choose sides rather than just playing together. I like to initiate games like Guess the Colour I'm Thinking, but Lisa never manages to get the right answer, while Matthew and I often guess correctly because we take the time to really concentrate on what might be in the other's mind. There are only nine basic colours allowed, so the odds of guessing right are pretty good. Lisa gets angry, accuses us of cheating, and insists we play Dodgeball or Monkey in the Middle instead; but then Matthew throws the ball too hard at both of us because I have agreed to Lisa's choice. Their battle for my friendship makes me so anxious that, during many recesses, I do not want to play with either of them. On those days, I would like to be Julie's friend, but she walks through the schoolyard encircled by five or six other girls who fence off my access as effectively as barbed wire. However, I doubt any of this will recommend me to Mr. Fluxcer, so I keep my thoughts to myself. Then I debate if he perhaps lost his friends when he had to sell his boat and camper. I have witnessed that kind of rise and fall in popularity at school based on who has a Gizmo plush toy and who does not; another domain in which I cannot compete, because the Gremlin creatures make Ina shudder.

A gentle cooing draws our attention to the back of the station wagon, so I am not required to answer. Mr. Fluxcer proceeds to take down the cage and open its door. Reaching in for Dovetail to alight on his hand, he signals that I should approach. He holds the dove close to his chest, bends down onto one knee, and instructs, "It is best to begin by stroking a bird gently from their head toward their back." He demonstrates with his finger and thumb. "Would you like to try?"

The Twistical Nature of Spoons

I inch my way forward, still clutching Daughterspoon against my chest with one hand as I reach forward with the other. I feel a surge of disbelief as I run my finger over Dovetail's soft head. Touching a bird, of all things! A giggle wells up inside me, and I pull away momentarily. As I reach forward a second time, I am surprised by the wispy rigidity in the edges of her back feathers. Still attached, they feel different than the one I found on the stairs. Dovetail's little eyes seem to be sizing me up, and then she raises her head and exposes her neck.

"She likes you," Mr. Fluxcer observes. "You can gently rub her throat. Downwards from her beak. She will not bite. She may decide to nibble at you."

Miraculously, she does just that.

Mr. Fluxcer chuckles. "She's preening. Returning the favour."

Up and down my fingers, her little beak is intent on grooming me despite my obvious lack of plumage. I look up at Ina and she seems content not to comment. At that moment, Dovetail reaches forward and gives Daughterspoon a few pecks. The hardened tip of her beak, with its slight downward turn, raps at the metal as if posing a question. Is Dovetail just curious about the shiny patina of a new object, or can she sense that real magic exists in the world and knows that my spoon embodies it?

Mr. Fluxcer affirms, "I can see you and the doves will get along just fine."

But when I smile up at him, he has already drawn himself away, holding the bird as if to shield his heart. It troubles me that his encouraging words do not match his demeanour. As I listen to the rain letting up, I hope that Mr. Fluxcer's sadness is not being compounded by magician-versus-real-magic envy.

There is little time to ponder. My first task as the assistant of the Magical Influx Show is given to me that very afternoon. It is not directly magic-related, but I am beyond joyful. Mr. Fluxcer puts me in charge of supplying the doves' supplementary food two or three times a week. My assignment is to chop vegetables and fruit, place them in a clean dish in the cage, and then remove them the same day so they do not spoil and make the doves sick. I am permitted and encouraged to hand-feed them their bits of leafy greens. Because the chopping requires using a knife, I have to wait for Ina to supervise, but she does not interfere. After a short time, she does not even bother watching me, but remains in the kitchen, attending to her own tasks. I lament her lack of interest at the same time as I crave the independence it provides me. And every night, I bestow an extra good-night kiss on Daughterspoon's handle for her lottery ticket idea. Even though it almost led to disaster, it granted me my wish instead. In one way, it is inexplicable—unless that is what Ina means about bad luck not existing—in another way, it feels like it was destined to be.

More responsibilities are rapidly added in preparation for the first scheduled magic show. Mr. Fluxcer is patient as he teaches me what is required, and never fails to be encouraging as I practise. I note that when he is in magic mode, he does not lumber and I do not fear for his disintegration. On the third floor of our house, in the doves' room, I learn how to fold slippery silk handkerchiefs, arrange props on a small side table with exact placement, and set the decks of cards and special coins in the proper pockets of Mr. Fluxcer's tailed tuxedo coat. The best part, however, is placing a dove back in its cage after Mr. Fluxcer has produced it from his tall, black top hat. Joy and trepidation swirl through me each time. With the bird perched on my fingers, I slide my whole hand through the cage opening ever so carefully, and then ensure I latch the door shut and drape the black cloth over the wire. Their return to the covered cage ensures that when we perform for boisterous children, the doves do not suffer undue stress. Dove Out of a Hat is Mr. Fluxcer's best trick and the show opener. Its placement, off the top, is to serve as an audience attention-grabber and to release the dove at the first opportunity. Although we practise the hand-off

The Twistical Nature of Spoons

much more frequently than the entire trick, I worry about the birds each time we fully rehearse it. Mr. Fluxcer assures me that the doves are not frightened by the trick. The way they flap their wings upon emergence makes me speculate to the contrary. My only reassurance is his obvious concern for the doves' well-being. He ought to know, I conclude, but I wish I was the one performing the trick so I could be certain for myself. Maybe I will. Maybe, some day, I will perform the greatest dove magic tricks of all time with not a single feather ruffled. In the meantime, at least I get to experience a feeling of relief each time I safely return Mortise or Tenon to their cage.

The day before our first library show, Mr. Fluxcer invites Ina to a run-through so we can complete it from start to end for an audience. The prospect of performing in front of my mother makes my stomach flutter out of control. While scrambling to learn all my responsibilities, I had lost the acute awareness that our rehearsals would culminate in a presentation to an actual audience. Performing in front of Ina means the real thing is just around the corner. I can barely make myself double-check all the props. I want to tell Mr. Fluxcer that I do not want to do the show anymore, but I am equally afraid of missing out. In the midst of being pulled in two different directions, I hear Ina calling me downstairs. I cannot believe she is interrupting my pre-show routine.

"I think you'd better go straightaway," Mr. Fluxcer admonishes when he sees the look of protest on my face.

"But ..."

"We must be prepared for interruption. On performance days, we can't control our environment or those in it. Dealing with disruptions is part of our task," he says knowledgeably.

I sigh and bound down the stairs.

Ina stands in the kitchen, scowling, arms crossed. "Just because you're a magician's assistant does not mean you can skip making your bed."

I am tempted to huff and stomp past her to my room. Why is she adding to my turmoil? But I know without a doubt that one word from Ina and I will be out of the Magical Influx Show. So I hang my head and march, withholding complaint. Wondrously, my bed is already made and atop it lies the most beautiful small black velvet dress. A plain, straight, sleeveless sheath adorned with silver sequins around the neckline and hem. When I pick the garment off the bed, the sequined trim glints and ripples. I hold it at arm's length and squeak with delight.

Ina is standing in the doorway; her former demeanour was clearly a ploy. She babbles, "I hope it's not too hot in those libraries. That's why it's sleeveless. If you have some winter shows, I can make a little cape. I bought an entire bolt of the fabric. It was deeply discounted because people went so gaga for velour, but velvet is superior, and it's what a magic show deserves."

I turn and fling myself at Ina, hugging her waist and sobbing into her shirt.

"And Blisse," she adds, unlatching my grip, eager to show me an added detail. "There's even a secret pocket sewn inside, in case you want to practise your own magic trick." Without taking the dress from me, she shows me the little vertical pocket attached to the side seam.

Through blurry tears, I hiccup, "No one would ever know it is there. That is sneaky."

Ina brushes at my tears with the palm of her hand. I brace myself in case I feel the ridge of her bumpy scar, but it is not noticeable against my cheek, and I am relieved. I feel my nervousness drop away and declare, "I am going to hide a good luck charm in this pocket."

Ina cocks her head, questioning.

"Please, let me, Ina. We both know the perfect thing."

"Hey, you don't need good luck, Missy Blissey, because you have practised so much. You don't—"

The Twistical Nature of Spoons

I cut her off. "I know. I know, Ina. I am aware the *pretend magic* is determined by how well you do the steps of the trick. But please, Ina," I beg, touching the sparkling trim, noting how each sequin has a tiny hole for the stitch that holds it in place. "This whole dress could be a good luck charm."

I am dismayed that Ina seems more excited about the discounted savings and fabrication particulars than the potential added wonder of the dress, especially if it were concealing a spoon. I add, "I think my dad would let me."

I see momentary bewilderment pass across Ina's face, and then she turns her attention back to the dress. She gently pries it from my fingers. "Okay. Okay," she says and nods. "Okay, Blisse, just try it on. I still have time for alterations after this dress rehearsal."

It is impossible not to stand straighter, to feel elevated above the ground when I am sheathed in the sequined dress. It is as if the garment's lining is enchanted with tickling silk; my stage smile no longer feels fake and pasted on. The velvet's lustre whispers assurances that I am a small spectacle in my own right. Perhaps the audience children might even envy me. I pat at the dress's side seam to confirm that the secret pocket is the perfect size to house the souvenir spoon.

Mr. Fluxcer joins us downstairs and applauds when he sees me. He is then overcome when Ina presents him with his own gift of a framed fabric sign. Painted red letters, outlined in silver to match my sequins, announce: *The Magical Influx Show*.

He declares, "It almost looks like a living thing, Ina."

"The natural effect of painting on black velvet," Ina confirms. "Kind of pops like 3-D, doesn't it? Eye-catching. I ignore the critics who call it a tacky art form."

Mr. Fluxcer adds, "It confounds our vision just like magic does. How thoughtful, Ina. It's like seeing my name in lights," he chuckles.

My mother beams.

The unexpected generosity of Ina's gifts produces another electric surge of happiness, smoothing away the last of my pre-show jitters. The magnitude of my first performance seems manageable. Maybe Ina is right and I do not need luck because I am already the luckiest girl alive! Yet despite my new feelings of invincibility, I am surprised when a sense of alarm creeps in, and then, as if a red handle is yanked down, starts clanging inside me. Although I do not have the precise word to describe it, I am experiencing a feeling of disloyalty. And I do not quite understand to whom I have been disloyal. Should I not have insisted on combining the evidence of my father's real magic with Mr. Fluxcer's performance of mere tricks? I refuse to succumb to self-interrogation. I do not have to answer my own questions. I dash away to my room and duck under the bed to pull the box out from underneath. With the lid opened, and my silver family all in a row in front of me, I cover my ears against the high-pitched whine of guilt and the echoey reverberations of the unknowable. I can tune out the clamour. I reach past the dove feather to pluck out the original spoon and tuck it into the secret pocket of my dress.

Ina

flounders

Emerging from the Three Sheets bathroom, I bent a strip of chewing gum into my mouth to chase away the taste of bile. I straightened my barmaid apron, smoothing it down over my still-flat belly.

Antony took a hard look at me and said, "Hey, so I wasn't planning on bringing this up, but you've seemed off ever since that guy showed up—the one who smashed a glass outside the door."

My body tensed. I nodded. Noticing a spot on the bar, I wiped at it with a cloth, my hand shaking.

He continued, "Yeah, so he came back, banging on the door after closing time, asking for you."

"Oh," I said, forcing my voice to sound uninterested. The last thing I wanted was for Antony to know I was knocked up, at least until I started showing and couldn't disguise it any longer. I desperately needed time to figure things out. "How'd you know it was the same guy? I didn't think you even saw him."

"Well, first thing, before he even says your name, he pulls out a five-spot—fesses up that he owes me for a broken glass."

"When was this?" I said.

"Pretty sure it was the next night. The night after I put you in the cab home." He nodded with certainty.

Trying to unstrangle my voice, I asked, "So what happened?"

"I told him you weren't here. He's got this big duffle bag slung over his shoulder—looks like it contains all his worldly possessions the way he's hanging on to it—but I figure he's about to haul it off and swing it at me when I say you've gone home. That's when I figured he likely threw that glass *at* you. Am I right?" He doesn't wait for my answer. "So I go to shut the door in his face, but he's freakin' quick, pushes his way in. Says he has to see you. How can he find you? Starts spewing shit about destiny. 'She's my destiny,' he keeps repeating."

I pulled a face at Antony like I couldn't believe what he was saying.

He forged ahead. "Did you tell him your last name is Rhymeswith? I swore he said, 'I must see Ina Rhymeswith.' But I can't remember half the shit he said. He musta been high or off his nut, so no way I'm telling him where you live. Especially if you gave him a fake name. So I give him a choice. He can vamoose, or I can call the cops. He pulls out a plane ticket, says he has no choice but to vamoose because he's booked on the first flight out in the morning."

I blinked hard, trying to keep my eyebrows in check. "To where?"

"Damned if I know. He's waving the thing around like it's burning his hand. Then he says he's also had enough of the law for one night. Well, I didn't need someone who'd already had a run-in with the cops standing in my bar after hours, so I say I've had enough of *him* for one night, and he better make himself scarce if he knows what's good for him. Nutcase actually sits down at the bar, all

The Twistical Nature of Spoons

cavalier-like, and asks if there's really a need for pistols at dawn. Pistols!? That got me riled—not to mention a little worried about what he had stashed in that duffle bag. So I hand him a coaster and a pen and tell him to write you a note. Assure him I'll give it to you. Even hand him his fiver back—no hard feelings."

I nodded and shifted away to wipe down the handles of the beer taps in an attempt to curb my anxiety. Barely trusting my voice, I asked, "Did he?"

"Did he what?"

"Write a note?"

"Yeah, he did. I fired that coaster right into the garbage the second he was out the door. Good riddance to bad rubbish."

I wanted to scream bloody murder. But instead, with what little breath I had, I agreed. "Yeah."

After a brief pause, Antony seemed satisfied that I didn't much care. Shrugging, he added, "Just thought you should know. You've been real jittery since that night, but I doubt you have to worry about him ever showing up here again."

My breath caught in the spot where my heart was newly lodged. "I'm lucky you looked out for me, Antony."

My boss puffed up his chest and patted the bar like he'd saved the day. I was relieved when he sauntered over to chat up a table of customers.

Taras had returned! The universe appeared to be playing an additional sick joke on me. The strain of supressing my pregnancy symptoms and not reacting to Antony's disclosure gave way to anxious giddiness in my head. As I tried to avoid my boss for the rest of the shift, nonsense popped into my brain, making bizarre little circles:

A man walks into a bar with a spoon.

Bartender says, "Sorry, we have a policy against *serving* spoons."

Man says, "Oh, my spoon is a *tea*-totaller, so even if you brought a drink to the *table*, she could only keep it as a little *souvenir*."

Ba-dum tss! I wasn't exactly *ladling* out top-shelf *punch*lines, but I was in no mood for carefree laughter anyway.

The next day, after a sleepless night, but buoyed by the fact that Taras had come back to Three Sheets, I decided to hop on a bus and return to Lakehead U. By early afternoon, anchored down with fatigue, I forced myself to stride through campus, hoping that no one would question my presence. There was only a smattering of students in the main building. It had to be spring or summer session. I didn't know which. I arrived at the door to the studio where Taras and I had spent our fateful night together. A wave of queasiness hit me as I tried the door handle. I hadn't allowed myself to remember how good it had felt to be with him; I was afraid re-entering the room would make me start bawling from a lack of Taras. The lock held tight.

Plan B was to find the office of Taras's colleague. I didn't know Dirk's surname, so I tried to recall if Taras had mentioned any physical traits. Nothing came to mind. I wandered down a couple of halls, glancing into open doorways, trying to avoid eye contact with anyone. My demeanour must have been shrieking "dazed and confused" because a middle-aged woman stopped me. She wore a pair of paint-spattered overalls, but her stance was that of a *Vogue* model, slim and pouting, when she drawled, "You need directions?"

I took a deep breath. "Actually, I'm looking for a person. A fellow named Dirk."

"Dirkland Quinn?"

I nodded, thinking it unlikely a Dirk and a Dirkland worked in the same building.

"Well, if he's still around, you might catch him in his office." She leaned in toward me as if confiding gossip. "He's headed to BC. Summer research grant. Lucky bastard. Seriously, what glassblower deserves that? At least they turned him down at Harvard. There'd be no living with him if he spent the summer with that

The Twistical Nature of Spoons

Glass Flowers collection." She shook her head and then thrust her chin in the opposite direction. "Office 11C. Seriously, he blows molten sand into ashtrays and calls himself an artist. Likely blew someone for that grant, if you get my drift."

A part of me wanted to defend glassblowing, explain how I loved the play between light and coloured transparency in my stained-glass classes. How could she deny the beauty of that? Glass was a magical medium. With a pang, I realized that Taras would understand what I meant, and my need to find him ballooned a few sizes. I started in the direction she pointed.

Dirk was locking his office door, an artist's portfolio squeezed under one arm, a bulging briefcase at his feet, and an army surplus canvas backpack slung over one shoulder. The bags seemed to overwhelm his too-thin frame, like an overburdened stick figure. At that moment, my teensy womb-dweller turned into an oxygen hog. Gulping for air, and relieved I hadn't missed him, I called out, "Dirkland?"

At the sound of my voice, he swung around, which dislodged his portfolio. He fumbled about, trying to prevent its unzipped contents from spilling out. Without looking at me, he stated, "I'm afraid you've missed my final office hours."

"No, I'm not here for ..." I searched for the words and continued toward him. "I actually need your help."

He stole a hard look at me, then surveyed the hall as if the explanation for what I was doing there could be found somewhere behind me. "I'm running late. You could seek assistance at the main office. They're happy to help." He picked up his briefcase and wrestled it into a position that allowed for rapid escape.

"No. I ... I need some help locating a friend of yours."

"A friend?"

"Taras ... with the masks. He was here doing a workshop for you."

He squinted at me. "How do you know Taras?"

"Well, we met and he brought me here to see the masks."

"Here? He brought you to our studio?"

I decided to go all in. "He said he was staying here because you and your wife had just had twins and he didn't want to impose."

Dirk set the briefcase down again. Annoyance lapped over his wariness. He unlocked his office door and ushered me in. "You are …?" he asked.

"Ina."

"Well," he began, straightening his back, "Taras and I are professional associates only. So I—"

I interrupted, "He said you were old friends."

Dirk shook his head as if he could dispel my words with his own assurances. "We became acquainted back in our undergraduate days, but we were never regular collaborators. You say he brought you here?"

"He brought me here one night to see the masks," I confirmed.

Dirk's forehead creased. He glanced at his office door. It was clear he wanted to shut the outside out, but was equally reluctant to shut himself in. He reached around me and closed it, stepping back. He gripped his office chair, trying to look composed. "And you wanted to see them? That night? You agreed to see his masks?"

"Um. Yes."

"So which faculty? You're not enrolled in this department."

"No. I'm not a student here."

"Ahh. All right then," he concluded. Dirk's demeanour oozed relief. He stopped short of winking when he added, "We make adult decisions, eh?"

When I didn't respond, he offered, "He doesn't live in the Lakehead area."

I nodded again, finding it harder to catch my breath in the cramped office, as if it lacked breathable air.

He frowned. "Do you need to sit down?"

I remained standing. Given his shred of concern, I thought I

The Twistical Nature of Spoons

might try a different tack and tell him we shared an interest in glass. But it seemed smarter not to try his patience. "Do you know where he is or how I can get ahold of him? It's important."

"Well," he began, dragging a hand through his hair, "He's likely touring. Summer festivals. But you could try his *wife*. She'll know."

"His wife," I dumbly repeated.

Dirk nodded in response, then slid into his office chair and leaned back.

I added, "The same wife who slept with her advisor guy?"

His forehead creased again, but he continued to lean back. "Uh, yeah," he stalled.

"So although you're irregular collaborators, you know about his wife screwing around?"

Dirk shrugged. "Taras overshares when he drinks. What can I say?"

You could say you're an ass, and you'd get no argument from me. My thoughts must have shown on my face and made him uncomfortable because he shrugged as if it would be better to just give me the goods and get me the hell out of his office. He said, "She ditched the new guy, called to inform Taras on his last day here. That's how the masks got stolen."

"What?" I exclaimed.

"Hey, wait a minute," he declared, sitting up straight. "You said he showed you his masks." He snapped his fingers and pointed at me. "You're the one who took them! Where are they?"

I scrunched my face at him. "What are you talking about? How were they stolen?"

He looked doubtful I was telling the truth. "Taras was on the phone with his wife. It was clear she was begging him to take her back. I left to grab a cup of coffee and give him some privacy. After the call, Taras was totally discombobulated—beyond his normal weirdness. We went back into the studio so he could pack up and discovered someone had made off with half his masks. Taras blamed it on the phone call, but of course, it was his own fault. He left the studio door wedged open."

I nodded my head, remembering the wedged-open door that let us into the building on the night we spent together.

Dirk looked at me with more suspicion.

I said, "I swear I don't have the masks."

"We searched for hours, alerted security, called the cops. Sometime after midnight, Taras bailed, said he was late to meet someone. I assumed his wife had hopped on a flight here. I haven't heard from him since." His withering glare held me for another long moment. "And you don't have them?" he asked one last time.

When I shook my head, he sniffed and shrugged. "Probably students pulling a shitty prank. Well, in that case, Ida, we're done here."

I didn't bother to correct him. It was more important to make sure I breathed. Had my baby's father gone back to his wife? I knew I should leave, but Dirk was the only person who could shed more light. I could get answers if I just asked the right questions.

"Are you taking the twins with you?"

He blinked hard, not comprehending.

"The woman who directed me here said you were going to BC. Are you leaving your wife stranded with the babies?"

"Je-sus," he muttered. "Not that it's a total stranger's business, but they're coming with me."

I nodded. I felt some meaningless relief. My hands hung at my sides, and I felt my palms turn up, as if I needed to show him they were empty. "That's good," I said.

Dirk assumed our meeting had come to a close. He practically leapt out of his chair, reached around me, and opened the door.

My mind urged surrender, but my body stayed put. It was as if my little embryo had its own questions. I said, "So you're a new father. How would it be for you if you had a child in the world and didn't know about it?"

The Twistical Nature of Spoons

He huffed. His patience was wearing thin. He crossed his arms, refused to engage.

I ignored his hostility and pressed on. "Do you have any inkling how Taras might feel in the same situation?"

"Taras?" he said, incredulous.

I nodded.

"Taras?" Dirk repeated. "Is that why you came here? To claim Taras made you pregnant?"

"He did—" I began.

Dirk threw back his head and roared with laughter, cutting me off. "Wow. A-plus for dramatic effect. He sure knows how to pick women."

I stared at him.

"Taras is sterile!" he squawked. "That's likely why his wife cheated on him. I imagine the doc's report pushed her over the edge. Clock is ticking."

"Sterile?" I said, stunned.

"Yeah, for such a hyper guy, his sperm are uber-lazy. Apparently, near motionless. Test was repeated. Second opinion confirmed very low motility." Dirk seemed to be enjoying himself. "Leave it to Taras to say, 'If only my indolent sperm had four servants and a palanquin to convey them to their destination.' He must rehearse that stuff." He looked at me, tossed his head back, and laughed again. "But why would you choose to hustle Taras Petryshkovych? I mean, he's a brilliant, creative guy, but his head's in the clouds. Most months, he barely scrapes together his mortgage payment. He has more than one upward mobility issue."

I opened my mouth to assure him that Taras's sperm must have taken swimming lessons when a squiggling sensation churned in my abdomen. My heart leapt. Did I just feel my baby move for the first time? I reasoned it was too early to be feeling anything, but I couldn't help but focus on my midsection, waiting for it to happen again, only half listening.

Dirk motored on. "His own wife, before embarking on her temporary fling, said it was a good thing Taras was infertile because any kid that had to grow up with him as a father would surely choose to stab him dead. Right in the heart!" Dirk shivered dramatically. "Guy has his faults, but what kind of woman spews out venom like that? Taras labelled that a 'seriously cursed pronouncement'—seemed genuinely terrified."

"Pardon?" I said, trying to follow what he was saying.

Dirk spoke right over my question. "Personally, I hope he rushed off to finalize those divorce papers, but I doubt it. She has a real hold on him, almost hypnotic. Anyway, you want my advice? Unless the guy's in jail, go find your kid's *real* father."

I could have sworn that the floor tilted because I had to put one hand on the office wall to stay upright. I pressed my scarred palm to the flat of my stomach as if I could cover my baby's ears.

Dirk must have thought I was playing for sympathy because he sneered, "You need to vacate my office, Ida. Or do I call security to escort you?"

Recognizing my own impotence, I realized I now had nothing to lose. I narrowed my eyes at Dirk. "Go ahead, call a guard, but I can guarantee that the two of you will be more terrified than me," I said, echoing what Taras had said of those paid to be brave.

He glanced at the phone on his desk, but didn't reach for it.

Then, as if my improbable, squiggling little embryo was cheering me on, I added, "Your paint-spattered colleague is right. You blow, Dirk!" I turned on my heel and left him gaping after me.

A moment later, I regretted my lack of escort. I was shaking, and I couldn't remember the way out. I could've used a firm hand gripping my elbow. When I managed to stumble out an exit, I was blinded by the scalding June sunlight. I headed toward a large spruce tree and kneeled in its shade, gulping in deep breaths of evergreen tang. A squirrel let loose a furious barrage of chattering at me.

My mind tried to recap. Taras, sterile? Who messed up those

The Twistical Nature of Spoons

lab results? Twice? A hungover tech? Self-medicating doctor? Names switched on test tubes? Taras's last name couldn't actually fit on a test tube label, could it? What had Dirk said? Taras Petro-somethingorother? Why didn't I ask him to write it down for me? I wrestled back to my feet. Dirk said the people in the main office were helpful. Someone there would know the name of the man who came to lead the workshop. The man who was late showing up at Three Sheets. Why had Taras come at all? To tell me his masks had been stolen? That he'd spent the night searching in vain? That although they were gone, his no-longer wife was back? If I'd seen him at the bar, would he have clutched his heart, waved his plane ticket, and apologized for returning to the arms of the hypnotic Mrs. Petro-somethingorother?

As I attempted to return to the main building, the world started drifting in and out of focus. The overhead branches blurred and the sky lost its blueness, and then it all pulsed back with such defined vividness that I couldn't recognize my own shoes. Where was the entrance? What if the lab results were correct? What if I had been impregnated by an infertile man? Taras's great-grandmother leapt to mind. Did her predictions really involve my baby? Could a gash from a broken lemon gin bottle be the thing that brought my baby into being? What had Taras gleaned from her words? That he would be cursed if he chose a wrong wife. Great-granny never told him what the curse would be. Taras chose badly and bam—cursed with sterility. He had to look for a hand marked like mine. He found me and bam—baby on the way. The sunlight continued to blind. I licked my lips and tasted ozone, as if lightning had struck nearby, though the sky was cloudless. And was Taras back with his wife? Could she know that I broke the curse? Could she get pregnant now too, and then live happily ever after with Taras? I raised my foot to take another step across the campus lawn, but my shoe never touched the unreachable, greying ground. Narrowing ... narrower ... then nothingness.

When I came to, there were a couple of concerned students hovering over me.

"Whoa, you just crumpled like a rag doll."

"You passed out. Have you eaten today? It's really hot out here."

"Good thing you didn't hit your head."

I felt only the fading whispers of that in-between space. It was a safe place to be. I raised my shoulders, as if to move toward it, but got no further.

"Can you stand?"

If only I could just drift back into nothingness. Be left alone.

"Should we get an ambulance?"

But I wasn't alone any longer. There was another being inside me. "Uh … no." I raised myself to a sitting position. The grass was green. I made myself stand up on it. The group pressed closer, as if to ensure I'd stay upright, but I could sense their reluctance to touch me. I blurted, "I'm pregnant. That's all. I'm okay." My hands clutched my stomach, but there was no discomfort, no indication of harm.

"Oh!" One of the female students stepped back, as if pregnancy could be spread as easily as the common cold.

Although I was a little unsteady, I shooed them away. "Thanks, I'm all right."

As they dispersed with their textbooks in hand, all I could do was put one foot in front of the other until I reached the transit stop. I climbed aboard the bus, sat, and placed my forehead against the cool glass pane. I was frightened. My hands trembled. My body was betraying me. The pregnancy had taken charge. I had to rest before my shift. I needed to drink water and eat something healthy, then work my ass off that evening and pretend nothing was wrong. My body flushed hotter, and I shivered in the heat. I had to put the crazy thoughts out of my head. I sought out my reflection in the bus window to ensure it was me. When I saw that it was, I felt some relief.

The Twistical Nature of Spoons

I reached home to find the front door ajar. Charlene should have been at the salon, so I figured Denny must have stopped by. Maybe he was fixing something. Charlene liked to give him tasks on his days off; otherwise, he'd be fishing all day and in a beer-fog by the time she got off shift. I imagined his hairy hands wielding a hammer as I pulled open the screen door.

But it was Charlene who came rushing at me. "Regina!"

I was startled by her use of my full name.

"Where have you been? Oh, God." She was more pale and shaky than me. "They called me at the salon. My number must have been in her purse. Ina. Your mom. She's … she's gone."

"My mom?"

Charlene clutched me. "She died this morning. I'm so sorry, Ina. I can't believe this."

"What?"

"She collapsed at work. They rushed her to the hospital by ambulance, but she didn't make it. An aneurysm, they said. Poor Aunt May."

"Aneurysm? What is …?"

Char shrugged helplessly. "First my mom. Now yours."

Now is the time to faint, Ina. Feel free to faint now. But I didn't. I opened my mouth, gulped air, felt my heart rise to my throat and delay oxygen's progress for the second time that day. I sat down on the sofa, clutched my belly, and felt the sides of my head tighten as if they'd been clamped into some instrument of torture. A scene from my childhood welled up inside me: My first-grade classmates are playing Mother, May I? I am confused by the game. I can't understand how they know my mother's name. What do they have to do with my mother, May, and me, and why are they attaching their *Is* to our lives?

As the memory blinked away, I said, "What do I do, Char?"

"Denny will drive us to Winnipeg. He already booked time off. I spoke to Antony because I thought you went to work early or something …" Her voice trailed off. She sighed. "We need to pack."

My mother was dead. I was expecting a baby that shouldn't have been, but was, and my mother, May, was dead. I felt the word "curse" slither over my skin. I rubbed hard at my arms in its wake.

6

Blisse

potion notion

I am eight years old, and I decide that when I grow up, I will marry Mr. Knowlton Fluxcer and continue to be his magic show assistant. It does not matter that he is a middle-aged man, and I do not recognize that he will continue to age as I pass through my teen years. It is enough that he is kind and patient and owns doves, and that when I move into the upstairs rooms with him, Ina will continue to have our company, not to mention a way to maintain a roof over her head with the continuation of Mr. Fluxcer's rent cheques. When I am certain I am out of earshot, my spoon family enacts the engagement, wedding, and honeymoon trip to Hawaii. I think Mr. Fluxcer would benefit from the sunshine. I sustain my intentions for over a year, but by the time I am ten, I waver. Partly because a new boy arrives in our classroom, and although I am too tongue-tied to speak to him, he is my first classmate crush, but mostly because I am starting to realize that Mr. Fluxcer does not believe in real magic. He loves the illusions in his magic show and is quite taken with the physical apparatuses that create them, but he shrinks away from my hints that authentic magic exists. I am concerned we are not a perfect match. With Valentine's Day looming, the billboard advertisements prompt me to contrive another plan: Ina should marry Mr. Fluxcer instead. Ina was lucky enough to have had her perfect match with my truly magical father, but she has been alone for some time now, and Mr. Fluxcer might be the next best thing.

 I tally the evidence. Ina does nice things for Mr. Fluxcer. Things that she has never done for anyone else—like the fan and the sign and the fresh muffins she leaves for him on the mantel every month when he pays his rent. They always speak respectfully to one another. Mr. Fluxcer is willing to help Ina out in a pinch when she needs transportation or assistance with heavy objects. Mr. Fluxcer never mentions his ex-wife, and Ina has not gone on a single date to my knowledge. The pairing of Ina and Mr. Fluxcer seems a reasonable solution to their solitary states. In fact, it is puzzling to me that they are not already engaged. And it feels as if letting go of Mr. Fluxcer as my own intended groom is not only necessary, but noble at the same time. I trust that my destiny in finding a suitable partner will be fulfilled, while Ina might not otherwise, given that her social existence is mostly limited to other craft-sale vendors on the days they sell their wares.

 One evening, as I do my homework at one end of the kitchen table while Ina sits at the other, stuffing her handmade potpourri into the silk-and-lace sachet pouches she has fashioned, I broach the subject.

 "Ina, you and Mr. Fluxcer should go see a movie together. It would be fun, and I am now old enough to stay home alone for an evening."

 Without looking up, Ina responds, "You have to be twelve to stay home alone." She ties the sachet shut with ribbon, snips the ribbon ends at an angle, sets the filled pouch aside, and reaches for another.

The Twistical Nature of Spoons

"Technically, I have to be twelve to babysit. I believe the law is okay with ten-year-olds on their own."

Ina sits back in her chair, even though there are several dozen more bags to be filled. "What put this into your head?" she asks, suspicion creeping into her tone. "What is it you're planning to get up to while we're out?"

I have started wearing glasses, and although their penchant for fogging up renders me momentarily fearful of some unseeable foe whenever I come indoors from the cold, I also feel they make me look more grown up. I take the time to adjust them before answering, "Well, you both work so hard. I mean, for the past few weeks, our house has smelled like a perfume factory. This potpourri stuff is nice, but it is nonstop."

"Sachets are selling like hotcakes right now," Ina insists. "I am not missing this boat."

"Okay, but you can take one night off before the next bazaar," I say. "What about fun, Ina? I mean, poor Mr. Fluxcer. The Influx shows are *his* fun, and we have only one booked for spring break, and then it is a long wait for summer."

Ina narrows her eyes at me. "Has Knowlton been sad lately?"

I stop to think. "Probably."

"Probably?"

"Highly probable?" I add.

"Blisse, you are taxing my patience here."

"Do you like Mr. Fluxcer?"

"Of course. He's a wonderful man," she responds.

"Well then, why will you not have a date with him?"

"A date?" Ina guffaws.

I bite my lip. I have misjudged Ina's potential reaction. My cheeks flush with my miscue. I squeak out, "Yes. Why not?"

It is Ina's turn to flush. "Well, Blisse, it's best to be attracted to someone you date."

"I am sure he finds you very attractive."

Ina covers her mouth so her words are muffled, but audible. "Yes, but Mr. Fluxcer is a fair bit older than me, Blisse."

"But not too old. He is not retired or toothless, Ina. Not like my school friends' grandpas."

Ina shakes her head. She picks up a sachet bag and adds a scoop of dried petals. "Blisse, if you date someone, it means you would consider them for a boyfriend. I don't want to be Knowlton's girlfriend. Understand?"

I wrinkle my nose. My glasses slide. "He is not romantic enough?"

"I have no idea," Ina sputters, "but we don't have a romantic relationship."

"You could not fall in love with him?"

"Nooo," Ina insists. "I already fell in love, remember?"

"I see," I reply, feeling a jab of guilt that my enthusiasm has overshadowed what Ina has maintained about her love for my father. It strikes me, however, that she does not speak of it as frequently as she once did. She has stopped mentioning how their wedding vows were exchanged in the courthouse atop the hill—the most grandiose building in all of Thunder Bay—where she said you can look out the windows and see a giant asleep in the water. It has been some time since she stressed that they spent their honeymoon at the nearby waterfall—not the famous Niagara one, but one with a name that sounds just as interesting—Kakabeka. I could barely remember the last time she admitted that if it were not for my birth, she would have believed her own life to be over after my father took ill and died when he was away travelling. In short, there have been no recent declarations of her undying devotion to him. I think I have construed this to mean she is ready to find new love. Perhaps she is ready, but is not willing to admit it to me, as she would not want me to think she no longer loves my father. But I understand, by virtue of no longer wishing to marry Mr. Fluxcer myself, that feelings can change, and it does not mean

The Twistical Nature of Spoons

you are a bad person. I am certain that my mother could keep my father's memory with her always and love someone new.

She cuts into my thoughts. "Oh my gawd, Blisse! He didn't put you up to this, did he? Getting you to wheedle out information about my feelings?"

"No!" I declare. "Cross my heart."

Ina looks relieved.

I stick my pencil in my mouth and taste the spent bit of eraser that remains. I turn the page of my scribbler, avoiding eye contact with my mother. I mutter, "As I said, I am sure he finds you attractive, but he does not look at you googly-eyed from what I can tell."

I feel deflated when, instead of this statement giving Ina pause, she lets out a sigh of relief. I imagine a large D-minus at the top of my blank scribbler page for my matchmaking skills. I make myself cough. "I think I should go breathe some unscented air," I say. I close up my books and trudge to my pantry bedroom, where the smell of Ina's flowery mixture is only slightly less potent.

It is distressing to be stuck with the most uncooperative mother in the world. Standing atop my bed, I stomp my feet as hard as I can possibly stomp them, each footfall sinking into my saggy mattress, and know that if Ina comes in and tells me to stop jumping on my bed, I will have a caustic and defendable retort. *I am not jumping. I am stomping! Jumping requires an element of elevation above the mattress and I am accomplishing the opposite by sinking into it.*

Somehow, above my frustration, I sense the quiet beckoning of Grannyspoon—the least opinionated of all the spoons—from under the bed. I clamber down, drop to my knees, and pull the canteen out.

Grannyspoon surmises in a quavering, near-whisper tone, *She's not opposed to Mr. Fluxcer. She just needs a prod from Cupid's arrow.*

I do not reply in my own voice. A response seems pointless. I stare at the twisted handle's tarnishing daintiness.

Grannyspoon persists. *In my day, we fixed that with a love potion. Or maybe a spell.*

"Do you believe spells and potions are real?" I refute, "Ina would call that being 'suckered by superstition.'"

Your mother married a man who mind-bends spoons.

"Ina says psychokinetic powers are in a magical category of their own."

Potions work, Grannyspoon says with assurance. *People have been making love potions for hundreds of years.*

I have to shush her mounting excitement by blurting out, "I saw recipes for them in *The Unlimited Holiday Fun Book* that Ina purchased last year at the thrift shop."

Grannyspoon nods her bowl-head and dances in a circle. *That book is still in the parlour. Go get it.*

I kiss the tip of Grannyspoon's bent handle and creep out of my bedroom. Ina is absorbed in her flowery sacks and does not notice me sneak around her and into our cramped front room, which we rarely use other than to deposit odd items that are destined to collect dust alongside my deceased grandmother's possessions, which include, among other things, a Tiffany-style lamp, a broken clock, and a ceramic ashtray embellished with two partridges taking flight. I do not care for the room. When I am in there, my skin feels crawly, and my spine prickles with the sense that my grandmother's spirit does not want me poking around her old belongings—that I am not welcome. We continue to refer to the room as the parlour, propping up its yesteryear identity, but that seems like too special a word for such an uninviting place. It takes me only a moment to locate the book and scurry back to my bedroom.

I turn to its Valentine's Day section. Scanning the first potion recipe, my spirits sink again. What in the world is "vervain"? Plus, our foyer fireplace is fake, and I do not have a cauldron. Scratch that potion. The next one must be the inspiration for the "Love Potion No. 9" song because it calls for nine ingredients multiplied

The Twistical Nature of Spoons

nine times. It comes with a warning that its powerful results cannot be reversed. I figure I could only secure the nine apple stems and the nine drops of vanilla anyway, and Ina would be livid if she discovered I used more than a drop or two of her costly pure extract. The next concoction requires bully tree bark. That sounds more likely to poison than attract someone, bringing an abrupt halt to a romantic evening. Still, I am surprised to find that none of the active ingredients in the potions are as gruesome as I might have imagined: no frog brains or ground sparrow beaks. It makes me question if any of the elixirs would be effective, or if they are included merely as intriguing diversions which do not threaten the book's objective of harmless holiday fun.

I hear Ina's voice from the kitchen. "Did you finish that homework, Blisse?"

"Yes," I say and hold my breath, waiting to see if she is coming to check it.

"Is it neat? Your teacher said you could improve on your handwriting if you don't rush."

I mutter so my mother cannot hear, wobbling my head for emphasis, "My teacher finds petty excuses to complain about me, in case you have not noticed, Ina. I think sometimes she looks afraid that she has run out of things to teach me and will lose her job if I tell the principal." I wish Mr. Fluxcer could replace my bossy, schoolmarmish grade-four teacher. But I still strive to be the best student in the class in the hope that she will award me with the lucky-penny paperweight she keeps on her desk. I covet the maple-leaf-side-up copper coin in its ball of moulded plastic. Once, I offered to give her a pure white dove feather in exchange for it. She slipped an extra worksheet out from under the paperweight and told me to take my seat.

I respond louder to Ina this time, "Yes, my homework is very neat."

"Okay, lights out, then."

I grab my scribbler and look over the spelling list I have written out. To my spoons I say, "My cursive writing is just fine! It is called *hand*writing, not *manufactured* writing, for good reason."

Grannyspoon speaks up, *Did you say 'cursive' writing?*

I nod my head, jumping up to switch off the light in case Ina notices it still shining under the door.

Grannyspoon's shiny outline is still discernable in the dim light from the back lane lamppost. She trills, but keeps her voice low, *Do you remember the time Cousin Char came to visit and told the story of how Denny proposed?*

I nod again, unsure of how to connect the dots.

Grannyspoon prods my memory. *The spell!* she insists. *A teacup reader cast a spell on a piece of paper for her. Remember how you were embarrassed when she teased that you could get a nice boy to fall in love with you?*

"And I pointed out to her that I could not participate in that kind of spell because we had not learned all of our handwriting letters yet."

Grannyspoon adds, *And she told Ina how adorable you were, and that she couldn't wait to have kids of her own, but not until she and Denny were out of debt. Maybe one of them buys too many gambling tickets too.*

I hold up my free hand to prevent Grannyspoon from getting too far off topic, but her comment also serves to remind me that when I have followed spoon advice in the past—despite there being a potential for disaster—it has proved to be very beneficial. I can see that my desire to concoct a *real* magic potion might not sit well with Mr. Fluxcer, and Ina might surmise that being a magician's assistant has driven me to experiment with things that are dangerous. I might be stripped of my role in the Magical Influx Show and never be allowed to see the doves again! But I choose to put my belief in the spoons' sage recommendations.

I hold Grannyspoon close to my face so our voices will not be

The Twistical Nature of Spoons

heard. "I remember that spell because it was so easy. The teacup reader wrote Char and Denny's full names three times, alternating between them, and then she circled the letters that appeared in both names. Next, she told Cousin Char to concentrate, focussing on her wish, and to write, without lifting her pen—which was why you had to know cursive writing—the words 'propose to me' continuously, turning the paper, until their names were totally encircled. Then she told Cousin Char to fold the paper in half toward herself three times, and either tuck the folded paper in her bra or under her mattress for one week, preferably at the end of her period. Cousin Char did both, wearing it all day and sleeping on it all night, and claimed that the end of her monthlies aligned in her favour."

Grannyspoon interrupts with a chuckle, *Good thing Ina had that talk with you this year because that period business went right over your head when Cousin Char first told the story. You thought she meant the written phrase had to contain punctuation.*

I clear my throat to let Grannyspoon know I am not appreciative of the reminder. I do not like feeling dumb, nor am I looking forward to finding blood smears on my underwear. Ina told me I was all grown up when I was still in kindergarten, but I continue learning about new, laborious grown-up markers I will have to meet.

I change the subject, lamenting, "But where can I find a teacup reader? Ina will obviously refuse to participate anyway. And how could I begin to ask Mr. Fluxcer to write 'marrymemarrymemarrymemarryme'?"

Grannyspoon whispers directly into my ear, *Do it yourself. 'Getmarriedgetmarriedgetmarriedgetmarried.' Look no further than the twist in me as evidence of the power of the mind.*

"But I need not remind you, that was my father's doing," I insist. *You are his daughter.*

I twirl Grannyspoon between my palms so she can show off her twist, then dust off her nooks and crannies with my dove feather. She laughs from the spinning and tickling—a croaky, hissing laugh. She seems very out of character. Pushy, even. I am not sure it is becoming for a spoon her age, but she has probably seen a lot in her many years, and I put my trust in her being the wisest of the spoons. Plus, her opinion about my magical abilities aligns with Daughterspoon's, which I was not able to test because I abandoned the plan to purchase lottery tickets.

The next day, with the aim of enhancing the spell's potency, I wait for Mr. Fluxcer to come home from work and for Ina to be in the same room as me before commencing. I sneak a peek into the bathroom cupboard to check on Ina's supply of feminine products in the hopes of pinpointing her cycle, but do not know exactly what to count. Nevertheless, with my targets in place, I prop up my spelling workbook as a shield—with Grannyspoon helping to keep the pages open—and pretend to write out a word list. I start with alternating their names before circling their five shared letters. I focus on approaching a trance-like state to add to the spell's power, but without quite knowing how to accomplish that, I settle for picturing Ina in a flowing wedding gown, with Mr. Fluxcer by her side in his magician's top hat, exchanging gold rings. I complete the encompassing final touch without once lifting my pencil:

getmarriedgetmarriedgetmarriedgetmarried

I write a duplicate spell, one for each of them. While folding the pages, I recognize the real challenge will be getting access to Mr. Fluxcer's bed. He only permits me upstairs for dove care while he is present, even though he allows me to work independently. Getting Ina's key ring would be a cinch, as it hangs on a hook next to our kitchen window, but finding the right opportunity and summoning the courage to trespass will prove more difficult. If I do it one day after school, I am at great risk of being caught by Ina, or facing the untimely return of Mr. Fluxcer himself.

It is all I can think about until a fortuitous heavy snowfall two days later presents the opening I need. Ina gets bundled up to shovel our porch and walkway because she says Mr. Fluxcer will surely be stuck in standstill rush hour traffic and should not have to come home to the extra work on top of it. I seize my opportunity. I prepare a reasonable lie to tell if Ina catches me upstairs: concern for the doves because she herself said that Mr. Fluxcer will be delayed in traffic. I take the steps two at a time—careful to avoid tearing the decorative strings of hearts Ina has woven around the banister—with a paper spell tucked under my shirt. I unlock his door, listening for Ina's shovel scraping the front walk.

Entering the bedroom, I do not expect to find Mr. Fluxcer's unmade bed, nor a pair of his pyjama bottoms lying on the floor. The intimate unsightliness of it makes me falter. Was I about to curse Ina to a life of nagging marital frustration, rather than bless her with a fulfilled, uncomplicated life of love and companionship?

I hear the shovelling stop. Ina is stomping the snow off her boots on the porch. There is no time to reconsider. Avoiding the pyjamas, I reach forward, shove the note between the mattress and box spring, and dash out. I neglect to relock the door. Racing down the stairs, I get back to the kitchen and replace the key ring just as Ina enters, a blast of cold air billowing into the foyer and through the kitchen doorway. While she sheds her coat, scarf, hat, and mittens, I scuttle into her bedroom and place the second note under her mattress, nearest to where I think her sleeping heart will be positioned overtop of it.

From the foyer, I hear Ina carp, in a voice huffing from exertion, "Nasty work!" Her words reverberate through the main floor like an accusation.

I call back from the kitchen, "Can I fix you a hot chocolate, Ina?" My voice sounds as sweet as the instant package contents.

Ina blows her nose, but declines. "Nice of you to offer, though, Blisse."

My heart continues to thump so hard against my ribs that I am certain Ina can see it through my shirt, but she says nothing. As the week drags on, she also seems to remain oblivious to the lure of love. There is no date that week, or the next. Mr. Fluxcer does not alter his routine for closer proximity, other than shovelling the walk for Ina when a second flurry of snow blows in. Ina meets him in the foyer afterward and offers only her thanks. That is when I decide it is time to check on the paper spells.

When Ina fills the bathtub that evening for a warm soak, I enter her room. I slide my hand under the mattress and feel around for the spell. I cannot locate it. I boost the mattress and peer beneath it. No sign of a note. I proceed to check the entire perimeter of the bed, lifting and looking. I shoulder the mattress to raise it as high as possible. There is no evidence that a folded piece of paper has ever been there. I have to wait for Mr. Fluxcer's Saturday morning grocery excursion, with Ina in the basement doing laundry, to risk a second break and enter into his bedroom. With the exception of his room being much tidier, I detect no sign of a blossoming Romeo. My eyes dart about the sparse room. There are no boxes of chocolates or floral bouquets, no new cologne scent or evidence of excessive grooming accoutrements. There is also no paper spell that I can find, not between mattress and box spring, nor elsewhere. *Croo-CROOK-croo.* One of the doves startles me; its call like a probing query from the third floor. I hightail it back down the stairs, replace the key ring, and feel my stomach churn. Have the intended bride and groom discovered the notes? Are they waiting until they can agree on an appropriate punishment before summoning me? Have the spoons tricked me into putting my faith in them and risking

The Twistical Nature of Spoons

what has become the highlight of my week—caring for the doves and rehearsing my role in the show?

For two days, I cannot eat breakfast and only pick at my dinner. Ina does not seem particularly concerned about my loss of appetite, noting that my school lunch is devoured. When a week comes and goes with no mention of a shared discovery on Ina or Mr. Fluxcer's part, I wonder if the written spells, given their failure to produce a love connection, have merely vanished into thin air. When I solicit Grannyspoon's opinion, she reveals her suspicion that the adults have uncovered the spells and are having a laugh at our expense, and although this should build a bond between them, she doubts it will cause them to fall into each other's arms. When I suggest we try something more powerful to persuade them, she informs me she is feeling poorly, is taking to her bed, and is not to be disturbed. Grannyspoon nestles into a slot in the wooden cutlery box and turns mute on the subject. I am dismayed by her cowardice, but do not have the resources to bolster the both of us. Plus, I am wise enough to recognize that, should I pursue another round of doomed matchmaking, my meddling might not be indulged a second time. I have to accept responsibility for the failure, but I do not understand its source. If a teacup reader could produce a successful spell, then why have I failed?

As I am about to lower the box's lid, Mommyspoon clears her throat. *Have you considered that you might have missed something? Ina claims she fell in love with your father on the night they met. Sounds to me as if a spell was cast. A powerful one. Did you imagine you could undo a spell your father cast? That is misguided, young lady.*

I cock my head at her.

Daddyspoon pipes up, *Perhaps, as you suspected, your paper spell did disappear. Your father's original spell destroyed it. Poof!*

I ask, "Are you suggesting that I should not be messing with things I do not understand?"

Lodgerspoon offers, *That is a consideration.*

Patti Grayson

A shiver skims across my spine. "But I am my father's daughter."

Daddyspoon responds. *So prove it. If you want your powers to develop, best get to work.*

I grab Petspoon and place it on my dresser. I stare at its tiny purple stone and its crooked handle. This was the spoon my father gave my mother on the night they met. This was the spoon that sealed their love for one another. If I can make it move without touching it, then perhaps I can have access to its power. And if not, my parents' love will endure for all eternity. I focus every molecule of my energy into nudging the silver souvenir across the hard surface. When, minute after exhausting minute, it does not budge, I am surprised I do not grow discouraged. Instead, with every failed attempt, I feel more empowered. The spoon's resistance indicates to me that my father loved my mother as much as she loves him. All of Ina's claims are truer than true. When I finally crawl under the covers, I am awash in a sense of well-being. I accept that Mr. Fluxcer and Ina are perfectly suited to lodger and landlady. The bond between my parents is eternal. And just because I cannot make the original spoon move does not mean I lack inherited powers—they are merely waiting to be awakened.

Ina

delivers

After the funeral, Char and Denny gifted me money to get a flight back to Thunder Bay once I'd settled legal details and put my mother's house on the market. Char froze meal-sized portions of the casseroles that friends had dropped off, and left me with phone numbers for movers and real estate agents. In the two weeks that followed, however, both my appetite and ability to focus on practical details were nonexistent. When I wasn't lying awake atop my mother's bed, or sitting next to the toilet bowl, flushing away my morning sickness, I sat alone in the kitchen of my inherited two-and-a-half-storey childhood home—window propped open to the warm outdoor breezes—staring into the void. The traffic noise from nearby Broadway, a couple of long-distance phone calls from Char, and the weekday steps of the mailman on the rickety front porch were my only reminders that normal life was still going on without me.

Late one night, I forced myself to stay put at the kitchen table and concentrate, but I couldn't make sense of the words on my mother's death certificate, will, or life insurance policy. I wondered if half my brain cells had been upchucked along with my dry toast and tea. It was as if my head was a monkey cage and all my jittery thoughts were swinging from rubber trees and screeching out their ridicule. *And don't put me in an early grave by coming back home knocked up.* Was my pregnancy responsible for my mother's passing? Did May croak so she didn't have to hear me confess I'd be giving birth out of wedlock? If Taras's great-grandmother had cursed his marriage to the wrong woman, was it possible my mother had cursed herself? Why wasn't May's collection of upturned horseshoes, peroxide-soaked wishbones, and cross-stitched four-leaf clovers enough to counteract her own ill will? I had to entertain the thought—despite what I wanted to believe—that malice trumped good every time. And if so, had Taras returned to his wife? The one who wanted him dead but then wanted him back? Dirk had mentioned Taras's divorce papers. If I could just get my own documents sorted, I could get back to Lakehead U and track down Taras. After all, he'd abandoned searching for his stolen masks to come find me. If he'd chosen divorce, then I'd be free to tell him we'd produced a miracle. But how much power did his wife wield over him?

Just as I was imagining their phone conversation, during which Taras's masks were stolen, the chiming of my mother's seven-day clock caught my attention. It was striking twelve, but I could have sworn it had already done so. I turned and checked the time on the stove. It was 1:00 a.m. I got up and went into the parlour to wind the clock on the end table. It was totally disorienting that May wasn't there to do it herself. She loved that clock. She would never wind it again. Hesitating at first, I picked it up, inserted the key, and started to crank. There was a sharp recoil as a spring snapped inside. I turned the key around and around, but it would no longer engage. The broken clock, raging pregnancy hormones, choking grief, and severe lack of sleep all combined to snap something

The Twistical Nature of Spoons

inside of *me*. I flung the key across the room and slammed the clock back down onto the table. In the dim light of the parlour, I sobbed, "Stupid, cursed thing! Cursed, cursed, stupid thing!" And that's when the words "cursed pronouncement" were exhumed from the buried depths of my brain and rose up like sulphurous gas.

The words spoken by Taras's wife. What had Dirk reported them to be? It was a good thing he was infertile because any kid that grew up having Taras as a father would choose to stab him dead?

With the clock no longer ticking, the parlour was quieter than I'd ever remembered. A swallow-you-alive silence that spit out a horrible thought: What if my baby had been cursed by Taras's wife, a woman able to make masks disappear via phone call alone? Was my child doomed to kill their own father? For months, I'd been trying to shed my belief in Taras's great-grandmother's clairvoyance and Taras's freaky psychokinetic powers. I rubbed hard at my face and told myself his wife could not pose a supernatural threat. But what had they said about her? Taras had called her bewitching. Dirk said she was hypnotic. Could it be that when Taras spoke of her inventive ways of cursing him to death, he was referring to the cursed pronouncement? I'd been a tad preoccupied, but I was certain Dirk said that Taras was terrified. Terror was a strong response, unless Taras believed that his child *would* plunge a knife into his heart if his wife foretold it. Did he understand the full extent of her reach, her malevolence? What if Taras wasn't just a bitter cuckold relaying the angry jeers of a deceitful wife? What if she really did have otherworldly powers?

I shuddered. It was all sinking in. Taras hadn't been cursed with infertility. How was I pregnant otherwise? The real curse was marrying the wrong woman and opening the way for her to blight his offspring. He'd set his great-grandmother's prediction in motion by marrying a woman who was capable of hexing him, and now he was doomed to death by the hand of his own child. Our child. My child. If only he'd found me first! How could my baby survive its own unthinkable future?

I ran to my mother's bedroom and threw the quilt over my head. Prison bars appeared behind my closed eyes. I could feel my scarred hand gripping the hard wooden armrest of a courtroom chair while I watched my child getting led away in handcuffs. How scary would juvenile detention be? How often could I visit? I tossed and turned in what had been May's saggy double bed, unable to shake free from imagined headlines, scowling prison guards, solitary confinement, Taras's grave. In the middle of the night, I drifted off, convinced I could smell institutional cafeteria food. And on the brink of reawakening, I rose out of my own body, looked down, and saw not me, but my tormented child, lying on a thin mattress, reliving the nightmare of plunging a knife into their own father's heart.

Daylight did nothing to bleach out the abyss. That evening, I filled the kettle, and instead of setting it down on the stove to boil for weak tea, I watched as the element ring heated up to a bright red. I thought about setting my hand on the coils. I imagined the searing hot pain. Its simplicity. A surefire way to obliterate my second lifeline. And while I stared at the glow, I realized I was no longer right in my head. My thoughts were becoming more and more unthinkable. I backed away, my heart thumping. I caught sight of my reflection in the darkened kitchen window. Though I wouldn't have said I was showing, I somehow looked pregnant for the first time. I reached forward, set the kettle on to boil, and gazed down to see if my shirt buttons looked strained around my belly.

With that one small action, I realized I was still capable of rational thought, because if I was really going off the deep end, I would've been burn-unit bound instead of assessing the tightness of my shirt. One thing became clear as I smoothed the fabric over my belly: it didn't matter whether my wild theories were the

The Twistical Nature of Spoons

product of a grief-fuelled spiral caused by my mother's death, or the result of my own maternal instincts kicking into overdrive—I had to shield my growing little one. And yes, maybe buying into the predictions of a palm-reading crone and a soothsaying femme fatale seems unbelievable and irrational, but I believed them. Without a doubt. After all, if Taras had chosen to confide in *me*, I had to find the fortitude to believe in my *own* trustworthiness. It was all I had left. That tiny little turn-around in my perspective triggered a fresh flood of clarity—I'd been looking at the situation all wrong.

There was a reason that Taras's great-grandmother had told him to seek out a woman with a hand like mine. I was the one who would prevent the curse from being fulfilled. I'd felt the mind-boggling connection between us from the moment we spoke in the bar. Taras claimed we shared an intimacy beyond sex. And even though our encounter had been so brief that his features were fading from my memory, I would never forget the full-blown, miraculous bliss of the preamble to conception. My scar was the earthbound sign of something meant to be.

I understood, right then and there, that our unborn baby's absolute innocence had to be maintained. Our child would not go to prison for murder. I was the right person to bear Taras's baby because I already loved them both so much that I was willing to do anything to keep my child and my child's father safe—even if it meant protecting them from a cursed fate. Taras's wife had said his offspring would want to stab him dead if they grew up with him; all I had to do was keep them apart for my baby's entire childhood. It fell to me, Regina Trove. I could do it. That wasn't an eternity. What was the exact duration of childhood? Twelve, sixteen, eighteen years? Doable, even briefer if I thought about it in terms of seasonal markers. I could manage twelve New Years, or sixteen Valentine's Days, or eighteen Halloweens.

Good fortune was already on my side. I was safest staying put.

Dirk believed I was a mask thief who tried to exploit the first interesting guy who came along; he wasn't likely to mention me to Taras the next time they spoke. If Taras showed up at Three Sheets, Antony would send him packing. Taras didn't know my full name, or specifics about Char and Denny; and they, in turn, were the only people who knew my current address. Taras would need a whole flock of clucking chickens and one gigantic crystal ball to know I was in my mother's house, a province away from where we'd met.

And I could take advantage of the familiar. Rather than claiming there'd been no earthly father at all, which was doomed to be a very hard sell, my best bet was to adopt widowhood as my reality. I'd been raised by my own widowed mother in that very house. I could rely on what I already knew, and try to be better at it. And so what if my future no longer meant sailing abroad in search of messages in glass bottles and columns of medieval stained glass? There was no lack of the unknown ahead. It was going to take creative measures to keep my child hidden from their father, while not allowing them to believe he was a deadbeat, or worse.

I considered next steps. Going back to a serving job was not an option: raising a latchkey kid was a risk if they were home alone and Taras somehow discovered our whereabouts. I took a look at my assets. There wasn't much, but it would be enough: a house, some insurance funds, my travel savings, and some crafting skills. A plan began to take shape around budget calculations. With some of the insurance money, I hired a local handyman to add doorways on the second- and third-floor landings to separate the two upper levels from the main floor. Then I had him add locks to my kitchen and parlour doors, to allow me to secure and seal off my own living space from the main-floor entrance foyer. I bought a mini fridge, a hotplate, a toaster oven, and a new twin bed, then stuck up posters at the nearby university to advertise I had an upstairs suite to let. I hoped that by fall, I would have a nice, quiet student lodger. The very next day, an older woman called—a cafeteria

The Twistical Nature of Spoons

worker who'd been living with her son's family, but was looking for affordable, independent accommodation. It was a relief to have a mature woman move onto the second floor; I believed she'd be more tolerant when a newborn arrived.

With the last of my travel funds, I bought my first bagful of yarn and started knitting kids' toques and crocheting granny squares to assemble into one-of-a-kind diaper bags. The plan was to have a stack of hats and totes ready in time for holiday craft bazaars to see if I could turn a profit. The soft textures and pastel colours were soothing, and safer than glass projects. The repetitive work lulled my fretting brain into a state of relative calm, provided an excuse for avoiding old friends, and kept me busy while I waited to give birth. It also presented a good reason to walk to the Cornish Library, where there were racks full of crafting magazines, and where I could sidle over to the stacks of paranormal books to try to find some explanations for the mysteries that had barged into my life.

One evening in mid-January, I grew restless. I was beyond agitated. The thought of casting any more stitches felt too taxing. Spurred on by a surprising profit from my holiday sales, I'd already started churning out spring beanie hats. I knew that production would fall off with the imminent arrival of the baby, but that night, I couldn't motivate myself. Instead, I squeezed into my oversized winter coat, which barely wrapped around my huge bulge, laboured into my winter boots, and set out through the cold and dark for any distraction the library could offer. I was grateful the sidewalks weren't slippery; I could manage a brisk waddle without fear of taking a fall.

By the time I entered the old brick-and-limestone building, I was winded and overheated. As I unwound my scarf and dropped off my returns, a little foot thrust upward under my ribs. With the womb gymnastics about to begin, I doubted I'd be able to sit comfortably with a magazine; better to stay upright and head to the stacks, where I could lean against them for support while browsing. I wandered into the fiction section, pretending it held some interest, while I waited for a chance to divert to the 100s and 200s without being too obvious. There was no chance I could borrow anything that visit and hope to return it on time. I wanted to share a joke with the librarians about overlapping due dates, but they'd recently stopped making eye contact with me at the checkout. My growing girth, my ringless left hand, and my selections from the psychic-phenomena stacks had them clearing their throats politely and may even have prompted the current arrangement of parenting books on the centre display table. From their tight-lipped expressions, I couldn't pinpoint what they felt more strongly, unease or pity, when I bypassed colic and diaper rash and headed for crystals and telekinesis. Perhaps they questioned why the churning mayhem of knees and elbows belonging to the little karate expert living just below the surface of my belly skin wasn't enough mystery for me. On a previous visit, I'd overheard one of them mumble, "Oh look, the Pregger Express to Kooksville is here." I snuck a glance at her tall-heeled boots and expensive wool suit, and had to resist the urge to rearrange an entire shelf out of Dewey decimal order just to gall her. It scared me that someone like her—or any of my old friends I'd promised to get in touch with after they'd turned up at May's funeral—might out-and-out judge me as an unfit mother in the making. It made me more desperate to avoid contact and find solace in the mysticism stacks. Perhaps May would have been proud of me after all, because the paranormal books—filled with claims that some elements of our universe were beyond rational explanation—soothed me. I finally appreciated why she embraced her daily horoscope and believed in séances. When my fears ran wild with curses and predictions and fate, the books assured me to trust my intuition. And spiritual contemplation stopped me from dwelling on the frightening practical aspects that came with pregnancy—like the reality of a dinged-up second-hand crib parked

The Twistical Nature of Spoons

next to my bed, and the fact that I was the only one who showed up to prenatal class without a birthing partner.

After a few moments of meandering, I sidled into the non-fiction stacks and slid out a book about unblocking the chakras. I opened to the first chapter and felt a warm gush between my legs.

"Cripes!" I exclaimed aloud.

"Shh," I heard from somewhere, but I was too concerned about the damp blotch spreading down the inner thighs of my men's size sweatpants to look for the scolder.

My first thought was to wrap my coat shut and head to the washroom so no one would see I'd wet my pants, but I suspected my bladder wasn't the culprit. With enough volume to topple an encyclopaedia cart, I shouted, "Oh my gawd. My water broke. Somebody?"

Two librarians came running. Thankfully both wore sensible shoes, and their faces registered genuine concern. They spoke over each other and latched onto my arms, one on either side, leading me away from the stacks.

"Are you having contractions?"

"You have to get to a hospital."

A third librarian, who'd remained behind the circulation desk, waved her arm about wildly as she called me a cab.

"I can walk," I insisted. "It's across the street."

"Your legs will freeze!" one of them exclaimed.

"You could faint or something!" the other warned.

I assured them I was fine and not feeling the slightest twinge of contractions. They insisted on splitting the cab fare three ways for me, and several pairs of hands eased me into the back of the taxi when it arrived, the librarians' combined breath rising in a frosty billow above us. It was the briefest of rides, but it reminded me of the cab I took en route to my baby's conception. How easy it had been to make the driver take me elsewhere that night. Should I convince the cabbie to divert to the Westminster Motor Hotel, where I could dance the night away to aid the progression of labour? Instead, I bumbled my way out of the back seat, accepting the driver's assistance to the doors and offering my sincere gratitude. It seemed as if my taste for rebellion had been expelled along with the amniotic fluid.

"We think it's necessary to begin induction," were the words I remember most vividly before things turned weird. Contractions started shortly afterwards as I lay propped up in a maternity ward bed, and before too long, I said yes to the pain drugs. A few hours later, two saints appeared and introduced themselves to me. When I apologized for not having a clue who they were, they replied in unison, "We met before, at a stained-glass workshop, if you recall?" "Before my paralysis," Catherine of Siena added. "And before my beheading, of course," said Saint Panteleimon. I insisted they must be mistaken, but despite my protests, Catherine took up a position at the foot of the delivery table and offered to write letters on my behalf, and Saint Panteleimon squatted near my head, unwrapped a black cloth to reveal a scalpel, and assured me that should he have to use it, his training dated back to the third century. Their halos were so large, they rose to the ceiling and touched the walls, emitting a sound like a lightsaber whenever either of them bowed their heads. "Now, push," they insisted.

Blisse entered the world, wailing out her first squalls in the daintiest of ways, but accompanying them, I swore I heard a cry of "horse and hattock!"—an overriding but distant cry which convinced me witches would fly in and whisk her away, right off the scale upon which the delivery nurse had placed her. The saints switched a bright moon on and pointed it at my perineum to lessen my concerns. They insisted that brooms were never allowed in the delivery room, so there was no need to whimper about my baby's whereabouts, adding that my hallucinations were an extremely rare side effect of the medication, the likes of which they had never witnessed before.

The Twistical Nature of Spoons

When my stitches were complete, and the saints were absorbed into the large wall clock, the nurse put the wrapped bundle in my arms. My infant daughter—blinking against the out-of-womb light, puzzled by her first unsubmerged sounds—thieved the air from my lungs, as if still in need of my oxygen. But I knew, without question, my life was now dependent on *her*.

I whispered, "It's because she's special."

The saints flocked back, and everyone gathered like a church choir of seagulls, wings spread as if to catch an updraft. "Of course she is. She's your newborn baby girl."

"No, I mean *really* special."

The bright moon reared its head and said, "Yes, but she's not exactly born with a silver spoon in her mouth, is she?"

"Oh, but she is," I insisted. "A *really* special spoon."

"She's a little miracle," the saints hummed.

"She's heaven-sent," the nurse chimed.

We all chorused in agreement, "She's sheer bliss!"

I declared, "She is, isn't she? But I think I will drop the 'sheer' bit, and keep one of its *e*'s."

Everyone concluded it was the best naming party they'd ever attended. Their tinkles of laughter dripped down the delivery room curtains. They captured their excess mirth in their gloved hands and sprinkled it about, making the room smell of antiseptic and sound like the squeaking of rubber shoes. I touched Blisse's cheek and told her there would be many more things to hear, like chirping birds and melting ice cream. Her head turned in response. She opened and closed her little mouth—soundless—but hungry for nourishment and elucidation alike.

I didn't need pregnancy books to tell me my birthing experience wasn't exactly normal; it went a long way to confirm that forces beyond my understanding remained in play. Blisse was over five months old before I finally returned to the library. She was starting to teethe and was cranky and whiny. Desperation turned me outdoors, doggedly putting one foot in front of the other on a beautiful spring day, walking to who knows where. Robins were hopping around the lawns of every other yard we passed, as if cheering us on our way. I wondered if it was easier to keep straight which squalling mouth received the next worm than it was to get the hang of successful breast-feeding. And did robins—with their habit of rising early—ever close their eyes and sleep in their nests? Because I had learned that waking up to feed Blisse, and lying awake, listening for her cry to be fed, were really just two different states of not being asleep.

I was surprised when I found myself standing in front of the library. I pulled my sweatshirt hood up to prevent any librarians from recognizing me—especially those who had assisted me and paid my taxi fare. I didn't want to introduce my baby to them when my hair hung in limp, unwashed strands, and I had no extra cash to pay them back. Slouching my way into the non-fiction section, I checked the carpet on the spot where my water had broken. No lingering trace. The smell of the books in the quiet, still air did, however, trigger the memory of the night of Blisse's birth. I loitered in the religion section, looking for a volume that might explain the visions I'd had during delivery. Blisse slept against my chest in her homemade sling without uttering a peep, while I paged through books on saints and martyrs. The words were a blur; I reshelved the books, lacking the energy to ensure their spine labels were in order. I had to save my juice to care for my baby girl. I trudged back home, ignoring the robins' optimism.

That evening, Blisse's flushed cheeks, her inability to sleep, and her resistance to being soothed even with teething drops, all made childbirth seem like a piece of cake. I was pacing the bedroom floor with her when I stopped to reach up to the top shelf of my closet, and for the first time since the day of my mother's funeral—when I'd removed it from my purse and hidden it there—I grabbed down Taras's bent souvenir spoon.

The Twistical Nature of Spoons

"Look at the pretty spoon," I said, waving it in front of her.

She reached for it.

I know what you're thinking. What kind of mother would give her infant daughter a spoon that was an obvious choking hazard? Well, I tried a game of peek-a-boo to start with, pretending to hide behind the tiny metal bowl. Blisse scrunched her eyes, arched her back, stretched both hands toward the spoon, and wailed. I pretended the spoon was a squawking seagull, a hopping kangaroo, a motorboat, and a choo-choo train—all in an effort to keep it from her grasp. She wailed louder with each attempt. I worried that my upstairs lodger would assume child abuse and call the police.

"Shh, shh, shh, you want the spoon?" I asked. She stopped crying. I handed it to her, and she promptly stuck it in her mouth, her body relaxing as her little tongue and lips explored. "Too late to wash it," I said aloud. Blisse smiled around the spoon. I smiled back. She giggled. I responded in kind and felt a wave of relief. "Can Mommy have the spoon now?" I asked, with palm outstretched. She pressed her sore gums down on the hard metal. "Okay, we have to put the spoon back to bed now," I said and tried to gently pry it from her fingers. She was having none of that. She opened her mouth and screamed, as if I'd turned into the devil. "Shh, shh, shh. Okay. Okay. But Mommy wants the spoon." I tried to look sad to see if she might share it. Turned out she was a little young for empathy. She looked quite self-satisfied that she had it and I did not. Her tears dried up. With her imperfect coordination, she took the opportunity to rap me on the forehead with it before stuffing it back in her mouth.

Any time she fussed from teething after that, the spoon—with its amethyst swallowing hazard—provided her with immediate relief and would not be surrendered until I pried it from her little fist after she'd fallen asleep. I did my best not to fret.

One night at bedtime, while I was draped over the bars of

the crib, rubbing Blisse's back, I told her the story of how I got the spoon. She responded by manoeuvring herself into a sitting position, unaided. Seeing her sit up on her own for the first time gave me such a jolt of joy that I asked if she wanted to hear the story again. She mouthed out, "Mamamamam." That was all the convincing I needed to repeat it nightly. Before too long, Blisse enunciated her second word: poon. She'd query, holding it aloft, "Poon?"

"Spoon," I'd confirm enthusiastically. If I tried to skip the story, she'd squeal a string of *eeee*'s at me.

I tried out different versions, including how I found the spoon in a bottle on the shore of Lake Superior, and how a bird landed on Cousin Charlene's porch with the spoon in its mouth. I assumed Blisse found the sound of my storytelling voice soothing as she drifted off to sleep, but that she wasn't old enough to comprehend the words. After weeks of variations, however, she started to frown and fuss if I didn't share the version in which her father bent the spoon with the power of his mind and then gave it to me to keep forever. Eventually, any deviation, including one in which Taras used sleight-of-hand techniques to swap bent and unbent spoons, caused her to scrunch her eyes and shake her head. She took to wailing in protest, pushing her little hand over my mouth, and refusing any alternate accounts by covering her ears. That was how she took her first steps—not to me, but away from an unwanted variation. Blisse showed her appreciation for her preferred version in heart-melting ways: happy clapping, hugging me while humming, or saying "nie-nie" as she lay down to sleep without further fuss.

With her first birthday looming, I started to panic. I'd believed her fixation on the "poon" and its story was a just a passing phase, but then I started to worry it was becoming problematic, like a case of recurring cold sores. I doubted parenting books would have a chapter on how to successfully wean a child off a story. I didn't

The Twistical Nature of Spoons

know how I was going to manage Blisse's withdrawal symptoms if I stopped the telling cold turkey. Prior to her birth, I thought the hardest part about keeping her and her father apart would be ensuring that Taras never found us. I thought I'd only ever tell Blisse the skimpiest of details about him, and only when she was grown enough to ask. But with her unwavering attachment to the spoon and its tale, I realized that the much harder part was going to be keeping her from learning the truth about him. Until she was born, I didn't realize how much independence a child would assert. First, she was part of me, smack dab in my womb, and the next thing I knew, she had a personality and will and mindset that had nothing to do with me at all.

By making the mistake of telling her the spoon story, I realized I'd stumbled onto a valuable insight. In the future, I'd have to be more strategic. Whatever I told Blisse from that point on should encourage her to love her father with every fibre of her being. Because what child who loves her father would ever want to stab him in the heart? And what seemed to boost her joy and bring out the sweetest parts of her nature? The spoon and its love story. I believed I was onto something—maybe Blisse needed her own spoons.

7

Blisse

final denial

For months, I look forward to the landmark of my twelfth birthday. I anticipate it not just because Ina has finally agreed it will be time to go shopping for my first real bra, but because I suspect it will be a birthday of other revelations. I feel I am on the brink of something. And it is the birthday of the last spoon. Ina told me over the years that my father sent twelve spoons in total. That seemed like an endless number when I was younger, but as the bestowing of the final gift approaches, I wonder what it will be like to receive it. How will I feel? Will it be more special? Will it provide insight into my father's extraordinary ability? Ina is always putting off answering my questions. "When you're older" is her usual response. When I turn twelve, I will put my foot down on the "older" excuse and demand she tell me. Perhaps it will help explain why, despite my best efforts, I have not been able to make anything move using the power of my mind. No matter how hard I focus, no matter the duration of my sessions, not one of the spoons will move a centimetre. I cannot even make a dove feather move. I have breathed extra heavily just to witness a result, but there is no satisfaction in tricking oneself.

Even when I tried combining methodologies a year earlier, I was unsuccessful. I placed my plastic wastebasket upside down over Babyspoon, and then used Grandpaspoon—a tablespoon with a long handle bent in the shape of the golden arches—as a magic wand. I tapped the basket three times, and with the most focussed concentration I have ever mustered, incanted Mr. Fluxcer's magic words: "and voilà!" Babyspoon neither disappeared nor adjusted its repose.

The frustration of those failings has led me to focus almost exclusively on real sleight-of-hand tricks since then. That, in turn, has landed me in trouble. Last month, I was called to the principal's office for making my classmates' milk money disappear and not giving it back. I explained to the principal that I have not yet mastered the production of vanished items, and I cannot simply return the money or the illusion of the trick will be ruined. How will my classmates believe I have caused the money to disappear into thin air if I simply return it? She did not appreciate my explanation, and threatened to call Ina in for a conference unless I relinquished the funds immediately and agreed to "no more tomfoolery." I was sent to my classroom to retrieve the cash from the cloakroom, where it was hidden in my jacket pocket. On my return trip to her office—seething at the lack of regard she demonstrated for my craft, wishing my father was alive so he could come and, with just a glance, twist her desk lamp into a mangled, sparking hunk of scrap metal—I opened my palm and had the urge to spit on each coin before returning them.

Something happened as I debated performing this small act of revenge, working up saliva in my mouth. The coins grew warmer. I am certain they did. A quarter became so hot, I yanked my hand out from under it and the coins went spilling down the hallway. I chased after them, and with my entire body flushed from both the

The Twistical Nature of Spoons

shame of my contemplations and the elation of *something* at work beyond my ken, I handed the booty over, minus my spittle.

I have neither manifested nor witnessed real magic since then. I hope my upcoming birthday will help me understand why, and divert my energies because, despite my bravado, I did not like sitting in the office waiting for the principal to see me. The radiator hissed in there and the overhead fluorescent lights made a weird humming noise, as if someone had turned on an electric chair. In my heart of hearts, I know I have inherited some part of my father and his abilities. Ina said once, when I was sick with a fever, that the bright intensity of my eyes matched his. And because she has tried to wiggle out of elaborating, I sense this is significant. If there is no connection, why did he believe I was special before I was even born, and why do I sometimes feel energy emanating from the objects on the Influx Show props table, and why would normal coins grow hot with my spite, and why does my everyday life leave me wanting more?

When the big day arrives, I wake early. The dawn light is barely a glimmer outside my little bedroom window, which is frosted partway up the pane. It is a Saturday, which makes my birthday extra special since I do not have to go to school, though admittedly, not as special as when it falls on a Friday—Ina likes to remind me that I was born thirteen minutes after midnight on Friday the thirteenth and that is another reason why she knows I am beyond remarkable, since I defy all superstition by being the luckiest thing that ever happened to her. My stomach thrums with excitement. I pad into the kitchen and find that Ina is already at the counter, dressed in her chenille housecoat, mixing pancake batter. There are chocolate chips and bananas waiting to be added.

"Happy birthday, Blisse!" she exclaims. She rests her wooden spoon on the bowl and opens her arms. She hugs me, bestows a kiss on the top of my head, and flatters, "Pretty soon I won't be looking down like this. Next birthday, I'll bet you'll be taller than me."

My shoulders hunch forward. I cannot understand why adults must remind children that they are growing. When our sleeves and pant legs are too short, we understand we are growing. The commentary is akin to explaining the punchline when everyone is already laughing at the joke. Unnecessary. I do not want to spoil my birthday, though, so I hug Ina back, and notice the two wrapped boxes on the kitchen table. I am surprised they are of comparable size. This makes me so nervous that I feel myself flushing. Might there be two spoons? That would make thirteen birthday spoons from my father, but fourteen spoons in total, and this is concerning as Mr. Fluxcer's influence has caused me to grow less appreciative of even numbers.

Ina sees me staring at the boxes and says, "The one on the left is the last spoon from your father. The other box is my gift. Go ahead, open your spoon," she coaxes.

I pick it up and hold it a moment. It feels heavy, so I envision it as larger than the dainty coffee spoon from the year before. I unwrap a soup ladle with a single right-angle bend in the handle. At first glance, it has the appearance that it might have been designed in that bent way, but when I hold it aloft, it is clear there is no natural balance left for its functionality. It wants to tip in a most mischievous, soup-spilling sort of way. I cannot hold its absurdity without smiling.

"The biggest spoon for his grown girl," Ina squeaks, and she turns to hide the fact she is tearing up. "Twelve years old is considered the actual end of childhood," she adds. "It's a big deal. Agreed?"

"Is this the final time you are going to tell me I am a grown-up, because I actually am now?" I ask, clutching the spoon with both hands.

"I don't mean you're an adult, Blisse," she shakes her head. "But

The Twistical Nature of Spoons

no longer a child either," she says, and I expect her to elaborate, but she just stands there beaming at me the same way Mr. Fluxcer does when a trick goes better than planned.

I let out a deep sigh. Some of my excited anticipation seems to have drained off with Ina's sermonizing. I wish I had agreed to the pizza party with my friends that she offered, but I was certain that Julie would turn down the invitation again, and Matthew would get teased for being invited to a girl's birthday, so it would come down to just Lisa and me, which I wanted to avoid because of the way she refused to pick a card—any card—from the deck she was offered at my party the previous year, claiming that playing cards were the devil's picture books and were banned in her home. But most of all, I suspected I would not want to share this day—the day of the last spoon—with anyone outside our household. I feel myself flushing again.

I blurt, "If I am no longer a child, then I must be old enough to be told how my father got the power to bend this?"

Ina's eyes widen, and she hesitates. "That … is a … mystery, Blisse." She fusses with the frying pan, inspecting it for cleanliness before adding some butter to melt. When she turns from the stove, she says, "All I know is that his great-grandmother was like a clairvoyant, and he believed she could move objects without touching them. He remembered being a child and feeling a weird buzzing in his brain when she kissed his forehead." She turns to swirl the melting butter in the pan before confirming, "So I really have no idea."

I think of my father's good fortune to have encountered his great-grandmother. The only extended family I know is Cousin Char, and although she smothered me with hugs and kisses the time she visited, I recall no buzzing. Her affection did produce hair static, which she promptly remedied with salon products from her suitcase. If there was ever to be brain buzzing, it would have to originate from someone on my paternal side. Looking down at the bend in the spoon, I apply counter-pressure, first with my thoughts, and then with my fingers. My shoulders droop when I produce no reaction.

Ina says a little too brightly, "Would you like to open your other present before I put the batter in?"

A knock on the kitchen door saves me from answering. Ina removes the pan from the heat, snugs up her housecoat belt, and steps forward to open the lock. Knowing it must be Mr. Fluxcer at the inside door, and suspecting that he will grow uneasy—as he always does at the sight of one of the spoons—I rush the ladle to my bedroom. I stroke the bent handle and say a silent thank you to my deceased father before placing it on my bed and dashing back to the kitchen. Mr. Fluxcer is waiting near the door, holding a shoebox wrapped in the coloured Sunday comics. He offers it to me and clears his throat before wishing me a very happy birthday.

I thank him profusely, forcing one of my magic show smiles onto my face. I want to focus on the kindness behind his present, but I am besieged by the need to process what Ina has revealed: further evidence that my father's powers might be hereditary. Perhaps the sole reason I have not been able to channel my own abilities is because he did not live long enough to kiss my head and buzz my brain. I wish I could ask Mr. Fluxcer's opinion on my theory because, lately, I feel certain that my father would be disappointed in my lack of powers, and I would like to be assured otherwise. It is difficult to focus on what is in front of me, but I unwrap the comics carefully so I can read them later. Inside the box is a pair of pink slippers, each with a large, plush bunny head over the toes. The bunnies have wiry whiskers, eyeballs that shake inside their clear plastic casings, and soft, floppy ears. On the back of each heel is a fluffy bunny tail. When I slip them on, not only are they the perfect size, but they immediately warm my feet from the cold kitchen linoleum.

"They are super cosy," I exclaim.

The Twistical Nature of Spoons

"I should have bought you a pair two years ago when your birthday was the coldest day of the year," he acknowledges. "Remember that?"

I nod as I look over my shoulder at the tailed heels. "These are the most fun slippers in the world, Mr. Fluxcer. Thank you."

He nods his head, and I am glad that it remains firmly on his shoulders. He makes apologies a second time, "I could not find slippers with doves. Just rabbits. Close enough."

I traipse to and fro in the kitchen, even hop a bit to activate the moving bunny parts.

Ina pats Mr. Fluxcer on the shoulder. "Cute," she says. "Will you stay for pancakes?"

"Can't this morning. But I will be back later to take you up on the offer of cake, thank you."

"Can you please bring the doves down for my cake party? Just this once?"

"I suppose I could, seeing as it's a special day," he agrees.

I beam at his acquiescence. "It is a troll doll cake," I confirm.

"Mercy," Mr. Fluxcer says. "I thought your mother shuddered at the thought of troll dolls."

Ina pipes up, moving the frying pan back over the heat, "I suggested a round snowstorm cake with coconut-topped white icing, but no dice."

"You said it was my choice," I say, to let Mr. Fluxcer know I was not being unreasonable.

Ina confirms, "And Blisse's choice was for me to design a hideous, purple-haired-fiend cake. It's wearing overalls, at least. I refused to leave it naked. Our teeth will be stained by the amount of food colouring I used."

I protest, "Just because something has a grotesque appearance does not mean we should condemn it."

Ina says, "Oh, I don't mind their ugliness; it's the weird déjà vu feeling I get when I'm around them."

"Did you play with those dolls when you were a kid?" Mr. Fluxcer queries.

Ina waves her hand as if she wishes she had not spoken and drops some batter into the pan. It sizzles. She turns down the heat.

Mr. Fluxcer announces, "Well, we'd best eat that troll cake before the troll eats us. I will see you later."

I follow him to the foyer, thank him again, and shut the kitchen door after he exits, all the while feeling guilty at my relief that he is not staying for pancakes. I want to open my last present, but more than that, I want to ask Ina questions. There is no easy way to steer back to the topic, so I just say point-blank, "Ina, I have now received my final spoon, but I do not even know my father's last name. You said when I was old enough you would tell me and explain how he died …"

She sets a plate of pancakes in front of me. "Well, it's very complicated. Are you sure you want to know?"

"Yes," I say.

She sits down at the table and flashes a smile to reassure me. It comes across as inauthentic, but it seems to bolster her enough to start. "I told you that your father died when he was abroad, right? Well, it was in Ukraine … at a hospital there … He'd returned to visit family. His own parents, who had immigrated to Canada, had passed away, so his only living relatives were back in the old country. He'd been planning the trip for … he'd saved up a long time. I couldn't travel with him because we were expecting you." Ina stops and gnaws on the corner of her lip. "Are you sure you want to hear this today?"

I nod.

"Okay," she says, and resumes with less hesitancy. "When he arrived, there was a large welcome party with extended family; lots of aunts and uncles and cousins came to celebrate. They caroused late into the night. Your father was excited to reconnect with his relatives since he was about to become a parent himself."

The Twistical Nature of Spoons

I imagine a room full of potential brain-buzzing forehead-kissers and smile at Ina, finding it odd that she ignores my gesture.

"Your father confided to his family members that he could bend spoons just by staring at them. He showed them that he had many silver spoons with him in his duffle bag, and he bent one for them. He thought they'd understand since they were all related to his great-grandmother. One of his second cousins, very religious and drunk on too much vodka, took it into his head that Petey must have been possessed by the devil. He picked up a knife and wounded your father in the chest."

"My father was stabbed?!" My imaginary, benevolent, magical extended family lurches out of my head.

Ina nods. She pauses. Reaching for the syrup, she pours out a large glug. We both watch as most of the liquid gets absorbed by the pancakes, while the excess forms a circular pool on my plate. "The wound was not life-threatening, but an infection set in, and he quickly became very ill. He wrote me a letter stating that if I was reading it, a kind doctor had posted it, and it would mean he hadn't survived. It explained that the accompanying twelve spoons had been bent especially for you, and were to be given to you, one per year, on your birthday. No one from his family came to see him in the hospital. He suspected they were trying to protect the relative who'd stabbed him, or they were all afraid of his powers. In the letter, your father insisted I protect our identity, so that no one in his family could ever find us if they came looking for any reason. He swore his love to me and asked me to do the same by keeping you safe forever. That's why you have my surname. Luckily, I'd kept it when we married—not because I was big into feminism, but because his was too hard to spell," she says with a shrug. "It was also lucky he hadn't told his family my name. They don't know who we are and never will."

"Can I see the letter?"

"Uh, well, here's the thing, Blisse. Not long after I received it, your grandmother died, and I rushed here from Thunder Bay, where I'd been living. I was pregnant and in double-shock by then, and I decided to stay here in this house. Char and Denny were kind enough to pack up the belongings I'd left behind and ship them here, but somehow, in that move, several big-deal documents, including my only photos of your father, our marriage certificate, and the letter, were all lost. Thankfully, I'd brought the spoons with me, but those papers were never found. Char said if I hadn't kept important stuff in shoeboxes, she wouldn't have accidentally thrown them out. I was broken-hearted to have lost his last words to me. But after a while, I believed it was for the best. Although your father never told me to destroy the letter, he wouldn't have wanted anyone finding written evidence of his spoon-bending ability." Ina reaches over and rubs my hand. "Your father was a big believer in fate. He said his life had been blessed and made perfect with the knowledge that his unborn child would come into the world and know they were loved. And you are, and you do! So all is as it should be."

I chew and swallow some pancake. It does not want to slide down my throat. The idea of my father dying from a stab wound hurts my insides. I wish I had never asked Ina to tell me what happened, but it is too late, and I cannot fathom my mother's optimism. "Yes, but really, was he blessed? Or were his relatives right?"

"Hmm?"

"Was my father possessed by a devil? Is that why he could bend metal?"

"Oh gawd, no, Blisse! Your father's heart was good. He wished no one harm." Ina jumps up and paces around the kitchen. "Do you think we're good people or bad people?"

I shrug, unsure of how I am supposed to answer.

"Well, do we steal, or hurt others intentionally, or cheat at gin rummy?"

The Twistical Nature of Spoons

I shake my head, glad I never took any of Ina's float dollars, despite contemplating it. I mentally excuse my school escapades as "borrowing for the purpose of demonstration," not theft.

Ina presses, "Do you think Mr. Fluxcer is a good person?"

"Yes. He is patient and kind to me, and to his doves too."

"Right. And he thinks the world of you, Blisse. So if your father was evil and you're his offspring, do you think Knowlton would want to be our friend? And buy you bunny slippers?"

I shake my head.

"Right. There you go. Simple."

My spirits lift slightly. I poke at my pancakes. "I guess my father must have been weird, though."

"Weird doesn't equal evil, Blisse. Weird can be wonderful. Your father was that and more."

"Yes, but lots of people do not like weirdness. Lots of kids at school think I am weird, and they do not like me. Maybe that is what I inherited from him."

Ina's voice quavers as she enunciates, "Well, then count yourself lucky, Blisse. I'd rather have weird genes than small-minded ones." She sits again.

I set down my fork and insist, "Yes, but when you think about it, Ina, do you not agree it was a bit of a misguided idea to bend spoons for his unborn baby?"

"They were tokens of his love, Blisse! And it couldn't have been that misguided. You screamed bloody murder whenever I tried to take the first spoon away from you."

I stare at Ina.

She acknowledges, "Bad choice of words," then affirms, "I'm certain you could sense your father's love in that spoon when you were a baby."

My eyes burn from the strain of holding my emotions in check. The metal of spoons and knives can be set to such different purposes. Contemplating the violent impulse to wound flesh makes me queasy. I insist, "But now that I am grown up, I wish he had never bent those spoons."

Ina gets up from the table and fills the sink with hot, soapy water before she announces, "Well, good thing he only bent twelve of them, then." She turns off the tap, straightens her back, and sniffs. "The perfect age to stop. Not one more spoon will be coming your way."

It is clear the discussion is over when she dries her hands, pushes the unopened birthday gift toward me, and plunks down with the tea towel slung over her shoulder.

I unwrap the box. Inside is a slender watch with a golden bracelet and small, square face the size of a piece of Chiclets gum.

"Oh, Ina," I say, exhaling as if I have been holding my breath underwater.

She says nothing but looks pleased as I slip it on and attempt to latch it. At first, I fumble, but then I succeed in closing the clasp. I hold it at arm's length. It is the most beautiful item I have ever owned.

"What if I break it?" is all I can think to say.

"You won't," Ina replies. "You might need to take it off for gym class, though."

"What if I lose it, Ina?" I say, overcome by what it must have cost.

"You won't," she assures me again. "You're old enough to take care of it."

"It is not for kids, that is for certain. Thank you," I say, staring at it. "It is eight thirty-four," I add before flinging myself at her.

She pulls me into the circle of her arms and says, "Don't worry, Blisse. It comes with a two-year warranty."

I know that presents are not supposed to make you sad, but mine do. I have a weird sense that each of the three gifts represents a part of me, but none of them can tell me who I am. Perhaps, however, I do know what I do not want to be … and that is endangered.

The Twistical Nature of Spoons

With the bunny ears of my slippers flopping on my feet, and my elegant watch encircling my wrist, I scurry to my bedroom and scrutinize the bent soup ladle.

"I cannot leave you nameless," I say to it. The new spoon's single, right-angle bend now seems harsh and unyielding. My father's extended family flashes in my mind. The name Cousinspoon takes an abrupt redirection from the cousin I know. Was this spoon the final one my father bent before he died? Perhaps it sapped what was left of his energy. He might have planned to make several more bends, an elaborate zigzag of turns, but could not summon the power to do so in his weakened state. I open the chest to place it inside, along with the others. Their collective silvery glints seem hostile, as if the arrival of Cousinspoon is not an occasion for celebration. My last birthday spoon. A traitor in their midst. If becoming a person who controls objects with their mind means I end up getting murdered, then perhaps I should stop staring at the spoons, willing them to move. It might be best to not even look at them, nor ask another single question about their origin. I extract the dove feather and pluck out Petspoon, whose history is separate. The twelve others remain speechless as I close the chest, push it back under my bed, and vow to leave them there from that day forward. I assure myself it will be absolutely fine to wish for something normal—maybe even a dove of my very own—when I blow out my candles later.

Ina

grapples

It wasn't as if the curse was my constant companion. Day-to-day life had to be lived, and in the same way that the intensity of grief or betrayal fades over time, my fear of the curse lessened, replaced by the joys of raising Blisse. There were surefire triggers that dredged it up, like walking into the parlour after midnight, where I'd flashback to the clock breakage and relive the dreadful moment of realization. Or inexplicably, I'd shudder if a desk phone rang while I was at an appointment in a cramped office, convinced that Taras's wife had pinpointed my whereabouts and was on the line, demanding to speak with me. I avoided those situations as much as possible, because they left me feeling unsettled for days.

As Blisse's sixteenth birthday approached, however, the curse started a low boil in my brain again, mostly because I was anticipating the thrill of being out from under it. I figured if my daughter was old enough to marry somebody with my consent, then her childhood was officially over, which meant she hadn't spent a minute of it with her father. I'd managed to keep her safe from doing him harm. On the morning of her birthday, I actually threw off my covers and stepped on the bathroom scale to see if I'd lost the weight off my shoulders. Down a pound. A good start. I checked the mirror to see if my appearance had altered. A new grey hair at my temple, but even that seemed like a good omen. I went straight to the foyer to hang Blisse's birthday banner before she woke up. The soft sound of the cooing doves drifted down the staircase, encouraging me to spread my own wings and catch the day's updraft. I remembered to set out the little beckoning ceramic cat on the mantelpiece. Miss Chen had left it on our staircase when she moved out. Her parting words were, "Give it to your little girl. She needs the luck more than me." Blisse loved that cat, but I was too ashamed to look at it. Not displaying it also made me feel guilty, so I agreed to set it out for Blisse's birthday, once a year, claiming that had been Miss Chen's instructions. Birthday luck. That morning, I gave it a high five and forgave myself for tossing my past lodger's belongings out the window. Blisse's sixteenth birthday was going to mark the end of my fretting—terminate my itch of unease. Despite the long years that had passed, the threat of the curse had never completely left me. It was time for Regina Trove to be free and clear.

After she woke up and unwrapped her new sweater—neither of us mentioning presents from the past—Blisse headed for high school, and I blew up additional balloons until my head felt dizzy. I could have done that all afternoon if it meant making her day extra special.

When she returned home later that afternoon, I gushed, "I've invited Knowlton down for cake. He's going to an early movie first so as not to intrude on our whole evening. In the meantime, do you want to order in or go out to celebrate?"

"Actually," she said and paused, dumping her backpack on the counter. "I have a situation."

The Twistical Nature of Spoons

I raised an eyebrow.

She continued, "Lisa told me today at school that she has not been invited to a single birthday party for several years. I explained I was not having a party, but she started crying anyway."

"Well, she's welcome to come for cake."

"She is not comfortable coming here anymore because of the foyer decorations."

"What?" I demanded.

"They just make her sad because her church does not allow Christmas or Halloween. Our foyer reminds her she is missing out."

"But there are only birthday decorations. Christmas is cleared out and packed away. Is she not allowed to celebrate her own birthday?" I argued.

"I try not to pry, Ina. I do not want her to feel disadvantaged by her restrictions, nor do I wish to encourage her attempts to convert me. She asked if just the two of us could go out for all-you-can-eat spaghetti tonight. Her treat. I did not have the heart to tell her that I would be happier spending my birthday with toddlers who refuse to obey bedtime—"

I interrupted, "You can't spend your sixteenth birthday babysitting, Blisse."

She held up her hand. "I knew you would say that. That is why I refused a last-minute job offer and caved to Lisa's suggestion."

"Well, it's important to hang out with friends."

"You set the bar very high, Ina."

I chose to ignore her jab at my lack of a social life. How could I explain that I kept to myself because of circumstances—the unrelenting need to keep her safe from curses and from discovering my coverups—without letting on that I knew she struggled to relate to her peers and vice versa? I'd never suffered from a lack of friends at her age; the last thing I wanted was to make her feel ashamed of her own unpopularity. With enthusiasm, I added, "And we'll have cake afterward."

"It is all-you-can-eat pasta. Can we save the cake for tomorrow?"

"But your birthday wish!" I exclaimed, as if she were still in elementary school.

She wrinkled her nose and squinted through her glasses at me before replying, "They never come true anyway, Ina."

"Blisse!"

She shrugged and headed to her bedroom.

Fighting to keep my buoyant mood, I called, "The cake turned out of the new mould perfectly, you know. The icing is pure white. Aren't doves a Christian symbol too?"

She didn't reply. She'd already closed her door.

After she departed for her mini-party at the neighbourhood restaurant, I dug a paring knife out of the utensil drawer and busted a few balloons, just to scare the emptiness out of the house. I could feel the loud bangs in my ribcage and urged myself to go down to the workshop to stop my popping rampage. Nothing could be gained from resenting Blisse's independence. It was what I'd been waiting for.

I picked out some paint to mix in a cup. I'd started working with glass again—pour-painting on antique windowpanes. The ripples in the glass reminded me of Lake Superior, and although I would completely cover the surface with acrylic paint, the flaws in the old cylinder glass could still be detected on the reverse sides. I had a deeper appreciation for the actual finished pieces knowing they contained this covert detail. It was like detecting an original image beneath a painted-over canvas—uncovering a secret from the past.

I considered my chosen palette. The colours did nothing to inspire me. What I really wanted was to see more of my daughter on her birthday. Why not just add to the cloak-and-dagger nature of my life with a few brief moments of sweet-sixteen spying?

I bounded up the stairs, bundled up, and bustled out in the direction of the eatery where Blisse was meeting her friend. As I approached the restaurant, I slowed my pace. From across the

The Twistical Nature of Spoons

street, I could see them seated in front of the large window. An overhead wicker fixture and a candle stuck in a bottle cast a subdued light, enough to illuminate them. Outside, the air was freezing, but I stayed put, marvelling at how some things looked clearer at that distance. Blisse had no idea she'd grown into a beautiful teenager, judging by the awkward way she adjusted her specs by grasping the arms with both hands and pushing them into place. Framed in that frosty-edged window, her studious, responsible, innocent nature was on full display. She deserved a trip to Disney World, a coming-out ball, a car of her own. She wouldn't be getting any of those.

I knew, standing on that spot, stamping my toes against the cold, that the thing she deserved the most was the truth. The whole truth and nothing but. But did I even know the whole truth? I certainly didn't know how to tell it. I wasn't sure if the extreme cold was causing the tears to well up or whether it was just responsible for their iciness on my cheeks; either way, the day was not going to let itself pass without reminding me that since Blisse's twelfth birthday, four years earlier, when I'd relayed the concocted story about her father's demise, she hadn't spoken of him once. Not a single word. She'd also taken to waltzing out of the room if I brought him up. I wished I'd stuck to my original plan of telling her the actual truth when she turned twelve—that age when she was technically no longer considered a child. Instead, the story I'd told her about Petro's stabbing just came spilling out of me once I started, as if it might have been the truth. At least I'd always kept that one kernel of honesty by assigning Taras a fake ID based on what I could recall of his actual surname. And after all, he *could* have returned to his great-grandmother's village. And because I was keeping him safe from his own child, he might have met his destiny at the hand of someone else in his bloodline instead. For all I knew, my trumped-up story could have matched his actual terrible fate.

The story must have been believable enough, because twelve-year-old Blisse had shoved her box of spoons under the bed, and I hadn't seen her take it out since. She even stopped sneaking a birthday spoon to school each day. The souvenir spoon was the only one missing whenever I yanked the box out to check. She still carried that first spoon around, sometimes fiddling with it absent-mindedly, but it was small and discreet, unlikely to attract teachers' attention, which meant I could stop worrying that family services might show up at the front door to investigate my daughter's abnormal upbringing. I'd braced myself for Blisse to generate new questions; wondered how she simply accepted what I'd told her. I don't think I would've believed me. But Blisse did.

Regardless, there'd been an abundance of sleepless nights fretting about the possible damage I'd done to her psyche. I'd head downstairs to the oversized table that Knowlton had helped me construct in the basement and try to work away my anxieties without waking Blisse. I had to convince myself that what I'd been doing was for the best. Even though I hated the saying "ignorance is bliss," I did believe that my biggest achievement was Blisse's blissful ignorance of the thing I feared. So not only had I kept her from committing a terrible act, but by having her believe someone else was to blame for her father's death, I was protecting her from having to wrestle with the horrendous idea that she might be fated to be his murderer. She didn't even know that gratitude was owed to me. That fraction of selflessness on my part had to be worth something. I'd continued to cling to that.

As I peered across the street, watching Lisa making broad gestures and chattering away, I smiled into the frigid night. Blisse sat upright in their booth, straightening the cutlery and offering the basket of breadsticks. She adjusted and checked her watch. I hoped she wasn't counting down the minutes until she could leave, that she was having *some* birthday fun. At the very least, I hoped she recognized her own good heart for not turning down

The Twistical Nature of Spoons

the invitation. When Lisa squeezed out of the booth and headed to the restroom, Blisse held her wristwatch to her ear. She'd often mentioned how she loved the faint sound of its ticking, like it held the secret of time for her alone. She listened briefly. As she brought her arm down, she knocked something amiss on the table. I saw her lift the salt shaker, pour some into her palm, and touch her left shoulder with it, warding off the bad luck while trying not to be too obvious.

Before she could glance out the window and spot me, I turtled my head and turned away, glad to have witnessed those innocent glimpses of my birthday girl. Perhaps her upbringing had left her superstitious and with a shortage of close friends—influenced as it was by my whacked-out shams and Knowlton's pretend magic—but at least she wasn't roaming mall stores for shoplifting kicks, or skulking in darkened alleyways buying hard drugs, right? I could be thankful for that, couldn't I?

The question was too unsettling. There was a slow leak in my celebratory mood. I didn't want to return to our empty house. I longed for a simpler time, before the lies, and realized I could detour to the library instead of heading straight home. If I could just stand in the spot where my labour had started sixteen years earlier, maybe nostalgia could cheer me up again.

I reached the library's entrance and felt a familiar notion wash over me—that the old wood-and-glass doors demanded a secret password, or an answer to a riddle, or a knock-knock joke to allow entry. The best I could come up with was: A woman walks into a library. Librarian says, "What'll you have?" Woman replies, "A baby." Cue the drum sting: *ba-dum tss!* There was no point in sharing that joke aloud. None of the librarians who'd helped me on the night of Blisse's birth still worked there. That struck me as lucky. I didn't need a reminder of how much time had passed—of how much of Blisse's childhood I'd wished away in my race for her to grow up.

I entered and took a deep breath. One of the best features of that library was its bookish smell, but that evening, the place reeked of mothballs and strong menthol lozenges. January in Winnipeg. I considered hightailing it back out, but I'd been outdoors too long, and the burning thaw of my toes convinced me not to walk home without first warming up. I pulled my scarf up closer to my nose, preferring the smell of my own stale breath on damp wool. I headed toward the stacks and paused, trying to picture my pregnant self leaking amniotic fluid onto the carpet. As I stood there, the sensation that one of the librarians was watching me took hold. I turned around, but no one was there. I unwound my scarf to get some air. The feeling intensified. I checked over both shoulders to see if some pervert was creeping on me. The only nearby patron was intent on opening and closing card-catalogue drawers, oblivious to my presence.

My feet were no longer cold. I deduced that I might be having my first hot flash. Or perhaps, as it had been years since I'd been near the books on mysticism, I'd forgotten that they could somehow influence people by proximity alone. Unbuttoning my coat, I reasoned I'd spent enough time down memory lane for one night. I started to skedaddle in the direction of the exit but stopped dead. In front of me, on the New Arrivals table, was a glossy hardback book that made my heart thud so heavily, I was certain the librarians could hear it at the circulation desk. On the cover was a mosaic of masks. Full and partial masks. Wood, fabric, paper. Smack dab in the middle was a leather Tartaglia, its round, owlish, empty-eyed openings peering at me. At first, I just gaped back at it. Then I stepped forward and read the book's title: *Immask*. By Taras Petryshkovych.

As I lunged for the volume, I knocked a few other books down. I scrambled to set them straight again, but quickly abandoned the task. I picked up *Immask* and turned it over. The author pictured on the back cover was disguised. The upper half of his face was

The Twistical Nature of Spoons

clad in a leather mask. Its long, beak-like nose curved downward toward the man's mouth. Clearly, no one had yelled "say cheese!" when the shutter clicked. My gasp, in the quiet space, sounded more like a strangled sob. The card-catalogue browser glanced over. I could barely focus on her, though—beyond the book in my hands, the room had turned into one-dimensional grey shadows. I coughed out loud, as if something had stuck in my throat, and scurried toward the ladies' room. The cubicle door bounced open from the force I used to slam it shut. Fumbling, I managed to secure the latch.

I stared at the author photo. The book shook in my hands. Could it really be him? So much time had passed since the one brief night we'd spent together. It seemed illogical to search for proof—how many Taras Petro-somethingorothers in the world would write a book about masks? Still, I scanned the photo hoping to know it absolutely. The author had a close-shaved beard; I couldn't quite reference the jawline. The hair seemed to be the same dark colour as Taras's but was curtain-styled in a way that was currently all the rage with male movie stars. A single hank of hair draped over the forehead of the mask, deliberately unkempt. Whoever was staring into the camera from the mask's drooping eyeholes took melancholy to a whole new level; I hadn't seen such a forlorn expression since Blisse lost the little amethyst stone from the tip of the original spoon. And there it was. Clinched. No one could duplicate that expression other than her own father. It was him. Taras. My hands trembled so violently that I could barely crack the pages open. The intensity of the reaction was akin to my water breaking all over again. The panic made sense. My arousal did not. What was to be born from this?

I yanked my scarf over my nose, bandit-style, and shoved the book under my coat. If alarms were going to start clanging, I planned to outrun anyone in pursuit. I darted out of the ladies' room, past the circulation desk, and slammed into the heavy entrance door so hard, I was afraid its window might shatter. I braced myself for the sound of smashing glass but did not stop. Heading in the opposite direction from home, I ran across the street and into the fancy-ass neighbourhood adjacent to the Cornish Library. I beelined straight for a backyard and hoped it wouldn't have a six-foot fence topped with metal spikes or a large black dog wearing a collar with a similar design. I got lucky. The property edge was bordered by a sparse, bare lilac hedge. I squeezed through its gaps and hid behind what might have been a carriage house back in the day. Finally, I stopped and listened. I caught my breath before I dared peek around the corner. The road was empty, save for the shadows cast by tree branches. In the backyard, there was an absence of streetlamp light, and the sliver of moon wasn't bright enough to give up my whereabouts. I slid the book out from under my coat, careful not to drop it in the snow. For a split second, I thought of ditching it in a back-alley trash can or a big dumpster bin, but I knew nothing would ever convince me to part with it.

I crossed through another couple of backyards before making my way to the next street over and ducking behind a huge elm trunk. In the faint streetlight, I stared at the author photograph. Seeing his eyes again, I felt certain that even if Blisse had not been the result of our one night together, he would still have been permanently etched inside me—as if he'd sandblasted my soul.

Sixteen years. What kind of cruel curse would keep us apart all this time? What kind of messed-up fate was this? I wished the photograph could answer.

The book sucked the warmth from my mittened hands. As my breath fogged the air in front of me, I couldn't stop remembering.

Taras had told me that he believed we can't escape our fates. If our fates had been sealed—by his great-grandmother's warning against the wrong wife's curse, and his wife's subsequent curse against Taras and his offspring—then could I really have undone anything? How could a simple cut on my hand stop fate? And

The Twistical Nature of Spoons

since the cursed pronouncement hadn't come to pass—Blisse hadn't stabbed anyone, to my knowledge—then could it really have been our destiny? Had I been the ultimate, asinine idiot guarding against something that wasn't fated to be?

A dog let loose some spirited, high-pitched barking from several backyards away, adding to the jangling in my brain.

Had it just been easier—far easier—to make up a really good story rather than face the sad truth of my situation? I'd spent a night with a man—a stranger, still legally married, who walked into a bar—and he knocked me up. That was the truth of it. Maybe I just needed to feel some power over my own circumstances, so I invented a destiny that I could control, that allowed me to ignore the truth of my reality. And to think, my powerlessness originated with Taras empowering me. For a few magical hours, he made me feel extraordinary. He demonstrated that living out your destiny comes with both pain and wonder.

I suppressed a bitter laugh and continued staring at his face on the back cover. But now my reality was all … what was that word he used? Twistical? It was all one twistical mess because I couldn't see a way out of the lies I'd told. Telling Blisse the truth now could only do more harm than good. Because despite it all—despite our odd, out-of-step life—Blisse was thriving in her little cocoon, ready to emerge with spectacular adult wings. When she wasn't doing magic shows or babysitting, she was reading stacks of books and tutoring other kids. She wanted to study literature. I tried to talk her into accounting or nursing, but no dice. Taras's keen intelligence and off-kilter appeal radiated from her. She didn't know much about her father—but then, did I? I knew enough. In one night, I learned that his chilled heart wasn't cold by nature; he was just preserving it on ice. Our daughter inherited his heart's expanse. I couldn't risk smashing that onto the rocks. And now, there was even more she couldn't know—her father was an author, and her mother was a book thief.

A shiver ran down the back of my head, urging me to trash the book. I held on tighter and zigzagged my way home after re-tucking the tome under my coat, in case someone was out searching for the bandit.

Knowlton was untying his winter boots in the foyer as I dashed inside. Conversation could not be avoided.

Because I'd been out in the cold for so long, my lips had trouble forming words. "Oh, you're home from the movie?"

"Yes," he nodded, his spirits high.

"What did you see?" I asked, one arm pressed against my stomach so Taras's book remained in place under my coat as I sidled toward my kitchen door.

"*Mrs. Doubtfire.*"

"You liked it?"

"It was funny-sad," Knowlton answered. He chuckled. "I'm going to have to fight the urge to call Blisse 'Poppet.'"

"Poppet?"

"It's what Robin Williams calls the children."

"Cute," I answered, inserting the key into my lock.

Knowlton sounded puzzled. "I thought you already saw it with Blisse?"

"Yep," I said vaguely.

He switched topics. "Is it time for candles and cake?"

I explained the change of plans in as few words as possible. He looked disappointed, so I paused to reassure him we'd eat cake the next night, and as I turned back to push my door open, I felt the book sliding. I couldn't stop it from crashing to the floor. Scooping it up, I pressed it against my chest, smothering it with crossed arms.

"Ah, library trip?" Knowlton asked. When I didn't answer, he said, "Whatever is wrong, Ina? I agree it's sad … Delayed cake isn't as much fun. She's definitely not a little girl any longer. But at the same time, it's wonderful. She's growing up."

The Twistical Nature of Spoons

I shook my head and put my chin down on the hard edge of the book. I felt the pull of unburdening. "I'm a bit of a mess, Knowlton."

He waited.

"I stole this book," I blurted.

"You what?"

"I did. I took it without checking it out."

Knowlton sat with one boot dangling from his hand. "Well, it's easy enough to return it. Put it in the chute after hours. No harm."

"I can't return it," I said. "I had no choice but to remove it. I didn't want Blisse to somehow see it there."

He wrestled his second boot off with the toe of his stockinged foot. He stared at me for a long moment. "This isn't connected to … Is it a book about spoons?"

I opened my mouth to answer.

He stood and held up his free hand like a crossing guard. "Stop. I don't need to know. Please don't tell me."

I swallowed. "I understand, but—"

He interrupted, "But! But … I won't shoulder another secret, Ina."

I sniffed. "Good thing you don't know the half of it then, Knowlton."

"Good thing," he agreed. He rubbed a hand over his forehead. "Life is stranger than the movies," he muttered.

Turning my back to him, I closed the kitchen door quietly behind me. My stomach clenched. He was right. His movie plot was less far-fetched than my life: a normal woman keeps her children away from their father because he's a deadbeat, not because she's terrified of bizarre curse possibilities. And even Knowlton, with his generous nature and willingness to help—and with only the most limited knowledge of Taras—did not want to be privy to any more of the craziness in my life. It would've been such a relief to explain the whole thing to someone without fear of judgement or consequence. As I listened to his footsteps ascending the stairs,

I knew Knowlton had taken himself out of the running for the role of confidant to Ina the Muddled.

I went straight down to my basement workshop and hid the book in the rafters above some ductwork. Blisse would never reach her hand up there if there was a chance of encountering gross filth. Cleaning out the newspaper from the bottom of the dove cage sometimes made her gag.

I ran back up the stairs, stripped off my outerwear and street clothes, donned pyjamas, and crawled under the blankets on my bed. Lying there in the dark, waiting for Blisse to return home from her birthday celebration, I recognized that Taras was out there somewhere, for real. We had a daughter who I'd kept from him. More than anything, after holding his book in my hands, I wanted to confess and have us live happily ever after.

But, then I thought of the possible humiliation—the risk of his potential anger and rejection. What if the curse had turned into something worse?

8

Blisse

graduation fluctuation

I am in Mr. Fluxcer's woodworking shop at school. He is using the electric jigsaw to cut a magic box—with a man inside—in half. I stand nearby, a dove in each hand. Mr. Fluxcer removes his safety goggles and undoes the box latch. The man springs out, whole and intact, a treasure chest in his hands and a patch over one eye. Approaching me, the man takes a bow and says, "Guess my name." Ina, wearing a cap and gown, calls out, "It's a trick! Don't fall for it!" The man opens the chest. It overflows with a jumble of spoons—tarnished and bent. I sense my own spoons are lost within, and I reach for one. The doves fly from my hands into the rafters. The man snaps the lid shut and insists, "Guess my name," and although his eyepatch moves from one eye to the other, his face is not unkind. He invites me to sit at a workbench to dine. I say, "If I had known you were coming, I would have hidden the sharp objects."

As I wake, for one delicious moment I believe my father is alive. I feel buoyant that harm was not inflicted upon him for that which set him apart. I anticipate him arriving for my high school graduation that afternoon. The drone of a neighbour's lawnmower begins to expunge the warm, dreamy feeling. I try to hold on; bask in the whimsy of standing, diploma in hand, next to my father. It has been so long since I allowed myself to think about him, and although I have not done so for six years, it suddenly takes Herculean effort not to bring the canteen out from under my bed and stare at the spoons in the hope that they will move. Blocking out thoughts of my father and his violent end seemed essential; the uniqueness of being his daughter was deadened as a result.

He was so alive in the dream.

Even if he were alive, how would I even recognize him? What did he look like? Who was he really? I scrub at my eyes. Lately, I have the sense that I do not know Ina, the person; that I have never really known her. But at least I know something of Ina, the mother. The only capacity in which I know my father is through Ina's unwavering dedication to him, and the presence of my birthday spoons. I wonder about his favourite colour. Convertible or pickup? Ham and eggs with hash browns or swills of black coffee? Stephen King or Richard Ford? Parka or peacoat? And what attracted him to Ina in the first place? Her penchant for wisecracks or the way her eyes glint amber when she becomes miffed?

It is pointless to entertain further wistfulness. Instead, I return to wishing the day were already over. I know this is also not the way I am supposed to feel. My classmates have been planning for this day for months with an exuberance I do not share. It is not that I lack appreciation for the end of high school—I am delighted it is over and done with. Rather, it is that I do not wish to celebrate any part of it. Especially not in full view of others, especially when my emotions are so charged and contrary. Why are times of celebration so fraught?

Ina has made certain my milestone event is on full display for our neighbourhood. Our foyer decorations spill out onto the

The Twistical Nature of Spoons

porch and front lawn. Blue and white balloons and streamers are strung everywhere, and a garish *Grad on Board* sign is staked near the walkway, without the least hint of irony on Ina's part. The fact that we have no car on which to properly display such a placard, and that we continue to depend on Mr. Fluxcer whenever public transportation will not suffice, seems lost on her. Similarly, the fact that we have never sought out relationships with our neighbours, and it is doubtful anyone outside our household cares whether a graduate resides herein or not, also seems not to matter one whit to her.

When I hear the soft tap on my door, I roll over and pretend I am still asleep.

Ina is not fooled. "Good morning, my grad star!"

I mumble acknowledgement but stay put.

She declares, "I'm done. I almost shook you awake at three in the morning but thought I'd better not. Didn't want you falling asleep during speeches. It still shocks me that the valedictorian is not the person with the highest marks."

With my face to the wall, I sigh, "I already explained, student votes decide the valedictorian. My high grades do not translate to popularity." I brace myself for Ina to remark that the kids at school do not know their asses from holes in the ground. For some reason, I find that the most offensive of her expressions.

She merely sniffs and changes the subject. "So what do you think?"

I roll over to face her. She is holding my grad gown on a hanger in one hand and the matching choker she created in the other.

I try to muster an enthusiasm to match hers. She was so thrilled when she read in a magazine that velvet was a voguish fabric choice for grad gowns this year. She insisted on designing my outfit from scratch. I just wanted to go to the mall and purchase a short skater dress, but Ina insisted on a gown fit for a red-carpet diva. I would have pushed back harder if it were not for her strange behaviour over the past few months since my eighteenth birthday. The dress project seems to have brought her back down to earth and diminished the way her leg starts jiggling from out of the blue, as if she feels a need to run away. She sometimes seems genuinely afraid of something. I worry that she cannot adjust to her own growing success, as her pour-painting pieces are selling so well that customers are beginning to commission them in advance. Maybe the pressure of that is getting to her. She not only has to do the art, but also needs Mr. Fluxcer to shuttle her to antique stores and around older neighbourhoods to try and find houses under renovation in hopes of sourcing some free or cheap cylinder glass—a finite commodity. Why new float glass will not suffice is confounding to me. I think she might be pushing herself too hard because she doubts my tuition savings are sufficient. At least she stopped crunching numbers when the dress project overtook her. I am glad it forced her to bring the sewing machine upstairs into the kitchen. The electric thrum combined with her intermittent humming was quite comforting to me while I studied for finals, and I think the daylight is healthier for her.

Ina says, "Maybe slip the dress on now." Before I can object, she adds, "Just to double-check the measurements. I still have time to alter it."

I acquiesce. But despite the dress's sophistication and its perfect fit, it can do nothing to cure my dateless grad status. I sense this bothers Ina more than me. She tried so hard to pretend she was not upset the day I came home from school and informed her I would be attending solo.

I said, "It is not worth agonizing over for the next two months. I listen in the hallways and during class, and all I hear is, 'Will hunky so-and-so go with so-and-so, or do you think I could get his friend so-and-so to hint that I want to go with him instead?' At least once a day some girl is so worked up about it that she starts crying, and the guys are hiding in Mr. Fluxcer's workshop over

The Twistical Nature of Spoons

lunch hour—because he lets them—and avoiding their friends who are egging them on to ask out someone with whom they barely converse."

"Oh, Blissey," she responded. "Do you like someone who you think doesn't like you back?"

I did not confess that on the previous day, when Matthew asked Julie to grad instead of me, with an entire corner of the cafeteria within earshot, I wished bad things would happen to him. The next minute, someone noticed his fly was undone and his bright red underwear was bulging at the zipper. His face turned a crimson to match, and the cafeteria erupted. Matthew and Julie were teased mercilessly for the rest of the day. A secret part of me wished that it had been my powers that telekinetically opened that zipper and exposed his embarrassment. I immediately admonished myself for wishing ill will on my long-time childhood friend, which left me no appetite for finding a date, even if, by some miracle, I could get one.

I ignored Ina's question and pressed on with my argument. "I also hear others confiding that it is too close to grad to break up with their boyfriends, but they do not want to date them any longer."

"Well, there's still time for broken-up couples to find different dates," she managed to counter.

I shook my head. "Ina, are you suggesting I get caught up in another couple's drama? Not a chance. Plus, most of them are not asserting their own choices. At least I am doing that. And I did not break Julie's heart by going with Matthew."

"He asked you?"

"Well … I knew Julie was dying to be his date."

Ina started gnawing on the inside of her cheek, a sure sign she was struggling. "You are considerate beyond your years, Blisse."

I was not sure I had convinced her and added, "I am thankful you encouraged me to think for myself. It is the best lesson you have taught me."

That seemed to do the trick. She has not mentioned my date status since.

When Ina hands me the choker neckpiece, even though I do not care for the dangling glass crystals that she hand-picked to adorn it, I gush my appreciation for their considerable sparkle. I still feel a niggling obligation to compensate for any disappointment she might be feeling. I slip it around my neck and fumble with the hooks. Ina reaches around to help me and then steps back.

I say, "It is very special, Ina."

She responds, "Only because of who's wearing it."

I cannot deny that I am pleased by the sincerity in her voice.

"Knock, knock," Mr. Fluxcer calls from the foyer. As Ina heads through the kitchen, I hear him say, "I have to dash to the school to help with preparations, but I have the corsage."

My mother coos, "Oh, it's gorgeous, Knowlton. She's going to love it."

From behind my bedroom door, I call, "Thank you, Mr. Fluxcer." I am uncertain if he hears me before he departs the house.

Droplets of water glisten on the cluster of orchids and rosebuds, as if they were just plucked from their misty habitats and attached to the wristband. My heart swells. I am mortified Mr. Fluxcer has chosen such a beautiful gift for me while I was wishing something would arise to prevent him from joining us at our grad table. It has been bad enough being his magic assistant in my senior year, but to have the woodworking teacher accompanying me and my mother to my grad dinner will surely generate more snide remarks. There have been a host of them recently, and although I have learned to pretend that they do not faze me in the least, and have refused to allow them to affect our act, the embarrassment they spawn must still be endured. *Fluxcer actually lives in your house? Is he bonking your old lady or something? No, man, that old dude just screws boards. Get it? Yeah, but what about his magic wand? Oh, that's sick. Hahaha!* Sometimes, I counteract their comments

The Twistical Nature of Spoons

by generating new yearbook captions for them in my head. Most likely to become the driver of a circus Volkswagen. Most likely to become a props assistant in the porn industry. Most likely to illustrate the Peter Principle upon receiving their promotion to Dog-Poop Inspector for the Canadian Parks Service. My conscience tells me the universe is not impressed by my cattiness, and so I suffer both the shame from their comments and the guilt from my own. This morning, Mr. Fluxcer's kindness adds yet another layer. I wish the day would just vanish in a puff of smoke.

•—•—•

After the ceremony concludes, I feel tremendous relief, as if I have survived time in the trenches, dodging enemy fire. Thankfully, no one booed or snickered when I crossed the stage to receive my scholarships and various awards. Their polite applause acted as a tension reliever, which, in turn, made me ravenous. At our hotel banquet table are Lisa, her parents, her date (who is from her church and a grade behind us), Ina, Mr. Fluxcer, and me. The spare chair seems to be making itself heard above the surrounding hubbub, especially since Lisa seems smug about it. I am a little sad that we no longer hang out since she started dating, but mostly I welcome the reprieve from the pressure to remain steadfast friends in our outcast corner. I wonder how I would be feeling if our bond had been based on a more positive, mutual synchronicity.

 When a banquet server places my chicken Kiev in front of me, I devour it too quickly and then consume the extra bread roll from the napkin-lined plastic basket. Before coffee and dessert are served, several school staff members come by the table to greet Mr. Fluxcer and offer me an extra round of congratulations. These same teachers ignore Lisa, and she responds by putting her head on her date's shoulder. He looks pleased with himself and nuzzles her cheek, which makes the veins in Lisa's father's neck pop out. The moment the dishes are cleared, Lisa's father announces a curfew for his daughter and drags his wife to the exit. Moments later, the canned music starts. Lisa and her date hit the dance floor and do not return to the table. I did not even know that Lisa was allowed to dance. Five songs pass and no one asks if I would care to do the same. It seems the perfect opportunity to complain of a mild stomach ache from the overly rich dinner and suggest we venture home.

Ina objects, offering me an antacid from her purse, but Mr. Fluxcer, recognizing the actual source of my reluctance to stay, interjects, "I'm with Blisse," and then provides misdirection by adding, "we do have that summer carnival show tomorrow afternoon—unfortunate timing for it, but the generous pay more than compensates."

He offers to fetch the van—a recent upgrade from his old rattle-box station wagon—and meet us out front. I agree to Ina's request for final snapshots in front of the photo-op backdrop. The picture-taking session seems to appease her; we head to the hotel's front door without further protest.

"Oh," I say and turn. "I forgot my programme at the table. Go catch up with Mr. Fluxcer. I will be right there."

When I am sure Ina is gone, I return to stand just inside the banquet room entrance and take a long, hard look around. Maybe Matthew or Julie or the exchange students I tutored in English class are searching for me, not wanting me to go. Music and dancing and laughter make the room pulse. No one notices me there at all, other than the fit man with the security armband, who nods in acknowledgement and then averts his attention. Apparently, I pose no threat. A thought niggles at the back of my brain that it is fortunate I do not possess psychokinetic powers after all; if you place any credence in genre fiction, this would be the perfect time and place for their unleashing.

The Twistical Nature of Spoons

I head out into the warm June night. Lawns have been freshly mowed. Has Ina noticed the fresh scent, or is she too distracted by our early departure? I do not bother to mention it in case she insists on scrambling back out of Mr. Fluxcer's van to sniff the air just as I cram my gown-clad body into it.

"Did you find it?" Ina swivels around to ask.

For a moment, I do not know to what she refers. Remembering my fabricated excuse, I say, "No, but it does not matter."

Though I have attempted a brave face, my tone must convey an absence of the appropriate graduation jubilation because Mr. Fluxcer's next words smack of a need to provide me with sympathetic compensation.

"Blisse, I think for tomorrow's show, you should take another milestone step … You should *graduate* from assistant to magician for the cup-and-ball trick. What do you say?"

"Oh my!" Ina exclaims.

He adds, "Your abilities have surpassed my own."

My heart sinks. I want to ask Mr. Fluxcer if he has ever once wished that one of the balls would disappear from under a cup of its own accord, but I do not. I answer, "Well, first, thank you for the compliment. But no! It is one thing to demonstrate the trick for you; it is a different matter to perform it for an audience. I am perfectly happy being your assistant."

"Well …" he pauses, "if you're certain."

I want to say I am not certain about one single thing, but I smile and nod.

I am surprised Ina does not insist I give it a try. It does not take long, however, to discover that her ultimate compliance, both with our departure and my refusal, is because she has planned another component to round out my celebration. From the back of our refrigerator, she pulls out a bottle of champagne and a small box of chocolates. As we have no stemware, Ina pours out three small portions into her special hand-painted juice glasses and admits that, while she admires the new concept of the *dry* grad, she believes there can be no harm in sharing a toast on such a momentous day now that we are safely home. I imagine that this is the point in time when other students might be free to reveal some of their illegal drinking escapades to their parents. I, on the other hand, feel the need to safeguard the tales of my abstinence—not that there have been many opportunities for me to decline an alcohol offering.

Ina raises her glass. "To Blisse!" she salutes and leads the clinking.

To acknowledge Ina's gesture, I take a sip. The bubbles feel energetic and their sharpness is not what I would have expected from such a renowned, coveted beverage; but its edginess also seems to suit the day, and the immediate fuzzy sensation above my eyebrows is not unpleasant. I finish my glass and Ina refills it to the brim.

Mr. Fluxcer samples a chocolate before raising his hand and saying, "I'll be right back." I take several large swigs before he returns with a wooden box. "I made this for you, to store your high school keepsakes."

The container is crafted from dark, rich wood with perfect dovetail corner joints. The lid fastens shut with a brass hook latch.

I hear myself squeal, "A treasure chest!"

Mr. Fluxcer nods and then shows me that he has built it with a secret compartment beneath its false bottom. "To always remind you of our magic act." He clears his throat. "It's been a joy … an honour … to witness your successes. Congratulations, Blisse."

I toast him with my thanks several times and polish off what might be my third glass. I am finding it difficult not to blurt out the coincidental detail of dreaming of a treasure chest that very morning. I am struggling not to giggle from the stress of being the centre of attention. I am fighting back tears knowing that Petspoon can now reside in a room in full view, yet never be discovered.

I manage to say, "You have helped me so much, Mr. Fluxcer, since you moved into our house."

The Twistical Nature of Spoons

"It's been a two-way street," he replies before bobbing his head. "And I think graduation makes it official—you can now call me Knowlton."

"I will try ... Knowlton." When I cannot say anything more, he pats my shoulder and, sensing my struggles, chooses to depart. He bids me good night with a kiss on top of my head before heading for the staircase.

Ina calls out after him that his gift is splendid as she empties the champagne bottle into my juice glass. I stare at the bubbles racing to the surface. They are in such a hurry. I hold the glass to my ear. I expect a louder audible hissing, but perhaps the effervescence is not angry at all.

In the distance, I hear Ina say, "I'm so very proud of you, Blisse."

From an equal distance away, I hear someone ask, "Do you think I will be a dork there too?"

"What?" Ina demands from an echo chamber.

"At university. Will it be the same dorky me in a different place? This choker is strangling me."

Ina reaches around to unhook it, all the while chattering like a tree squirrel. A tree squirrel whose eyes are leaking tears. "Of course not. No! You're going to find other people there—accomplished, interesting people—who are going to love that you're unique and that you don't dumb yourself down to be popular or go gaga for the right label on your clothes. That doesn't make you a dork. It's only assheads who think you're a dork, Miss Blisse. There will be wall-to-wall non-assheads on campus, excited to meet you."

I laugh and snort champagne bubbles up my nose. To try and counteract the tickling sensation, I gulp down what remains in the glass. I stick my tongue in to lap at the last few drops, in between asking, "Assheads? Definition, please?"

"Fools," she answers.

I nod. The world swings on a hinge. I point with my empty

glass. "I want you to know, you are no asshead. You are the best mom, Mom!"

Ina removes the empty juice glass from my hand. Perhaps she remembers more of my grad night. I do not.

Ina

diverts

I picked Blisse's gown off the floor, where it lay in a heap, and hung it up. As I switched off her bedroom light, I noted that her nightshirt was on backward and inside out, but she was already fast asleep with Knowlton's gift propped between the wall and her pillow. What a day it had been. Blisse was the belle of the ball with her scholarships and top student award. She oozed confidence attending grad without a date, and displayed such responsible behaviour by leaving early for the sake of the Influx Show obligations. And the kindness she showed Knowlton by refusing to one-up him in a public performance … There should have been an award for the highest maturity level attained amongst peers. But having her call me "Mom" again—the *best* Mom—and then listening to her tipsy ramblings about how she loved her father with all her heart even though she never met him … Those were my biggest, unexpected rewards of the night. I smiled into the darkness and shut her door. There was such a sweet relief inside me. Maybe I could permanently shut the door on all the wacky fears from the past eighteen years. Especially the one that had originated at the police bicycle auction—the day I took the wild notion into my head that if Taras tracked me down through a private detective, who overheard and reported five-year-old Blisse calling me "Mommy," Taras could do the math, surmise she was his child, abduct her, and set the doom-clock ticking.

I was so grateful for Blisse's champagne-induced proclamations. So why, then, was something not quite right with me?

I brewed a pot of coffee and padded down to my basement work table. Although it had felt good to be called upon to provide reassurances that she'd be fine at university, for the past few months, Blisse had refused to accept any of my offers to help with her post-secondary decisions. She was on the brink of starting a life that would grow more separate from mine, turning the last corner away from childhood. She'd called me "the best Mom," but I'd already messed up plenty. It was time for me to stay out of her way. But what was I supposed to do if steering my daughter's life to safety was no longer at the top of my list? There was a nagging sense inside me that my purpose in life was fading out, like fabric left too long in the sun.

I looked up into the rafters where Taras's book was hidden. For two years, I'd been too anxious to remove it, not even for a peek—both scared out of my wits Blisse would spot it and afraid of the feelings that had been churned up inside me the night I'd stolen it. From its cobwebbed hiding spot, the book had still managed to derail my daily thoughts. The promise of seeing Taras's words on its pages beckoned to me in a way that made my pulse jitterbug. My resistance had won out for a long time, and I'd forced myself not to think about his absence throughout Blisse's momentous day, but I yearned for just a brief glimpse of Taras's masked face again. With my resolve crumbling, I rationalized that if nothing else, the book might provide a shred of distraction from wondering what my sorry ass was supposed to do next.

The Twistical Nature of Spoons

I stood on my work stool and brought it down. Was this how Eve felt when she grabbed hold of that apple? If so, it's no surprise she bit into it. There was no way to resist after cracking open the first page. Within minutes, I'd squirreled the volume upstairs into my bed, confident that Blisse wouldn't be waking from her alcohol-assisted sleep anytime soon. At dawn, with the daylight urging caution, I snuck it back down to the rafters.

That afternoon, as soon as Blisse and Knowlton left for their first of many summer shows, I pulled the book out from the rafters again and picked up where I'd left off. I stowed it again for the evening and waited until after midnight to re-extract it. The next day I did the same. And the day after that. The book was mesmerizing. I read it cover to cover, and then reread it, forward and backward. I skimmed over the death and funeral masks, revelled in the disguises of the masquerade, and lingered over the theatrical varieties—ancient Greek, Javanese *wayang wong*, and Japanese Noh. And most of all, the *commedia*. It was as if the pages of Taras's observations and revelations were being spoken directly into my ear. His personal mask lore, meant just for me. A second seduction. Memories from our studio intimacy resurfaced, flooding over me like pounding surf.

And I couldn't stop myself from trying to read between the lines: Was he lonely? Was he in love with someone? Or worse, still married? When he wrote the passages on disguise, did he want his reader to think about secret longing? Did he remember me? Or was I nothing but a vague can't-put-my-finger-on-it notion that stirred inside him when a woman wearing my perfume walked by? Even with the passage of years, it stung to think that I had handed every bit of myself over to Taras, but had no way of knowing if, to him, I'd been anything more than a forgotten lay.

I started to fret that, with all the late-night reading, I'd fall asleep with the book splayed open in full view for Blisse to find the next morning, so I drank extra coffee each night and napped in the afternoon. When Blisse came home from her shows, I could barely concentrate as she chatted about the kids' reactions. And my trepidation increased; if Blisse so much as caught sight of the book, she'd surely recognize her father, deduce he hadn't died from a stab-wound infection, and decide her mother was a madwoman for claiming it. What was the use of being out from under the curse if I couldn't be free of my own lies? And I wasn't free. The untruths that I'd told were now holding me hostage because I couldn't undue them without enormous risk. Would Blisse ever speak to me again if I told her the truth about the spoons—if she discovered her father was still alive? She might disappear out of my life. In the past, I'd been horrified at the thought of her jailed in a cell, but the prospect of not knowing where she was living at all was even more gut-wrenching. With a whole new set of fears anchoring me down, instead of doing the smart thing and destroying the evidence, I clung to it like a life preserver. I forced myself back to my work table during the day and stayed up with Taras's words well into the night.

The resulting sleep deprivation was no doubt responsible for the idea that blundered into my brain. I suspect that a well-rested mind wouldn't have written Taras a letter. It was not meant to be a confession. I just wanted to connect, to communicate something—anything. Once the idea took hold, it wouldn't budge. Like a window painted shut. I tried to force it out of my head, knowing that all I had to do to stop myself from writing to him was to simply not write to him—but I couldn't withstand the promise of a small mercy should he write back.

Call it a reckless decision, but my plan was to write anonymously and stay out of harm's way. What could go wrong?

I addressed the envelope first, care of his UK publisher. It seemed like the only way to reach him. The brief biography on the flap of the dust jacket made no mention of Taras's personal life, no marital or family status, only that he wrote the work while

The Twistical Nature of Spoons

residing in Italy. Early the next morning, without having a clue what I would possibly reveal to him, I caught a bus downtown and secured a mailbox in the main post office for a six-month period. I returned home and practised a neutral signature that wouldn't arouse suspicion: *Regina*. I acknowledged it might be delusional to believe he'd even remember me if I signed *Ina* instead, but I wasn't taking any chances. I dashed out the letter in one fell swoop:

Dear Mr. Petryshkovych,

I have my fingers crossed that your publisher forwards this to you. I've read and reread your book Immask and I wanted to tell you how much I enjoyed it. It's educational and also inspiring. I like the way you write about theatrical mask use in different cultures. It's also an interesting coincidence to me that I've dabbled in black velvet painting and your book features a painting of a woman wearing the moretta mask (which you explain was often covered in velvet). I might try my hand at constructing one of those simple ovals, but I think I'd like to paint on its cheeks and forehead. Would that be some kind of sacrilege in your mind? Do you approve of the glitter-up of masks for Mardi Gras and their ghoul-up for Halloween? A mask project might give me new perspective on my current work. I am pour-painting on old windowpanes and often feel guilty "disguising" the glass. (I have a bottomless pit of guilt and could do a better job getting rid of it.) In your book, I especially like your quote from Oscar Wilde: "Man is least himself when he talks in his own person. Give him a mask, and he will tell you the truth." Do you think that applies to physical masks? Are you more capable of the truth when you slip one over your face? Or is it easier to deceive someone when you are hidden behind one? I can say that, maskless, I've spun some doozies, so it's an important question to me, even if you feel your answer is none of my business. For what my opinion is worth, I think the way your book describes masks and mask-making is quite seductive, so I'm glad I came across it.

Yours truly,

Regina

Later, close to midnight, after I was certain Blisse was asleep, I dropped the letter in the corner mailbox. As soon as I heard it hit the bottom of the container, I jerked the handle open in a panic, wishing I could retrieve the envelope. Resting my head on top of the box, I took deep breaths. I debated waiting there until the following day to intercept the mail truck, and wondered if it was a criminal offense to prevent a postal worker from emptying the box's contents. If they discovered me draped over the bright red bin, asleep on my feet, would they take pity and accept a bribe to fish it out of there? When the thought of starting a small fire in the mailbox crossed my mind, I started walking home, taking some comfort in the stories I'd heard about letters getting lost in processing.

I reviewed the letter in my head over and over, trying to determine if I'd written anything that could be tracked back to the Ina he'd once met. I regretted using the word "seductive" in the final sentence, but I also wished I'd admitted to pleasuring myself one night, lying next to the masked author photo on the back of his book. I fluctuated from reassuring myself the letter would never be forwarded to him, to convincing myself he'd sit down to write back the moment he received it.

I started checking my mailbox long before enough time had elapsed for a response to arrive. The box yawned empty for several weeks. It gave me a jolt the day I opened it and an envelope lay inside. Was it from Taras, or his publisher? There was no return address. I ripped the lightweight airmail envelope open in the post office foyer and read it on the spot.

The Twistical Nature of Spoons

Regina,

Thank you for your letter. I have received several from peers since the publication of my work, but none as thought-provoking as yours.

To answer your first question, I had the good fortune of moving to Italy on the brink of the Venice Carnival rejuvenation, and I did a stint assisting university students in the creation of masks for the celebrations. Although I am proud these were not mass-produced versions, they were still aimed at the tourist trade and not purely motivated by artistic pursuit. I dare not pass judgement on the endeavours of others. If you choose to paint on a velvet servetta muta, by all means!

I have a colleague in Canada who I am certain would be intrigued by your use of glass as a canvas. May I put you in touch with him?

As for masks allowing for the conveyance of truth? A complex question. My experience centres on creating character, mostly. When I slip on the mask, the intention is to actualize the character. However, I believe for any portrayal, we must access some truth within ourselves; perhaps the mask facilitates that more readily. As an aside, I once witnessed a beautiful truth surface in the eyes of someone who donned one of my masks. It was very powerful. But that was a singular experience, a long time ago, and imprecision is memory's least attentive, but most persuasive, handmaiden.

I will not presume to comment on your "doozies," but I do struggle with the advice, "the truth will set you free." I wonder, what does it set you free to do? Imprison someone else with your unburdening? Perhaps you have suggestions to enlighten me?

Please keep me apprised of your own work's progress.
Taras Petryshkovych

PS I am grateful you found my book seductive. I am steering away from the physical realms of performance and construction, and concentrating more on the written word. This, at times, is tumultuous for me; your sentiments, therefore, shored me up in a visceral way.

The light airmail paper trembled in my hands. My eyes skipped back and forth from how my praise pleased him, to the statement about the powerful moment with someone who wore one of his masks. Could he have been referring to me? And why would he tell a complete stranger that story? Unless he suspected? Could his glass colleague be anyone other than Dirkland? Had Dirk told him about my visit? Did Taras want to put us in touch to unearth my whereabouts in a roundabout way? Panic rising, I read the page a dozen times on the transit bus, and when I arrived home, I tucked the letter into his book and shoved both into the rafters. If I hadn't scribbled out an immediate response—which I didn't take the time to reread, but ran straight to the corner mailbox—I would never have replied. Mentioning Blisse was both a dumb-bunny risk and a churning necessity.

Dear Mr. Petryshkovych,

I only half expected to hear from you. Please don't bother your colleague on my behalf. Really! Not my thing, at all. Even this letter feels like I'm pushing my luck, but I wanted to tell you it was nice you wrote back. Your letter means a lot to me. I've managed to complete one moretta mask. There were numerous failures to start. My local library research only turned up

The Twistical Nature of Spoons

instructions for rudimentary mask construction, so trial and error followed. It was hard for me to scrap the rejects because, man oh man, can they look accusatory! I've been naming them all first—Rumplechin, Chipcrack, Lopsider, Cheekmess, Socketsag—and then wrapping them in a piece of cloth before stacking them in the garbage. On the sole survivor, I painted bright green trails of ivy and blue-winged birds. The black oval by itself struck me as quite sinister, even after I built it with no imperfections, and so adding flora and fauna was an attempt to counteract that—to express a sense of playful innocence. What surprises me is how much I want my daughter to be impressed by the piece. I haven't had the courage to show her yet; I don't want to seem desperate in case it prompts her to be dishonest with me and heap on compliments she doesn't mean. Obviously, I haven't confessed any of this to her (although I confide in her father). I did build the mask in the authentic manner you described, with the button bit that gets clamped between the wearer's teeth. That definitely shouted creepiness to me when I tried it on. (No wearer could be talking truth or telling lies with their mouth muted like that. Why not just cut out your tongue while you're at it?) I hope my ramblings aren't too ignorant. I'd hate to think I've insulted you in some way. Good luck with your writing.

Yours truly,

Regina

PS With respect to being set free by the truth ... I'm not sure I'm the best person to offer an opinion. I wonder about parallel questions, like: is it worse to be a prisoner of your own mind or to be thrown into an actual jail cell?

Patti Grayson

I deliberately stayed away from the post office for two weeks. I wasn't sure what I feared more—a response or no reply. The next time I checked, a second letter was waiting. A flat envelope, hot-wired to my central nervous system.

> Regina,
>
> A subjugator of the sinister? How marvellous! I wish I had access to the kind of talent that wrangles darkness from our days. It sounds as if your child has informed your creative pursuits, and that the surviving visard is the beneficiary of that inspiration. I cannot say why, exactly, but this fills my heart with a bracing hope.
>
> Perhaps my reaction is restorative, providing an extra boost to my own writing. I am adding the finishing touches to the third act of my drama, and I do feel energized as of late. At times, my words feel otherworldly, as if the Muses themselves are refilling the ink in my pen. Even so, self-doubt is known to raise its serpentine head, and I wish I knew the piece's fate. And, of course, it yearns for a stage somewhere before it can be fully realized. Luckily, I am no stranger to yearning.
>
> Taras
>
> PS I'm not troubled by your comments, Regina. On the contrary, your letters intrigue me. So much so, that I find myself pondering more personal particulars. Forgive my curiosity, but do you enjoy the winters in Winnipeg, or do you dread them? Of course, here in Venice, we prepare to face the acqua alta and the risk of flooding. Perhaps there is no perfect place on earth to call home. Do you live a nomadic existence with your postal box address?
>
> In your artistic life, do you choose the single moniker "Regina"

The Twistical Nature of Spoons

(like Banksy or Madonna), or are you deliberately omitting your surname to mask your identity? I find it is often the wealthy that choose to remain anonymous. Perhaps while you enjoy our communications, you wish to avoid becoming my patron. Rest assured, I have sufficient income to meet my corporeal needs, and my soul's girth is plumped daily with the tea and cakes of creativity (my aforementioned yearnings are sourced elsewhere). Or perhaps you just prefer to fashion an allure of mystery. If that's the case, you are succeeding.

And now my postscript length surpasses that of my letter, so I close. Ciao.

It took me several days to respond. I ripped up pages and pages before settling on a few sentences.

Dear Taras,
While I've enjoyed our letters, I am unable to continue writing to you. Good luck. And thank you again for your informative book.
R.

I thought there would be no further communication. I had no intention of checking the box again, but with Blisse starting her new studies that September, I found walking past the university cheered me up. If I extended my route all the way to the post office, it was easier to deal with the added emptiness of the house, especially on those days she stayed late to study. And once I was downtown, it seemed senseless not to double-check. Another letter had arrived.

Regina,
I am aggrieved I shan't hear from you again. I conclude that

either my mention of monetary matters insulted you, or, more likely, that this is a personal decision based on your husband's lack of support for our burgeoning pen-pal liaison. (Forgive me if I've surmised incorrectly, but that appears the most logical reason to halt our communication.) I am most respectful of your wishes; however, I am compelled to confess that I feel our correspondence has been spoon-feeding me creative elixir. So it is I who must express gratitude. Grazie!

Taras

PS I must also add I regret that, on the brink of my return to Canada, I will not be afforded the opportunity to make your proper acquaintance. Arrivederci.

The bittersweetness of it being his final letter was overshadowed by the array of alarms it sounded. *Spoon-feeding. Return to Canada.* I crammed the new letter into his book with the others, slammed it shut, and shoved it into the rafters. I swore to never bring the book down again and imagined someone discovering it there long after my death. I cancelled my post office box. No forwarding address. My routine of working well into the night, seated below the book, and dozing during the day, became more set. I was glad Blisse was preoccupied with her university lectures and that Knowlton was back teaching. I tried to act like my normal self when I was with them but found myself shaking uncontrollably at times. My mind wandered. Had I said one single thing that might lead Taras to know who'd sent him the letters? Was there a chance he'd venture to Winnipeg to try and track me down? Could I ever convince him that it was *his* cursed story—and not me—to blame for his daughter being hidden from him all this time?

There was nowhere to direct my nervous energy other than into

The Twistical Nature of Spoons

the masks I was building. It became harder to assert their innocence. I had to "subjugate the sinister" within myself. My struggle improved the work. I consoled myself with the masks' progress, because cutting ties with Taras a second time made me want to stay in bed with unwashed hair and take endless walks that led to nowhere and accomplished nothing.

One night, as I settled in at my work table, a sudden urgency gripped me. It wasn't my usual antsy response to approaching holiday craft-sale deadlines. It was a yearning to distance myself further from Taras and his inspiration, while somehow expressing the sway he'd held over my life since we met. I dug through unpacked boxes of my Thunder Bay belongings, which Char and Denny had shipped years earlier, and found three stained-glass sheets. Donning some safety goggles, I tossed the glass. I flung my arms in the air like an official signalling a touchdown as the sheets smashed on the concrete basement floor. I also held my breath, waiting to see if I'd roused the household. All remained quiet overhead. I circled the destruction. It made me queasy and giddy at the same time. The delicate, vulnerable breakage didn't fool me as I sifted through the shards; I knew danger lurked on every edge.

Right then and there, I decided to make masks with stained-glass eyes. Masks that served a traditional role of shielding the wearer from being seen, but that also prevented the wearer from seeing clearly.

Did that not perfectly sum up my life?

I dug through the *morettas* and found one to sacrifice. I lopped off the bottom half, stylized the eye sockets, and held up some pieces of glass behind the holes. I figured I could fill the eye cavities of Colombina half masks—the celebrated mask which originated with the "little dove" maidservant of *commedia dell'arte,* and evolved into the customary adornment for masquerades.

Could a crown buckram framework support the weight of glass eyes, or would I have to embed the glass in a thick papier-mâché form? Linen—the cloth of death masks—was my first choice. I had a feeling that the masks would end up unwearable—relegated to pieces of window decor. They would have to be ass-kicking exquisite to compensate. I'd never felt the need for an artistic statement before, but I knew it was perfectly suited the moment it popped into my head: *Refusing to See What's Right in Front of Me.*

9

Blisse

Tweed read

I witness my second aura during my inaugural week of university classes. It is the first morning of Comedy and Tragedy—my half-year elective course—and a young man strolls through the seminar room doorway, encompassed in a blue aura that summons the words "body halo" to my mind, the effulgence of which leaves me breathless. I speculate that auras which do not dissipate immediately—like Mr. Fluxcer's did—must feed on the oxygen intended for those who catch sight of them. I emit an almost audible sob as I gulp for the air that his aura has not yet usurped. The visual disturbance that surrounds his lanky frame proceeds to both ignite and calm me. I press my hands atop the hard surface of the seminar table, just to be certain I am not dreaming.

Although the aura man, along with a red-headed female classmate, are a full five minutes late, Professor Honeywell greets them as if their arrival is a rescue mission intended to free him from a smouldering pile of plane wreckage. The professor waves off the younger man's apology. "Oh, no problem, Theodore. Delighted to have you back in one of my classes."

With his fawning deference, I wonder if the professor also detects the blue aura. But glancing around the room, I have the strong sense that I, alone, am aware of this Theodore person's envelopment. I can only assume that my singular receptivity is the result of inherited traits on my paternal side. My heart quickens as I realize the hovering blue shimmer may indicate that my father's legacy lives within me after all.

Professor Honeywell continues his enthusiastic greeting. "If you'll take a seat," he motions them to empty chairs, "I'll take the roll call to sort out the rest of us. I'm acquainted with Miss Amberlyn Cache. Welcome. And with Mr. Theodore Halverden."

Someone reverently shifts from their own seat so that the spotlighted duo can sit next to one another.

Amberlyn purrs a greeting to the professor, and then, gesturing to her companion with her thumb, she addresses a comment to the rest of us. "He goes by Tweed, for those of you who don't know him yet."

The professor runs his pen down the class list to mark their presence, saying, "Thank you, Miss Cache. As all of you here *do* know, this class has no prerequisites; however, students further along in their drama studies, such as this talented pair, will have a slight advantage. Nothing that a little extra diligence cannot overcome."

Tweed repositions himself in his chair, and it is impossible to know if he is uncomfortable with being fawned over, or if he feels anointed by the professor's comments. He issues a nonchalant two-finger salute to the group and scans the room in an assessing manner. I avert my eyes before he looks in my direction, hoping he cannot detect my befuddlement. He waits me out. When I do look up, he dips his chin in an acknowledging nod.

"Blisse Trove?" Professor Honeywell says a second time before I recognize my own name.

The Twistical Nature of Spoons

"Uh, here. Present."

"That's reassuring," the professor says, ticking his list with an exaggerated flourish. The class titters, with the exception of Tweed, who looks my way one last time, and does not, as far as I can ascertain, so much as glance in my direction for the rest of September.

I, however, watch his aura wax and wane over the month. My ability to concentrate on Euripides, Sophocles, and Seneca is often diminished by the blue smudge surrounding him. Depending on Tweed's engagement in class discussion, the colour of his aura ranges from thoughtful summer-sky azure to debate-laden faded denim to bored dusty-elephant-hide slate. I catch myself wondering: If I were to reach my hand toward his chest, would my fingers be repelled or sucked forward? If I were close enough, would I detect an emanating sound—the whisper of sea foam or the rustle of bluebird wings bathed in mist? It continues to surprise me that, unlike Mr. Fluxcer's aura, which only appeared momentarily, Tweed's is ever-present. That is, until he speaks to me for the first time.

It is the day after Thanksgiving. I spent the extended weekend studying, and ruminating over Ina's refusal to roast a turkey with all the trimmings. It is obvious she is preoccupied with her upcoming exhibit, but that is still several months away, and she has created enough masks for two solo shows. Individually, I find the visards both enigmatic and exquisite; en masse, however, I find them a tad overwhelming. It is as if, in multitudes, they have the power to peer into the darkest recesses of my soul. I almost wish Ina had stuck to her crowd-pleasing, homey crafts. While I appreciate her desire for more meaningful creation, I am concerned they are beginning to negatively impact her as well. Often, her entire body shudders, and although her penchant for festive decorating might have slightly dwindled since I became a teenager, she never once forsook a holiday celebration until the mask work started. Or perhaps I have not been paying close enough attention; I have so many new distractions. I did offer to try and make the harvest dinner happen myself, reasoning that, having reached adulthood for real, the responsibility had somehow transferred to me in some unspoken rite of passage, but Ina insisted we dine at the Nobleman's Hotel restaurant, where my grandmother had worked until her passing. By way of explanation, Ina marvelled at the fact that she had not set foot in the place for twenty years and was curious as to how it could remain a viable business. She invited Mr. Fluxcer to join us. He accepted, and I was glad he came along. His gracious manner kept me from remarking that the decor of the hotel restaurant could not have been updated since my grandmother worked there; I did not wish to appear unappreciative when a show of thanks was the holiday requisite. While in line for the congealed-gravy buffet, Mr. Fluxcer asked Ina if he might join us for our pumpkin-carving sessions at the end of the month. I sensed he was unnerved by the prospect that Halloween might be on the chopping block next to come and go under-celebrated. Ina's response had been, "Sure! Knock your socks off!" in a distracted manner which caused Mr. Fluxcer and me to raise our eyebrows in unison.

 As I walk toward class, my mind skimming over the significance of the weekend's events, Tweed Halverden catches me off guard in the hall.

 "Hello there. It's Blisse, right?"

 I face him, and his amused aquamarine aura pops like a balloon. "Cripes!" I exclaim.

 Blinking hard at me, he stops in his tracks. "Whoa! Didn't mean to startle you."

 I clutch my books to my chest like a shield. "Yes. Sorry. I am Blisse."

 He glances down at my tabbed binder, pocket dictionary, and copy of *Doctor Faustus*. A dove feather is holding my page as a bookmark. Tweed reaches forward and touches it, as if testing its authenticity. When he withdraws his hand, I fidget and shift my

The Twistical Nature of Spoons

books down to my side, struggling to align them neatly. "Theodore, correct?"

Nodding, he says, "Call me Tweed. Everyone does."

"Not Professor Honeywell, I have noticed."

"Indeed," he replies. "The guy loves the drama of extra syllables, doesn't he?"

"Ha!" I sound off in agreement.

He dives in. "I have a favour to ask. My friend Amberlyn and I have major theatre class auditions later today, so we need to skip Comedy and Tragedy. Would you mind sharing your notes with us later? Normally, we'd ask someone we know better—Amberlyn knows everyone—but we've noticed you're the diligent one in our midst. Head down, recording the imparted wisdom." He smiles, making sure I register his words as complimentary.

I want to tell him that I only take notes to avoid staring at his aura the entire class, but that is not wholly accurate, nor does it seem like a prudent thing to reveal. And besides, his aura has evaporated now anyway.

He tries a different tack. "We'd be glad to buy you a coffee, or a beer, if you prefer? Some pizza to go with it?"

In an effort to camouflage my eager willingness, I say, "Hold out for the bribe. I have noticed that it usually comes."

Tweed throws his head back and laughs. "Indeed! Do we have a deal?"

"I doubt you will decipher my handwriting, but by the time you realize it, I will have consumed the bribe. Caveat emptor."

Tweed opens his mouth and closes it again before he draws himself up and grins. "I'll take my chances, Blisse. You don't strike me as a swindler." On a scrap of paper, he scribbles out a note with a time and place to meet them later, tucks it into my binder, and issues his lackadaisical two-finger salute before bounding for the escalators, briefly glancing back over his shoulder at me.

I remain in place, dumbfounded that he looks even more

attractive without his outer blue glow. I breathe in deeply. There is more oxygen to go around, and with it, a lingering trace of recently dry-cleaned wool. I suddenly want to skip class too. I have the urge to follow Tweed, despite knowing the promise of his company is dependent on generating classroom notes. I start toward the seminar room, then stop. A warm, tingling flood spreads in parts of me that have, thus far, existed in a state of hibernation. I contemplate catching transit home to check if the box of condoms that Ina tucked into my underwear drawer a year earlier—and which I flung under the bed in chagrin-fuelled incredulity—is still there. I imagine myself at a drugstore, having to replace it. But would Tweed not be readily stocked? Perhaps he will read his audition script to me afterward when we linger in bed. Whose bed? I could never bring him home to the twin-size in my back-pantry-off-the-kitchen bedroom. I rest my forehead against the wall outside the seminar room. Since when could a mere glance generate such a problematic debate? How can I possibly scribe notes about tragic soul-bartering and denied redemption when my brain is devolving into runny, sexually charged poached egg?

I reach into my jacket pocket, digging past the wad of unused tissues. My hand closes around the warm and solid metal of the original spoon. I finger the spot where the amethyst used to be. The tiny stone fell off one winter, partway through high school, and was never recovered. I recall the kindness Ina displayed the day I came home, distraught from having lost the stone. It was technically her spoon, but there was no reprimand. She merely took a deep breath, kissed the top of my head, and proclaimed, "A mystical-ass miracle it stayed intact this long." I appreciated Ina's attempt to make light of it—and could not stop the lopsided grin that cut through my tears in response to her newly coined term—but I longed for Petspoon to be whole and intact—at least, as intact as a spoon with a twist could be. As I stand in the hallway, I recognize the irony of carrying my father's gift to my mother around

The Twistical Nature of Spoons

with me for comfort, while at the same time ignoring its origins over the past several years. I push it back down into my pocket and enter the seminar room. Mind over matter—even when the matter is a guy whose aura just burst before my eyes.

•—•

Tweed's note specifies the name of a restaurant on Corydon Avenue, in the heart of Winnipeg's Little Italy, where I am to meet them. Since they are treating, I do not mind that it is not exactly convenient for me. I board a bus that does not run on my familiar route as the autumn dusk sets in. I am relieved they are already seated in the dining room when I arrive. Tweed rises from his chair as I approach the table, and in the dim lighting, I scan to see if his aura has returned. It has not.

"Hey there, Blisse. Good you could make it."

"Sit here," Amberlyn says, indicating the seat next to her, rather than one on Tweed's side of the table.

I obey and launch in. "I have your notes. I photocopied two sets. At the library. I did not know those machines can make change now." I dig into my backpack.

"Yes, indeed they do," Tweed says, an eyebrow raised at what I guess is my awkwardness.

Amberlyn gathers her cascading curls and sweeps them off her shoulders as she breathes out, "Oh, right. Copying costs money."

Tweed reaches into his jeans pocket. "We must compensate you."

I shake my head. "Oh no. This invitation is my compensation."

Tweed fishes out a five-dollar bill. "I insist."

"But it only cost one dollar and fifty cents."

"No need to make change," Tweed states.

"Oh," I say, too embarrassed to reach for the cash. I should never have mentioned anything monetary. I manage to say, "Let us leave it for our server, then. Thank you." As I pass each of them the notes, I add, "Professor Honeywell sulked at your absence. I believe he was on the brink of cancelling class. Are the two of you privy to where he buried the body or something?"

Tweed and Amberlyn glance at one another, taken aback.

Feeling my cheeks flush, I say, "I suppose gallows humour is not everyone's cup of tea."

At that, Tweed smirks, and turns his attention to the wine carafe our waitress is placing on the table. "Perhaps an alternate libation?" he suggests and starts filling Amberlyn's glass.

She looks relieved and drawls, "Looove some!"

"Just a bit, thank you," I agree, but do not elaborate on the fact that it is only my second time drinking alcohol, and that the first time ended badly. "What I meant was, Professor Honeywell seems to adore you both to the point of obsequiousness."

"Whoa!" Amberlyn leans forward, raising her hand to the side of her mouth to feign confidentiality. "Tweed, you didn't tell me I'd need a dictionary tonight." She proceeds to swill the contents of her glass and then holds it up for a toast. "To Professor Honeywell's obsequiousness."

As we clink glasses, I sputter, "Oh, and your auditions …?"

Tweed says, "Cast list will be posted tomorrow. Until then, we wait."

"Which play is it?"

"*Harbouring*. You won't know it. We're premiering it, actually."

Amberlyn chimes in, "The playwright sent our director the script this summer, and our class workshopped it all September. Tweed and I were extra psyched about it, and we were assigned to read the lead roles more often than not. We're shoo-ins."

I say, "Oh, the leads! I will buy a ticket to see it."

"Isn't that sweet, Tweed?" Amberlyn says and reaches across the table to touch his hand.

The Twistical Nature of Spoons

"Indeed." Tweed looks down at her fingers lingering on his before addressing me. "You're a first-year, right? It's on the syllabus that you're expected to contribute backstage, and it's compulsory to audition next year."

"Oh, no," I clarify, "I am not a theatre major. I am enrolled in English Literature. Comedy and Tragedy is my elective."

"Ah! Too bad," he responds, his tone tinged with genuine disappointment. "But the production department always needs volunteers if you're interested. No experience required."

Amberlyn shakes her head at Tweed's suggestion. She peers at me through her glass before tipping it back for a full swig.

I take a sip of my own drink, feeling that I somehow am not measuring up. I blurt, "Well, I have been on stage from a young age."

"Do tell," she insists, taking another gulp of wine.

"Ah, well not in a true dramatic capacity. I am a magician's assistant. Amateur, well semi-professional, I suppose. We do some shows gratis for charity—"

"Indeed!" Tweed interjects.

"But we are paid for most others," I rush to conclude.

Amberlyn sets down her glass. "How unique. Ever dined with a magician's assistant before, Tweed?"

"Can't say I have. Here's to tricks!" he says, raising his glass.

She smirks and slaps his free hand. "You are so naughty, Tweed."

"Oh, no," he says, looking apologetically at me. "I didn't mean it that way at all."

"You did so," she insists.

Tweed refutes her a second time, "No offense intended, Blisse. Though I'm afraid things will only get worse as we progress through this wine, so you'd better keep pace with us." He tops up my glass despite my protests.

Amberlyn holds hers up, empty.

By the time the extra-large pizza arrives, it is accompanied by a third carafe. The wine has made me morose, while also emboldening me. "How can you be so confident you are both cast in the play? What if one of you gets a lead and the other does not? Horrible, horrible thought. Would you still be friends?"

Amberlyn has started responding to everything I say with the same sense of delight that one exhibits when watching pets perform commands. "Isn't she adorable, Tweed? Caring so much?"

Tweed replies, but his voice does not have the same mocking edge. "Indeed," he agrees. "Rare attributes."

"And she's only just met us," Amberlyn says, balancing her pizza slice in both hands and biting in with gusto. Her eyes open wide as she chews and swallows before exclaiming, "So delicious!"

Tweed raises his glass and tips it forward, as if saluting me. "That is an apt word. I couldn't agree more."

"You haven't even tasted it yet," Amberlyn complains.

"Oh … you meant the pizza. I thought you were referring to …" he allows his voice to trail off intentionally and smiles at me before using his knife and fork to cut into his slice.

I feel the room tilt slightly, certain it is not the wine, but rather Tweed who is causing my disorientation. I resume my previous subject. "Well, I hope you both get lead roles, so there are no hard feelings."

Amberlyn sets down her pizza. "Geez, stop worrying, okay?" She wipes her hands on a cloth napkin and digs into her purse, producing a very tired-looking, orange-hued rabbit's foot. "I never audition without my lucky charm. I can't help but get the part."

Tweed smirks. "Oh Lord, Ambs. I can't believe you're still carrying that thing around."

She looks hurt, and turns angry when Tweed scoops it off the table. "Give it back, Tweed!" she insists.

He holds it over his head. "Not until you repeat after me: I, Amberlyn Cache, don't require a rabbit's foot for luck. I have formidable natural talent."

The Twistical Nature of Spoons

Amberlyn turns a deep crimson, but stays silent.

Tweed looks at me. "She's a standout when the curtain rises, and she knows it. Why she continues to carry this thing around with her, I haven't the slightest idea. Though, I suppose actors *do* cling to the strangest superstitions. I can't wait to utter 'Macbeth' backstage this year."

"Don't you dare!" she cries. "You'll jinx the whole show."

"It's a university production of an unproduced script, Ambs. It's half jinxed already."

"Ha! You know the script is brilliant, and you're hungry for a good review. Now, give me back my rabbit's foot, Tweed."

"You haven't completed your pledge."

Amberlyn gives up on retrieving her talisman. She slumps back in her chair and takes another long pull of her wine. "You're a dickhead, Tweed. You're the star and you know it; you're just fishing for compliments in front of Blissful here."

"Wouldn't dream of it," Tweed counters, and reaches across the table, rubbing the soft rabbit's foot down the length of Amberlyn's bare forearm before placing it back in her hand. "I doubt Blisse is impressed with the likes of us."

His actions unnerve me. I exclaim, "Oh, but I am!" Aware that I am speaking with my mouth full, but unable to restrain myself, I add, "I am so very impressed."

Amberlyn wraps her fingers around the rabbit's foot. "And here's where we pledge allegiance to the Mutual Admiration Society." With her free hand, she raises her glass again. "She claims she's impressed, but she's toying with us, Tweed. She's been an entertainer for years. Abracadabra!" Amberlyn waves the rabbit's foot in the air as if it were a magic wand, knocking the pizza server off the raised tray.

Tweed catches it before it upends our wine glasses and checks over his shoulder to make sure management is not about to ask us to leave. This sets us all laughing.

An overwhelming feeling of camaraderie washes over me—a tide augmented by alcohol. I reach into my jacket pocket and brandish the original spoon. "I have a good luck charm too," I proclaim. "I store it in a secret pocket in my costume every time I step on stage." I giggle, trying to focus on it.

"What the fuck happened to that thing?" Amberlyn demands, looking at its contorted twist. She reaches for it.

I sober in a split second, horrified that I have revealed the spoon to virtual strangers. I jerk it out of her reach. "Uh, puh-uh …" I stammer, "it got jammed between equipment boxes. It twisted … but survived. That proves it is lucky." I change tactics. "But Amberlyn, you do not need a talisman. Trumpet fanfare, please! Your talent … what is it they say? You are the whole package. Talent *and* beauty. Agreed, Tweed?" I ask, feeling my eyebrows stuck somewhere high on my forehead.

Tweed does not immediately answer. He watches as I bury Petspoon deep inside my backpack and leans forward. "That spoon is a one-of-a-kind original." He nods, then adds, "Yes, talent, beauty, and a tad off-kilter," but his gaze is still levelled on me, as if he is not thinking of Amberlyn at all.

From the corner of my eye, I see Amberlyn flick him a look that is a notch below affectionate. A trickle of venom follows as she says, "Oh, you and your superior judgement, Mr. Halverden. You, who languish in a state of unfulfilled ennui despite all those inherited tweed jackets, and the random apartment blocks and suburban strip malls that were put in trust for you along with them. Poor misunderstood soul. Perhaps what you need, what you are lacking, my Tweedy Bird, is your very own lucky charm."

I find it the most intriguing of coincidences that I often thought of my father as Petey Bird whenever my mother referred to him by his nickname, and now the fellow I cannot stop thinking about has been called "Tweedy Bird." To stifle a giggle, I must summon my stage face.

The Twistical Nature of Spoons

Tweed is smirking, as if Amberlyn's attempt to bait him pleases him to no end, but when he catches me beaming at him, his expression alters, turns pensive. He sits back to remove his wallet from an inner pocket in his jacket, but keeps his assessing gaze locked on me. His scrutiny makes me wriggle in my chair. He does not even glance in Amberlyn's direction when he responds, "Ambsie, you should know by now, if I get any luckier, I might burst."

Ina

grasps

Blisse blew past her place setting at the kitchen table, her backpack strap snagging on a chair spindle. As she untangled it, I blocked her path to the door.

"What about your dinner?"

"I have to go back to campus to do some research for my paper."

"But you'll be starving."

Blisse patted her bag. "I have garlic-free snacks."

"Your library carrel will be offended by chilli breath?"

"I might go out afterward."

"Where?"

She shrugged.

"With who?"

She adjusted her newsboy cap's brim to shield her eyes. Her long, fine hair was brushed to a shine, and she fussed with it to straighten the strands she'd disturbed. "With some university friends," she answered. Her hand movements sent forth a watt of perfume.

My little cocooned butterfly had emerged. With gladness swelling in my heart, I resisted prying and changed tacks, sniffing the air. "Is that the sample?"

Blisse nodded, and offered up her wrist. "Yes, thanks for getting it."

"Doesn't smell like sunflowers to me," I said.

"Despite its name, I do not believe that is the intention," she responded, pulling her arm away to check her watch. "If I do not leave now, I will be stuck waiting for the next bus or will have to walk."

I opened the kitchen door and noticed, not for the first time, that the Halloween decorations in the foyer were still waiting for me to pack them away. "When will you be home, Blisse?"

"You do not have to wait up, Ina." She clutched her backpack strap as if bracing herself. "As you point out, ad infinitum, I am legally an adult now."

There was a part of me that wanted to block her way again. Instead, I followed her to the front door and forced a cheerful goodbye. "Be careful out there."

She was already bounding off the porch before she answered, her farewell flung out to the open sidewalk. The silence that followed was wounding. I closed the door behind her and squinted through the stained-glass windowpane; watched her traipse down the street, through the skiff of snow and rotting leaves. To stop myself from waving, I pressed my fingers against the cold glass.

Avoiding the ghouls and caved-in jack-o'-lanterns, I headed straight for the basement stairs. If I could just get to the point where my hands were working, I could maybe stop worrying about Blisse out alone at night. I rolled my shoulders, let the next worry settle in. I'd been down there most of the day and several evenings already that week, but the physical toll wasn't as bad as the panic I was feeling from having actually agreed to mount my first gallery show—a commitment that I'd ducked until I revealed

The Twistical Nature of Spoons

the *moretta* mask to Blisse for the first time and she said it was the most magical thing she'd ever seen, and that I should make a million more and sell them around the globe. Admittedly, at the time, she might have been preoccupied with her first essay deadline, and a compliment was the quickest way to be rid of me. I chose to take the praise at face value. It was gratifying to have her approval. A thousand paying customers couldn't have equalled it. And if she hadn't continued to admire the new pieces I showed her, I might have turned chicken, pulled out of my co-op gallery membership, and cancelled my upcoming show—content to return to craft-booth rentals. It was as if her endorsement of my work completed a miraculous circular connection to Taras. He'd roused my yearning—my need to create something meaningful—and Blisse's words stoked that ambition, helping the fear fall away.

In my workshop, there was barely space left to move. Aside from the rows of completed masks, the room was crammed with bolts of linen and velvet, pots of paste, buckram rolls, stacks of newsprint, spray paint cans, spools of copper foil, and sheets of stained glass. I should have stuck to one medium and one mould, but I wanted to stake my own claim within the domain of mask-making, without agonizing that Taras's work would nip at my heels until it chased me off his territory.

I moved some sketches off my wooden shop stool and perched on it. I was about to spend my first night completely ignorant of Blisse's whereabouts. The masks seemed to be expressing their disapproval of my parenting skills. But who were they to be critical? I'd designed the early pieces to emulate Blisse's childhood innocence. They should have been reassuring me instead of adding to my anxiety.

Since the arrival of Taras's final letter, his book had remained untouched in the rafters. But that night, it beckoned like a bad addiction. My feelings of inadequacy and terror needed a fix. I moved my stool, reached up into the rafters, and brought the volume down, clutching it to my chest. With Blisse out for the night and the masks staring at me, I wanted to be near my daughter's other parent; to be reassured there was nothing to fear. His letters slipped out from between the covers and scattered. I stuffed them back between the pages. Selecting a *servetta muta* from a shelf, I placed it in front of my face. I held up the book and looked at Taras's author photo looking back at me through his mask. I wondered why I was so bad at foreseeing which moments in my life would retain meaning and grow disproportionately dominant, and which would drop away, meaningless and forgotten. My own naivety and dumbass ignorance astounded me. I'd taken another risk writing those letters, when what I really needed was to retain anonymity.

A new fear gripped my heart. I bounded up the stairs and dialled the gallery. Relief flooded through me when a person answered.

"Oh, hey, Ina. Lars here. We're just closing up for the night and headed out for drinks. Care to join?"

"No, but thanks for asking. Listen, I've had an idea. I need to literally stop the presses. I don't want my name to appear on any of the promo stuff. We settled on my artist photo being the one with me wearing a mask, right?"

"Yeah, but … hang on. Rosie, it's Ina. She says she doesn't want her name to appear on the publicity."

Rosie came on the line. "What's this shit, Ina? The whole point of publicity is getting your name out there."

"Just tell me, is it too late?" I asked.

"No, but what are we supposed to—"

"I want every piece of publicity to refer to me as Eye Trove, not Ina Trove. *E-y-e*, not *I*."

"Eye Trove?" she repeated.

"Yes. I mean, it's multi-layered. An 'eye' for an 'I.' *E-y-e* Trove is a play on my initial, I. Trove. The exhibit is also a 'trove'—a collection for the eye. And the eyes are the focal point of my masks. Some with, some without, some bespectacled. Do you get it?"

The Twistical Nature of Spoons

"Cool," Rosie said. "Yeah, I get it. *E-y-e* like it. But are you prepared to be known as 'Eye' in the future?"

"Why not?" I said.

"Well, then consider it done. But I repeat, apart from the poster, there's no budget for publicity. We depend on local freebies. If we're lucky, the media gives us a shout-out."

"That's perfect. Thank you." We ended the call, and I returned downstairs to my work table where I rested my head, relieved to have another layer of disguise.

•—•—•

I woke with a start, my cheek damply clinging to an open page of Taras's book. I slammed the volume shut and listened. Something had startled me out of my sleep. The wall clock read half past two. It was the middle of the night. I bolted up the basement stairs and saw that Blisse's bedroom door remained wide open, with no sign that she'd slept in her bed. Where was she?

Muffled chuckling drifted from the front of the house. I flung open the kitchen door, spilling light into the foyer. Blisse was sitting on the floor, cap on backward, her long hair a dishevelled tangle beneath it. She was attempting to stifle her laughter. Her backpack contents were strewn around a ghoulish tombstone and its rotten, protruding hand, which seemed to be reaching for her lip glosses and highlighter markers.

When Blisse saw me, she uncovered her mouth and put an index finger to her lips. She whispered, a dribble of spittle accompanying her slurred words, "Shh, Ina. Knowlton is sleeping upshhtairs, shh. Look, I tripped. See?" She pointed to her feet. "On the bottom step."

"Blisse, how did you get home?"

"In the tax-eee."

I sighed.

"In the tax-eee that Tweed knows," she asserted. "He must know the tax-eee because I did not even have to pay! Tweed knows a lot of people in Winnipeg."

I frowned. "You were out with that couple from your class again?"

She straightened her back, and I noticed that the buttons of her plaid wool coat were misaligned.

She exclaimed, "No! No, they are not a couple. She is hishh shheatre friend. Did they tell you they are a couple, Ina? You are lying!" She cocked her head at me, crossed her arms over her chest, and pouted.

"Whoa, Blisse. No. I know nothing about their relationship. I've never even met them."

She brightened. "They are my friends. A *couple* of my friends. Not a couple. Just friends. I have never had friends who know soooo many people."

"They had a party, then?"

She tilted her head back and cooed up the stairs, "*Croo-CROOK-croo* … Shh, Ina, listen. I am home, dovey-loveys! Oh no, Pocket and Bishhcuit do not recognize my voice."

"They're asleep," I insisted, and then repeated my question. "You were at a party?"

"Indeed!"

"Indeed?"

"Indeed, it was an after-rehearshhal party."

"Oh," I said, and offered my hand to help her up from the floor.

She ignored my gesture and said, "Because, Ina, it happened after rehearshhal. They rehearsed and then the party. Simple." She nodded her head, evidently pleased with her imparted wisdom, and then pointed her finger at me for emphasis. "Indeed! 'Indeed' is what Tweed likes to say. It is not an affuck … Oops! Ha! It is not an … affectation. He is sincere when he says it. His name is

The Twistical Nature of Spoons

Theodore. Tweed is only his nickname. But if you ashhk me …" she paused. "Go ahead and ask me."

"Ask you what?"

"If you ashhk me, his nickname should be Indeed Tweed!" Blisse threw her arms back and laughed. Her hand smacked the banister hard, and when she brought it back down to cradle it, she knocked her hat over her face, tipping her glasses askew. I thought she was shaking with laughter, but tears were spilling down her cheeks.

I sighed and removed her hat.

"Oouchh, my hand, Ina!" she announced to the neighbourhood.

"Let's get you to bed, Missy Blissey. We'll talk in the morning."

"No, no, no, you cannot talk to me in the morning. Because I am in love, and in the morning, I will still be in love. I love him, Ina. Shh, no talking."

She looked up at me, her hurt hand nestled over her heart, her eyes glistening with tears, but her smile was so bright, it rendered her almost unrecognizable. She had perfected a fake smile for her part in the Magical Influx Show, but her expression at the foot of the stairs that night was sincere and transformative.

"Well, well," was all I could muster as I plunked down on the bottom step.

"Well, well," she agreed and continued to beam. "Sit down," she insisted and smacked the step next to her where I was already seated. She stopped. Her eyelids fluttered. "Do not be sad underneath, Ina. I am so very tired of shhad." She closed her eyes.

"What do you mean, you're tired of sad, Blisse?" I squawked.

But she'd conked out.

I hadn't noticed Knowlton on the stairway landing above us until he cleared his throat. Tightening the belt of his oversized velour housecoat, he murmured, "Need a hand getting her to bed, Ina?"

"She's three sheets to the wind, Knowlton."

He nodded and ran a hand over his thinning scalp as he descended a few more steps.

I spat, "And what did she mean, she's 'tired of sad,' Knowlton? Gawd help me."

"I don't think you can take … You shouldn't put too much stock in the last words she uttered before passing out, Ina."

"What about the part before that? The *being in love* part?"

"I didn't hear that," Knowlton said with delight.

"Not funny, Knowlton. This is not the first time this Tweed fellow has gotten her drunk. It happened two weeks back. Not to this extent. She was coherent that night."

"She's eighteen, Ina. You're lucky it took this long."

"I should never have encouraged this by pouring that graduation champagne."

"You are fully to blame," he responded, smiling. His attempt to calm me backfired.

"Well, call me a hypocrite, Knowlton, because even though she's the best thing that ever happened to me, I don't want Blisse knocked up, okay?"

Knowlton cleared his throat a second time. "Did you not give her those packets you asked me to purchase some time ago? And no doubt she's aware of more effective options."

"Like a chastity belt, Knowlton?"

He turned to head back up the stairs.

"Hey, I thought you were going to help me put her to bed?"

"It's probably best not to disturb her. All she needs is a blanket and pillow. I actually came down to speak to Blisse, but obviously that's not possible."

"What's up, Knowlton?"

"I don't want to burden you, Ina. It can wait."

"I have all night here. She could choke on her own vomit. I won't sleep."

He descended the stairs again, stepped around us, and stood

The Twistical Nature of Spoons

next to a plastic skeleton suspended from the ceiling. "Well, as you know, Blisse has been wonderful with Biscuit and Pocket. I'd never have replaced the others when old age overtook them without Blisse and her gentle insistence. She actually said, 'The show must go on, Mr. Fluxcer.' Thirteen-year-old wisdom. And training the new birds has been a great joy to me. Especially in Biscuit's case. He seems to thrive in the spotlight, like Blisse herself."

With my daughter lying passed out on the floor, I didn't have much patience for Knowlton's lingering melancholy over the passing of his three original doves, but I did my best to console him. "You give those birds a wonderful life, Knowlton. Blisse loves that you share them with her."

He nodded. "And I knew it would happen eventually ... She told me recently that she wouldn't have the time. Her studies. So she's stopped participating in the care of Biscuit and Pocket."

I swallowed hard. "She has? I've been so distracted. I ..."

Knowlton nodded. "It's fine, Ina. We agreed. University is a lot of pressure."

I let out a long sigh and rubbed the back of my neck, which was extra stiff from falling asleep at my work table. I tilted my head and noticed how Knowlton looked older in the partial light.

He gulped. "The thing is, I received a call today. A request." He stopped as if he was going to turn tail and head back up the stairs without finishing.

"A request?" I urged him to continue.

"From the Canopy Club Telethon."

"The one that broadcasts every December?"

Knowlton nodded. His eyes beseeched me to make the connection so he didn't have to say more.

"Wait! Does the Canopy Club want the Magical Influx Show on the telethon?"

He nodded vigorously.

"That's amazing, Knowlton! You're going to be on TV! What

great exposure, not to mention supporting an important cause." I clasped my hands together and laughed, then shushed myself so I wouldn't wake Blisse.

Knowlton murmured, more to himself than to me, "They admitted that another act cancelled. And it seems ridiculous for me to admit … but I've waited my whole life for such a moment."

"Well, I get that," I insisted. "It's a big deal."

"But, Ina, I've come to rely on Blisse. Something about her presence makes me feel like I'm a real magician."

"Well, you are, Knowlton." I narrowed my eyes at him. "You've been at this a long time. Kids love your show."

"No. You must understand, Ina. I rely on Blisse being a stickler for practical details, but I also know the audience senses her intangible mystique. And she says things like, 'Even if a show is flawed, we must congratulate each other for doing our best.' She is an old soul, Ina."

I looked at her on the floor. "Old soul succumbs to reckless immaturity," I muttered.

He shook his head before I could interrupt further. "The telecast is right before exam period. I'm certain it's harder to fool the camera. There isn't much rehearsal time to prep for that. I think … I am sure Blisse was trying to tell me she was quitting the show when she gave up the dove care, but just couldn't admit it all at once." He bowed his head.

I was about to tell him he was making assumptions when he added, "I can't ask her to join me now, Ina. Especially if she is dating. Her studies. Her first beau." He blurted, "Would you ask her?"

"Me? I think she would be more receptive to you …" I swept my hand toward her. "She's not really listening to my advice these days."

"I've decided I will happily retire afterward. Blisse will not be pressured to continue. And she won't have to officially quit either."

"Retire? Knowlton, that's crazy. You're supposed to retire from teaching soon so you can do more magic shows."

The Twistical Nature of Spoons

He shook his head. "My mind is made up, Ina. I will continue to dabble in apparatus construction. But no more shows. Biscuit, Pocket, and I can retire from the scene together. We're no longer spring chickens, you know?"

I couldn't help but smile at his attempt at humour, which seemed to give him permission to repeat his question. "Will you please convince Blisse to do this one last show?"

I gently urged, "Knowlton, just ask. She won't say no."

He did not look convinced. "I'm asking you to ask for me. I think you owe me that, Ina, for guarding your secret all this time."

I sprang to my feet and put a finger to my lips. With Blisse so close, even conked out, I had to stop him from saying another word. I nodded an okay.

"Thank you," he said, and set the bones of the Halloween skeleton clacking as he shuffled around us on his way back to his suite.

10

Blisse

ideal congealed

The Canopy Club Telethon will commence in the pre-dawn hours tomorrow morning. Mr. Fluxcer and I, along with all the other booked talent, are attending the final pre-production meeting. The television studio is abuzz with excitement, but I am wishing that the Magical Influx Show included a disappearing act. I have not admitted to Mr. Fluxcer the real reason why I agreed to perform one last show with him, allowing him and Ina to believe that my acquiescence was so that he could have his last hurrah—his swan song. His gratitude was palpable, and so it did not seem wrong to avoid mentioning, that by a stroke of serendipity, Tweed and Amberlyn were also making their debut at the same telethon event, representing the university with a short excerpt from *Harbouring*. Whenever I am near Tweed, a keen intensity vibrates between us, but as of late, play rehearsals have dominated his and Amberlyn's lives, making the pair even more inseparable; and although I have volunteered to do advance ticket sales and front-of-house ushering for their upcoming run, it has given me no more access to either of them than if I had remained glued to my studies in a library carrel.

I am unsure if the price of deceiving Mr. Fluxcer has been worth it. While I anticipated our event-in-common would generate further camaraderie between Tweed and me, there has been no such result. And now, with the revised final schedule in hand, and the discovery that our two acts have been placed within the same half-hour segment near the start of the live telecast, I fear that it will be Mr. Fluxcer who sits up and takes notice, realizing the thespians performing two acts before us are my classmates, thus deducing my real motivation.

As the producer wraps up the proceedings and bids us good evening, I attempt to hurry us toward the exit, both to avoid an encounter with my friends and to ensure Mr. Fluxcer gets some sleep before we return for our 4:30 a.m. call. The throng of people who remain milling about on the studio floor impedes our progress.

Then I hear Tweed's voice hailing me. "Blisse! We found you in this chaos."

My impulse to scurry in the opposite direction is matched by my desire to crash through the crowd and throw myself at him. I turn and wave. "Tweed. Amberlyn." I flash an Influx Show smile.

Tweed cranes his neck around a man toting an accordion case. I consider using the opportunity to lose them in the crowd as we funnel toward the lobby, but Tweed's satirical grin jolts that thought out of me. I consider heading upstream and losing Mr. Fluxcer instead, but he is not allowing himself to get too far ahead. Near the exit, the crowd thins, and we find a spot to pause as Tweed and Amberlyn reach us.

Tweed speaks first. "Hello, Blisse, and you must be Mr. Knowlton Fluxcer. Pleased to meet you."

I feel the need to take over the introductions as Tweed extends a firm business handshake to Mr. Fluxcer, who seems somewhat

The Twistical Nature of Spoons

discombobulated. I marvel at my awkwardness over such a simple task.

Mr. Fluxcer nods. "Hello, Theodore. Amber," he says vaguely.

"Amber*lyn*," I correct.

"Please, call me Tweed. All my friends do."

"Ah!" Mr. Fluxcer exclaims. "You are the duo from Blisse's early-morning class."

Before I can mumble further explanation, Amberlyn nods, and exclaims, "Enchanted! Aren't we, Tweed?"

"Indeed. Looking forward to watching your segment, sir."

Amberlyn's eyebrows climb her forehead. "You're staying after our performance, Tweed? I'm heading straight back to my bed after we're done our bit. You heard that producer—they want us in the green room a full hour before our airtime. That's indecently early!" she says, beaming under the influence of her own melodrama.

"Well, I'm sticking around for the *magic*," Tweed insists, and Mr. Fluxcer looks down at his own feet, flushing at what appears to be Tweed's genuine interest. When he does so, Tweed shoots me a look that intimates it is not the idea of pulling a rabbit from a hat that is capturing his attention. My heart rate spikes, but I hold his gaze.

Amberlyn responds with a narrow-eyed glare.

"Say," Tweed remarks, "we're meeting our director—she is in this throng of talent somewhere—and the other cast members for one quick drink in Old Market Square. It's a bit of a pre-broadcast celebration. Even our reclusive playwright is joining us."

Amberlyn brightens. "You'd love our scribe. His genius is hampered only by his hapless romanticism."

Tweed shoots her a sideways glance, but continues, "Why don't you both come along?"

Mr. Fluxcer's demeanour shifts from bemused to crestfallen as the truth dawns. "Your play is also part of this event," he states.

Allowing him to believe the best in me has been a betrayal I had not fully understood until that moment. As I imagine his potential hurt, my childhood apprehensions rampage: Will his legs detach? Will he crumple sideways, his abbreviated torso forced to balance on the lobby floor?

To steer the conversation to neutrality, I spew, "It would be a novelty to join fellow performers for a drink."

Mr. Fluxcer nods in a preoccupied manner, and I recognize my ineptitude at social manoeuvring. With a full bloom of anxiety unfurling inside me, I reach deep into my coat pocket and grasp the original spoon so tightly that its edges dig into my skin.

Amberlyn, not to be ignored, adds, "You should come. Our cast members are dying to know more about tomorrow's acts. The telethon scene is just Tweed and me. Did Blisse mention we are the leads?"

Mr. Fluxcer clears his throat. "Blisse seems very smitten by your talents."

Tweed responds, "And Blisse has expressed how fortunate she is to be part of your show."

There is a brief teetering as Mr. Fluxcer weighs the truthfulness of Tweed's statement. "She has?"

"Oh, indeed," Tweed confirms. "Blisse confided to me recently that you are not just a mentor, but her hero."

I scrutinize Mr. Fluxcer's face as he chooses to believe the words. To avoid throwing myself at Tweed in gratitude, I reach over and pat Mr. Fluxcer's arm. I cannot recall having made any such statement, but I do not remember half of what I said at the last party. And even if Tweed is telling a white lie, he is saving me from the consequences of my own deception. My anxiety regarding the separation of Mr. Fluxcer's legs and torso subsides.

Tweed persists, "Now, about that beverage?"

Mr. Fluxcer replies, "Oh, thank you. But with our time slot so early, I must head home. Try for some shuteye."

In my heightened state of relief, I cajole, "It is only one drink. Perhaps it will help relax us. Please say yes, Knowlton."

The Twistical Nature of Spoons

I startle at my own enthusiasm, which is quickly quashed when I hear Amberlyn mutter, "Slippers and warm milk for you, Gramps?"

I want to point out that, moments earlier, she was the one complaining about the early call time, but I remain silent, and Mr. Fluxcer does not respond to her either. Instead, he shakes his head by way of apology and says, "We should be off, Blisse."

"Um, I … I will not stay out late."

"It's no problem for me to drive Blisse home afterward if that helps." Tweed holds up his two-finger salute. "I'll even pledge to a non-alcoholic brew to ensure she arrives safely."

Mr. Fluxcer shifts from one foot to the other. I avoid his look of unspoken appeal. I know that I am committing a second act of betrayal, but I cannot help myself—cannot throw away the opportunity to spend time in Tweed's orbit.

"Well," Mr. Fluxcer concedes, clearing his throat. "I'll let you young folk be on your way. Should I let your mother know, Blisse?"

When I do not immediately answer, Tweed concurs. "Indeed. Kind of you, sir."

It might have been easier calling out a goodbye to Mr. Fluxcer if he had been adamant I return home with him. I could have then disobeyed and felt self-righteous. Instead, his display of magnanimity makes me further squirm with guilt. Despite being abandoned and betrayed, he is willing to face a surefire interrogation from Ina. He waves as he exits along with the dwindling crowd. To distract myself from the impulse to catch up to him and return home, I tap the spoon in my pocket until I achieve perfect unison with my own rapid heartbeat.

Tweed gestures, "Shall we?"

The three of us step outside to discover a deluge of huge wet snowflakes. A thick white coat blankets the grassy boulevards, while the pavement and concrete remain clear of accumulations.

"Wow," I utter.

Amberlyn ignores the change in weather as she queries, "Is Mr. Fucksir your great-uncle or something?"

"No," I say absently, reaching my hand out to intercept some large flakes, their intricate designs melting away in a blink. A small red welt remains on my upturned palm where the souvenir spoon dug into it earlier. "Mr. *Flux*-cer," I correct her. "He is our lodger." A prickly shame spreads over me with this admission. In haste, I state, "Big house. Just me and my mother, Ina, kicking around in it otherwise."

Amberlyn feigns a light smack to her forehead. "*Fluxcer*, not Fucksir. How dumb of me." Then she adds, "Divorce by-product?"

It is not clear if she is referring to him, our big house, or me. I know I should treat it as a rhetorical question, but I want her to drop her mockery and dismissive attitude. If she is Tweed's friend, I should want her to be my friend too. "No, no divorce." Summoning as much stoicism as I can muster, I add, "My father died before my birth." I gulp air, unaccustomed to speaking of him to anyone outside of my household.

As if charmed, my breath returns when Tweed places his hand on my back. It rests there for a moment as he says, "That's tough." He lets it fall with a soft stroke down my spine. "My father stands at the central podium of my life, touting my virtues." He shrugs. "At the same time, he's up there silently praying for a quick death to my artistic pursuits so I can join the family biz."

"Yes," Amberlyn nods, and adjusts her pace to fall in step alongside Tweed. "There are worse things than *no* father."

"It is fine," I say. "Ina kept him alive for me when I was younger, telling me of their love for one another, but now I feel as if I must let go. I do not want his absence to become the litmus strip by which I test all other potential resentments."

Tweed lets out a whistle. "Remarkable. What planet are you from?" He cocks his head as if searching my face for tell-tale traces of alien.

The Twistical Nature of Spoons

Amberlyn shakes snow from her hair. "Or, like, what's your therapist's number? I need to call their office."

I am uncertain if there is a trace of truth in my statement, or if my need to impress somehow generated it. I raise my coat collar to prevent wet flakes from dripping down my neck and to keep from admitting out loud to the disquiet that the story of my father's murder instilled in me. A wondrous halo of white around the adjacent parking lot lights grabs my eye, and I note how the snow falls with an earnest, but silent, enthusiasm. I stick my tongue out to capture some flakes as Tweed places a hand on my elbow, just long enough to indicate we have reached his car. Amberlyn pushes the passenger bucket seat forward to allow me access behind it. The squeak of expensive leather is somehow reassuring as I clamber into the low-slung back seat.

As soon as Amberlyn is settled in the front, Tweed peels out of the parking spot, the tires hissing on the slick pavement. He leans forward and looks up through the windshield. "This weather is something," he mutters, then says, "Ambs, I think I might have to skip out on this drink."

She is shrill when she answers. "What? You can't. We have to go." She turns to me in the back seat to explain her insistence. "On top of the celebration, the playwright's presence tonight is a not-to-be-missed opportunity."

Tweed taunts, "For you to practise your flirtation skills on an older man?"

"Oh, do I detect a hint of jealousy? Of his continental air? Of the way he exudes mystery from every pore of his body?"

Tweed guffaws. "Ambs, tell me you haven't already slept with him? What is it with you and older guys?"

She puckers her mouth and then sniffs. "It's not like he's Fluxcer-old. Seriously, I just want to talk to him about those beats in act 2."

"He said the pages are in our hands now. I'm good with that.

And I promised my parents I'd check my grandfather's place. You talked me out of it earlier this week, and now there's this snow …" His voice trails off as he slows for a red light.

"But exactly, Tweedy Bird! You can't drive out past Lockport in this. Wait until after the telethon tomorrow."

"Could be two feet of snow on the ground by then," he refutes.

"So wait for the snowploughs."

"I need to do this tonight. I'll be back home in bed before you even leave the pub."

"Oh, puh-leeze, Mr. Responsible …"

He shoots her a look and sweeps into the loading zone in front of a doorway lit by a coach lamp. "Please extend my regrets to everyone." He hops out of the vehicle and sprints around to hold Amberlyn's door open. "You can fill me in *very* early in the morning."

"Tweed, you can't be serious," she says, her seat belt still secured.

"Indeed, I am," he says in a tone that gives her no choice but to scramble out of his car. He pushes the bucket seat forward. "I promised Mr. Fluxcer I'd get you home, Blisse, so I'll do that first, unless you want to join Amberlyn."

I shake my head.

"Hop in the front, then." Tweed leaves Amberlyn standing on the curb as he signals to pull away. "You should buckle up."

I oblige and then crane my neck to look behind us. "This wet snow will ruin her curls if she does not go inside."

Tweed chortles. "Oh, she won't allow *that* to happen." As he approaches the next intersection, he says, "I'm sorry about curtailing the fun, but I really must see to this. Right or left? … Unless you feel like a drive?"

"Oh," I say, "I … I should get some sleep."

"Indeed."

I jam my hands into my pockets. My fingers close around the original spoon again. It feels warm, almost tingling, to the touch.

The Twistical Nature of Spoons

I run my fingers over its crooked handle and rub hard at its flaw. "Unless you would prefer to have company? Is it far?"

"Not really. I make the trip often. Snow tires are installed, if you're worried about being on the highway."

I blurt, "Ina and I do not have a car; those things never cross my mind."

"No car? How in the world do you get around?"

"On foot. Or transit. Or bicycle. Knowlton also transports us when necessary."

Intrigued, Tweed asks, "Have you cycled as far as Lockport?"

I shake my head. "Never outside the city."

"Is it possible you've never been to Skinner's? Never had a foot-long or ice cream cone there?" he asks, his voice tinged with incredulity.

I rub the spoon harder, unsure of how ridiculous I will appear in his estimation by admitting I have rarely passed the city's perimeter. I reply, "Uh, no. But when it comes to kids' birthday party foods, my primary focus is always the cake."

Tweed guffaws and glances over at me. "Well, the menu is secondary. It's the tradition—the jukebox selections right at your table, the bridge, the locks, the pelicans, the ritual."

"Ah," I say. "I understand."

He shakes his head in amusement. "Clearly, you don't, Blisse Trove."

I have craved Tweed's attention, and now I am uncertain what to do with it. All I know is that I would trade all the magic show applause in the world to hear his voice say my name in that tone again. A witty response eludes me.

Tweed shifts us back to neutral territory. "If I'm a bit overzealous, it's because the drive-in churns up the nostalgia of childhood visits with my grandparents."

I ask, "So we are heading over to check on your grandfather?"

"Just on his house. My parents are vacationing abroad, and the pressure of rehearsals had me putting this off." Tweed's voice wobbles a fraction. "Grandfather will be glad to see me driving past his ashes en route to keeping my promise."

"Oh, I am sorry," I murmur.

We are silent for a moment as we head north, passing through the railway underpass on Main Street, the windshield wipers swiping at the wet snow, which accumulates as fast as the blades can clear it off.

Tweed remarks, "My parents are squabbling over whether to move into the monstrosity or sell it. In retaliation for its undecided fate, the house sulks: it springs leaks, unhinges shutters, allows birds to roost in its chimney. The hullaballoo right now is whether the ancient furnace will give up the ghost."

"What was your grandfather's wish for the house?"

"Astute question. My mother complains old Alfred didn't care about the property, just that I inherited his Harris Tweed jackets."

"Hence your nickname," I declare.

"Indeed. I was in junior high the first time I borrowed one. My corny Sherlock Holmes phase. Somehow, the jackets became my trademark, and the 'Tweed' moniker followed me to campus. My grandfather loved to lend them to me. The first time I returned one freshly dry-cleaned, his eyes got teary."

"You exaggerate?"

"No, he was a tad obsessed. He actually suffered his stroke in the Outer Hebrides when he was visiting one of the Scottish cottagers who hand-weaves the cloth. We trust he died fulfilled."

I mutter a second apology, mystified by how openly Tweed has discussed his family members that evening. I anticipate that he would not consider a bent spoon family to be a legitimate branch on any genealogical tree, so I steer clear of mentioning mine. Instead, I offer, "My grandmother also died and left us her house." I pause and take a deep breath, unable to avoid the exotic, musky overtones of Amberlyn's perfume still clinging to the seat belt. "I believe you are the first person I have discussed that with."

The Twistical Nature of Spoons

Tweed accelerates from a stoplight and the car fishtails. He straightens it out without oversteering. "Getting a little slick out here."

The snow is no longer melting. Tire tracks down the middle of multiple lanes are visible, but all else on the roadway is obscured, blanketed in white.

He glances to the passenger seat. "Am I being selfish? Your segment airs after ours, but not by much. This snow is going to slow us down. Would you prefer I take you home?"

There is nothing I want more than to continue sitting next to Tweed. "That would only delay you more."

"Are you sure? Last chance," he says, and turns the windshield wipers up to a higher frequency.

I ignore my conscience, with its parade of Mr. Fluxcer's detaching body parts. "We should go ahead while we can."

By the time we reach the outskirts of the city, the wind is gusting; snow blows across the highway, forming drifts that finger their way from the shoulders onto the pavement. The farther we proceed, the more traffic diminishes, as do the streetlights. We come upon stretches that are fully snow-packed. The only trustworthy indicator that we are not in the ditch is a single pair of tire tracks leading us forward. In the glow of the car's headlights, the falling snow appears to be sealing us off from the world, but in such a manner that infinity itself seems contained inside Tweed's car.

The undercarriage is beginning to scrape against some snowdrifts, but Tweed does not seem concerned. "Your lodger reminds me of my grandfather. Men who are passionate about odd things, by normal standards—not tracking football or hockey stats—and they pursue that passion, possibly at the peril of other parts of their lives."

"For instance?"

"Relationships. My grandmother scoffed at my grandfather's

closet. Granted, it expanded to the point that it filled an entire spare bedroom. After she passed, he lived without companionship."

I rise up in defence of Mr. Fluxcer. "Oh, but Knowlton's wife had a gambling problem."

"Perhaps a result of her frustration with the time he spent perfecting magic tricks?"

I bow my head, letting my hair screen my face. "Perhaps." I regret having revealed such a private detail of Mr. Fluxcer's life and scramble to deflect attention from him. "Perhaps you are right. And perhaps it is not just men. My mother does not date, and she is consumed right now with mask-making."

"Seriously?" he demands.

"What? You think masks are weirder than tweed clothes or magic tricks?"

"No. It's just that our playwright did mask work in the theatre. What are the chances? As Amberlyn likes to say, 'small fucking world, hey?'"

At the mention of Amberlyn's name, my chest constricts. I thought we had left her at the curb, but she seems to be along for the ride. "Would it bother you if she sleeps with the playwright?" I ask.

Tweed glances over. "Should it?"

Taking a calculated risk, I respond, "To quote my friend Theodore, 'indeed.'"

Tweed smirks in response. "Your friend says that, does he?"

I dare to add, "My *good* friend."

"Lucky Theodore. Let's hope he can live up to your classification of him."

A mutual silence descends as we both think our own thoughts. The whiteout swirls around us.

It is Tweed who clears his throat and breaks the silence. "What types of masks is your mother into?"

"Evolving," I reply.

The Twistical Nature of Spoons

"Evolving? Like a new mask species?"

"They started out as oval *moretta* masks, made from dark velvet and adorned with lush paintings."

"Black velvet painting, like Elvis portraits?" He raises a dubious eyebrow.

I feel myself bristle on Ina's behalf. "Well, Tweed, the history of the art form extends further back than the secular portrayal of a modern pop-culture idol. Orthodox priests painted religious icons on velvet, and I consider Ina's work to be more closely aligned with this early tradition, despite her deviating into the pagan world and depicting elements of nature."

"I beg your pardon, Blisse," he says, contrite. "Didn't mean to imply … Please continue. It's fascinating."

If he is being disingenuous, I cannot detect it. I continue, "And then, from out of the blue, she started making linen half masks with stained-glass eyes. Just recently, I was rummaging through a drawer and held up a pair of my glasses from when I was a child. Offhandedly, I asked if any of her masks were near-sighted. Ina proclaimed me a genius and switched to creating elongated, blank-eyed papier-mâché *bauta* masks wearing exquisite stained-glass spectacles.

"She is self-conscious and private about them. When she does share, she resorts to self-deprecating humour about her 'unifying vision' for the collection, and hums that 'Sunglasses at Night' song. But the masks are impactful, giving off the uncanny impression that they harbour hidden insights."

Tweed cocks his head. "Wild!"

Emboldened, I say, "You should come to her opening."

"I'll be sure to attend. I want to see just how your genius contributed." He covers my hand with his own, his fingers curving into mine.

"Just because my mother thinks it does not mean I am a genius," I snort nervously. I try to ignore the electricity of his touch by continuing to talk. "If I inspired her, it was just a weird fluke of circumstance."

Tweed says, "You don't believe in serendipity?"

I tsk out loud.

He presses on. "We're not *destined* to be here together on this road in this snowstorm?"

I glance over at him. He takes his eyes off the road to assess my expression, and I stare straight ahead again to ensure he resumes focus on his driving, but my fingers tighten around his. "I have ceased believing in fate, Tweed."

"So is your universe random? No religion? No karma? What about your lucky spoon?"

"Uh, well," I hesitate, "I admit that was a clumsy attempt on my part to relate to Amberlyn. I wanted her to like me." What I had really wanted was for Tweed to run my good luck talisman down the length of my arm, like he had done for her. It feels necessary to distance myself from Amberlyn, so I state, "I try not to heed superstitions."

This does not begin to cover the complicated nature of my beliefs. How could I possibly explain to him that I spent years trying to move spoons with the power of my mind, because I believed it was my destiny? I am struck by the separation I have created between me and my father's legacy over recent years. A small pocket of hollowness opens inside me, despite the fact that I can feel Tweed's thumb stroking the back of my hand.

I confess, "My father gave that spoon to my mother on the night they met."

"Ah, a romantic memento."

I feel my heart racing, realizing I have once again shared too much. To counteract my blunder, I blurt, "Romantic or random. If we accept we are all just atoms, bumping headlong against one another, it can be more than enough."

Tweed considers this before responding, "You're quite the

The Twistical Nature of Spoons

conundrum, Blisse Trove. I would have sworn there was something otherworldly about you the first time we spoke; yet here you are, proclaiming science drives the universe."

"Otherworldly?" I loosen my grip on his hand.

He allows me to slip it away, but insists, "Please don't misconstrue that as anything but complimentary."

"But you also reject good luck charms."

"If you're referring to Amberlyn's rabbit's foot ... sometimes I can't resist taunting her. She plays mad so well. I really must apologize to her first thing ..."

Amberlyn again! Though the car pushes forward through the snow, I have the sensation I am skidding out of control. I take a reckless, desperate stab at banishing her from his thoughts. "So if I told you that on the first day of our acquaintance you were bathed in the most arresting blue aura, which was visible to me alone, what would you think?"

He adjusts his rearview mirror until it's angled on my face. I want to hide from the glow of the dashboard. His thumb drums on the wheel. "I'd think that is the most oddly flattering and inexplicably provocative thing anyone has ever said to me."

I sit perfectly still and watch as the windshield becomes tinged with a perceptible fog. The car's heater blows it clear again before I squeak, "That is really what you think?"

He clasps my hand a second time, drawing my fingers to his lips like he's swearing an oath on them, and answers, "Yes, it is." He gives my hand a playful shake before pressing it to his chest. "But is that true, Blisse?" he asks, as if enchanted.

I lean toward him. "Well," I begin, trying to uncinch my vocal cords, "you know what they say: nothing up my sleeve."

"Indeed," Tweed responds. "I'd very much like to verify that for myself."

Ina

defies

The wind rattled the kitchen windowpanes as I paced in front of them. Half the time, I mistook my own reflection for someone outside the house. Wishful thinking.

"That's all of them?" I asked Knowlton. "You're sure there's no other spelling for 'Halverden'?"

Bent over the telephone book, he squinted as he ran his finger down the *H* columns. "I can't see any other possibility. I've checked several variations. There's just C. T. Halverden, no answer, and B. Halverden, angered by the wrong number. Maybe it's unlisted. He continued to squint as he glanced up at the kitchen clock, which read 2:40 a.m.

I said, "Tell me again, what exactly did the Amberlyn girl say when you finally found the pub she was at?"

He sighed. "She said Tweed had felt obligated to go check on his grandfather's house, out past Lockport, because of the bad weather, and that his stated intention was to drop Blisse off at home first before heading out there."

"But she didn't know exactly where that was?"

"I specifically asked her. She said she'd never been there. Seemed put out by that."

He rubbed his hand over his face and I heard the rasp of his bristly unshaven jowls.

"It's past two thirty, Knowlton."

"You've mentioned that several times, Ina!"

I don't know if the irritating scratching sound or his unusually abrupt response was my ignition point, but my anger—which I'd wrestled down earlier—flared again. "Don't get huffy with me, Knowlton. You left my daughter to go pubbing with some goofballs, and now they're out joyriding in a snowstorm. More likely in a ditch someplace."

Knowlton sighed and closed the phone book. He pushed it forward to indicate he was done. "I know, Ina. I am aware."

"I'm sorry," we both apologized.

I started again, "And you don't remember the girl's last name?"

Knowlton shook his head.

"And you said an older guy sitting with the theatre kids in the pub looked familiar. A former student, maybe?"

"No, a former student would've called me by name. When he invited me to join them, it was clear he didn't know me."

"Where else could you have recognized him from? Think, Knowlton!"

"Ina, do you not believe that I'm thinking? Blisse and I are due at the station in less than two hours for the broadcast."

I sighed. "I know. I'm not blaming you. You couldn't have physically dragged her home." With the tension ratcheted down, I slid into my chair at the table. My leg jiggled.

Knowlton patted the chrome edge of the tabletop as if it needed calming. "Ina, I am certain … I have no doubt she is safe."

"Tell me again about this Tweed character," I said, picking at the loose Band-Aid that covered a finger slice from my glass work earlier that day.

The Twistical Nature of Spoons

"Polished manners. Self-assured for his age. I still should have given Blisse cab fare."

"I would've paid you back," I agreed.

"There would have been no need, Ina. You haven't raised my rent in five years."

I didn't want to start an argument about who owes whom, considering all the things that Knowlton kept running in our house. My concerns were elsewhere. "Damn storm."

Jumping up from the table, I passed through the foyer and opened the front door to peer outside. The wind stole my breath. The world was white. White roads, white branches, white rooftops, white heavens. I shut the door, turned around to face the kitchen, and caught Knowlton wiping his eyes with the palm of his hand. He'd become teary while my back was turned.

Without looking up, he said, "I won't be able to live with myself if …" He did not finish his sentence.

I wasn't sure how to react to his emotional outburst. It seemed outrageous that I had to comfort him; I was her mother! But I couldn't bear to see him suffer either. "She's fine, Knowlton," I insisted, and then couldn't help whimpering, "it would just be good to know where she is right now."

He cupped his forehead in his hands and rocked from side to side. It appeared I hadn't sidelined his guilt.

I suggested, "Let's go to the parlour. We can watch out the front window from a soft seat."

Ever since that night, nearly two decades earlier, when I'd deduced what the cursed pronouncement might bring down upon us, I'd avoided spending time in the parlour. Apart from the items that were stored in there to be out of the way, nothing had changed in the cramped space since I was a child. The faded upholstery of May's threadbare armchair was still disguised with a draped blanket, the old brocade sofa was still worn shiny, and there were two blotches on the area rug where the jute backing showed through. I'd never tried to have the broken clock repaired. It remained on the end table. I'd surprised myself by suggesting we occupy the parlour, but then I figured it made good sense. Blisse had avoided the room most of her life too, so there was very little of her precious self in there to ramp up my anxiety. And I'd managed to decipher what I'd needed to do to avoid catastrophe in that very same space eighteen years earlier. Perhaps I could ward it off again.

After a few moments, Knowlton, who had seated himself in the armchair, coaxed, "Ina, there will be nothing left of that rug if you don't stop pacing."

I sat.

He sighed, "If only the problems stayed small. Like the time she tried that matchmaking spell on us and we had no idea … no idea what to do." He shook his head.

I felt some lightness in my chest, and a titter escaped despite my anxiousness. "We never said a word."

Knowlton chuckled.

I sprawled out on the couch facing the window, determined to spot Blisse the moment she started up the walkway.

Knowlton shifted about in the armchair, chose a cushion to clutch against himself. "What do I do, Ina?" he asked. "The show must go on. But how can I leave without her, knowing she could be in trouble? I should go back out, drive the highway this time. Although, the grandfather's house could be on either side of the river; it would take hours to cover both sides. Can you think of another option?"

I took a deep breath. "At this point, I'm going to sit here at this window and wait for her. And you're going to go get ready. She told me …" I stopped and cleared my throat. "She thinks you're the cat's ass, Knowlton. She wouldn't want you blowing your big TV appearance. You'll have to leave for the studio and do your best without her. Go finish packing the van."

The Twistical Nature of Spoons

He stood up like a hundred-year-old man. I heard his footsteps shuffle up the staircase, pause on the landing, and then descend back down. I expected him to return to the parlour, but instead he shouted at the top of his voice, "Ina, look out there!"

I jumped to the parlour window. An old jeep had pulled up to the curb. Two figures were wading through the foot of snow that had accumulated on the boulevard.

I scurried to the foyer. Knowlton had his hands cupped around his eyes and pressed to the glass, nudging aside the suspended stained-glass panel at the front door.

"It's Blisse! Thank the stars," he declared, patting his chest as if to ensure compressions weren't necessary. He opened the inside door and we both looked out through the storm door. "What the devil is she wearing?"

We watched as Blisse, draped in a woolly throw blanket, together with a companion, who was decked out in an old-fashioned, full-length sheepskin coat and hat to match, trudged up the unshovelled front walk, stamping the snow off their feet on the front porch before entering the foyer. They burst in, along with a draft of cold air.

All I could muster was her name, said with the same relief I'd felt when a Zellers store clerk returned my three-year-old to me after she'd wandered out of the shoe section.

Blisse spoke first, holding up one hand to prevent us from saying anything more, while maintaining a firm grip on the blanket with the other. "I am sorry. I was hoping you two were sound asleep and not worrying."

Her companion removed the sheepskin hat, and Knowlton yelped, "Theodore! I had no idea that was you."

Blisse said, "Ina, this is Tweed Halverden. Tweed, this is my mother, Ina."

"Pleased to meet you," Tweed said, extending his hand. "I am to blame for Blisse's late night, and I came in to apologize for that."

I shook his hand, and then crossed my arms over my chest, glad to still be fully dressed.

Blisse began an explanation of how they'd set out to check on Tweed's grandfather's house. "But the storm was worse outside the city, and we arrived to a defunct furnace."

Tweed nodded, and addressed both Knowlton and me equally. "My first concern was the threat of pipes bursting. I got fires started on both upper floors, and one in the basement wood stove, and started calling furnace repair technicians. Thank providence one agreed to come out so late and in such weather, but it took several hours."

"Tweed's parents are away," Blisse clarified. "He was responsible for the house. It is a beautiful heritage home. It would have been tragic if it were damaged."

I interrupted Blisse, whose main concern seemed to be doing justice to Tweed's heroics. "Why didn't you call me?" I demanded.

"I debated it, but I was afraid the ringing phone would wake Knowlton." She turned to him. "You needed your rest before the telethon. I hoped you would both be fast asleep," she repeated.

Tweed added, "I ensured Blisse got some shuteye on the couch while we waited."

"I did doze off while you kept that cozy fire going," she said, and I saw a flush start to creep up her neck.

"But you have to perform as well, Theodore," Knowlton stressed.

Tweed raised his hand. "I'm a night owl, sir. Late nights don't faze me."

Blisse chimed in, "Tweed arrived at the house just in time. There was enormous pressure for him to be at the pub for the cast gathering instead." She narrowed her eyes and tilted her head at him. "It was as if you just knew you had to get there."

Tweed raised his eyebrows. "Well, it helped that Blisse was such a good sport. I doubt I would've been so accommodating if I'd been the person along for the ride in that foul weather." The corner

The Twistical Nature of Spoons

of his lip twitched as he looked at my daughter. "Perhaps it was you who had the furnace premonition. But then, how do you reconcile any of that with those random atoms?"

During their unified-front explanation, I'd bit the inside of my cheek to keep from interrupting a second time. I couldn't decide if Tweed practised snobbery or if he came by it naturally, but when his attitude changed to one of easy banter, I started to seethe. He wasn't taking the situation seriously enough. Calling him out on it, however, would embarrass Blisse beyond words. My skin prickled from the effort of self-restraint. It helped that Knowlton, rocking on the balls of his feet, stood next to me and also remained mute.

Blisse continued, "The best part was Tweed jump-starting his grandfather's old jeep. I do not believe we would have made it home through the snowdrifts in his car."

Tweed shook his head. "It will require some major digging out," he said. "But the snowploughs are clearing the city streets, thankfully, so our rides to the TV station should be uneventful." He stopped then, his attention diverted to the foyer mantel. He reached toward the row of snow globes arranged there—the first step in my holiday decorating.

"May I?" he asked me, reaching for the most ornate one.

Surprised, I nodded and watched as he shook the globe and stood momentarily transfixed as the fake snowflakes whirled above the miniature park bench and tree-laden sled.

"Not at all problematic when you contain it under glass," he mused. "Quite beautiful, that one." He returned it to its exact place before addressing Knowlton and me. "At any rate, I must head home and get ready." He checked his watch, gave a low whistle. "There isn't much time ... Once again, my apologies for what must have been a worrisome night for you both."

He extended his hand to Knowlton, who cleared his throat and allowed, "The important thing is no harm ... She is home safe and sound. We'll all make it."

Blisse beamed at Knowlton as she unwrapped the blanket from her shoulders to hand to Tweed.

"Oh, do keep the mohair throw," he insisted. "A memento … guaranteed to keep you warm and itchy this entire winter."

I could not believe my ears when I heard Blisse giggle in response. She had not been a giggler since the days when I nibbled on her toes during diaper changes. But it was the expression in her dark eyes when Tweed murmured directly to her, "I really have to go," that made me audibly gasp. Her distinct, melancholic glance was a perfect match for the one that peered out from behind the mask on the back cover of Taras's book. Blisse's paternity had never been so evident.

Neither Blisse nor Tweed paid the least amount of attention as I coughed to cover my reaction. She followed him out onto the porch. With her back to me, all I could see was Blisse extending her hand toward him. Tweed reached for it and, without so much as a self-conscious glance around the neighbourhood, raised it to his lips. The gesture was so intimate, I had to look away.

Knowlton, who had witnessed it all, but was mostly assessing me and my cover-up cough, said, "Ina, I need coffee. I didn't feel my exhaustion until she was safely through the door. Come upstairs. I think you should … you really should join me. Then I'll pack the van. Let Blisse get ready."

His request was a godsend. An offer of coffee was uncharacteristic coming from Knowlton, but I knew he was extending it as a lifeline. I had no idea how I was supposed to react to Blisse when she stepped back into the foyer, so I took the opportunity to flee. I mounted the stairs ahead of Knowlton, certain I was leaving a trail of my cowardice behind me.

Once upstairs in the kitchenette, Knowlton set about filling the kettle and placing it on the hotplate. From a jar, he measured out heaping teaspoons of instant coffee into matching brown mugs. He placed a half carton of cream and a chipped sugar

The Twistical Nature of Spoons

bowl on the small table in front of me. It felt strange to be in a space that was now his but had once been my parents' bedroom. I didn't have any memories of my father, and I stopped regretting that once I reached my teenage years and May revealed, in an offhand way after a late-night shift, "He hit me a couple of times when he'd been drinking, so I can't say I miss him all that much. But I didn't wish him dead neither." For some reason, it dawned on me that I was sitting in the room where my parents had had intercourse. Parental sex and progeny sex competed for space in my brain; I didn't want to ponder either. I gulped the coffee as soon as Knowlton handed it to me and burned my tongue.

"Damn it," I blurted.

Knowlton looked at me with real concern. I set the mug down on the table to try and ward off his pity. We both heard the shower taps turn on below us.

"Look," I said, "I know you have to go. And I don't want to upset Blisse before the telecast, but I don't believe a single word they said."

Knowlton raised his eyebrows.

"Okay, so I believe they headed out to his grandfather's house, but 'defunct furnace' is fancy code for 'had sex.' Blisse is right. He's a good actor. It was a well-rehearsed story."

Raising his cup to his lips, Knowlton took a cautious sip. "It's possible. Perhaps not. That Amberlyn girl also fancies him. Perhaps they're a couple, despite Blisse denying it."

"Do you think they are?" I demanded. "And would that really stop him? That's worse!"

He shrugged. "It's clear Blisse is enamoured. She's smitten with the fellow."

Ire rose inside me. "What? So you're saying Blisse is to blame?"

"Of course not, Ina. Is there someone at fault when two adults consent? There may be … regret might follow."

"Two *baby* adults, Knowlton. Just because you're old enough to attend university doesn't mean you know your own mind."

Knowlton took another sip of his coffee. He wiped his mouth with the back of his hand and stared into the cup, refusing to meet my eyes. "But perhaps she is old enough to hear the truth, Ina." He drank again, producing a noisy slurp.

"The truth?"

Knowlton nodded.

"About … ?" I stalled, my pulse racing. I reached for my coffee, but set the mug back down without raising it to my mouth.

"Ina," he said gently. "Ina, you fear Blisse isn't telling you the truth. And it pains you to think of her as a liar."

I stared at the wall. I knew what was coming, but counted on Knowlton not having the courage to say it aloud. I studied the calendar hanging in front of me—the cheap glossy edges curling up from nearly a year of use. Knowlton hadn't turned to the new month yet; the deer stag was still surrounded by colourful foliage.

Knowlton stood up from the table. As he placed his cup into a plastic basin on the counter, his hand shook. "I have never . . . never once have I so much as hinted. But perhaps it's time Blisse learned the truth, Ina. The spoon truth." He stopped and tapped at his forehead with his fist, as if he needed to knock some sense into himself. "I've got to get Blisse to the studio."

"Knowlton, you gave me your word!" I spat out, fear and anger mounting.

"I did. But something about the stress of this night … Ina, I don't know how much longer I …" He stopped himself, swallowing down the last words.

My body was so tense that I felt if I turned my head I would split in half. Air became the enemy, as my lungs could neither expand nor contract with it. I choked down a wail that had the potential to wake the dead. How dare he think he could tell me what was best for my daughter. With teeth clenched, I ground out, "I want you gone from our house, Knowlton. Pack up your cooing moulters and get out!"

11

Blisse

devastation detonation

Standing in the shower, steam amplifying the pungency of Tweed's and my mingled scents, I squirm at the idea that Ina, with her bloodhound senses, might have detected the evidence of our sexual encounter. Perhaps the acrid aroma of wood smoke acted as my olfactory ally. Still, I want to slather myself in the perfume of our act, not soap and shampoo. I want to bathe in the goose-flesh tingle of our bare, chilled skin; in the light chuckle Tweed emitted when I disclosed that the oil portrait on the living room wall had changed its expression from statesman to peeping Tom when he removed my clothes; in the gallant way he draped the mohair throw over the ornate picture frame to address my discomfiture. I shiver with the anticipation of seeing him again at the TV studio, and hearing more about the proper first date he intends for us—a country sleigh ride and a romantic French dinner for two. I want what will follow. With the hot shower spray dousing me, I marvel that Tweed's moments of intimate vulnerability were as rarefied and tender as a dove exposing its neck for a caress.

Thinking about him makes the hard, unyielding metal part of me soften into something malleable.

I quickly dry my hair and pack my velvet high school grad dress into a tote bag. When we surmised the gown would perfectly suit the telethon occasion, I insisted Ina add a secret pocket to fit the original spoon. I am grateful now for the dress's sophistication. I want Tweed to be impressed by me. Providing we can do it well, I am counting on his approval of our Magical Influx Show segment. A pang of guilt cuts through me. I doubt Mr. Fluxcer slept at all. But we have rehearsed to perfection over the past few weeks, and I am confident he could perform the tricks in his sleep. I am not just ready; I feel as if I could levitate, unassisted by any magic show trickery, from having been in Tweed's self-assured orbit overnight. I weigh less in his gravity.

Ina is not waiting at the door to wish me luck as I dash outside, but there is no time to debate whether she remains angry that I stayed out late. When I clamber into the van, there is barely a spot for me to sit, but I fail to ask Mr. Fluxcer why the vehicle is jam-packed with boxes that are not part of our show because I have to double-check that one of his ears has not gone missing. He appears to be sweating, and I hope this is due to the overly warm temperature in the van, cranked up to prevent the birds from getting a chill. None of this explains why, when he brakes at the first intersection, Mr. Fluxcer's knee wobbles like a broken wheel on a child's wagon.

My throat feels dry. I say, "I really did not imagine you would be waiting up for me, Knowlton. I am sorry."

He sighs. "Do not fret, Blisse." Then he musters, "Let us turn our thoughts to what comes next."

"Absolutely," I agree. "It will be great! I am very excited."

When I pick up the corner of the birdcage's black cloth to check on the doves, however, I sense they are also out of sorts, especially Biscuit, who, more than any of the past or present birds, has always

The Twistical Nature of Spoons

seemed the keenest to perform tricks. When I make kissing noises at him, he opens his eyes, but they are dull. He remains puffed up and still, without his usual inquisitive energy. I say to Mr. Fluxcer, "I do not believe the doves care for this very early hour. Good thing we have a wait before our time slot. It will be closer to true morning by then."

Mr. Fluxcer agrees, and after a pause, he adds, "Shall we run through the order of the tricks?"

I am relieved to do so. It replaces the awkwardness between us and helps calm the jitters that have started brewing inside me. When we arrive at the TV station, we trundle our props through the snow into a backstage holding area where orchestra members are unpacking their instruments. The studio is crammed with crew technicians preparing for the start of the live telecast. A production assistant checks our names on her clipboard, and leads us to separate dressing rooms. Mr. Fluxcer insists on taking the small dove birdcage with him and I falter, concerned that my recent behaviour has provoked him to distrust me. Once we are in costume, we are shuffled to a green room. Several televisions simultaneously display a trio of jigging Irish dancers warming up in the studio. I expect to see Tweed and Amberlyn in the green room, only to learn that there are two other holding areas for the acts that are set to come and go throughout the duration of the broadcast. Fatigue creeps in behind my eyelids as Mr. Fluxcer and I are ushered out, down a flight of stairs, and into a corridor lined with chairs, where we are asked to wait for hair and makeup. A whirlwind of people bustle around us, ranging from harried and tight-lipped to relaxed and chatty. There is a heightened, surreal, escalating energy, and I am uncertain if I should seek reassurance or emit professional stoicism. With the minutes ticking by toward our on-air performance, I have to search for hidden pockets of confidence within myself. Mr. Fluxcer pats my hand as we are pointed in the direction of a door that leads to a mirror-lined room. Powder and hair spray are administered to counter shine and tame stray wisps. I act appreciative, although my face feels parched, and my hair, cemented.

By the time we are escorted back upstairs, the telethon has gone live, and Tweed and Amberlyn are in front of the cameras. My heart thumps in my throat. I am nervous for Tweed and nervous because of him. I can barely concentrate on their short piece, but it seems flawless—a tender love scene, shot mostly in close-ups—and so convincing that it is painful for me to watch. For a moment, I forget my own trepidation about our upcoming performance and attempt to discern how Tweed could portray those emotions and not be in love with the recipient. Is that the nature of acting? Or is he *always* acting, including recently with me?

The screen switches to a shot of volunteers manning two rows of telephones, and then to a host who sweeps in to announce the mounting total of pledges. I pace in the cramped green room, stopping to lift the cage's cloth to ensure the doves are comfortable, and am no longer certain which of my anxieties is predominant—that of waiting expectantly to catch a glimpse of Tweed off-set, or of knowing that I will soon be standing in front of live cameras. We are led immediately backstage to start prepping our act. A barbershop quartet is performing live in the studio, and as I prepare to help Mr. Fluxcer transfer Biscuit, I fear the melody might prove too enticing for our avian partner. What if he decides to coo along? Will he interrupt the singers? But Biscuit remains calm and obeys the *On Air—Quiet Backstage* signage. I whisper a thank you to him as we place him in his secret panel, which causes Mr. Fluxcer to whisper an automatic, "You're welcome." I am not sure if he is issuing it on behalf of his dove, or if he thought my gratitude was intended for him instead. I let it go, chiding myself for obsessing about inconsequential matters, and focus my full attention on quietly unfolding our props table, locking its tripod legs, and covering it with black cloth.

The Twistical Nature of Spoons

As a pre-taped segment airs, showcasing telethon-supported youth programs, we are hustled into the studio. Two floor assistants help move our table into place. Making final adjustments to our familiar props grounds me, and watching Mr. Fluxcer go through his own pre-show rituals—double-checking his tuxedo pockets and limbering up his fingers for the more delicate sleight-of-hand work—calms me.

The floor director gives us a two-minute warning; we'll be live following the break for station ID and promos. We take our places on a set of floor Xs that mark our spots for ideal focus. I double-check my dress's secret pocket for the original spoon; press it against my thigh to feel its firm and reassuring twisted contours. Despite everything that could have thrown us off-kilter, all is as it should be for our final performance. Nearby, in front of a different camera, the host stands ready as the floor director silently counts him down from five on his fingers. With infectious enthusiasm, the host welcomes viewers back to the live show and introduces our act. And then, the light above the large lens in front of us turns red. We are on!

Mr. Fluxcer takes a deep bow, flashing the crimson lining of his cape with the grandest of gestures. He extends his hand toward me for his magic wand. I hand it to him with a showy flourish, an excited smile plastered on my face as I try not to squint under the bright studio lights. Mr. Fluxcer brandishes the wand, and then stands stock-still. His hand is poised mid-air, as motionless as if he had turned to stone. It seems an eternity, but I understand that mere seconds are passing. I make an elaborate gesture toward him, as if I have to present him for consideration before he can perform his first trick. When he remains frozen, I gesture toward his hat, as if the audience should focus on it. More seconds tick by. The small orchestra's accompanying melody continues its upbeat tempo. It is as if Mr. Fluxcer has fallen asleep on his feet. Or perhaps what I have feared since the first day I met him is actually happening. Mr.

Patti Grayson

Fluxcer's mind has surely fallen out of his head. With every fibre of my being, each of my own poised muscles screaming, I focus my thoughts on Mr. Fluxcer's arm and I will it to reach up and remove his hat. I almost whoop for joy when he takes it off and I see that his head remains intact. I close my eyes and will his other arm to wave the wand over the hat's brim and then tap it three times. When I dare to look, Mr. Fluxcer's arm is doing my bidding and Biscuit is released all aflutter. Relief floods my body. I reach for the sweet dove as Mr. Fluxcer holds his hat aloft, and I present Biscuit to the second camera that has swung away from the host to cover our close-ups. I whisk Biscuit into his covered cage to join Pocket, who was brought along as an emergency backup, and then immediately gesture toward Mr. Fluxcer to ensure the director will switch cameras back to the star of the show. Mr. Fluxcer bows again, but only after I force all of the energy in my body to bend him at the waist. When he straightens, we make eye contact, and I see the blank bewilderment in his expression. I cannot believe what is happening. I grit my teeth and set my mind to make him extend his arms toward me and remove three large golden coins in a row from my hair. In the next instant, to cause their subsequent disappearance from Mr. Fluxcer's hand, I simply wish them away into thin air. Poof. The camera does not catch any movement of Mr. Fluxcer's gloved palm; the coins have seemingly vanished. I feel an expanding power inside me. I surmise I will need to control the Ace of Spades card trick, the appearance of the flower bouquet from Mr. Fluxcer's sleeve, and the long strand of silk handkerchiefs that seem to originate from his ear. When Mr. Fluxcer looks at me again, the cameras alternating to focus on our every move, I see the overwhelming gratitude he is attempting to convey to me. I want to shrug my own bewilderment at him, but instead I flash an even brighter smile as he takes his final bow.

The host steps into our two shot, his microphone poised in one hand and his other arm extended to emphasize our magnificence.

The Twistical Nature of Spoons

"The Magical Influx Show, everybody. Mr. Knowlton Fluxcer and his lovely assistant, Miss Blisse. Now folks, these fine people know that even their best magic can't make those phones ring. Am I right?" I nod my head enthusiastically and note that Mr. Fluxcer is just barely moving his own head in confirmation. The host continues, "We need you good people, watching this morning from the comfort of your living rooms, to pick up the phone, dial the number that is scrolling across the screen right now, and make a pledge. No denomination is too small. Every dollar …"

The remainder of his words are lost on me as I stand transfixed in this bizarre moment, my mind racing, my smile so tight that I think my face may never relax again.

"We'll be back with the sixth annual Canopy Club Telethon after these words from our sponsors …"

The red light on our camera switches off. "That was awesome, you two. Thanks so much for being part of this." The host is shaking our hands. Our props table is being moved off set. I rush forward to grab the birdcage so the doves will not be jarred. Mr. Fluxcer remains standing on his X, basking in the momentary attention of the floor director and camera operators. I follow the floor assistants, clutching the cage for dear life. What just happened? I cannot say, but I am filled with an elation that is indescribable.

A moment later, Mr. Fluxcer is standing next to me backstage, gushing, "Oh, my dear girl, I could never have done … It seemed impossible …" He stops and then starts a third time, "I am so grateful to you this morning. Thank you, Blisse!"

A backstage assistant prevents me from answering Mr. Fluxcer. She indicates we must pack up our gear and vacate, just as another assistant rolls a large harp past us. Moments later, we are led back to a hallway adjacent to the green room, where we are invited to help ourselves to tea, coffee, and doughnuts. I spot the backs of Tweed and Amberlyn before they see me. They are talking to someone who could be a supermodel; she is taller than both of them in her spike heels. I shuffle in their direction, still clutching the covered portable dove cage. Mr. Fluxcer hangs back, helping himself to the goodies.

"Hi!" I say a bit too loudly, and when they swivel around, there are spontaneous outbursts of congratulations and compliments. The supermodel excuses herself, and I attempt to lead Tweed and Amberlyn away from the food table.

We move to the end of the hall and, although their scene has made me envious, I praise their performance. "Your dialogue was so convincing. I cannot wait for the full production."

"Thank you," they chorus.

When Tweed adds, "Looking forward to the run now that this is out of the way," Amberlyn nods and beams at him.

Tweed switches focus. "But Blisse, your segment was mystifying!"

Amberlyn laughs. "Glad I didn't head straight home as planned. I wouldn't have wanted to miss Mr. Fucksir going into that bizarre trance. Does he always do that?"

I shake my head, bursting with the need to confide in Tweed. "No! This was the only time." Then I murmur, "He froze, actually."

"He did?" Amberlyn exclaims, her eyes widening.

I put my finger to my lips to shush her, and although I wish she was not present, I admit to her, "He blanked, I think."

"Like he couldn't remember what to do?" she squawks.

I nod.

"It happens. Poor guy," Tweed says. "But you covered it beautifully. It just looked mysterious to anyone watching."

"Well, thank you … I … had to take over. It felt like a kind of *rescue*, actually."

"Quick thinking on your part with those gestures," Amberlyn admits, with a bit of reluctance.

More than anything, I want Tweed to understand the astonishing thing that has transpired. I appeal to him, my voice barely above a desperate whisper, "Yes, but I had to literally take over. I

The Twistical Nature of Spoons

had to make him move his arms and wave the wand and produce the coins."

Although Amberlyn has to lean in to hear me, she interposes incredulously, "What?"

"She's kidding," Tweed says, and places his hand on Amberlyn's shoulder.

I stare at his fingers resting there for a beat too long. "No. I am not kidding," I insist. "Not at all."

Tweed crosses his arms over his chest, and Amberlyn looks from me to him and back again. She barks a laugh.

I meet Tweed's eyes and hold his gaze. "I had to control Knowlton with my mind to get through our performance. My father had psychokinetic powers. Mine have been … I suppose … dormant?" I say, thinking back to my childhood efforts. "I have tried to move spoons to no avail."

They are both staring at me without comprehension.

"My spoon, remember?"

Their eyebrows rise in unison.

I cannot stop the words from tumbling out of me. "But this morning, it was as if …" I think of the original spoon in its secret pocket. "My abilities were awakened!"

Amberlyn throws back her head and laughs so hard that she has to lean on Tweed for support. "Oh, Blisseful, you had me going there."

I stammer, "Tweed, you … you know I am telling the truth, right?"

His mouth alternates between trying to form a response and smirking. "Well, Blisse, I think it's cool you have this magic persona. You are quite convincing. Compelling, even."

I shake my head. "It is for real. Do not mock me." I shift the cage in my arms to create distance from them.

"Okay, seriously, just confirming here," he says. "You believe you somehow made Mr. Fluxcer do your bidding by controlling him with your mind?"

I nod with relief that he understands. "Yes. My father bent spoons with his mind, and it is finally evident that I managed to inherit some of his abilities. The blue aura … ?" I say to remind him.

Without hesitation, Amberlyn says, "Well, this was fun, but nobody has had any sleep, and you're acting like a lunatic right now, Blisse. Give it up! Let's go get some real breakfast. I draw the line at shoving those free doughnuts into my mouth at this hour."

While she speaks, Tweed looks past me and down the hall, as if deep in thought, then meets my gaze again.

"Say you believe me, Tweed," I insist quietly.

He lowers his head and rubs both his eyes vigorously, as if trying to wake up. "Uh, indeed." After a long beat, he adds, "I can't say that I do, Blisse."

"Ditto!" Amberlyn agrees.

"Stay out of this!" I direct my surge of anger at her.

Tweed raises his hands in a placating gesture.

She spits, "Take a chill pill, Blisse. We should go, Tweed."

"Advisable under the circumstances, Ambs," he agrees. "Blisse, I think you should definitely get some sleep."

"Oh, should I? And who prevented that?" I demand, my incredulity slashing at him.

He shoots me a look that pleads with me to relent. When I mouth, "It *is* true," pity flashes across his face. He shakes his head, as if I am a grave disappointment, and manoeuvres around me, beckoning Amberlyn to follow him down the hall. As I spin around, I see them nod at Mr. Fluxcer and continue right past him without slowing their pace.

I do not follow them. A blind fury overtakes me. Assheads! I turn in the opposite direction, rush down the corridor, and crumple as I round the corner. I want to wail aloud like a wounded beast. Desperate for comfort, I uncover the doves' cage. Pocket ignores me. Biscuit is tucked low into his feathers, but his eyelids

The Twistical Nature of Spoons

are open a crack. "You believe me, don't you, Biscuit?" I whisper. He raises his head, emits a low coo. I open the carrier door, reach in for him, support him in the crook of my arm, and stroke his soft head. Instead of feeling comforted, I continue to seethe with anger. Dread takes hold. They acted as if I were insane. Damn them to hell!

At that moment, Mr. Fluxcer comes around the corner. As I look up at him, I witness a deep sadness overtake him. He cocks his head to the side and asks, "Is he gone?"

I can feel my lip trembling as I admit, "He left with Amberlyn."

"Uh ... Oh ..." he begins again, "I am sorry about that, Blisse." He pauses. "But I was inquiring ... has Biscuit passed on?"

I leap to my feet, still cradling the dove. "Nooooo!" I cry out.

Mr. Fluxcer stretches his hands forward, and I pass the limp body to him.

"Oh, what have I done, Knowlton?" I wail. "I killed Biscuit!"

"Shh, Blisse," he insists as he holds the bird against his tuxedo and checks over his shoulder to ensure we are still alone in our section of the corridor. "You didn't kill him. He has been slowly getting weaker over the past few weeks. I hoped he would have this one last chance to shine."

"No, Knowlton!" I persist, "I killed him. With my anger!"

Mr. Fluxcer's voice turns stern. "Blisse, you're talking nonsense!"

"But I did," I insist, my face awash with tears. "He was alive when I took him from the cage. And then I was so angry at Tweed. My angry thoughts must have killed him, just like my thoughts controlled our show. I controlled you when you froze in the studio. You felt me move your arm, right? And I ... I just killed an innocent creature with my mind!"

Mr. Fluxcer takes the cage cloth and wraps Biscuit's body in it, placing it gently atop the cage. Pocket turns an inquisitive eye upward. Mr. Fluxcer steps forward and encloses me in his arms.

I sob against his chest. "Do you suppose my father did evil? Is that why someone stabbed him? To stop him?"

"What?" Mr. Fluxcer demands.

I take a deep breath and enunciate each word. "Do you think my father, Petro, only went about innocently bending spoons, or did he wreak havoc with his powers?"

Mr. Fluxcer releases me from his embrace, places his hands on my shoulders, and steps back. "Blisse, listen to me now. You did not kill Biscuit. I'm infinitely relieved to know he passed comforted, cradled in your hands."

I try to focus on him through my tears.

He looks shaken and pale, but determined, his body pulled together tighter and more defined than I have ever seen it. He says, "It's time you heard the truth."

I sniff hard and swipe at my wet cheeks.

"Blisse, your spoons …" he waits until he is sure I am still listening to him before he continues. "Your spoons were not bent by your father's mind. Your spoons were bent by Ina in my workshop at the school."

I stare at him. The world seems to have stopped spinning on its axis. My body turns rigid under his hands.

He gently pats one of my shoulders. "Your mother was one of my students. She was the only girl in my shop class. A first."

I shake my head, uncomprehending.

He waves one hand in the air and addresses himself as much as me when he says, "But that doesn't matter." He clears his throat and continues, "When you were just little, she showed up at the school one day. I hadn't seen her since she graduated. She asked for my help. That first time, she pulled you all the way on a beat-up wooden toboggan. You wore this oversized blue snowsuit you could barely stand up in. You were desperate to be walking."

I frown at him.

He continues, "Ina wanted you to believe the best about your father. She wanted him to be a hero for you. She couldn't anticipate the consequences back then. It was pure innocence. She never

The Twistical Nature of Spoons

intended twelve spoons in the beginning. It started with just your first birthday, and then another and another. She believed you'd grow out of the story by the time you turned five or so. Like Santa. No serious harm done. She loved you so much. And then each year afterward, as you grew more attached to your spoon family, she didn't want to disappoint you. After I moved in upstairs, we completed the final six all at once. She clung to the belief that if you discovered the truth, you would see her absolute love for you in her gesture." He flounders, tears welling up in his eyes.

"I have been duped?"

"Not duped, Blisse." He covers his face with his hands. "Oh my. I promised Ina I would never reveal any of this to you."

"My father never sent the spoons for me … for me to receive on my birthdays?"

Mr. Fluxcer refuses to look at me, but shakes his head with the most imperceptible movement. "No, it was your mother." He takes a deep breath and explains further, "There were times that I tried to dissuade her from continuing. But she insisted. Said there were things I didn't understand. Things she couldn't bring herself to reveal, even to me, but that with each passing year, those things mattered less. I accepted that and continued to support her. I didn't want to pry. I imagined what I imagined, regarding what she might need to hide, and left it at that. Hearing that your father was stabbed … that explains some things I didn't understand."

"You thought he was still alive?"

He shakes his head, but then shrugs, and shudders. "I thought … well, I'd thought … the very worst … But it doesn't matter now what I thought." He cannot bring himself to say more.

I look over at the black cloth on top of the cage. It is as if my soul is wrapped up in it next to the dead bird.

"Blisse, believe me," Mr. Fluxcer insists, "Biscuit died of natural causes. You did not kill him with your mind, sweet girl." He rubs at the strands of hair-sprayed wisps over his balding head and moans.

Resisting the urge to reach for it in my secret pocket, I ask, "What about the original spoon?"

He shrugs. "Ina maintains your father gave it to her. I don't know."

I just barely hear him as I head back down the corridor to gather my coat and walk out into the cold morning.

Ina

succumbs

I whipped up blueberry pancake batter, opened a fresh package of bacon, squeezed real oranges for juice, and set out a bottle of maple syrup for the post-telethon brunch. I even brought out the remaining Christmas decorations and hijacked a couple of stars to make a table centerpiece for the two celebrities. My morning party plan had a dual purpose: to congratulate them for making it through their television debut—I'd broken into a cold sweat during Knowlton's episode of momentary paralysis—and to make amends for my indecent behaviour when I'd ordered him to move out. I should have apologized before he left the house instead of going down to the basement to break small pieces of glass. I was counting on his post-performance high to put him in a spirit of forgiveness when I olive-branched him brunch and explained I'd just been spouting off stupidity.

I sat at the kitchen table nodding off and springing awake for several hours after their segment aired. A few hours after that, despite having no food in my stomach, I'd lost my appetite. Brunch turned to dinner. I paced the floor, seesawing between being crazed with worry and dulled to a dead-weight stupor. I couldn't believe it was happening again. Where were they? Several times, I got as far as putting on my coat to catch a bus down to the TV studio, but then reasoned I would miss their return, our paths crossing in opposite directions. I figured they'd been swept up in some kind of telethon afterparty, but that didn't excuse them from dropping a quarter in a payphone. If Blisse tried to pull the lame excuse again that she didn't call in case I was catching up on my sleep, I'd explain that I knew my ass from my elbow, and that I wasn't falling for it. As the late-afternoon dusk gave way to darkness, I ladled sludgy batter onto the griddle and choked down a pancake. Though it sat like concrete in my stomach, I grabbed my ring of keys and trudged up to the second floor—my guilt over barging into Knowlton's private space surpassed by my outraged concern. I didn't know what I was expecting to discover when I unlocked his door, but I was hoping for a clue.

The hinges creaked as the door swung open into the kitchen. The cupboard door was ajar and the shelves were empty. Knowlton's few dishes were gone, as was the kettle and the coffee supplies we'd used that morning. I rushed to his living room. His small television and some magazines were still there. I felt a wave of relief as I made my way to the bedroom, but when I threw open the closet door, not one stitch of clothing hung there. The dresser was likewise emptied. One tiny dried leaf remained on the windowsill where Knowlton's single houseplant had resided. I reached for the doorframe to steady myself, and then raced back to the staircase and up to the third floor, praying that the round table still housed the large birdcage. It did not. The scratched and chipped tabletop was as bare as a yawn, with the exception of a ring of keys. While I'd been sulking in the basement, Knowlton had managed to clear out most of his meagre belongings before departing with Blisse.

I left his doors wide open behind me as I descended three

The Twistical Nature of Spoons

flights of stairs and staggered to my work table—the one Knowlton had fashioned for me. I resisted the urge to pound on its surface and tried to calm myself, my heart beating so hard that my eyes throbbed, the edges of my vision pulsing in time, as if my brain was expanding and contracting in disbelief.

And maybe I deserved it. I'd had the chance to apologize and didn't. What else did I expect? Knowlton was gone, and if he'd told Blisse that I evicted him from our home, she'd be furious with me. Were they conspiring to keep me in the dark out of spite—revelling in their day's celebrity—deliberately indifferent to my rising tide of distress?

"Acckk!" I screamed, "kiss my royal ass, Knowlton!"

Despite my desire to rage on, the repercussions of my actions started sinking in. Without Knowlton's rent money, would it be necessary to find another lodger? How could I trust someone else to live in my house? The thought made my stomach lurch. The months I'd spent working on masks now seemed like a complete waste of time. What if I didn't sell a single one at the show? How would I recoup my expenses? I could've been creating pour-painting pieces instead of drifting off course in my bizarre artistic pursuit—nothing more than a wacko attempt to link myself to Taras. I'd likely have to abandon the masks altogether and get back to popular, quick-selling crafts to make ends meet. That notion left me doubled over and breathing as if I had gills instead of lungs.

I forced myself to straighten up and reached onto the shelf for a half-finished, elongated mask. The papier mâché felt delicate in my hands. Its stained-glass spectacles still had one empty lens, while the other was a narrow, cat-eye strip of jewel tones. I held the facade over my face and closed one eye to look through the multicoloured stained-glass lens, hoping to see into my own future. Had I reached a point where I couldn't keep my world intact? That's what it looked like.

I plugged in my soldering iron. My hands trembled as I tried to assemble the glass pieces I'd previously cut to fill the other lens. My unsteadiness threatened to ruin the work. I had to set it down numerous times and shake out my fingers. I almost sent the whole piece crashing to the floor when the phone started ringing in the kitchen. I bounded up the stairs two at a time, afraid the caller would hang up before I could answer.

I grabbed the receiver. "Hello? Hello?"

Knowlton did not say hello. "We're fine, Ina." He cleared his throat. "Blisse is fine. I know you must be … We're fine."

I steadied myself by placing my scarred hand down on the counter. "Where are you? What happened?" Before he could answer, I accused him, "You moved out!"

"You ordered me out."

"Cripes, Knowlton," I said, wrapping the telephone cord around my fist. "You weren't supposed to … Where *are* you?"

"I have obtained temporary lodgings. Blisse is here as well."

My heart swelled. All I could picture was Blisse and her pale fairy hair. "Where?" I demanded.

There was a pause. "I can't … It's better for now that …"

"Where the hell are you, Knowlton?" I repeated.

He cleared his throat. "You were right, Ina. The Tweed character broke her heart … He said unkind words. She doesn't want to come home. She's distraught and doesn't want to burden you … with your show and all. So she's staying put for now. I have space enough."

"What are you talking about? Burden me? Knowlton, put her on the line!"

"She can't speak to you right now, Ina. Please, try to understand. She needs to pick up a few things tomorrow. Late afternoon or evening. I have everything I need for the time being. I'll get the rest when I'm resettled. But please, for both your sakes, go to the parlour when Blisse arrives. Don't come out to speak to her."

"What? You're telling me I can't talk to my own daughter? I'm

The Twistical Nature of Spoons

just supposed to let her sneak in for her stuff and leave? Look, where are you calling from? I'll come there."

"We're at a payphone at this particular moment. This line of questioning is …"

There was rustling, some muffled words behind a covered receiver, and then Blisse's voice came on the line. "Stop hassling Knowlton! It is not his fault."

"Blisse, are you okay? What happened? What did that snobby guy say to you?"

"Oh, Ina," she croaked, and there was a long, strangled pause before she composed herself. "I believed you, but you are a liar. I must have chosen to wish that you were not."

"What? Why would Tweed say that? Why call you a liar?"

There was no reply.

I tried again. "Is he with that Amberlyn girl? He's been leading you on. That makes *him* the liar! Blisse, this makes no sense."

"Really, Ina? You pretend to not understand me?"

There was such rage in her voice that I couldn't believe I was speaking to my daughter.

I heard her intake of breath, as if she was about to say more, just before the line clicked.

"Blisse?"

The dial tone buzzed in response.

I stood with the receiver in my hand, her statements running undecipherable loops through my head. What was going on? She must have fallen hard for him. I could only hope that her extreme anger would blaze itself out, that she wouldn't resort to self-pity. I needed to tell her to forget him—to forget the jackass in the tweed jacket.

In a frenzied stupor, I walked directly out of the kitchen and started unpacking every single Christmas ornament we owned, placing each in its reserved spot. I was determined that the foyer would welcome Blisse home when she came for her belongings the next day. Festive and joyous and nary a care in the world! I would make hot cocoa and let her cry out the tears from her first broken heart. After the decorations were all arranged, I returned to the basement and constructed one black velvet eyepatch to replace the unfinished spectacles on the *bauta* mask. When it was affixed, I slumped over my work table and slept in fitful starts.

First thing in the morning, I dialled Knowlton's high school. The secretary answered. I could hear the hubbub of students in the background.

She said, "I'm sorry, Mr. Fluxcer called in sick. He has decided to take a short leave of absence until his retirement kicks in at the end of term."

"Retirement?" I repeated. "Already? Since when?"

The secretary sounded young and flustered. "Well, his retirement is official as of Christmas, but he has some sick days owed. Mr. Mack was available to start immediately, so Mr. Fluxcer won't be coming back in. Would you like to speak with Mr. Mack?"

I stared out the window. Snow was falling in heaps again. Nothing was right. The world was whiting out. I don't remember saying goodbye before hanging up the phone. I thought about going to the university and asking for directions to Blisse's classes, but what if she chose to come for her things while I was out searching for her? It was better to sit tight. The afternoon passed alongside my daydreams of Blisse and Knowlton coming up the walkway through the blurred whirl of snowflakes, laughing and shrugging off all the misunderstandings, to join me for tea and shortbread cookies.

With dusk starting to settle, I went out to clear fresh snow from the front walk. I wasn't sure where to find the shovel; Knowlton had been taking care of these things without the slightest fuss for so long. It was in the garage, one of the few items in the empty stall where he'd parked his vehicle for over a decade. There was the sad little oil stain that had stubbornly remained on the concrete from when his old station wagon went kaput. I thought about my

The Twistical Nature of Spoons

upcoming opening, with no one to drive my masks to the gallery, but it wasn't a lack of transportation I was mourning—just the absence of Knowlton's willingness to support.

How badly had I abused that willingness? It had been so damn reassuring in the beginning to have someone else believe in the power of magic enough—be it the real thing or an illusion of it—to agree to help with my harebrained idea of bent-spoon birthdays. It was his willingness to assist me with the heating and bending of silver cutlery that forged more than a metal bond between us. He seemed to comprehend my need for the spoons to represent some grand, romanticized version of love, but he never commented on my determination to endure a life without the real thing in it. He rarely pried. When I'd arrived at the school to fashion the fourth spoon—which was not that long before his divorce—my doubts were swirling, and I'd said aloud, "How is this ever going to replace actual love from her father?"

Knowlton had responded, "Well, Ina, what is love if not the surprising, constant ache of it? Absent. Present. When it comes to love, does it matter which?"

The statement sounded so much like Taras that I'd been doubly convinced I was doing the right thing. I ended up working harder on that serving spoon than on any of the others. I bent a complete, near-perfect circular loop in the handle. On her birthday, Blisse had marvelled at its size, exclaiming, "It is biggest, Mommy!" But she was most entranced by the loop, tracing her chubby fingers around and around it for days afterward, a Ferris wheel of love.

I grabbed the shovel, and as I rounded the corner of the house, I saw footprints in the snow. My heart jumped. Blisse! But it wasn't her. A young man stood at the front door, trying to peer in and around the stained-glass panels. He turned around at the sound of my approach. I wanted to tell Tweed to get the hell off my property, but managed to demand what he was doing on my step instead.

He held up a hand in a weak attempt to forestall me. "Ms. Trove, please, I don't know what Blisse told you, but I regret what transpired yesterday morning. Would you be so kind as to let her know I'm here?"

I shook my head.

He added, "I'll wait outside."

"She's not home," I growled, and felt the urge to swing the shovel at him. I sliced it into the snow beside me. It stood upright, on guard.

He looked unconvinced and said as much. "Is she ill? Sleeping?"

"Blisse has not returned home since the telethon. I was hoping the likes of you might have a better idea of her whereabouts since you seem to be the reason she decamped."

He frowned. "I don't know where she is. That's why I'm here. She wasn't in class today, nor did she show up for our production's final volunteer meeting. Ms. Trove, I understand she likely feels hurt by my reaction, but I assure you, I had no intention of causing Blisse pain. And I'm worried about her."

"You call my daughter a liar and expect it won't hurt her?"

"Oh, I most assuredly did not call her a liar." He removed his hat for emphasis and swept back some unruly strands of hair. "I admit I found it hard to believe what she was telling me, and I should not have left like I did, but … Look, I want to help her …" his voice trailed off, but then he continued with renewed conviction. "If she needs to see someone, I can steer her in the right direction."

"What? See who?"

"A professional. A therapist. My family knows a good one."

"Are you suggesting Blisse needs a shrink?" I blurted.

"At first I thought she was kidding around. We share the same oddball sense of humour. But when she became so adamant, so frantic, insisting she'd controlled Mr. Fluxcer with her mind to get them through their on-air segment …"

"She what?"

"And I totally understand the fascination with telekinesis, but to believe you've inherited the ability … I find that concerning."

The Twistical Nature of Spoons

I staggered backward and reached for the shovel to steady myself.

Tweed bounded down the porch steps toward me. "Are you all right?"

I held up my hand to stop him. "Oh gawd." I took a deep breath, my mind racing. "Listen, she's not … oh gawd … she's not insane, Tweed. Perhaps you should come in. I can explain."

He was emphatic. "I have dress rehearsal. I should be there now."

"I can explain," I repeated, feeling my throat closing. I choked out, "This is all my fault, not hers. Just trust me. She might need to talk to someone, but Blisse is fine."

He dug his hands into his pockets as if he could only spare a brief minute more.

"Look," I said, "when she was little, I made up this story. Well, in a way, she chose the story, right from infancy. It soothed her when I told it. She never met her father, so I made up his character for her. Some fact. Some exaggeration. Her father did bend spoons." I paused and decided to rephrase, realizing how crazy it sounded. "Well, I now assume he did sleight of hand with bent spoons. He wasn't a magician like Knowlton, but he performed. He had a *commedia* troupe." I stopped, waving my hand as if I could make that detail disappear. "Doesn't matter. The story I told Blisse was that he bent spoons with his mind and before … well, before he passed away … he bent twelve of them to be given to her each year on her birthday." I paused again. "Saying it out loud, I know it sounds messed up … but it didn't start that way. It was an innocent story to let her know she was loved. I'm her mother. I'd have done anything to assure her she was loved."

Tweed raised his eyebrows and drew a hand through his hair again. He waited.

"Blisse is a very sensible girl. She's never once talked about telekinetic powers. But she's also inexperienced when it comes to guys, and she's smitten with you—that's obvious. No doubt she was trying to impress you with a cockamamie story of her own."

Tweed's complexion coloured, and for the first time, his polished personality seemed dishevelled. "Did she really say I called her a liar?"

Blisse's words re-looped in my head. I stared at Tweed as they sunk in. I leaned harder on the shovel. "Oh, no. Now I see," I said, comprehension dawning on me. "She was referring to me. I'm the liar. That's why she didn't come home. Knowlton must have told her."

Tweed looked as if his brain had gone into overdrive. "Did you say *commedia*? But Blisse's father is dead, correct? He passed away?"

"You're missing the point, Tweed. Blisse will be perfectly fine as soon as I straighten this out."

He scrutinized my face until I grew uncomfortable. I could not tell what he was thinking, but I could see how Blisse could have fallen for him. Everything about him was a riot of contradiction; he was equal parts self-assured prig and pensive gentleman. But did he truly care about Blisse, or was she a charity-case project to him?

He held my gaze. "Indeed, how curious. I wish I didn't have to dash …" He pushed his coat sleeve up to check the time and looked alarmed. "I must go. When she does return home, please tell her I came by."

As he sped away from the snow-banked curb, I abandoned the shovel and went inside. I sat down in the parlour armchair to wait for her, filled with dread. How could I possibly explain the past to her? It was as if my body couldn't handle one more stressor and shut down for my own sake. I fell asleep.

Awakening to the sound of a door opening, I startled out of my chair and dashed to the foyer. Blisse already had two large shopping bags crammed with stuff, one topped with the mohair throw Tweed had given her. She was on her way out the front door.

The Twistical Nature of Spoons

"Wait!" I yelled.

For a split second, I thought she was going to break into a run. I could see Knowlton's van idling out front. Standing with the door open, she declared, "We have nothing to say to each other, Ina."

"Oh gawd, Blisse, I have so much to say. So much to explain. I know you know. Shut the door. Stay. We need to talk."

"You want me to talk to you, Ina?" She set the bags down and crossed her arms over her chest. "Okay, how about this, then? You lied. My whole childhood. And now, your stupid, stupid lie has just ruined my life!"

I swallowed. My mouth formed a small O, but no sound followed.

Cold air billowed in from outdoors.

"Is that enough talking, Ina?"

I stepped toward her. "The spoons. I know it seems—" I managed to say before she cut me off.

"Yes, the spoons, Ina. My ridiculous birthday spoons." She was shaking her head. Tears were zigzagging down her cheeks. "Who executes something so crazed and tells their child such rubbish? And now you expect me to talk to you?" She picked up the bags again.

"Blisse. Blisse, wait. It was a story. I mean, like Santa. Parents do that. Tell kids about Santa." I pointed all around me at the Christmas decorations that were crammed into every nook and cranny. "I meant to explain it—the truth of it—years ago. I'll tell you now. Please come in," I begged. I took one step forward with my arms outstretched. "Please, can I just have your forgiveness, Blisse?"

She flinched. Before I could take another step, she dropped one of the bags and kicked it hard. The canteen spilled out of it. It tipped sideways and the lid flew open. Silver spoons clattered onto the floor. As I bent down to gather them, Blisse shoved me. I didn't have the chance to even flail. I crashed straight backward into a heap of elves, their ceramic bodies smashing all around me. I saw

Patti Grayson

the look of horror on her face and heard our shocked wails mingle. As I struggled to sit up, I winced, and fell back again. She didn't stop for a second glance before the door slammed shut behind her.

12

Blisse

romance askance

A few days after I sent my mother sprawling, I summon the courage to use the payphone in the hotel lobby where Mr. Fluxcer has secured a suite for a month. My fingers are shaking as I drop a quarter in and dial. When Ina answers, I cover the mouthpiece.

She repeats "hello" a half-dozen times and then says, "Blisse, is that you? Please, just say something already. Look, I know it's you and not some pervert asshole, otherwise there'd be heavy breathing."

I hang up the phone and feel light-headed with relief. Despite the edge of desperation in her voice, she is in top-notch Ina form, so I can stop losing sleep over the idea that she is hospitalized with her injuries.

As I push the elevator button to ride back up, my thoughts turn to the *Harbouring* run. It is closing night. As the elevator doors open, I repeat to myself that it is best to stay completely away from the production. The possibility of encountering Tweed and

Patti Grayson

Amberlyn and suffering a second round of humiliation is too great a risk. I shove the key into the suite's lock. My stomach lurches with hunger. For the entire day, the only thing I consumed was a bruised apple from the bottom of my backpack. I am reluctant to eat Mr. Fluxcer's food. It is enough that he is allowing me to stay on the suite's day bed at his expense; I cannot be the reason his first pension cheque does not last to the end of the month. That can fall on Ina's head.

I do not have robust options. I will not go back to live under Ina's roof, and my own father apparently did not provide support—not even by way of bent spoons, as it turns out. My resentment toward Ina has not stopped simmering—not even after shoving her to the floor.

Stepping into the suite, I listen. There is a delicious silence in the main room, though I can still detect the whirr of a vacuum from housekeeping out in the common hallway. Mr. Fluxcer must not be back from apartment hunting yet. I unzip the large, oversized parka he lent me to wear to classes and call his name to double-check. No reply. I am relieved. It has been hard not confessing to him that I left Ina in a heap the night we returned to the house. I do not want to risk him insisting I go back home immediately. He has already made my stay conditional on finishing the last few days of the semester. I agreed to do so, but stipulated I could not attend my class with Tweed and Amberlyn. We compromised. I donned a disguise of sorts to wear on campus, and Mr. Fluxcer agreed that I could appeal to Professor Honeywell to allow me to take my Comedy and Tragedy exam early and independently, due to a death in the family. Mr. Fluxcer even offered to forge documentation, if necessary, but my nearly swollen-shut eyes and unwashed hair must have persuaded the professor when I showed up at his office. I did not mention to him that the death was a metaphorical one—the demise of a *version* of my father. I wanted to tell Honeywell I found it a fitting irony how my own life was suddenly

The Twistical Nature of Spoons

more instructive on the comedy-tragedy front than his lectures. I refrained from doing so, lest he assume I missed the point of his classes and assign me a failing grade. I also wanted to tell him he exhibited poor judgement of character, but who was I to offer that criticism? The hardest part of eluding the dismissive duo was bailing on my volunteer responsibilities for the production. I used the same death-in-the-family excuse but felt delinquent and unworthy. It makes my obsession with attending closing night all the more confusing.

    I pull the black toque off my head and bury my face in it as I collapse onto the day bed. The hat's scratchy wool irritates my skin in the most satisfying way. I keep it against my cheek as I lie down. One of its fibres catches on the corner of my glasses frame. I try to pull the toque away, but it is stuck. I have to remove my glasses to untangle the hat. The fibre pulls out of the toque's weave, a blemish to its knitted uniformity. How perfectly apt. I had never felt completely defined by the belief my father had psychokinetic abilities; it was more like a single thread that contributed to the fabric of me. Now that the thread has been plucked out, the resulting ugly snag is ruining everything, threatening to grow into a gaping hole. But at least some things have been explained—like why Spoonfamily members never slid across the top of my dresser when I stared at them. What is not clear is how I am to live down the humiliation of declaring to Tweed that I inherited that non-existent ability. What if Tweed believes I was claiming my abilities were awakened because I had lost my virginity to him? I cringe, feeling a flush crawl over my entire body. Why had Ina believed in her right to deceive—to weave in that weak and damaged strand—without considering how the fabric of me would unravel when I found out it was actually she who bent the ridiculous spoons? I cannot fathom her deception. I lie back down, pull my knees to my chest, and tuck the hat under my chin. I close my eyes. I am so weary of my own confusion.

I have no utensil with which to eat my snowflake soup. While I search for a spoon, the bowl threatens to take flight. I try to lift it to my lips to sip, but my face is masked. Why can I not remove it? Who have I become behind it? I tug. Yank. Twist. Bursts of pulsing, crimson candy hearts clatter out with each pull, burning holes where they touch the wool of my sweater. I must find a spoon to scoop them back in before my clothes burn away, and I am left naked and exposed.

Mr. Fluxcer is calling my name and arranging takeout boxes on the coffee table in front of me. He says, "I got all your favourites and brewed us green tea."

My eyes well up with gratitude, and the delicious aroma makes me salivate. "Oh," is all I can say.

"Chopsticks or fork?" he asks.

It is an innocent enough question, but I have become touchy about the subject of eating utensils. My dream resurfaces, along with images of garments floating to the ground. I imagine the high school workshop, with heated torches and protective shields covering faces. In my half-sleep stupor, I am overcome by panic and suspicion. Mr. Fluxcer may not have dreamed up the scheme, but he played his own co-conspirator role in Ina's subterfuge. Something, no doubt, he wishes I would forget. The takeout dinner suddenly feels like a bribe.

Instead of answering his question, I hurl a volley of my own. "What possessed you to help her bend those cursed spoons? Why not tell the truth? Explain to me again why Ina fabricated that nonsense?"

Mr. Fluxcer continues to dish out our dinner. As he struggles to find the words, his hands are on the brink of falling off into the fried rice. He ignores the personal attack, and as we have been over this same territory already, he tries the same approach as Ina to

The Twistical Nature of Spoons

defend the past. "Blisse, parents tell children about Santa Claus, a man coming down a chimney with a sack of elf-made toys. And—"

I cut him off. "Okay, but no parent keeps up that charade past adolescence."

"The spoons did stop at twelve," he offers.

"The falsehood did not. It was expanded upon!" I taste the tea. It steeped too long, and I balk at the bitterness.

"Yes, well, then consider religion, Blisse. Millions and millions of people believe in something they cannot see or experience directly. That is not wrong. It is human nature to have faith."

"That is not the same, Knowlton. This was a story about my actual father, not a deity. Was I supposed to worship my murdered parent?"

"Well, no. Ina never claimed your dad was a god. Just that he could bend spoons. Others claim it. That one fellow is a millionaire, isn't he? Governments are rumoured to be conducting experiments on psychokinesis. And there is still the matter of that first spoon Taras gave her."

"Taras," I harrumph. "Was that even his real name? Or did she make that one up too, like she did Petro? Petey. Her Petey Bird—oh, how she crooned about him to me—her one true love."

Mr. Fluxcer's ears are loosening and drooping off the sides of his head. He says, "Taras is his name as far as I know. It's unclear to me why she told you otherwise."

"And you are not keeping his surname from me?"

"She never told me his surname. I never asked." He raises a forkful of chow mein to his mouth.

"Did Ina even marry my father?"

He sputters, his fork clattering as he drops it on his plate. "Heavens, Blisse, I thought we'd been over this." He turns his attention to his tea, slurping it loudly.

"For my whole life, she claimed she married my father, but you are not certain she did."

"I only thought it strange that there was nothing else left to her other than a souvenir spoon. But that was before I knew he was stabbed overseas." He takes a second sip to avoid looking at me.

"But if the spoon story is a flat-out lie, why would its embellishments be true? You said yourself that you believe her claim that she met my father in the bar where she worked."

He states firmly, "Plenty of brief encounters lead to serious consequences that don't include marriage, but that doesn't prove that a wedding ceremony was not performed for your parents."

The blush that creeps over my face travels right up to the roots of my hair.

Mr. Fluxcer pretends not to notice, and adds gently, "I've told you what I know, Blisse. Everything. Which isn't much. And while I agree your anger and bewilderment are … they are very understandable … I hope they'll pass with time. And you must speak to her yourself."

"But will she tell me the real story?"

"I think when your mother is not in control of a situation, she often creates havoc. That's not criminal. And it is forgivable. I've also seen her do the exact opposite. Give her a chance to do better." He picks up his fork again and twiddles with it for a moment before pushing noodles around on his plate.

I try my hardest not to ask, but I have to know. "Within this havoc, do you think there is a chance that my father is not dead?"

Mr. Fluxcer sighs. "She's never wavered from her widowhood claim. I believe it was your father's death that made her heart unmendable."

I want to admit that the idea of their love has been a bright joy inside me, and I am afraid of having it extinguished. I say nothing. We finish eating in silence. I shove entire chicken balls into my mouth and do not care if I choke on them. I feel sweet-and-sour sauce drip from my lips and down my chin before I wipe it away.

When we have both finished second helpings, Mr. Fluxcer

The Twistical Nature of Spoons

changes the topic. "Is that day bed comfortable? I would sleep on it instead. I'll be glad to get permanently resettled, especially for Pocket's sake."

At the mention of the surviving dove, I sigh, feeling contrite. Mr. Fluxcer has reassured me many times in the past few days that I am not responsible for Biscuit's demise; that he is to blame for not telling me about the veterinarian's diagnosis, as he did not want me to fret with my exams looming. I have stopped mentioning it for fear that my repetitive claim might turn the tables—that I might convince Mr. Fluxcer that I *had* actually killed the bird.

"I am fine, Knowlton. Thank you for your concern. And for dinner."

He nods and starts to clear the remains of the meal. "I'll wash these up, so you can get to your studies."

It irks me that his kindness runs so deep. It is hard to stay angry at his role in Ina's deception. I consider smashing my plate instead of passing it to him. I blurt, "Why did Ina kick you out, Knowlton? Did you come on to her?"

He straightens up and shakes his head, his jowls waggling and in danger of being flung apart in tiny bits. "Oh, Blisse," he says. "If you must know, I urged her to tell you the truth about the spoons. She feared this result—being estranged from you—more than anything in the world." He takes the plates to the kitchenette, puts them in the sink, and retires directly to the bedroom.

It is the sight of Mr. Fluxcer turning his back on me that makes me scramble for my parka and backpack. I scribble *Gone to the library* on a napkin and sprint out of the suite. Once outside, I slow down to take my bearings. But it does not matter where I am because there is nowhere to be. My life is akin to the pile of scattered alley trash I walk past. Too bad I left the chest of spoons behind; it could have been dumped right here. I kick at an apple core that lies atop the packed snow and decide I have nothing to lose by sneaking in to watch Tweed's play. Can doing so possibly exacerbate the mess that is my life? Unlikely. It is not clear whether this decision is simple masochism, or if it is a necessary diversion from thinking about Ina and who my father might have really been. More than that, however, I just want to see Tweed. I want my senses to take in the reality of him. The memory of him is not enough.

By the time I make the cold trek to campus and reach my preferred library carrel to hide out in until curtain time, the doubts creep back in. Do I dare subject myself to watching the dismissive duo declare their love for one another on stage? It is all such a muddle in my head. The only thing I know for certain is that I wish, with all my heart, that Tweed had never turned his pity on me. How much more bearable this would all be if I had not seen that expression cross his face. It is best not to see him again. I spread my notes and books open on the desk, determined not to waste precious study time. I check my watch—hold it to my ear and listen as it ticks away the misery-laden seconds of my life. It is almost curtain time. Stuffing everything into my backpack again, I head straight to the escalators. The metallic and rubber churn of the moving stairs is the only sound in the building. I imagine the gliding underside of the mechanism; its endless loop matches the whirlabout of my thoughts.

Outside, lively voices carry over from the university's expansive front lawn. Theatre patrons are making their way into Wesley Hall. I hesitate, then follow them in. In the circular snarl of my thoughts, I deduce once again that there is nowhere else to be.

A short line has formed at the theatre doors. I pull my toque down lower over my eyebrows and ignore the easel stands of cast and crew biographies and photographs. When it is my turn at the ticket table, I shove a ten-dollar bill forward without speaking. I accept the change and hear the loonie clunk against the original spoon as it lands in my pocket. A volunteer, who has likely taken over some of my intended responsibilities, tries to hand me

The Twistical Nature of Spoons

a program. I avoid eye contact and do not accept it. I recognize the usher from one of my classes, and I sidestep out of the line momentarily, hoping that he will turn his attention to help someone else to their seat so I can slip in unnoticed. Despite my avoidance tactics, I feel anticipation building inside me; I long to be in the same room as Tweed again. Will I be able to give my full attention to the play and stop wondering what possessed Ina to be such an inept parent? Will I have to flee the theatre during the tender love scene between Tweed and Amberlyn? Will the play distract me from questioning the naive mindset which allowed me, for my entire childhood, to readily accept a premise as truth which, in hindsight, was so obviously absurd and unbelievable?

Behind me at the ticket table, someone asks, "Will there be an intermission?"

I freeze. There is no mistaking my mother's voice. I check over my shoulder to confirm what has set my ears abuzz. Ina is holding her ticket in one hand—which appears to have a gauze bandage wrapped around it—and awkwardly shoving her wallet back into her shoulder bag with the other. My eyelids flutter with guilt. I am responsible for her bandaged hand. Fury quickly replaces all other emotions. In a split second, I am bolting toward the main doors before she can raise her head. While the risk of Tweed spotting me in the audience was low, Ina's presence is a completely different matter. There is a swarm of patrons filing in, and I have to detour around them. I slam into the exit crash bar. It *ka-thunks* a metallic objection. When I hit the cold outside air, its sting is stunning, but I am relieved to have escaped. I shove my hand into my pocket, seeking out the souvenir spoon. It is entangled amongst my ticket and coins and a small dove feather. I fumble to isolate the spoon as I head straight for the landmark rock at the front of the campus grounds. My resentment at Ina's unexpected presence burns so ferociously within me that the spoon stays warm in my trembling hand. When I reach Portage Avenue, I take a moment to lean against the rock and catch my breath. Ina is likely only attending the play to corner me. She must have assumed I would be volunteering and that I could not avoid her in public—a desperate move on her part, but one that has also successfully prevented me from seeing Tweed on stage. Tears sting the corners of my eyes. I don my mittens and swipe at them.

When will she cease sabotaging my life?

After several deep breaths that sear my lungs, I recognize my near miss is a golden opportunity. If Ina is at the play, hoping to catch sight of me, I can return home to collect more of my belongings. I look down the avenue and nearly yelp at my good fortune. A bus approaches, right on cue. I am about to board it and take my favoured seat up front when the holiday decorations on the lamppost make me wonder if Ina has cleared the damaged elves from the foyer. I do not believe I can face the destruction. Mixed into this turmoil is an onslaught of homesickness; a sense of nostalgia for the foyer, intact and merrily decorated for the holidays. Ina did that every year while I was at school. "Just for you, Missy Blissey. What do you think?" she would say when I came through the front door. Now, I do not know what to think, other than I am glad it is not quite the winter solstice. Ina would have set out every candle we own in the foyer to combat the darkness of the year's longest night, and I would be tempted to stay and light them all. It was one of my favourite rituals of the year. I turn away from the bus just as its doors hiss open. I do not board but wave my hand at the driver as if I have made a blunder about the route.

Just as it is pulling away, I hear Ina's voice calling from across the university grounds, "Blisse? Blisse!"

She must have spotted me after all and not gone into the theatre. My impulse is to run. I dash across eight lanes of traffic trying to put distance between us. A bus, going the opposite direction from my home, is opening its doors to let out passengers. I jump on

The Twistical Nature of Spoons

and will it to pull away from the curb before Ina can cross Portage Avenue behind me.

Four stops later, I hop off again and, checking over my shoulder, head toward the suite hotel. Once there, I tap quietly on Mr. Fluxcer's bedroom door and tell him that he must go help Ina set up her show in the new year as he promised. I confess to having pushed her down, but state that I cannot and will not go home for Christmas. I tell him that Ina's present is under my bed—a long, black split skirt intended for the opening night of her exhibition—and that he must be my holiday emissary. He agrees to it under one condition: that I attend the opening of her mask exhibit, like it or not.

Ina

opens

I should have been helping Knowlton unpack the stacks of plastic cups and punch ingredients, but I couldn't stop making minor adjustments to the mask displays. The black velvet *morettas* lined the gallery's white walls, while the sharp-chinned *bautas* and Colombina half masks were displayed on clear cube stands, lit from the inside so that their stained-glass eyes and spectacles could be best appreciated. I needed to touch them to ground myself, but I couldn't reach forward without checking whether the gash on the side of my hand was threatening to open up. It was mostly healed.

The way it extended my second lifeline clear down the side of my hand to my wrist was undeniably ironic. The absurdity of it was not lost on me. It probably should have had stitches, but how would I have explained my smashing into Santa's workshop to hospital staff? I refused to wear an ugly Band-Aid to my first—and likely *only*—gallery opening, especially as I felt the show was somehow putting the rest of my wounds on full display. At the same time, it wouldn't be ideal if I bled all over the place. I'd already caused extra work when I asked the co-op to change my name on the publicity materials; they'd want to evict me if I turned my opening night into a bloody horror show.

Mixed in with my nervous mask adjustments were brain loops of self-admonishment—I should never have stolen the book, or written the letters, or made a single mask, or bent a single spoon. Not any of it. I even wondered for the first time since Blisse's birth if I should have become a mother at all. At the very least, I should have used my injured hand as an excuse to cancel the show, but Knowlton wouldn't hear of it.

He must have noticed me checking the cut, because he abandoned the half-prepared punch and came to stand next to me. "It's not still painful, is it?"

I folded my arms over my stomach; my fluttering nerves were bordering on nausea and even that much pressure to my midsection wasn't a good idea. I took a deep breath. "I'm fine. Thanks, Knowlton."

He seemed reassured.

I chewed on the corner of my lip. "Why do I get the feeling you didn't talk to her?"

Knowlton shoved his hands into the pockets of his corduroy pants. "No, Ina. I couldn't tell Blisse that you don't want her here. Perhaps she'll decide not to come on her own."

"She'll be here. Too bad she didn't want answers when I tried to tell her in the first place." I knew I was striking out at Knowlton as a means of dealing with my growing alarm. Ever since the night Blisse pushed me down, the curse had risen back to the forefront. I couldn't shake the bizarre feeling that it wanted revenge on me for thwarting it. Had I set something worse in motion? Should I be afraid of my own daughter? The way she fled at the university made me wonder if she was terrified of her own hatred for me … and what it might have led to there on the

The Twistical Nature of Spoons

street if she had waited and faced me. Had my dear, sweet Blisse longed to push me in front of a bus instead of hopping on one to escape? When she'd refused to come home over the holidays, the curse didn't just timidly rear its ugly head; it jack-in-the-boxed right in my face.

It didn't help when Knowlton took up her defence again. "Ina, I can't say it enough times: Blisse regrets what happened. She felt so guilty at the time that she couldn't even tell me."

I rolled my eyes. "I was there, Knowlton. She got into the van and you drove off."

"She's still a kid, really. She's been sheltered. And I don't mean to be unkind, Ina, especially tonight … but she was misled. We misled her."

I changed the subject. "And Tweed? Did you ever tell her he came by?"

He cleared his throat. "Ina, I've barely been back to the other suite."

Knowlton had moved back into his upstairs rooms, assisting me with preparations for the show and building my display cubes, while Blisse stayed on at his temporary lodgings, the whereabouts of which he had firmly refused to disclose.

"So that's a no," I said, before I pretended that a half mask across the gallery needed my attention. I felt conspicuous walking across the room in the slinky split skirt that Blisse had bought me, but I wouldn't have dreamed of not wearing it.

Knowlton didn't follow me, instead returning to his punch-table duties. Lars and Rosie joined him there. I overheard them making a fuss over the design of his display cubes, enquiring if he'd make more for an upcoming exhibit. Knowlton seemed tickled pink when he agreed, and then turned everyone's attention to the line that was forming outside. People were braving the frigid weather to see my show. When the doors opened, the place was flooded with coats and scarves and winter boots. People unwrapped themselves and grabbed a cup of punch. Chatter erupted and bounced off the exposed metal pipes and ducts near the high ceiling.

The work miraculously seemed to hold its own. People squeezed and crowded around the masks, pointing out details while maintaining a reverential distance. A momentary sense of fulfillment whirligigged me into giddiness. An *artist* walked out of a bar. Who could've *pictured* that?

Rosie caught my eye, and I made my way to a small platform where I thanked people for coming and described the masks as an attempt to express artistically what we choose to keep hidden. As I explained that the show would be up for two weeks and that sales helped support the co-op artists who kept the gallery open, I scanned the room for Blisse, but didn't spot her. I did, however, notice Tweed at the back of the room. I'd failed to deliver his message. He must have come looking for Blisse in person. I hoped he wouldn't upset her—or worse, provoke her—by mentioning shrink sessions before I had a chance to speak with her myself. I wished that he'd just part with some of his money by buying a mask or two and call it a night.

I decided to encourage him to do just that, but as I stepped off the makeshift platform, I was distracted by a man in a dark wool overcoat. A moment earlier, he'd been studying the *moretta* pieces, but he'd turned toward me and started making his way through the crowd. His progress was hindered by others jostling about.

The years had changed his appearance, but the essence of him wasn't altered at all. I had what felt like an infinite amount of time to turn and run before he stepped out of the past. But instead of fleeing, I drank him in. His eyes locked onto mine. My next intake of breath stopped before it reached my lungs. When he stepped close enough, his voice confirmed his identity.

"Eye-nuh," he drawled, shaking his head slowly in a kind of disbelief tinged with wonder. "I would ask if you remember me, but the trails of ivy and blue-winged birds …" he said, gesturing to the

The Twistical Nature of Spoons

wall of masks, "assure me that it is you who wrote the letters." He tilted his head. "Otherwise, Regina-Ina, swear to me that this is some cosmic coincidence."

I stared at him. I couldn't answer.

He glanced past me, as if the next thing to say could be found displayed elsewhere in the gallery. After a brief survey, he offered, "Your work, it's very good." He seemed relieved to have come up with the pleasantry.

When I still couldn't find my voice, he looked resigned. He was about to excuse himself.

I thrust out a hand and touched his sleeve. "Uh … th …" I managed.

He looked down as I pulled my hand back. He offered, "I especially like the *bauta* creations."

I nodded, not registering his praise.

He continued, "They're my favourite full masks. It's fascinating how specific identity arises from a disguise. But yours, with their playful, bespectacled touch, manage to eliminate the furtive edge, which I assume was your intention?"

When my only response was another nod and rapid blinking, he added in an exaggerated, complimentary tone, "Dare I quip, they are *spectacles* in their own right." Then he looked over his shoulder at a piece and murmured, "Surpassing yourself … the rapture it brings."

I finally spoke. "Taras." It felt otherworldly to say his name with him standing there. "How did you find me?"

He looked relieved that I'd managed a sentence. Before answering, he said, "I've imagined this moment many times, but never quite like this." He looked apologetic and continued, "An acquaintance—a young actor—he thought I'd find the show interesting. He didn't provide context but insisted on accompanying me."

"Tweed?" I countered.

"Yes, Theodore. He referred to the exhibit as an 'eye trove';

never mentioned masks or your name. I was flattered he offered the invitation after our production wrapped, so I neglected to ask for particulars."

"Production?"

"Of *Harbouring*. My play."

"You're the playwright?" I thought about the night I tried to attend Tweed's performance. Might I have spotted Taras there if I'd stayed? Would Blisse have encountered him if my presence hadn't chased her off? I shook my head. "Your play. That's how you came to be here? Standing here?"

Taras nodded. "I would never have inserted myself like this had I comprehended the source of Tweed's insistence." He paused, presenting an opening for me to explain my relationship with the young man.

As I tried to make sense of Tweed's involvement myself, a trio of Doc Martens-clad twentysomethings, with full punch glasses, barged in next to me, professing their admiration for the masks. "We really love your stuff. Are some made from paper? Like that art stuff we used in grade school?"

I bumbled through answering their questions, not allowing Taras out of my sight. I feared he'd take the opportunity to disappear. As soon as the trio moved on, I signalled for him to follow me down a corridor. He hesitated, looking around the room apologetically, as if he shouldn't take me away from the public. He must have sensed I was about to stamp my foot and throw a fit; he changed course and followed me down the short hall to the gallery's tiny back office. As I closed the door behind us, I leaned against it for support. He took a moment to get his bearings.

After a long beat of observing me, he drawled out my name again. "Eye-nuh."

I sighed at the sound of his voice, coming back to me all these years later, knowing there were a million things to say, but only one thing to tell him.

The Twistical Nature of Spoons

He cleared his throat and smirked, then placed his hand over his overcoat lapel to indicate he was speaking from the heart, but not in a serious way. "A lot of time has elapsed. Are we about to live out déjà vu in this cramped back room? Will it be *your* masks that bear witness tonight?"

I wasn't expecting such an abrupt proposal. I jerked backward in response and smacked my head on the door behind me.

He winced and rubbed his eyebrow before bending his head in apology. "I wasn't … I was merely attempting to break this high-wire tension. And I can no longer count on my physical acrobatics; they aren't what they used to be."

Despite the tears that had sprung to my eyes from the bump, I visualized him handstanding in my shoes all those years earlier. I chortled. The corners of his mouth turned up in response.

Tears started to flow in earnest. "Oh my gawd." I was laughing and crying.

He said, "And this. This, Ina, I did not expect either." He patted his coat for a handkerchief, but found none. He surveyed the room for a box of tissues, but there weren't any. He said, "I should have pursued finding you as soon as I arrived in the city, but my show was being mounted and you'd terminated our correspondence. I wanted no part in homewrecking. Besides, I put my niggling suspicion down to foolhardy wishful thinking. Why I didn't twig to Tweed's odd invitation, I don't know, but this is clearly not the time or place for me to just show up …" His words trailed off.

I sobbed louder. He took a step forward, but I held out my hand to stop him. He stared at my palm, noticing the new cut on the side of it. I crossed my arms, straitjacket-style, and hid the wound behind my opposite elbow. I insisted, "No, Taras! You'll wish you hadn't tried to comfort me when I tell you what I have to say."

"Ina?" he said, his tone turning to uncertainty.

"The night we were together. You obviously remember it."

He nodded. "Of course. I—"

I cut him off and blurted, "I got pregnant."

He narrowed his eyes at me, but his expression altered only slightly. The skepticism I expected to flare up remained in check.

I stated, "I tried to find you."

He rejoined, "I went back to the bar. But when you never got in touch—"

I spoke over him. "Antony didn't give me the note you left. Your friend, Dirkland, told me my baby couldn't be yours. That you couldn't father children. That you'd returned home to your wife."

"Dirk? He never once … We lost touch when I left the country … But back then … Those feeble excuses for men!"

"No, Antony was just trying to protect me, and Dirk was honestly trying to protect you. He certainly didn't believe me. Gawd knows what he thought." I waited for Taras to interrupt again, but he stayed mute. I confirmed, "We have a daughter."

He shook his head.

"I'm sorry. Believe me. *You* have a daughter."

His words were hesitant when he finally broke his silence. "You kept this to yourself all these years? Even after you found my book?"

"I wasn't sure it was your book. Perhaps another Taras … You're masked in your photo. Disguised," I floundered. "One night. I knew you one night!" I felt as if I was trying to wriggle my way out of my own life.

Taras raised a questioning eyebrow at me, while the rest of his expression remained unreadable. "That's why you wrote the letters? To confirm my identity? And even then, you chose to say nothing?"

I took a deep breath. "I thought you'd returned to your wife."

His demeanour altered. "Is that really true?"

"I swear."

His eyebrow arched higher.

The Twistical Nature of Spoons

"Look," I said, "I know it's a lot. What must you be thinking, right now? But Blisse is your daughter."

He repeated "Blisse" in an awestruck tone. "A daughter." But then he shook his head vehemently. "You avoided finding me because you thought better of entwining your life with mine. Who could blame you?" His expression clouded. "My ex-wife had nothing to do with it, did she, Ina?"

I swallowed hard. "You're very wrong about that!"

He raised his voice, his words laced with sarcasm. "Come now. You didn't want to wreck my happy home, so you kept the secret of my child from me? Is your altruism so pure?"

The bitterness of his accusation caused a second torrent of tears to pour out. I couldn't look at him. Moving away from the door, I covered my eyes and choked out the words, "I thought there was a curse!"

Taras was struck silent. Chatter drifted in from the gallery space. Everything that was going on outside of that small office seemed to have lost all meaning. I croaked out, "I tried to find you through Dirk. He wouldn't help me, but he told me about the cursed pronouncement—that your wife had said if you had a kid, they'd stab you dead. And your great-grandmother said you'd be cursed if you married the wrong woman. Remember? You told me. You told me that, Taras." I was having trouble catching my breath, but I didn't stop. "I was alone and pregnant with your child, and I thought that child was doomed to murder you. You hear about kids killing their parents. And I thought I'd killed my own mother by getting myself pregnant." I uncovered my face and swiped at my tears. "Well, try and convince me that wouldn't screw up a person's head!"

Taras stared at me. His own face had turned ashen. Wordlessly, he lurched toward the door. He flung it open, but then leaned heavily against the doorframe. There was a small, strangled sound, as if someone had punched him in the stomach, before he exited into the hall.

I scrubbed at my face again. A mirror hung over the small desk, and I stopped long enough to wipe away the mascara streaks before I heard Taras yell something unintelligible about socks. I rushed out of the office to discover he hadn't yet made it down the length of the short hallway. At first, I thought he was waiting for me, but he stood with one hand against the wall, using its support to remain upright.

"Taras?!" As I rushed toward him, I spotted Blisse across the room, on the other side of the gallery. I felt a spark of joy at the sight of her, but then my head whirled. Now what? Was this the way she was meant to meet her father? I placed my hand on Taras's shoulder, but he attempted to take a step away. When that failed, he faced me.

With the last of his energy, he threw his hands up and raised his voice, as if he feared I wouldn't hear him. "Oh, heavens, Ina, what … what?" His hands fell to his sides. He gulped for air and barely breathed out his next words. "Ambulance … Eye …" he said, before sinking to the floor.

I sprang to the office and dialled 911, shouting instructions into the receiver, and then raced back into the hallway. Several people had gathered around Taras, including Knowlton, who was about to kneel down next to him.

He said, "Who is this man, Ina? Why did he look familiar to me at the pub?"

"There's no time, Knowlton!" I shook my head and barked at the others, "Get back! Give him space. An ambulance is coming, Knowlton. Please, go outside and direct them here."

Knowlton hurried off as I crouched next to Taras. His eyes were closed. I didn't know if he was conscious, but I leaned in close and could hear his laboured breathing.

"Taras? Taras? Listen to me. Listen." I clutched his hand and held it to me. "Blisse, she's so much like you. So brilliant. And kind-hearted. I've never known her to hurt anyone." At least, that

The Twistical Nature of Spoons

had been the truth until she pushed me, and that had only happened when, unbeknownst to us, Taras was right in our midst. But if I could just tell her the truth!

I uttered what I hoped was not another lie. "Taras, your daughter couldn't stab anyone if her own life depended on it." I thought his eyelids fluttered. I raced on, "Listen now, listen. I fell in love with you. Since that night, I've never not been in love with you. Remember how you bent me the spoon? Blisse had an entire spoon family when she was a kid. She believes you loved us both. She told me she loved you even though she never met you. And she's an adult now. You can meet her. I told her you …" I stopped myself. "But she's not speaking to me right now. It's a long freakin' story, Taras, and I have to tell it to you. Please, you can't die. I have to tell her too. Hang on. You're going to be fine. Paramedics are coming. They're coming. Just keep breathing. For your daughter's sake …"

It wasn't until I clambered into the back of the ambulance—with the attendants monitoring for full-blown cardiac arrest—that the dread tucked itself in all around me. There was no blade, but Taras had been stabbed right in the heart.

13

Blisse & Ina
bend in the end

The pounding on the front door is so loud and relentless that it threatens to wake the neighbourhood. I cannot imagine who could be causing such a disturbance at this hour. For a few tense moments, I consider staying hidden in the basement. When I inch the door open, it is a shock to see him standing on the front porch. His bare hand is poised to knock again. A blast of cold outside air enters when I motion him inside.

"Tweed, what are you doing here?"

He shuts the door behind him, breathes into his cupped hands. "I was about to ask you the same question."

I am taken aback by the formality of his tone.

When I do not respond, his voice softens. "You've been avoiding me for weeks."

Confusion dilutes the thrill of being near him again. "I assumed that would be your preference."

He raises an eyebrow and, from that slight gesture, I understand he has not come to discuss the telethon, or our night of intimacy. I am uncertain if he expects to be invited in, or if he has just come to request the return of his grandfather's mohair blanket.

He says, "At least I found you." Before I can respond, he continues, "Mr. Fluxcer told me where you were residing and asked me to tell you that he would stay and clean up at the gallery. At any rate, I scoured the Health Science Centre's emergency room first. By the time I reached the hotel suite and started pounding on your door, I was convinced you were standing on the other side of the peephole, enjoying yourself at my expense. I only came here on the off chance you'd returned home—and only after I'd reasoned that exacting revenge was likely outside your wheelhouse."

Heat surges across my face. I think about all the plotting I have done to get even with Ina in the past weeks. "Misplaced credit."

"Is that your nice way of telling me to leave, Blisse?" Before I can shake my head, he startles and points behind me. "What happened there?"

I glance at the elf remains and quickly turn away from the damage.

Tweed steps over broken fragments and, from the rubble, picks up the snow globe that caught his attention the last time he stood in the foyer. He shakes it. As the pretend snow flurries about, he seems relieved it has survived. He says, "I'm going back to the hospital. I think you should come with me." Setting the ornament upright back on the mantel, he adds, "I feel very responsible for what happened tonight."

"For …?"

He rakes a hand through his hair. "And I don't understand why you're here and not there."

"Not where? The gallery? The hotel suite?"

"The hospital."

Without attempting to hide my bafflement, I say, "Well, Ina

The Twistical Nature of Spoons

insisted I come home, but that was after she implored me to follow her there, so I do not know—"

"Pardon?" he interrupts, looking stunned. "She told you to leave Health Sciences even though Taras was admitted?"

"Taras?" I repeat. A flash of blue aura encircles Tweed as he nods his head. I squeeze my eyes shut. When I reopen them, the hue is gone, but my disorientation remains. "The man who collapsed tonight? His name is Taras?"

Tweed's hand is suddenly supporting my elbow.

My voice sounds as if it is echoing through the length of a tunnel. "According to Knowlton, that was my father's name."

Tweed is still nodding. When he speaks, his words are quiet, deliberate, and soothing. "I believe that's correct, Blisse."

"My father is dead," I insist. I look into Tweed's eyes. "Is he not?" Fury rises up inside me. "Why am I asking you?" I tear my elbow out of his reach. "How would you know anything about my father?"

"I don't. With any certainty." He pauses. "It does all seem too incredible."

"Ina got into the ambulance with him ..."

"She did," he says, coaxing me to connect the dots.

"The man—this Taras—are you saying he is my father?"

"Possibly." He takes a long, hard look at me, before supplying, "Taras Petryshkovych." Urging, he adds, "We should go."

He helps me into my winter parka and leads me out to his car.

"You dug it out," I say in a daze.

"Indeed," he responds, opening the passenger door for me.

We both look up as another vehicle's lights pull up directly behind Tweed's car. It is Mr. Fluxcer's van. I skirt around Tweed and rush toward it as Mr. Fluxcer scrambles out and reaches to embrace me.

Mashed against his chest, I plead, "Tweed is claiming that man is my father." I cling to him when he tries to release me.

Mr. Fluxcer murmurs, "I've reached the same conclusion. I encountered him and something seemed so familiar. I realized tonight that I see you when I look at him."

I beg, "Please come with us to the hospital."

Nothing loosens when he shakes his head. "You go with Tweed. I'll wait here."

"Promise you will not go back to the hotel … or … or disappear."

"I promise, Blisse. Go, hurry now."

Tweed guides me back to his car. I slide into the cold bucket seat and take comfort in the familiar creak of the leather. My rapid, shallow breathing evens out.

Tweed starts the car and fishtails away from the curb. "You can blame Amberlyn," he initiates. "She's the one who first noticed. She said when you were talking to us after your telethon act, you had exactly the same expression on your face as Taras did when he discussed scenes from his play the night we … the night of the snowfall. To quote her: 'They've got identical eyes with this intensely intense intensity!' She stressed the likeness several more times—even asked me if you'd mentioned being related to him. I ignored her at the time; chalked it up to a bit of rabbit-foot fancy."

"He is your playwright?" I squeak.

Tweed nods. "I brought him to the gallery. I shouldn't have. The day after the telethon, when I came looking for you, your mother let it slip that your father had been part of a *commedia dell'arte* troupe. That's a central feature of Taras's bio."

"*Commedia*? With the *masked* characters?"

"Yes. That's when it clicked. What are the odds? And when I tried to confirm that your father had indeed died, your mother avoided my question."

"She told me—"

Tweed interjects, "That he bent you twelve spoons for your birthdays."

My rage can no longer be contained. I do not understand where

The Twistical Nature of Spoons

the screaming originates within me, but once I start, I cannot seem to stop. "How is this happening? Is she delusional? Why did I not notice? She kept me fed and clothed. She made birthday cakes and created freaking fairyland in our foyer! Maybe *I* cannot see what is right in front of me." I bang my head against the headrest. "Screw Ina! And you as well, Tweed! And why not Mr. Fluxcer to boot! Screw all of you! For my entire life, I was sworn to secrecy about my father and those freaking spoons. And now, he not only never bent them, but he also never died! All lies! And you know all about my spoons? And you know him? You know my father. And I do not. How?"

Tweed pulls over a few blocks from the hospital. He turns to me and makes shushing motions with his hands, putting a finger to his lips. "I'm so sorry, Blisse. So sorry. Look, you need the truth. Regardless of what happened between us. Taras might … He could …"

"Die? My father might freaking die! He has been dead my whole life. This is not possible." I scramble to get hold of the door handle to flee, but Tweed wraps his arms around me and cradles my head against him.

He lowers his voice and speaks into my ear. "Look, Blisse. I could take you home. Just say the word. But I'm in this with you. Let me drive to the hospital. I have no idea where you go from here, but I do know one thing: your mother loves you. Let's start there."

I counter, "You have met my mother for all of twenty minutes, and she convinced you of that? Not surprising. She is very convincing."

Tweed replies, "She didn't have to convince me. You radiate the by-product."

"You make it sound as if I am exuding hydrogen bomb fallout. But that rivals most compliments paid to me."

There is a pause. I expect Tweed to loosen his hold, but he murmurs into my hair, "That is something I will rectify; I promise you." He continues without waiting for any response. "Is it human nature to believe that while we're scrabbling about, doing our misguided best, others are just slacking off? If Ina were out there trying to alter the moon's cycle for you right now, would you be willing to give her the benefit of the doubt? It's easy to overlook her effort in favour of the result, but your heart knows better, Blisse."

I pull away and face the passenger window to avoid looking at him. He is making everything more complicated. I want to cling to my fury so I do not have to acknowledge that, despite the strangeness of my life—with its unfathomable deceit—I have never felt unloved. I need my fury so I do not have to face the gaping chasm of bewilderment that is threatening to obliterate me. How could my father and I have been standing in the same room? Who in the world is he? He did not seem to resemble my vision of Petey Bird. He could turn out to be just a man who collapses at a gallery and refuses to acknowledge my existence.

Uncertainty swirling, I turn to Tweed. "His aura was red."

"Indeed," Tweed responds. "To the hospital, then."

At the emergency desk, I do not comprehend how Tweed manages to gain the information we require, but I am grateful for his enquiries. When he turns down a hall, I turn. When he presses the elevator button, I stand behind and wait. He only steps aside when we reach the family waiting room in the cardiac unit. He indicates I should precede him into the small, dimly lit room.

At first, I do not recognize my own mother. She is pale and drawn and shrivelled, as if the hospital might have drained half her blood away for someone in need. Her head tilts up in our direction when we enter, but her eyes do not focus. I have never seen Ina look defeated before. My mother has been a never-ending stream of determined action for my entire life. Her state of motionlessness transforms my fury into trepidation.

The Twistical Nature of Spoons

I didn't acknowledge them when they entered the room. I thought they were the family of some other poor, heart-damaged soul. It wasn't until I was lifted to my feet and swallowed up in Blisse's parka-clad hug that it registered. I thought I heard her choke out a smothered "Mom," but couldn't be sure. She didn't try to escape when I clung to her. As relieved as I was to feel her embrace, my mind jumped to the conclusion that she shouldn't be there. I scrambled to find the right words to tell her to leave. With her near, the risk of Taras's angioplasty procedure turning fatal was higher. Wasn't it?

But before I could speak, Blisse blurted, "So, is he …?"

Her strangled tone shocked me. I tried to untangle myself to see her face. She let me go but turned away.

I explained, "He's undergoing a procedure for a blocked artery."

"No!" she said, indicating I'd misunderstood. "His family, Ina. I am asking about the man's family."

My brain churned. I glanced to the doorway. Suspicion crept over me. Had Tweed somehow figured out the truth? I kept my voice level and said, "He regained consciousness in the ambulance; I'm sure he told the hospital who to contact."

At that point, Tweed inserted, "He lives alone."

"Oh, Tweed, you brought him to the gallery … Can you shed some light—"

Blisse cut me off. "Enough, Ina!" She shook her head, and her wispy hair flew around her. She demanded, "Is that man my father?"

My perception of time suddenly shifted. The planet could have ground to a halt in midspace; the hands of the wall clock could have been racing in a blurred circle. There was no reference point for morning or deepest night. Infinity filled that hospital family room, and I found myself adrift in it.

I heard myself say, "He is, Blisse. Yes."

There was a sharp intake of breath as she slid onto the couch.

The floor refused to swallow me whole. I offered, "But he never knew about you, Blisse. He never knew you existed. Until tonight. I told him at the gallery …" I gulped down the rest of the words.

Blisse, wary, asked, "Will he recover?"

I didn't know the answer. I could smell my own fear—not unlike scorched metal.

Tweed offered, "He's in the best place to ensure that, Blisse." He looked at me as if he was a script prompter standing in the stage wings, ready to supply my forgotten lines.

I took his cue. "The doctor said he was lucky the blockage could be treated without full-blown surgery." I couldn't stop myself from admitting, "But the artery could collapse during the procedure. So perhaps …" I wanted to beg Tweed to take her home immediately so the curse wouldn't have its way with us, but I clamped my lips shut.

Blisse broke the awkward silence. "Regardless of his good fortune, finding out about me nearly killed him."

Eighteen years of my mistakes tsunamied over me. How could I save Blisse? I was going to need to grab on to more than flotsam and jetsam.

I said, "If it was a shock to him, then that is entirely my fault, Blisse. Not yours." I stammered, "But also … there's something else … Before you were conceived, Taras believed he couldn't father any kids." I backtracked, "So correction! Not a shock, but a dazzling surprise."

Tweed exclaimed, "Honestly? Indeed!" He sat down next to my daughter, but didn't crowd her. "It appears you're even more miraculous than I already believed, Blisse."

She didn't acknowledge his comment, but the physical space between them appeared to narrow. Tweed reached over and rubbed her shoulder. "Maybe I can rustle up some herbal tea, Blisse. Coffee, Ms. Trove?"

I nodded, thinking his presence was providing a much-needed

The Twistical Nature of Spoons

buffer and that Blisse would follow him out rather than stay in the room with me. "Two cream," I replied.

Blisse watched the door shut behind him and then said, "Why did my father just find out about me? Did you even actually know him?"

I took two steps toward her and then two away. All reasonable thought vanished from my head as it struck me how labelling that waiting space as a family room did little to disguise its purpose. Blisse was waiting for an answer in a room where families gathered to wait for death to make up its mind. My long-awaited fate was closing in. Blisse deserved the truth. And I deserved it if she stormed out and never returned once I admitted to my fears over the blasted curse—which, despite my best efforts, continued to plague me.

She cut through my thoughts, demanding, "How did he even find you, Ina? And why?"

My mind would not unknot. What if I told Blisse the misguided reason I kept them apart and then Taras didn't recover?

"Ina," she raged, "is that why you would not reveal his surname to me? Why you concocted the story about hiding us from his murderous family? You could not tell me his last name on my twelfth birthday because you did not even know it, right?"

How could I prevent Blisse from suffering even more because of my stupidity? "That's true," I blurted. "At the time, I didn't know his last name."

"Your one true love? Mr. Anonymous, I take thee to be my lawfully wedded husband? What utter dreck!"

"Hold on there."

"Please," Blisse spat, "spare me from more ludicrous lies! Widow, schmidow! You were never even married—"

I whisper-shouted over her, "No, but your father was the most fascinating person I ever met. No one had ever affected me the way Taras did. It was like I couldn't get close enough. And yes, it was a brief encounter, but I fell for him." I knew I sounded unhinged, but I didn't care. "Who's the latest TV guru these days on all things *love*? Call them up, please, so that I can be introduced and educated. But until then, I will not waver from my claim: I fell in love with Taras, and I've never fallen out."

Blisse sniffed at me, as if I should stop talking.

That spurred me on. "Look, Blisse. What happened that night between Taras and me was mutual. Why would I not be in love with the man who made you possible?"

It was clear she wanted the final word. "Maybe," she scrunched her eyes at me, "because almost everything you believed about him was just a fabricated idea in your own head?"

"Yeah, well, how exactly does that differ from love itself, Blisse? Do you think you fell in love with that young man who went to search for your tea in some other magical way?"

I waited for her answer. There was silence. It somehow gave me the space to set myself right and make a decision. There really was only love. In whatever form it happened to take. And by whatever means, we had to turn to it, not away. The real curse would be to continue denying love its chance at the helm. Blisse needed to meet her father. And I had to avoid planting terror in her. Fear was the enemy—not curses or the evil I could imagine residing in others. If I couldn't shake completely free of my own fear, then the best I could do was shoulder the burden of it without harming Blisse any further.

I said to her, "I knew Taras was still legally married the night we met, but he told me his marriage was over—his wife was living with another man. And then, when I knew I was pregnant and tried to find him, Taras's friend said something that led me to believe that Taras was reconciling with her. Even to this day, I don't know if he did, but I chose not to tempt fate and ruin lives. I didn't think past the here and now. It didn't help my state of mind that your grandma died at the same time." I paused before adding, "My life back then was focused on ensuring you felt wanted and loved."

The Twistical Nature of Spoons

She took a moment to consider before asking warily, "Is that the truth, Ina?"

"As best as I can tell it to you, Missy Blissey."

I was already thinking ahead. If Taras recovered and so much as mentioned the curse, I would deny ever having told him such a thing. I'd insist he'd dreamed it while unconscious before the ambulance came. I'd multiply my lies if it meant protecting Blisse from becoming aware that I'd believed she might somehow bring about the demise of her newfound father. I could see clearly in that moment that doing wrong for the right reasons wasn't okay, but I figured that at least love was the most right of the right reasons. Maybe that counted for something.

The door swung open, and Tweed rushed into the room, preventing Blisse from pressing me any further.

"I just spoke with a nurse. Taras came through the procedure. He's groggy, but his vital signs are good. They're moving him to a room right now. Apparently, he's asking for you, Ina. And for his daughter. You can see him shortly."

Blisse stood up and started pacing the room.

"They told you all that?" I asked, unable to hide my surprise.

Tweed didn't look at me when he answered. His eyes were following Blisse. He said, as if it was already an established fact, "I explained I was his daughter's boyfriend."

Blisse's head swivelled around. "My boyfriend?"

Indeed, Tweed, I managed to think before we were interrupted by the nurse's bustling arrival. She gave instructions on how to get to Taras's room and advised a ten-minute-maximum stay. "He'll need rest," she warned.

After she hurried away, Tweed said, "I'll wait here and drive you both home afterward."

Blisse was shaking her head. "I do not think this is the right time to meet my—"

I cut her off. "He's asking for you, Blisse. It's the perfect time." I knew that for her sake, I had to appear brave as I put one foot in front of the other and led the way to Taras's room.

He lay in the midst of plastic tubes and monitoring apparatuses. Relief flooded through me when I saw a faint smile appear on his face. His voice sounded hoarse when he breathed out a simple "Eye-nuh." He closed his eyes, and I strode toward him, frightened. They reopened when I grasped his hand in my own.

He took a few tentative deep breaths, as if trying out a new skill, then spoke slowly. "I requested a metal spoon for that cup of ice chips, but they said plastic was it for now. I told them I couldn't greet my daughter with bent plastic." His voice gained a bit of strength as his tone turned puckish. "Evidently, they don't understand the twistical nature of spoons. Their response was to assure me that the drugs would wear off soon."

Blisse stepped forward and raised a hand in a meek hello.

Taras's smile broadened. "Ahh, here you are," he said. "Hello, Blisse. It is my distinct pleasure."

"Hello," she replied.

They stared at each other for a long moment, attempting to recognize themselves in each other.

Taras broke the silence, his voice wobbling a bit. "They claim they repaired my heart. It does suddenly feel quite healed. I wish we'd met when I wasn't lying here in this state of decrepitude."

Blisse said, "There is no need to impress me." She reached into her pocket and brandished the original spoon. "I have your handiwork right here."

Taras squinted. With effort, he raised his upper body off the bed in an attempt to focus more clearly on the spoon from across the room. He motioned for Blisse to come closer.

As she approached his bedside, the corners of her mouth twitched up into a smile.

"But I don't understand," he said.

"Understand what, Taras?" I blurted.

The Twistical Nature of Spoons

He glanced at me, his eyes alight. "It was a long time ago," he stated, "but I would have wagered my life on it …"

I feared he was expending too much energy and urged him to lean back.

He settled onto the pillows again and turned his attention back to Blisse. "I am certain," he began, and his brow creased so deeply that his forehead resembled a furrowed leather mask, "that I gave your mother the bent one and kept the straight spoon for myself."

Blisse and Taras locked eyes. They wore identical expressions, as if they'd both just heard the punchline to a really good joke.

I did a double take as the spoon glinted in the dim hospital light. I reached out my scarred hand. You won't believe it—and you can call me a liar—but the little souvenir spoon that Blisse placed in my palm no longer had a twist.

And if my story ended there, you might consider it too good to be true.

Acknowledgements

Whilst taking full responsibility for potential errors and my flights of fancy, I acknowledge the following drama professionals for their elucidation, facilitation, and/or inspiration with regard to the theatre-centric passages: the late Reg Skene, Kay Unruh Des Roches, and Mary Neill. Also, the founders and affiliates of the Manitoba Puppet Theatre. Plus, Stephen LaFrenie, Cory Wojcik, and Chris Sigurdson.

The entire Turnstone Press team must be recognized for their energetic creativity and their ongoing dedication to this endeavour. I credit and salute my editor, Sarah Ens. With her keen capacity to spot pitfalls and possibility, she encouraged me to dig deeper and distil what emerged. My gratitude extends to my copyeditor, Melissa Morrow, who pinpointed many insightful ways to improve the flow of the prose, and also contributed to the appealing cover design. I reiterate my unwavering appreciation for Sharon and Jamis, who have provided expertise and direction.

For their helpful critiques, I thank fellow writers of the Selkirk Literary Guild: Liz W., Deirdre and Hugh L., Ruth A., and Roxane A., with an added hats off to Sheila McClarty, who has supplied decades of extra encouragement. Wayne Tefs is remembered for his guidance and mentoring. A shout-out is also owed to a former student, Brooke S., for advising me—with youthful wisdom—that if I continued to leave it untitled, I'd never finish writing the book. The title winged into place later that day.

My children, Phil and Miranda—along with their partners, Nicole and Kate—provided much valued support. In particular, I thank Phil for obtaining my access to Harvard's Special Collections at the Houghton Library, where I was thrilled to turn the pages of Flaminio Scala's book of *commedia* scenarios, *Il Teatro delle Favole rappresentative* (1611). And I'm forever grateful that Miranda read an initial draft of the completed manuscript, offering reassurances and thoughtful commentary at a crucial time.

Finally, I have a reservoir of gratitude for my husband, David, who deserves an ovation for listening to endless read-aloud loops of redrafted pages, and for dousing the flames of my self-doubt. He also earns credit for recognizing that directions in *Venezia* are of no consequence ... The wandering is enough.